Lattes and Lies

Wishes and Chances Series: Book Two

by

Suzie Peters

GWL
PUBLISHING

First Published in 2018
by GWL Publishing
an imprint of Great War Literature Publishing LLP

Produced in United Kingdom

ISBN 978-1-910603-57-4 Paperback Edition

GWL Publishing
Forum House
Sterling Road
Chichester PO19 7DN

www.gwlpublishing.co.uk

Dedication

For S.

Chapter One

Four Years Earlier

Emma

"You've gotta stop re-arranging the muffins." Emma jumped and looked up across the counter, straight into Nick's gray eyes. He was smiling at her. "You okay?" he asked, like he didn't already know the answer.

"Yeah, I'm fine." Even to Emma, her words sounded unconvincing, but maybe that was just her tone – her bored, dissatisfied, disappointed tone.

"Well, I believe you." Nick folded his arms across his broad chest and stared at her.

"What do you want?"

"For my sister to tell me the truth; that'd be real good."

"I *am* fine."

"Yeah, right."

She didn't reply, but picked up a cloth from behind the counter and came around his side to wipe down the tables, the same tables that she'd already wiped just fifteen minutes before. Nick grabbed her arm as she passed. "Em," he said, "you're not happy."

"Well, neither are you."

"We're not talking about me," he countered.

"Why are we talking about me all of a sudden?" she asked, biting back her tears. She glanced around the empty coffee shop. It was five-thirty. She still had another hour and a half until she could close up for the night… Her last customer had left just before five, and Nick would probably be the only other person she saw tonight. She could just tell him she was bored – it wouldn't be a lie.

"Because you've been like this since Cassie took off, and that was months ago now."

Emma glared at him, then looked down at his hand, resting on her arm, until he released her. He sighed. "Okay," he said, "don't talk to me, but mom and dad are starting to notice. Mom asked me yesterday what's been eating at you, and you know she's not gonna let up once she gets started. So, you can either tell me about it, or you can carry on as you are now and get the inquisition from them. Your choice."

"I'm such a failure," she mumbled.

"Excuse me?" Nick leant back on the counter, looking down at her.

Emma pulled out one of the chairs at the nearest table and sat down, facing him. Her brother wasn't like anyone else in Somers Cove, there was no getting away from that. He'd come back from law school four years ago, much quieter than when he'd left, and since then he'd worked with Tom Allen, the local attorney. He was good at his job, everyone knew that, but he didn't conform. Nick had never really conformed. He wore his dark hair long – just above shoulder length – and kind of disheveled, but with such an air of confidence, no-one ever questioned it. His eyes were light gray and piercing, and his stubble bordered on a beard, but didn't quite get there. He never wore a suit – not even in court – choosing jeans, a shirt, a tie, and a waistcoat. He had style… it was just a style unlike anyone else's. It was Nick's style.

"I said, I'm a failure," she repeated.

"I heard you. I'm just not sure why you'd say that."

Emma looked around her. "You're a lawyer, Nick. Cassie's working for a publishing company, *and* she's writing a book… and I work in the town coffee shop."

Emma didn't dwell on the fact that she'd been to college. She'd gone at the same time as Cassie and her boyfriend, Jake, and just about every other kid from their year in high school, all of whom had graduated earlier in the year – except for Emma. She didn't graduate. She hadn't even survived her first semester. She'd hated every second of college and had come home after just eight weeks. It was a subject the family avoided, because it nearly always ended in recriminations, resulting in Emma feeling like she'd let her parents down… again.

"And what's wrong with working in the coffee shop?" Nick queried. "You're providing a valuable service. Everyone needs coffee, Em."

She smiled up at him. "It's not exactly what I had planned."

Emma had always intended to go into catering. She was a brilliant cook and, in her dreams, she saw herself with a restaurant, or maybe a small hotel of her own… But they were dreams, nothing more. In reality, she worked for Mrs Adams in the coffee shop, and lived in the apartment upstairs.

Nick pushed himself off the counter and came and sat beside her. "I know," he said. "But who's to say you couldn't take over this place one day? You could turn it into whatever you want it to be."

"How?"

"You've still got the money you inherited from Grandpa Jonas. You could use that."

"Mrs Adams doesn't want to sell."

"Seriously? You've asked her?"

"Yes. When we first got our inheritances, I had the same idea."

They'd both inherited from their paternal grandfather about six months earlier. Nick had immediately bought a piece of land, about five miles outside of town. He wanted to build a house there – one day. For now, he lived on the site, in a trailer. It was something else for their parents to feel embarrassed about. But Nick didn't care about that; he just wanted a place of his own, that he'd created, in his style… and he didn't mind waiting for it.

"And she doesn't want to sell?" Emma shook her head. "That's ridiculous. She's never here. I mean, you practically run the place." It was true. Mrs Adams spent most of the cold winter months in Florida, where her son, Max and daughter, Ruth, both lived now.

"I know." Emma shrugged. "But even if she did, I don't think Grandpa Jonas's money would be enough. I'd be buying the building, *and* the business."

"Well, if she changes her mind, you should talk to the bank," Nick encouraged. "You'd have a substantial downpayment. They might lend you the rest."

"I don't know…"

"It might happen. And if it does, I'll help you with the paperwork. I'll come to the bank with you as well, if you want me to." He looked at her, holding her gaze for a moment. "That's not everything though, is it?" he asked.

"I miss Cassie," she murmured.

He leant over and gave her a hug, putting his arm around her. "I know you do. You two have been inseparable for years."

"Well, not as inseparable as she and Jake were."

Nick paused for a moment. "Yeah. None of us saw that one coming. Why *did* they break up?" he asked. "You've never said." It was a question the whole town had been asking for months. Jake and Cassie had been together for six years, but had been friends since they were six years old. And then they'd gone their separate ways when they finished college earlier in the year… just like that. They'd both left town on the same day. Jake had just disappeared without a word to anyone; Cassie had told Emma and her mom what she was doing and where she was going, but only on the understanding that they never revealed it to anyone else, and because of that promise, Emma hadn't even been able to tell Nick.

"I can't say, you know that. I was sworn to secrecy."

"Okay." He didn't push. "You know where she is though, so why don't you go and see her?" he suggested.

"I can't. Not at the moment. Mrs Adams has gone down to visit Ruth until after Thanksgiving."

Nick sighed deeply. "At least if you owned the place – or even ran it – you could take on more staff, and have a few days off. This way, she's got you as an unofficial manager, working every hour of the day, on a waitress's salary, with no-one to cover for you, because she decides who works here and when, while she swans off to Florida for weeks at a time."

She couldn't deny anything he was saying. Emma worked six days a week, until seven o'clock each night and had two part-time helpers. There was no doubt about it, Mrs Adams was taking advantage, but there was nothing Emma could do about it.

"Maybe you can get Cassie to come here for a visit?" Nick tried again.

"She won't be coming back," she said.

Nick stared at her. "Not ever?"

Emma shook her head. "No."

"Wow." He let out a low whistle, then leant in closer to his sister. "You're lonely, aren't you?"

She turned to face him, tears forming in her eyes. She nodded her head. "How did you know?" she asked.

He shrugged. "Takes one to know one."

"You're lonely too?" Emma blinked back her tears.

"Yeah, but like I said before, we're not talking about me." He smiled at her.

"No, and we're not talking about me either," she murmured.

Nick rested his elbows on his knees. "Okay," he sighed. "But you know where I am if you change your mind."

Emma leant into him. "Thanks," she whispered. Then she squared her shoulders and sat back in her chair, looking across at him. "Did you come in here for a reason?"

"What, you mean apart from proving that I'm the best brother in the world?"

"Yeah, apart from that…"

"Well, I've gotta work late tonight…"

"Nothing new there," Emma muttered. Nick had been really focused on his job since returning from law school, but now she knew he was lonely, she could understand that.

"Yeah, okay," he said, smiling at her. "And I was wondering if you could make me some macaroni and cheese to take back to the office."

She swatted his arm with her cloth. "It's always about food with you, isn't it?" She got to her feet and put the chair back neatly under the table. "And I don't do the cooking, in case you've forgotten?" That was another point that rankled with her. She could cook better than Noah, the chef, but she was employed to wait tables.

"It's your recipe, though," Nick pointed out.

"Yeah, but Noah gets the credit." She shook her head, just for a moment. "I'll go and ask him to make you some, and I'll bring it over to your office when I close up."

He stood up, leant down and kissed her on the cheek. "You're a star, Em."

"Yeah, I know."

Emma was running out of things to tidy. She'd sent Patsy home early; there seemed little point in both of them kicking their heels. Noah was cleaning the kitchen, and prepping for tomorrow's breakfast. Although it was quiet, Emma wasn't unduly worried. This was normal for a Thursday night in early November. People were tired at the end of the working week. They were either at home with their families, or they'd be in Mac's Bar. The coffee shop would get a little busier over Thanksgiving and, again, over the Christmas holidays and then there'd be another lull, before the tourists started to return in earnest in the spring.

She leant on the shiny wooden counter and surveyed the shop. It was a little tired, but the locals seemed to like it. The wood panelling gave it an air of old-worldliness that went well with the neat round, dark wood tables and matching ladder-backed chairs. There were booths running down one wall and, in the summer, they provided seating outside as well, along the wide sidewalk. Right now though, it felt kind of cozy in here, even if she knew she could do so much more with the place… if only it were hers.

She let out a sigh, turned and started cleaning down the coffee machine.

The door opened and closed again and, surprised by the late caller, Emma swung round… and her tongue dried, feeling like it was stuck to the roof of her mouth. The man walking toward the counter was the most gorgeous human being she'd ever seen. He was tall – very tall – with thick dark brown hair and a strong, square jaw. He wore jeans, a gray t-shirt, and a black leather jacket, none of which hid his athletic build.

"Hi," he said, staring at her unashamedly. "Are you still open?"

"Yes," she replied, nodding her head at the same time.

"Great." He smiled, and she felt a warmth in the pit of her stomach. That was weird. She'd never felt anything quite like that before. "I'm in need of coffee."

"Okay." She came closer as he sat down opposite her. "What would you like?"

His smile widened. "A latte, thanks."

"Coming right up."

She fetched a large cup from the shelf behind the counter and prepared him a coffee, as requested.

"Are you visiting town?" she asked, not turning round.

"Yeah. I'm here until next Wednesday… on vacation."

Now she flipped her head round. "At this time of year?"

"Why not?" He smiled again, and that warmth spread a little further.

"People tend to visit here in the summer, that's all."

"Well, I like to be different."

She passed the cup of coffee over the counter and he pushed a ten dollar bill toward her.

"Being as you're not exactly rushed off your feet," he said, looking around the deserted café, "why don't you join me?" He patted the stool next to his.

Emma felt that strange heat increase again. She lowered her eyes, feeling a little shy, but when she looked back up, he was still smiling at her. "Okay," she said. "Thank you."

She made herself a latte as well and came around the counter, sitting down beside him.

"Is it normally this quiet around here?" he asked, once she was settled.

"At this time of year, yes." She looked up at him. His amber colored eyes were mesmerizing. "People – tourists, I mean – they come here for the beaches. So, the summer's our busy time." She felt like she was rambling.

"Are the beaches any good?"

"Oh, yes." She smiled. "They're…" She searched for the right word. "Beautiful – really dramatic."

"You'll have to show me." His voice had dropped a note or two, his eyes pierced hers, and she felt herself being drawn to him. That warmth had now given up spreading. It had suffused throughout her whole body and, as she watched him sip his coffee, she wondered how those long fingers, now gripping his cup, might feel caressing her skin… How was this even possible? He'd been there all of five minutes and she'd turned into a simmering mass of need and emotions. And she didn't think it was just her either. The look in his eyes was one of complete desire, and he hadn't once taken them from her. "I'm booked into the hotel up the street…" He was still talking, and she dragged her attention away from her lustful thoughts and back to his words. "But they don't serve evening meals. So, is there anywhere I can get something to eat?"

"There's Fernando's," Emma suggested. "It's at the other end of Main Street." She pointed over her shoulder.

"Sounds Italian." He grinned and she twisted in her seat, trying to get more comfortable, despite the increasing heat of his gaze, but the movement just made her even more aware of how much she ached for his touch… What was wrong with her? How could she want him this much, this quickly?

"That's because it is," she managed to say.

"Any good?" he asked, moving just a little closer.

"Not bad." She shrugged and tried not to sound too negative. "Gino and Elaine are lovely, but they're not very adventurous."

"So it's a bit… safe?"

"That's a good way of putting it."

"Well, I guess safe isn't *always* a bad thing."

"No, but it can get a little boring."

He smiled again, and his eyes sparkled, like they were burning into her. "You're sounding like a woman after my own heart," he whispered, then he paused, opened his mouth, closed it again and finally said. "Look, I know you don't know me… and I've literally just walked in off the street, but would you like to have dinner with me tonight?"

Emma stared at him. The heat, the need, and the want were still there but, being sensible, he was right. She didn't know him. "Um… I'm not sure…"

He held up his hands. "I promise I'm not a serial killer, or a madman, or an ax murderer." He smirked. "But then I guess serial killers, madmen, and ax murderers probably say that all the time." He moved his hand along the countertop, closer to hers. "I'm really just an ordinary guy."

"It's not that," she murmured. It was in part, but he seemed so genuine.

"Then have dinner with me," he urged. All of a sudden a thought seemed to strike him. "Oh, I'm sorry," he said quickly. "I should've thought. You've probably already got plans for this evening."

"No, I don't have plans. I've got no-one to make plans with." Oh, God. Had she really just said that out loud… to a total stranger? She felt herself blushing, especially when she noticed the corners of his mouth twitching upward.

"Then you've got no reason not to eat with me."

"Except I don't know why you want to." Her head dropped. If this was his idea of a joke, she'd rather know now. She didn't need anyone else to humiliate her. It seemed she was doing a perfect job of that all by herself.

She felt his finger under her chin, felt him raise her face, until she was looking into his twinkling pale brown eyes again.

"Are you serious?" he asked.

"Well, yes," she replied. She was.

He sighed. "I want to have dinner with you because you intrigue me," he murmured. Then he stood, looking down at her. "And because we've already established we've got something in common."

Emma was confused, as well as breathless. "What's that?"

He leant in closer to her, close enough for her to smell his body wash. She thought it might be sandalwood and vanilla, but whatever it was, he smelt divine. His lips were only a few inches from hers, and she couldn't help but focus on them when he whispered, "We both think safe is a little boring."

Mark

She was the most beautiful woman he'd ever seen – and he'd seen some beautiful women in his time. How on earth could she doubt he'd want to have dinner with her? She was staring up at him, her deep brown eyes gazing for a moment into his. She was utterly bewitching. And he was rock hard; harder than he'd been in… well, forever. *Please let her say yes*, he thought. *Even if it's just dinner. She's enchanting.*

"Thank you," she murmured eventually. "I'd love to have dinner with you."

"Great." *Thank God for that.*

"I'll meet you at the restaurant, shall I?" she suggested.

"No." It didn't work that way, not where he was concerned. "I'll come back and pick you up."

"I've got a quick errand to run when I finish work," she said.

"Okay. Give me a time. I'll be here."

"Um… seven-thirty?"

"Seven-thirty it is. Shall I wait out front for you?" She nodded and he noticed how the light caught her hair. Now she was sitting beside him, he could see it was almost black, but with brown flecks, and had a natural wave. At the moment, it was tied, quite loosely, behind her head, with a few strands hanging down the side of her face, but he wondered what she'd look like with it left untied, wild… untamed. "Great. Well, I'll see you later," he said and started toward the door.

"Wait," she called after him, and he stopped, turning to her. "I don't even know your name… and you don't know mine."

He grinned at her – he couldn't help it. "I know," he said, and he opened the door and went outside, still smiling.

He walked down the street, feeling elated. Nothing quite like this had ever happened to him before, and it felt so damned good. He'd picked up all kinds of women in the past; he'd taken them to intimate dinners, to private clubs, and usually to his bed, but they'd always, *always*, known who he was. It got boring after a while – real boring. The 'coffee shop girl'… she had no idea. And that was what felt great – well, that and the idea of spending a whole evening looking into those beautiful dark brown eyes, talking about… *Oh shit*.

What was he going to tell her about himself? He stopped and looked up a the night sky, studying the twinkling stars for a moment. His instincts were yelling at him to tell her the truth. She was really special – different – and he certainly wanted more than the usual one night stand… He wanted a lot more than that. He may have only spent a few minutes in her company, but he'd worked that much out already… and lying to her wasn't a good place to start. But, could he tell her the truth? If he did, it'd be all over a small town like this before they'd even sat down in the restaurant.

He walked on more slowly, plunging his hands into his pockets.

He'd checked into the hotel as Mark Ellis, using his mother's maiden name, because he wanted a week of anonymity. If you said the name 'Mark Gardner' anywhere in New England, everyone knew immediately who you were talking about: the son of the owner of the biggest chain of hotels on the East coast, one of the hottest rising stars in the business world – set to take over from his father – and a very, very eligible bachelor. Mark was good at keeping his private life private. He was an expert at it, and he knew the press hated that, so given the opportunity, they made up stories about him, most of which were too ludicrous to be taken seriously by anyone. He saw a lot of women, but he took them to places they wouldn't be photographed, and where they could be alone, anonymous, and intimate – if they wanted to. And they usually wanted to. He rarely saw the same woman more than once though, simply because he'd yet to find a woman who wasn't more interested in his fortune than she was in him.

And he'd been burned... twice. A couple of years ago, it had been a young actress and, most recently, an up and coming model, both of whom had sold the story of their solitary 'night of hot passion' to the gutter tabloids. There had been lurid details and photographs – of the women, not him. Mark did everything in his power to avoid being photographed, but that didn't make the stories any less intrusive. His family consoled him that most people who mattered didn't read that kind of trash anyway. His friends – such as they were – consoled him that both women had been real complimentary about his prowess in the bedroom. He'd laughed; he'd made the right noises... but since the last time it had happened, back in the summer, he'd been wary. Well, he'd been more than wary. In reality, it had been over four months since he'd been with a woman...

Still, 'coffee shop girl' wasn't just your average woman.

He got back there ten minutes early, having showered and changed into casual pants and a jacket, with a button down shirt, and stood outside the now locked door to the coffee shop, which was shrouded in darkness. He waited patiently. It was cold, so he paced up and down, telling himself it was to keep warm, not because he was nervous. Since when did Mark Gardner get nervous on a date? Maybe since he was pretending to be someone he wasn't... and maybe since he was about to have dinner with a woman he already knew would forever haunt his dreams and fill his every waking thought.

At exactly seven-thirty, she appeared from a doorway just beyond the coffee shop. But... his heart sank. She wasn't alone. Walking beside her was a tall, muscular-looking guy. Even in the street lights, Mark could see the guy's hair was – frankly – messy. Although it was cold and the girl was wearing a knee-length coat, her companion was just in shirtsleeves, with a loose tie and waistcoat, over jeans, his hands shoved deep into the pockets. He looked kind of disheveled, and a little rough around the edges. *What the hell?* Mark thought.

They approached quickly, the girl's heels tapping on the sidewalk.

"Hello," she said quietly, as she came to stand in front of him.

"Hi." He looked from her to the man standing next to her. His eyes were steely and, although he couldn't see them clearly in this light, Mark guessed they were probably either blue or gray.

"This is my brother, Nick," the girl said. *Her brother*. Mark felt relieved and confused at the same time.

"I'm not stopping," Nick said quickly. "I just came to check you out." Well, that was honest enough.

Mark almost laughed, but managed not to. "Okay." He guessed it was a fair thing to do. He didn't know the guy's sister… Actually, at this point, he still didn't even know her name.

Nick looked him up and down. "Em told me her plans for this evening." He paused. *Em? Short for Emily, maybe? Or Emma?* Mark hoped it was Emma… it suited her perfectly. "And I told her I thought she was insane," Nick continued.

"Fair enough," Mark replied. "Would it help if I told you my intentions are entirely honorable?"

"No. I'd just call that bullshit." Mark laughed and noticed Nick's lips curl upward. "We both know a guy's *intentions* can vary enormously from his actions. If they didn't, I'd be out of a job."

Mark raised an eyebrow. "Nick's a lawyer," 'Em' explained, then she turned to her brother. "Okay," she said. "You've done your protective brother bit. Can I go and have dinner now?" She tilted her head to one side, her hand resting on her hip.

Nick looked from her to Mark, and back again. "Sure," he said, smiling. He bent down, kissed her on the cheek, and whispered, loud enough for Mark to hear, "Call me, if you need me."

She leant back and looked up at him. "Get going," she said, pointing back down the street.

Nick chuckled, shaking his head and turned away, walking slowly back the way he'd come, evidently immune to the cold.

'Em' turned to Mark. "I'm so sorry," she said.

"Hey… don't be. I think it's good you've got someone looking out for you. I'm sure I'll be the same with my sister, when she's old enough to date."

"You've got a little sister?"

"Yeah."

"How little?"

"She's not a toddler, if that's what you mean. She's ten years younger than me."

"Well, being as I don't know how old you are, that doesn't help much."

He smiled. "Sorry… she's fifteen."

"Um… I hate to tell you this, but fifteen is old enough to date."

"Yeah. I know." He smiled as he thought of Sarah. "She just hasn't gotten around to it yet, thank God." He grinned.

"Somehow I get the feeling you'll be even worse than Nick." She stared up at him.

"Probably." He took a half-step closer. "Now," he said solemnly, "I think it's time we introduced ourselves." He held out his hand. "My name's Mark…" he paused, just for a second, and made a snap decision. "Mark Ellis."

"Emma Woods." He was pleased. *Emma. Just as I hoped.* Her name felt right for her and he knew then that, unlike her brother, he'd never shorten it. She would always be 'Emma' to him.

She put her hand in his. Her skin was soft, delicate, and he felt the air being sucked from his lungs at her gentle touch.

"It's a real pleasure to meet you," he whispered.

They were shown to a quiet table at the back of the restaurant. There were a few people dining, maybe five or six other couples, and a group of eight, who were quite loud and – thankfully – seated as far away as possible. Emma removed her coat, handing it to the hostess – who Emma introduced as Elaine, the co-owner – and, as she turned back to Mark, his breath caught in his throat. In the coffee shop earlier, he'd noticed how her black pants had clung to her hips and he'd found it hard to ignore the way her nipples had shown through her thin white blouse. But now… Oh, my God… She was wearing a dark blue, knee-length, all over lace cocktail dress, which appeared to be see-through, but it wasn't. Mark could just make out a layer of skin colored material beneath the lace, creating the illusion. An illusion that made him hard again, in an instant.

He held her seat, pushing it forward as she sat down, and resisted the urge to touch her shoulders, or lean down and kiss her neck.

Over a 'safe' main course of spaghetti with meatballs, which they'd both ordered, Mark gazed into her brown, sparkling eyes and explained that he worked in the hotel trade. It wasn't a lie... well, not really. He did. His family owned dozens and dozens of hotels all over New England. The fact that he'd implied he worked in a particular hotel was beside the point. He avoided specifics and turned the topic of employment back onto Emma.

"So, do you manage the coffee shop? Or..." He left the question hanging. She seemed too young to own it, but she'd been the only person there, and it had felt like she belonged.

She shook her head. "No." She looked a little dejected. "I'm just a waitress."

He put down his fork and reached across the table, taking her hand in his. "Don't say 'just' like that," he told her. "You're not 'just' anything." Even as he said those words, he wondered what would happen if he took Emma home and introduced her to his family as a 'waitress'. His mom would be fine with it. Lisa Gardner was renowned among her friends as an incurable romantic. His dad? No... Michael Gardner would freak at the idea of his only son, the heir to his empire and fortune, dating a waitress. He smiled to himself. Since when did he 'date' – in the conventional sense, anyway? Or take women to meet his parents, for that matter? Never. Well, not until now, anyway. But there was something about Emma that was different... very different.

Emma was talking. "I wanted to buy the place," she was saying. "I inherited some money not long ago." She took a sip of wine, and he was momentarily distracted by her lips and the sudden urge to kiss them. "It's not enough though."

Mark sat forward. "You could borrow the rest, couldn't you? If you've got a big enough down payment, the bank would lend it to you." He'd happily give her the money, but he could hardly tell her that.

"You sound just like my brother."

"Well… couldn't you?"

"I don't know. I didn't inquire."

"Why not?"

"Because when I asked her, Mrs Adams – the woman who owns the coffee shop – she said she wasn't interested in selling at the moment, so there seemed little point in pursuing it."

"Then how do you know your inheritance isn't enough?"

"It's not just the business I'd be buying. Mrs Adams owns the building as well… so that's the shop, the apartment above, *and* the business."

Mark nodded. He didn't know how much money she'd inherited, or how much Mrs Adams was likely to be asking for the property and business, but he guessed it didn't matter if she wasn't interested in selling, and he sensed Emma's disappointment.

"Is it an ambition of yours?" he asked.

"What? Owning a coffee shop? Not really."

"Then why…?" He was confused.

She smiled. "Why even think about it?" He nodded. "Because at the moment, I do run the place, but I get paid a waitress's salary. And I figure I could make it so much… more, if I just had a free hand."

"In what way?" He was intrigued.

She sat forward in her seat, ignoring her food. "I'd redecorate, to start with; make the place more modern. And I think we should offer more home-made cakes and pastries – something a bit more unique – not the mass-produced things Mrs Adams buys in…" Her eyes lit up. "And then I'd change the lunchtime menu. I'd make it more… adventurous."

"Do you know anything about cooking?" he asked her.

"Yes. I love to cook. It's what I always wanted to do."

"Then why didn't you?"

She slumped back into her seat, her face falling. "I studied culinary arts at college," she said. "But I hated it… I only lasted half a semester and I came back home. I've been at the coffee shop ever since." She picked up her fork and started pushing her food around her plate.

"What didn't you like about it?" he asked.

"Pretty much everything." Emma didn't look up. He reached across the table and, placing his finger under her chin, just like he'd done at the coffee shop earlier, he raised her face. *Shit.* There were tears in her eyes.

"What's wrong?" he asked.

"Quitting, like I did… it's always made me feel like such a failure." She mumbled out the words, then clamped her mouth shut, like she regretted saying them.

"No-one's a failure… unless they give up on themselves," he whispered, leaning a little closer. Her eyes met his and he wondered, briefly, if she had. "You're young," he added. "You're… what? Twenty-two?" She nodded. He'd guessed right, that was something. "Most kids are just leaving college at your age, with no idea what working for a living involves. You've got huge advantages. You've got experience, understanding, expertise. You know your business, your field, your market…" He stopped, aware he was sounding too much like a businessman and not enough like a hotel employee. She was staring at him.

"Thank you." Her voice was barely audible.

"What for?"

"Apart from Nick, you're the first person to show any faith in me." She seemed to think for a moment. "Well, that's not true. My best friend was always really supportive, but she's left town now."

He wondered if she was lonely. She sure seemed to be unhappy… and isolated. It didn't sit well with her. It didn't sit well with him either.

"Just don't give up," he said. "Mrs Adams might change her mind one day, so keep the plans going. Keep thinking up the ideas."

She smiled. "Oh… I do. It's what keeps me going."

God, that was sad. Was that really all she had?

They didn't bother with dessert, or coffee. Neither wanted the former and when the latter was offered, Emma gave him an almost imperceptible shake of her head. While Elaine went to get the check, Emma explained that the coffee there was awful, which made Mark laugh out loud.

"You should know," he said, quietening down as he handed over the right amount of cash, including the tip. He didn't want to use a credit card while in town… the name wouldn't match the one he was using. And he knew it would get back to the hotel owner – and to Emma – probably before he'd even put his card back into his wallet, that Mark Gardner was in town and staying under a false name. He shook his head as he helped Emma into her coat, feeling guilty for deceiving her.

"This is me," Emma said as they approached the coffee shop again.

"You live above the shop?" he asked.

"Yes."

"And I guess that means you open up every day?"

"Seven o'clock sharp." She smiled.

"A twelve hour shift. How many days a week do you do that?"

"Six. I have Sundays off. That's when I sleep."

"And you do this for a waitress's salary?"

"I keep my own tips. And I have the apartment."

"Rent free?" he asked.

She shook her head. "No… but it's reduced."

He felt as though he'd quite like to sit down with Mrs Adams and give her a good talking to about employee relations.

Emma moved a half-step closer and he caught the scent of her perfume. It was floral, like jasmine, or something. "I've had a lovely evening," she said.

"Me too."

"I'd invite you up, but I've got an early start."

"That's okay." He moved closer still. They were almost touching. "Can… Can I see you again tomorrow night?" That wasn't a question he was used to asking.

There wasn't even a blink of hesitation before Emma nodded her head, a smile forming slowly on her lips. "I'd like that," she said.

"And… can I kiss you?" he whispered.

Again, she nodded. "I'd like that too."

He brought his hands up, clasping her face, and leant forward, gently brushing his lips across hers. At the moment they touched, his world stopped spinning. Just like that. Nothing moved or stirred… not even his heart. After a minute – probably less – he pulled back, staring down at her face as she opened her eyes, gazing up into his.

"I'll see you tomorrow," he whispered. She nodded and he let her go, watching as she went inside. Then he turned and walked away, feeling a little lost without her.

Chapter Two

Emma

Getting out of bed had been a struggle. On the cold winter mornings it always was, but today it was even worse. She'd lain awake for hours last night, just thinking about the strength of his hands on her cheeks, the depth of longing in eyes as they gazed into hers, the softness of his lips, molding gently against her own. She'd wanted more… a lot more. But he'd pulled away. Why was that? Didn't he want more too? His eyes said 'yes', she was almost sure they did… Eventually, she'd drifted into a restless sleep, filled with dreams where Mark was always just out of reach. And she'd woken in the morning to the noisy beep of her alarm, feeling as though her head was stuffed with cotton wool.

Two hours later, the coffee shop door opened and closed, letting in a blast of cold air, as another satisfied customer left to start their day.

During the winter months, breakfast was the busiest time. Locals came in for something quick and simple they could take away with them, like a muffin or bagel, or if they had time, they'd sit down, have a coffee and enjoy something more substantial, like french toast with bacon and maple syrup, or pancakes, or home fries, eggs and bacon, all served with a side order of gossip. Although Emma did her best to ignore the tittle-tattle, she still preferred this time of day. She liked the noise and bustle, the distraction of having plenty to do; and she found keeping busy helped when she was feeling as low as she had been over the last few months. And she really had been low.

Kathryn was on the breakfast shift with her today. Like Patsy, Kathryn had worked in the coffee shop for nearly ten years – longer than Emma – and, also like Patsy, she had no ambition to do more than a little part-time waitressing. Both women had teenage kids, who could look after themselves, and the money they earned supplemented the family income and paid for treats – nights out, weekends away.

"A cappuccino for table seven," Kathryn called out to Emma.

"Okay." Emma smiled. It had taken her months to persuade Mrs Adams to invest in a barista coffee machine, so they could offer a wider range of drinks, rather than just the filter coffee they'd always served before, and to offer a take-out option. Mrs Adams had baulked at the idea, citing the extra cost involved. However, when Emma had done the research and presented her with figures showing the potential for increased profits, she'd given in and leased the equipment – she wouldn't buy it, just in case it didn't work out. Emma had tried repeatedly to train Patsy and Kathryn to use the machine, but they both refused, which meant during busy times, like breakfast, Emma was stuck behind the counter. She didn't mind. She could still keep busy… and stay away from the gossip mongers.

She looked up as the door opened again, and her heart flipped over in her chest, a smile spreading across her lips. Mark didn't even look around, he just walked straight over and sat down on a stool by the counter – the same one he'd occupied the night before.

"Good morning," he said.

"Hello." She was surprised how normal her voice sounded, considering that her heart was pumping so hard she could barely breathe.

"It's a bit busier in here now."

She grinned. "That's breakfast for you."

"And there was me hoping I'd have you all to myself again."

"Well, you will later…" His eyes widened. They noticeably widened and she felt herself blush. She hadn't meant it like that. At least, she didn't think she had, had she?

"Yeah…" He looked a little sheepish. "So, I know we said we'd meet up again tonight, but…" he smiled, "… it seems I'm not very good at waiting when it comes to you. I woke up this morning and wanted to see you, and I didn't want to wait." He leant a little closer. "Not one more minute."

"Emma!" Kathryn's voice brought her back to earth with a bump as she passed by the counter, carrying two stacks of pancakes. "Table seven… cappuccino."

"Sorry." She looked at Mark. "Give me a minute."

"Take all the time you need," he said, smiling and looking annoyingly relaxed as he leant over to grab a menu. "I'm not going anywhere."

He studied the selection for a while, then when Emma had a free moment, he ordered French toast, but asked if he could have it with fresh fruit, not bacon, and no maple syrup.

She grinned. "That's a bit adventurous…"

"Hardly." He smiled back at her.

"It is around here."

He leant forward. "Well," he murmured and paused, just for a moment. "I've always been adventurous. I think it's so much more fun than being boring, don't you?" The heat in his voice was intoxicating, and she moved closer, nodding her head. "God, I wish it could be later already," he whispered, and the look in his eyes scorched through her. She was almost certain she heard herself moan as she stared at his lips.

"Hey, Em." The male voice from over by the door fractured the moment and she jumped. Mark moved back again, and Emma looked up and saw Nick approaching the counter.

"Hi, Nick." She took a step back and tried to appear normal, although she was aware she was flushed, and breathless. Had Mark done that to her, just with his words? Evidently.

And what was more, she wanted him to do it again.

"Everything okay?" Nick glanced at her, then looked back at Mark again, his eyes narrowing. Could her brother guess what was going through her mind? God, she hoped not.

"Everything's fine. And stop trying to intimidate him."

"I'm not… trying, that is."

22

Mark laughed and stood up. He was maybe an inch taller than Nick – who Emma knew was six foot four – and he didn't look even vaguely intimidated.

"I'm Mark Ellis," he said.

Nick looked down at Mark's hand, waited a long moment then offered his own. "Nick Woods," he replied. They shook hands. Even from her side of the counter, Emma saw Nick's knuckles whiten as he crushed Mark's hand in his.

"Stop it," she said. "I mean it, Nick."

He turned to her, releasing Mark, who didn't flinch.

"What do you want, Nick?" Emma asked him.

"A double espresso, to go, please." He smiled across at her.

"Okay. Is that your breakfast?" she asked.

"Yeah…"

"How late did you work?" She turned and started to grind the beans for his coffee.

"I think I finished some time around two. I was going over depositions."

"Then you should probably eat something," Mark suggested, sitting down again.

"He's right." Emma turned. "Even if you just take a muffin, or a bagel with you. Eat something, Nick."

Nick looked from one of them to the other. "Okay. I'll take a blueberry muffin… Happy?" He glanced up at Emma.

"Yeah." She smiled back at him. "I am… very." She held his gaze until he smiled back, nodded his head, and finally relaxed.

"Where are you from, Mark?" he asked, turning toward him.

"Boston."

"And what do you do?" Emma felt her shoulders drop. She thought he'd got the message. She was happy, she'd just told him that. He'd nodded. So why was he giving Mark a grilling?

"Leave him alone," she said.

"I'm just asking," Nick replied.

"It's fine, Emma." Mark looked at her, his eyes gazing deeply into hers for a moment. "I'd be the same if a guy was interested in Sarah."

Did he just say he was interested in her? Seriously? "Who's Sarah?" Nick asked.

"She's *my* little sister." Mark's eyes moved away from hers as he turned his head back toward Nick. The warm glow of his words remained, however, keeping that heat within her on a gentle simmer.

"You've got a little sister too?" Nick grinned. Mark nodded his head. "Pain in the ass, aren't they?" Mark laughed.

"Hey!" Emma went to swipe Nick around the head, but he caught her arm, just in time.

"Missed again."

"That's the last time I bring macaroni and cheese to your office at night."

Nick faked a sulk. "You know you love me."

"No, I don't."

She turned back to the coffee machine and carried on making his espresso.

"Yeah, you do." She looked over her shoulder at the two of them, sitting like co-conspirators, watching her… and she couldn't help but laugh.

Mark stayed for breakfast, and lunch, which he ate late with Emma, on her break.

"I know we agreed to see each other again tonight, but we didn't make any firm plans yet, did we?" he said as they finished eating.

To Emma's ears, he almost sounded worried. "No," she replied.

"And I know I've spent the whole morning here," he added. "I'd understand if you're bored with me——"

"I'm not," she interrupted quickly. "I'm not bored at all. It's been lovely having you here." She felt herself blush as a smile spread across his face, lighting up his eyes.

"It's been lovely being here," he said. "So… will you have dinner with me again tonight?"

"I'd love to." She didn't hesitate for one second. After all, he was interested in her. He'd said so himself.

"I'll drive us up the coast. We'll find a quiet restaurant somewhere."

"We could do that…" She thought quickly about what she had in her refrigerator. She mentally shook her head. It didn't matter. She could go to the store during the afternoon, when the coffee shop was quiet, and get what she needed. "Or I could cook," she said at last.

"You'll cook?" he whispered. "For me?"

"Y—yes… I'd like to prove I can."

He stood up, pulled her to her feet, and rested his hands gently on her hips. "You don't have to prove anything to me, Emma," he said quietly. "I already believe in you. But I'd love you to cook dinner for me, if you're sure you really want to." He smiled.

"I want to." She let out the breath she hadn't even realized she was holding. "The door to my apartment is to the right of the shop." She pointed. "Ring on the buzzer and I'll let you in."

"What time?" he asked.

"Come over at seven-thirty?" she suggested. "I don't finish until seven, so dinner won't be ready by then, but we can… we can have a glass of wine and talk, while I cook."

"I'll bring the wine," he offered. "Red or white?"

She thought for a moment. "White."

"Okay." He smiled, releasing her. "I'll let you get on with some work, and I'll see you later."

He was sitting at Emma's breakfast bar, wearing dark blue jeans and a white button-down shirt, watching her. It made her feel a little self-conscious, which she never normally did when she was cooking. This was where she was at her most confident… except when a gorgeous, sexy man was sipping wine and staring at her.

"It smells incredible," he said.

"I just hope the taste doesn't disappoint." She checked the oven temperature. She didn't need to, but it gave her something to do… not that she'd been idle since she'd finished at the coffee shop. She'd bought her ingredients earlier in the afternoon, and Kathryn had stayed a half hour later than normal, giving her time to do a little preparation, so the appetizer was already done and the dessert just needed a finishing touch. Then she'd put the chicken breasts in the oven as soon as she'd come upstairs, had the quickest shower in history, finger dried her hair and braided it loosely, put on her dark red cocktail dress, and set about making the carrot and kale salad, which she'd just finished when Mark arrived.

"I'm sure it won't," he replied.

She glanced at her watch again, and undid the apron strings behind her back. She knew it wasn't ideal to have greeted Mark wearing an apron, but she didn't want to spoil her dress either. As she pulled it over her head, she could have sworn she heard him let out a sigh and she glanced up to find his eyes raking down her body. She knew the dress was a bit of a risk. It was shorter than the one she'd worn last night – not much, but enough. Being dark red, against her nearly black hair, she knew the color always looked good on her, and because they weren't going out, it didn't matter that it was sleeveless. She wasn't likely to feel cold standing by the stove anyway, and the way Mark was staring at her, she could feel a heat burning from within too.

"You look… stunning," Mark said, and she felt herself blushing. She really wished she could stop doing that.

"Thank you," she murmured. "We can eat now, if you'd like to sit at the table…" She nodded in the direction of her living area. It was small, but functional, with a couch, coffee table, wall-mounted television and a small dining table and two chairs, set by the window that overlooked Main Street.

He went over and sat down, looking back at her as she followed, bringing the appetizers with her. She put the plates down before taking her seat opposite him and, just for a moment, he took his eyes from her to glance down at the food.

"It's parma ham, with melon and mozzarella, basil leaves, and a lemon and herb dressing."

"It looks incredible."

She'd taken a lot of trouble over the presentation and smiled up at him. "Thank you," she said again. "Enjoy…"

They talked while they ate, mainly about how good the food tasted, the combination of ingredients, and how the dressing complimented everything.

"It's a perfect balance," Mark said, placing his knife and fork back on the empty plate. "Any more lemon and it would have been too sharp."

"That's just about tasting as you go," Emma explained. "The most common mistake people make is to just trust the recipe."

"Isn't that what recipes are for?" Mark inquired.

"They're a guide. But personal taste has to come into it. I don't like things that are too sharp, so I've reduced the amount of lemon in the recipe, used a little more oil, and increased the oregano."

"It's perfect." His eyes met hers again and they sat, just staring at each other.

"I—I suppose I'd better get the next course," Emma said eventually.

"Yes…" His voice echoed her reluctance to break the moment.

She cleared the plates and, while she was preparing the final touches to the main course, and slicing the chicken breasts, he asked about her family.

"My parents own the boat yard," she said. "Around here, that's like saying they're the King and Queen, I guess… or that's the way they act, anyway."

"Oh…"

"Sorry. I shouldn't have said that."

"Why not?" She looked up from the kitchen and saw he was staring at her again.

"Because my problems with my parents are just that… my problems."

"If it helps to talk…" he offered.

She shrugged and went back to the job in hand. "I'll still be a disappointment to them, however much I talk about it."

"A disappointment?"

"Yeah. The college drop-out."

"Oh… And I guess it doesn't help that your brother's a lawyer."

"No, not even he escapes their criticism."

"Really?" She could tell he was surprised.

"Nick did really well at law school," she explained, adding the last of the garnish to the plates and bringing them over to the table. "He could've taken his pick from… oh, I don't know… maybe a half dozen law firms in Boston."

"And he chose to come back here?"

"Yes." She sat down again.

Mark looked down at the plate in front of him. "Wow." He smiled up at her. "Once again, this looks amazing."

She blushed. "It's chicken with roasted lemons and potatoes, and a carrot and kale salad. It's meant to be made with a whole chicken, but there wasn't time…"

"I see. Well, for someone who doesn't like sharp flavors, you use a lot of lemons."

"Ahh, but when you roast them, they become sweeter."

"Is that so?"

"Hmm… taste…" she suggested, nodding to his plate.

Mark put a piece of lemon in his mouth and swallowed. "You're right. It's hardly sharp at all."

They both started to eat. "So, why did your brother come back here?" Mark asked.

"He always changes the subject when I ask him that, so I don't really know. I think he had an aversion to those big corporate firms. He wanted to work somewhere he could help people more, but he could've done that in any small or medium sized town. He didn't have to come back here." She cleared her throat. "He's never said anything, but I think something happened to him at college. Something to do with a woman. I think he got hurt… badly. So, maybe he came back home to lick his wounds, and just never left."

"And does he live with your parents?"

"Dear God, no." He laughed. "Sorry, that came out wrong too."

"Not necessarily."

"It's just, we both got out of the family home as quickly as we could, so the idea of Nick still being there, or moving back after law school… well, it's diverting, to put it mildly."

Once they'd finished, Mark helped her to clear the table, then she shooed him into the living room while she made the coffee and whipped some cream.

"Whipped cream?" he asked as he sat down on the couch.

"Yes."

"I like the sound of that…" His eyes roamed over her again and she felt every muscle clench as she thought of him licking softly whipped cream from her naked body, his tongue exploring her… "For…?"

"Um… sorry?" She dragged herself back to reality.

"What's the whipped cream for?" He was smiling, like he knew exactly what she'd been thinking.

"That would be telling." She noticed him shift in his seat and wondered if he'd had the same thoughts about the whipped cream, and whether he was feeling the sudden heated connection between them as much as she was.

It didn't take long for her to make coffee and finish the mini ginger cheesecakes. Well, it didn't take long once she'd got her brain to stop fantasizing and focus on what needed to be done.

She set the tray on the coffee table.

"You made those?" Mark looked at her.

"Yes. They're really quick."

"They'd need to be." He picked one up and put the bitesize morsel into his mouth. "Oh… my God," he muttered as he swallowed. "It's official. I've died and gone to heaven."

She laughed. "I don't think they're quite that good."

"You haven't tried one yet. Here, let me…" He picked up a second one and, moving closer, he held it out to her. "Open up," he whispered, and she did as he said, opening her mouth to let him pop the mini cheesecake inside. His fingers grazed across her lips and he let them linger there as she closed her mouth again, their eyes locked.

"Good, isn't it?" he asked.

"Hmm." She nodded, swallowing.

"Can I kiss you?" he asked. She nodded again and he moved closer still, his hand cupping her cheek as he leaned forward and let his lips touch hers. Almost immediately, she felt the tip of his tongue brush against her lips and she gasped at the contact, her mouth opening to his. His tongue found hers and she responded to the urgency she felt in him. He changed the angle of the kiss, taking her deeper, leaning her back into the corner of the couch and bringing his other hand to rest on her waist. She felt him shift his weight on top of her, and reached up, her hands entwining in his hair, fisting there and pulling him down closer, harder. She heard him groan into her mouth. It was such a deep, sexy sound… all it did was heighten her need for him. He must've sensed it too.

He broke the kiss and leant back, taking his weight on his arms and looking down at her.

"I want you," he whispered.

"I want you too."

"You do?" She nodded. "You mean that?" She nodded again and he looked into her eyes, searching. "Where's your bedroom?" he asked and he stood up, then leant down, lifting her into his arms.

"Left hand door, off the hallway," she murmured, looking up into his eyes.

He moved quickly through her apartment, opening the door to her bedroom. It was in darkness, but the streetlights gave a rich, yellow glow to the small room.

Mark lowered her to the floor, standing her on her feet and, without saying a word, unzipped her dress. She wasn't wearing a bra and, as it fell to the floor, she was exposed. She heard him suck in a breath.

"Christ… You're beautiful," he whispered and he bent down, running his tongue gently over first one nipple, then the other. Emma let her head rock back as she felt the contact… for the first time ever. It set off bolts of electricity that ran through her body, mostly ending at the apex of her thighs, where she felt like she was on fire. She heard herself moaning, breathing hard, and she clutched his head to her as he used his teeth to nip at her, just gently. Just when she thought it was going to be too much, he stopped and knelt down, placing his thumbs in the tops of her panties, before lowering them to the floor. She stepped out of them and stood, naked before him.

"God, Emma…" he breathed. He knelt there for a long moment, just staring at her, and then he stood, clasped her face in his hands and kissed her really hard, walking her back to the bed. When she hit it, he lowered her gently, so she was lying across the mattress.

"I love that you're shaved," he murmured. "I want to taste you." He knelt between her legs and parted them, spreading them wide with his hands. "God... you're so beautiful." He looked up at her again before leaning down and, using his fingers to part her swollen folds, ran his tongue across her sensitive clitoris. Her hips bucked off the bed. "Stay still, Emma," he muttered, looking up at her again. She nodded, and then felt his breath on her, just before his tongue swept over her again... and again. She tried not to move. She tried to keep as still as she could, even though the sensations were driving her insane. He sucked on her, alternating that with soft, swirling licks and, before long, she was aware of a tingling feeling deep inside her. It came and went, building slowly at first, and then more rapidly, increasing in intensity, until an enormous wave of pleasure crashed over her, consuming her. She closed her eyes and saw stars bursting, her body convulsing and out of control as she screamed and cried his name. She struggled to breathe, her back arched, her head rocked, and still he kept up the movement of his tongue on her, swirling over and over, around and around, until slowly the sensations began to subside and she returned to earth.

She opened her eyes again and looked down. He was smiling up at her.

"That was... incredible," he said. "You taste so good." He moved off the bed and stood, and she watched as he unbuttoned his shirt, shrugging it off and dropping it to the floor, his eyes not leaving hers, not even for a second. His chest was hard, muscular, and she longed to touch it. He undid the buttons on his jeans, lowering them slowly, together with his trunks, and she felt her mouth dry.

Fear creeping over her, she instinctively closed her legs and scrambled away from him, across the bed.

"I can't," she said. He had to be kidding, right?

"What do you mean?" His voice was soft.

"I—I can't," she repeated.

"You can't what?" He knelt back on the bed again, crawling over to her. "What's wrong?" he asked and, looking up into his face, she saw nothing but concern.

"It… it's not going to fit."

He laughed softly. "It'll fit." He sounded so reassuring.

She glanced down at him again. His erection was a lot bigger than she'd anticipated – longer, much, much thicker, and harder. Not that she'd really known what to expect, but she was absolutely certain it wasn't this. She swallowed hard. "Are you sure?" she asked.

"Yeah, baby," he replied. "I'm sure." Did he just call her 'baby'? She looked up at him. "Trust me?" he asked.

She nodded.

"I won't hurt you," he added.

"I know."

He smiled. "Good." He paused for a moment. "Now – at the risk of being practical – do I need a condom? I'm clean…" He left the sentence hanging.

"So am I." Well, she would be, wouldn't she…?

"Birth control?" he asked. She shook her head. "Condom it is, then." He grinned at her and quickly leant over the edge of the bed, grabbing his jeans. He straightened, then moved back between her legs, using his to part hers again.

"You brought a condom? You knew this would happen?" She wasn't sure how she felt about that.

He leant down over her. "No. I *hoped* this would happen," he whispered. "And I brought more than one. Once won't be enough for us, believe me." She gasped and he kissed her, just quickly, before kneeling up again. "Bring your legs up," he murmured. She did as he said, then she heard the foil packet being torn and, intrigued, she raised her head and watched as he slowly unrolled the condom over his length. He leant forward, placing his hands either side of her head and he kissed her gently. She felt his erection pressing into her, right at her entrance, and she tensed. "Relax, Emma… I promise I won't hurt you." His voice reassured her and she calmed, just a little. "That's better, baby."

She closed her eyes, savoring the sensations as he pushed into her, by just the tiniest amount… then a little more. She felt herself being stretched, and then he stilled. She waited, but nothing happened, and she opened her eyes again. He was staring down at her and she couldn't read his expression at all.

"Y—you're a virgin?" he said.

"Um… yes."

He held still, not moving at all. "Seriously?"

She felt the urge to close her legs again, embarrassment almost overwhelming her. "Y—yes. Is that a problem?"

He smiled. "Not for me, no. I'm just blown away, that's all." Without moving inside her, he lowered himself down onto his elbows, studying her face closely. "I don't understand," he whispered.

"What don't you understand?"

"Why you've never had sex."

"Because I've never wanted to."

"Really?" She could see the surprise in his face.

"Well… no. That's not strictly true. I've wanted to. I've often wondered what it'd be like. What I mean is, I've never met anyone I wanted to have sex with." *Could this be any more humiliating?*

"But you want to… with me?"

"Well, yes. Isn't that obvious?"

He let out a laugh. "Yeah. I guess so." He raised himself up again. "You're sure?" he asked. She nodded. "Say it out loud, Emma. I have to know you mean it. It matters."

"I'm sure."

He smiled, and sighed softly. "You know I promised I wouldn't hurt you?"

"Yes."

"I take it back."

"Oh." Her face fell, and she knew it.

"Hey… look at me." He waited. "Look at me, Emma." She did. "I promise I won't hurt you any more than I have to. But this *is* gonna hurt."

She nodded. Then she closed her eyes.

He took a breath and then, very slowly edged into her a little further. She felt a sharp pain and let out a cry, opening her eyes and grabbing hold of his arms. He waited, then pushed in even more. It didn't hurt now. Was that it? She looked up into his eyes and saw her own pleasure reflected right back at her. "You're so tight," he whispered. She smiled. He was stretching her, entering her steadily and slowly, inch by inch, until she'd taken his whole length. She sighed out a long breath as he finally stopped and rested against her.

"How does it feel?" he asked.

"Good," she replied. "Really, really good."

"Hmm… You feel unbelievable. I love how tight you are on my cock."

She smiled again. She liked hearing his words.

"Do you like me saying things like that?" It was as though he'd read her mind.

She nodded, a little embarrassed.

"Hey… that's good. I like that. I like that I can say what I'm really thinking," he reassured her before he leant down and kissed her, and as he pulled back again, he muttered, "I want you to enjoy everything we do together, baby… all of it. I'm gonna fuck you now, until you come." He pulled his cock almost all the way out of her. "Really hard." And he plunged back into her again. She let out a cry, bringing her legs up higher, around his waist, as he started to thrust into her, harder and deeper, over and over. It was relentless… it was perfect.

"That's… Oh, God, Mark… That's so good." She could hardly control her breathing, and then she felt that tingling, quivering sensation starting to build inside her again.

"Oh, yes…" he called out. "Come for me, baby. Come now." He drilled into her, again and again, and she screamed out, as the pleasure drove through her, on and on, in never ending waves…

This time it didn't seem to be stopping. It just kept claiming her, controlling her. "I can't," she panted, trying to breathe. "I can't, Mark. It's too much."

"You can, Emma. I know you can." He kept going and her orgasm heightened again and, as she clamped around him once more, she felt him swell inside her, just before he yelled her name into the darkness, his body convulsing as he pulsed into her and then they both collapsed, breathless into each others arms.

"Cassie?" Emma was taking a five minute – well, maybe ten minute break – out the back of the coffee shop. It was freezing, but she didn't care. She didn't care a bit.

"Yes, it's me." There was a pause. "Are you okay, Em?" Her friend sounded concerned.

"Oh… I'm better than okay."

"Really?" She heard the knowing smile in Cassie's voice. "Wanna give me details?"

"Not details, no… but…"

"But what?"

"I think I've met 'the one'…" Emma breathed.

"Seriously?" Emma could imagine Cassie leaping forward on her couch in her small apartment in Portland… well, maybe not 'leaping' – she was just over seven months pregnant, after all.

"Yes. He's… he's perfect."

"Okay. Now you *are* going to give me details."

Emma laughed. "Alright." She leant back against the wall. "He's here on vacation…" she began. "He's from Boston, and he works at a hotel – I guess in the city, although we haven't actually talked about that much." She paused. "And I spent the night with him."

"You did?" Cassie squealed.

"Yes."

"And?"

"And it was incredible. I mean… Why didn't you tell me?"

"Tell you what?"

"How good it is…" Cassie laughed and Emma joined in.

"Are you seeing him again?" Cassie asked.

"Yes. He's coming over for dinner again tonight. And I don't think he'll be going back to the hotel afterwards." She felt the smile spreading across her lips. "He's just… he's *it*, Cassie."

"I—I'm… Ouch." There was a moment's silence. "I'm really pleased for you."

"Thanks… but why the 'ouch'?" Emma pushed herself away from the wall, suddenly serious. "What's wrong?"

"Oh, it's nothing. They told me I'd get these kind of practice contractions. I can't remember what they called them now, but they're like pretend ones… And I've gotta say, if this is just pretending, I don't want the real thing. I'll just carry on being pregnant."

"You're sure it's just pretend?" Emma asked.

"Yeah. It's gone now. I'm fine. I'm so excited for you. And pleased. I knew there'd be a perfect guy for you out there somewhere." Emma knew how sad this must be making Cassie. She was alone, pregnant, miles from home, lonely without her friends and family, and Emma finding someone had to remind her that Jake – the love of her life and father of her unborn child – had cheated on her.

"Thanks, Cassie," Emma said, feeling guilty all of a sudden.

"How's my mom?" Cassie asked. Emma thought she must have been right… Cassie obviously needed to change the subject.

"I haven't seen her for a couple of days."

"Well, if you do, can you tell her I've managed to get hold of a cheap crib for the baby. One of the women at work was getting rid of it. Mom was saying she was gonna ask around at home, see if anyone was selling off an old one…"

"How was she gonna do that, considering no-one around here even knows you're pregnant?"

"She wasn't gonna tell anyone it's for me."

"Oh… okay. Well, I'll let her know." Emma checked her watch. She'd already been out here for too long. "I'd better be going," she said.

"Time to get back to 'him'?" Cassie teased.

"No… he's gone to the store to buy the ingredients for dinner tonight. I've got to get back to work."

"Take care," Cassie added.

"You too."

"And stay in touch. Just because you've fallen in love, doesn't mean you can forget your oldest friend…"

"Who said anything about love?" Emma felt herself blushing.

"Me…" She heard Cassie laughing as she ended the call.

She wasn't about to deny it. She already knew Mark Ellis was the only man she'd ever love.

Mark

Mark knew from the moment he saw Emma that he wanted to make love with her. He also knew that making love with her would be different. He hadn't realized how different, though, and neither did he immediately appreciate the 'why' in all of that. It took him until Sunday to fully understand.

She wasn't like anyone else he'd ever known. She was a mass of contradictions. She was an adventurous, sexy, sensual, innocent virgin. Well, she wasn't a virgin any longer. She'd entrusted him with taking that from her, and he knew how much it had meant. He'd seen it in her eyes. How the hell she was still a virgin at twenty-two, when she looked the way she did, was beyond him... but now he'd had her, he was glad she'd waited. She may no longer be a virgin, but she was still innocent. She knew absolutely nothing about sex, and that thought made him smile. It was something very new for him, to be teaching her how to enjoy her own body – and his – and it was more pleasurable than he could ever have imagined. That said, she was also adventurous. She'd been willing to try everything he'd suggested so far, without hesitation, and she'd enjoyed it all, breathlessly. She was sexy and sensual. Hell, you only had to look at her for those attributes to be obvious, and as for what she could do with that divine body... it made him tremble just thinking about it, and he'd never reacted like that before, not with any woman. He'd also never been with a woman who could have multiple orgasms before... and nothing as explosive, or shattering as Emma's. Just keeping pace with her was challenging, but it was a challenge he would readily accept, which was just as well, because she was – evidently – insatiable. Within minutes of him taking her virginity on Friday night, she'd wanted to go again... and then again. He'd taken her really hard, up against the wall in the shower on Saturday morning, and twice more that night, once on the couch and again in her bed. He'd introduced her to the pleasures of sex. And now she couldn't get enough. Well, she couldn't get enough of him... and he really, really liked that, because the feeling was entirely mutual. There wasn't a moment in the day when he didn't want to be inside her.

On Sunday, they spent the whole day together, because that was Emma's day off. So, he didn't have to sit in the coffee shop and watch her working – not that he minded doing that. He'd happily sit and watch her sleeping. He didn't care what she was doing, he'd watch her do it. But a whole day together was just bliss. And by about half way through it, he'd finally worked out what it was about her that was so different; why she was special. He'd fallen in love. For the first time in his life, he'd fallen in love. It was that simple.

He kept smiling, all the time. He couldn't help it. And he noticed Emma was doing the same thing. It made him wonder whether she felt the same way. God, he hoped so.

He cooked for her on Sunday evening, so she could have a complete rest. His meal wasn't a patch on any of the things she'd made for him, but he did his best. She sat at the breakfast bar, watching him, not offering advice, or criticizing… just watching.

"Tell me your favorite movie," he said, peeling the outer layers from an onion. He'd worked out, while they were in the shower together earlier in the day, that they'd spent most of their time together, when she wasn't working, either making love or sleeping in each others's arms, and he wanted to get to know her a little.

"I've got lots," she replied.

"Okay… pick one."

"*Groundhog Day*."

He looked over at her. "Why?" he asked.

She shrugged. "Lots of reasons. I love Bill Murray, for one. But I think it's because I like the idea that you can screw up pretty much everything in your life, and get the chance to change and make it right again."

"Even if you do have to re-live the same day a couple of hundred times to get there?"

She laughed. "Yeah… even then." She paused. "Yours?" she asked.

"Hmm… I love war movies. I'd be torn between *Saving Private Ryan*, *Black Hawk Down*, and *Platoon*."

"Pick one." She echoed his words.

"You're gonna make me?"

"Yep." She smiled.

He thought for a moment. "*Saving Private Ryan*, I guess."

"Why?"

"For the first twenty minutes."

"You mean the bit where everyone dies?"

"Not everyone."

"Well, no… obviously. But it's…"

"Probably the best anti-war message you could ever see on film." She was staring at him.

"What about music?" he asked, lightening the moment.

"Favorite band?"

"Or musician, or singer."

"That's difficult. It depends on my mood."

"Okay… right now. The mood you're in right now." He stopped chopping the onion and looked across at her.

"Justin Timberlake." Her reply was immediate.

"O-kay." He'd expected something more… romantic, maybe. "Why?" he asked.

"My best friend and I have always danced around to his music," she explained. "And I'm so happy right now." She paused for a moment, staring at him. "In fact, I don't think I've ever been this happy. And… well, I just want to dance." She smiled.

"You're happy?"

She nodded. "Yes, I am. Very…" she mumbled, lowering her eyes. She did that a lot. She was so damn cute when she was embarrassed. He walked over, leant across the breakfast bar and kissed her.

"Me too."

"Really?" she whispered. "Here? With me?" How could she be surprised?

"Yes, here, with you. I'm happier than I've ever been in my whole life," he said truthfully. The air between them crackled with desire. The look of doubt on her face made him wonder if he should tell her how he felt, to convince her she was special… unique… The one.

"Your turn…" she murmured.

"My turn to what?" he asked, still staring at her.

"Favorite music?"

He smiled. "Oh. That's easy," he replied, standing up straight again. "Coldplay."

"Coldplay?" He could tell he'd surprised her – again.

"Yeah. Why not?"

"Aren't a lot of their songs a bit… sad?"

"Not always. They can be uplifting too. I'm not sure if they're meant this way, or if it's just me reading too much into the lyric, but I when I listen to their songs I often find I have a better appreciation for the important things in life. It's not about money, and possessions; it's about people, and living life to the full, and loving with everything you've got…" *Like I love you.* He stared at her, willing her to understand.

Emma got up and walked around the breakfast bar, coming up to him and putting her arms around his waist, her head resting gently on his chest. "That was a beautiful thing to say," she whispered into him. He held her close for a while.

"Here's another one," he said, still holding her. "It's one I don't really have an answer to, so it's a question just for you…"

She looked up at him, waiting.

"What's your favorite flower?" he asked.

She smiled. "I absolutely love daffodils."

"Daffodils? I thought you'd say roses…"

She shook her head. "No. Daffodils are so simple, and beautiful. And they come out early in the year, when everything seems so dead and dull, and they're just so alive, and bright, and they nod their heads, like they're talking to each other…"

He smiled. "Okay… Daffodils it is then."

The timer beeped on the oven, pulling them back to reality, and Mark reluctantly let her go and added the peppers, zucchini, onions and garlic to the potatoes that were already roasting.

"It's my turn now." Emma went and sat back down again.

"Your turn?" He looked over at her.

"Yes. We've done movies and music, and flowers. Now it's my turn to quiz you."

"Oh. Okay."

She seemed to be thinking for a moment. "Favorite and least favorite personality traits," she said eventually. "And, before you ask, I don't mean just in me. I mean, in general."

"Hmm… getting serious now, are we?"

"Not necessarily, I'm just interested."

He grinned. "Good." He liked that. "Favorite personality trait…" He thought for a moment. "I like a person to have sense of humor," he said, "especially about themselves."

"Right…" She looked thoughtful. "And least favorite?"

"Self-importance, I guess. I really hate it when people think they're superior, just because they're the boss, or because they've got more money, or a bigger house, or because they're stronger, or they're a guy, not a woman." He looked at her. "Or because they've got a better education… All of that bullshit really annoys me."

He felt her eyes piercing his, saw the slow, sweet smile forming on her lips, and mirrored it with his own.

"Your turn," he said, twisting black pepper over two salmon steaks.

"Mine are one and the same, really," Emma said. "My favorite personality trait is honesty, and my least favorite is dishonesty. I can't stand anyone who lies, or cheats, or is in any way dishonest… about anything. My best friend's boyfriend cheated on her. It's destroyed her whole life…" He heard the emotion in her voice, even as he shivered.

"Well, I guess there's lying and then, there's lying…"

She looked at him like she didn't understand.

"There's a difference between cheating, like your friend's boyfriend, and a little white lie, Emma."

"You think?" Now she was looking at him like he'd just kicked her pet kitten, and slowly but surely he felt his world grinding to a halt. "Is there such a thing as a little white lie?"

"Yeah… I think so. Would you tell your best friend if she looked really bad in an outfit that she liked?"

"Yes. I'd find a way to be kind about it, but I'd tell her. I wouldn't be a real friend if I didn't. Would you tell me?"

"Tell you what?"

"Tell me if I was wearing something that looked dreadful on me?"

He smirked. "I'm not sure that's possible, baby," he murmured. "You could wear a sack and look great."

"It's the principle, Mark," she persisted.

He thought for a moment. "I'd tell you. I'd try and do it without hurting your feelings, but I'd tell you."

She smiled again. "Exactly. You wouldn't lie to me... even to make me feel better. You'd be kind enough to tell me the truth." She hesitated just for a moment. "I know this is going to sound ridiculous, especially as I've only known you a few days, but I trust you, Mark. I know you'd never lie to me."

He tried to smile. "I... I'll be back in a minute," he said. "I just need the bathroom."

He moved quickly toward the door. "Should I do anything with dinner?" she called after him.

"No." He turned as he reached the threshold. "It's fine. I'll only be a minute."

He closed the bathroom door behind him, and leant back against it. Opposite him, his reflection looked back in the mirror. At that moment, he hated himself. He'd lied to her, built their whole relationship on a fiction, on a person who didn't even exist. And then he'd fallen in love with her... really, deeply in love with her. And now – after that little speech of hers – he knew, if she ever found out he'd lied, she'd never forgive him. He rubbed his hands over his face. What was he going to do?

The doorbell ringing pulled him out of his trance.

He heard Emma answer it, heard her talking to someone with a deep male voice. Who was that?

He came out of the bathroom and looked down the stairs to where she was standing by the open door. He could see a man's shoes and the bottom of a pair of jeans. Whoever it was, she wasn't inviting him in.

Mark went back to the kitchen and waited.

After a few minutes, he heard Emma climbing slowly back up the stairs again. He glanced up and immediately went to her. Her eyes were red, her cheeks stained with tears.

"What's wrong?" he asked, his own problems forgotten. "Who was at the door?"

"That was Nick…" She sniffled a little and he pulled her into his arms.

"What did he want?"

"He had a message. Do you remember my friend… the one I told you about?"

"The one who's boyfriend cheated?"

"Yes."

"What about her?" Mark asked.

"She's just gone into labor."

"She's pregnant?"

Emma nodded. "Except it's too early. There's still six or seven weeks to go…"

"Do you…" He paused. "Do you want me to take you to her?" he asked.

She shook her head. "She doesn't live near here anymore. She moved away."

"I don't care where she lives, Emma. If you want to be with her… If she needs you, I'll get you to her."

She leant back and raised her hand, cupping his cheek. "Thank you," she said. "But it's okay. She'd hate a fuss, and she's got her mom… well, she will have. That's how Nick knows. My friend's mom works for Nick's boss, but he's out of town at the moment. So she's just called Nick to say she won't be at work tomorrow – or for the next few days – and, even though the pregnancy has been a secret right from the beginning, as it was Nick, she told him why. Oh… Oh, God. What if…?"

"It'll be okay, Emma," he said quickly. He knew nothing about babies, early or otherwise, but she needed reassuring. "I'm sure they'll be fine."

She looked up at him. "That's a little white lie, isn't it?" she whispered.

He gazed into her eyes. "Maybe…"

She nestled into him. "Thank you."

Much later that evening, Emma got a phone call. She took it in the bedroom while Mark sat in the living room, worrying. After about fifteen minutes, she came out again, looking pale.

"What's wrong?" he asked as she sat down beside him.

"That was my friend's mom…"

He turned to her, preparing for the worst, ready to hold her and comfort her. "And?" he urged.

"She's had a little girl."

"Is she…?" He didn't want to finish that question.

Emma looked up at him. "She's in the NICU. She's real sick…" A tear fell onto her cheek.

"Let me take you. I mean it. I don't care where she is…" He hated seeing her like this. He'd do whatever he had to do to help her, even if it meant revealing his true identity and dealing with the consequences.

"She's in Portland."

"Okay." He pulled out his phone. "I'll check the flights…"

"Flights?"

He looked down at her. "Yeah… to Portland." He stopped. "We are talking Portland, Oregon, aren't we?"

She smiled. "No, Maine."

He laughed. "Oh… that's easy. You made it sound like she was miles and miles away."

"She is… to me."

He leant over and kissed her. "I'll drive you," he whispered.

Emma shook her head. "They said to wait a while. I guess they wanna see what happens."

He put his phone down on the table and pulled her into his arms. "She'll be okay, Emma."

The days went by far too fast. Emma had to work, but they spent their evenings together, made love into the early hours, and he held her all night long. Emma received regular updates from her friend's mom;

the baby had jaundice and was having breathing difficulties, but she was a fighter… things were looking hopeful. Mark tried to comfort her as much as he could, but his time was limited, and on Wednesday morning, he was due to go home.

They made love when they woke up, and again in the shower. And Emma clung on to him afterwards, crying. "I don't want you to leave," she sobbed into his chest

"We can make this work," he told her, stroking her hair as the water cascaded over their bodies, mingling with her tears. "I'm only in Boston. It's a three hour drive."

"I don't even have a car, Mark. I can borrow Nick's, but…"

"I *do* have a car, and I'll come back and see you, I promise."

She leant back, looking into his eyes. "When?" she asked.

He thought through his commitments for the coming days. "It's Thanksgiving in a couple of weeks," he said. "I've gotta spend it with my family, and I'm sure you have too." She nodded. "But I can come back here on the Friday, and spend the weekend… if you want me to?"

"I—I'd love you to." She leant up and kissed him, deeply.

They were standing by his car, which he'd parked behind the coffee shop.

"Nice car," she said, seemingly avoiding the inevitable goodbye.

"It's a company car." That much was the truth, and he hoped she wouldn't ask too much, because he knew he couldn't lie to her now. "I'll text you when I get home," he added quickly, holding onto her. She nodded. "And we can call each other." He cradled her face in his hands, staring into her eyes. "This isn't over, Emma."

"Promise?"

"I promise… faithfully. We'll make it work."

"Who the hell are you texting now?" Michael Gardner glanced across at Mark as they walked down the steps of their townhouse and across the sidewalk to his Mercedes, which was parked at the roadside.

Mark didn't reply. He'd been texting and calling Emma fairly incessantly since he'd got back from Somers Cove.

"I'm guessing this is whoever it was you met when you went up to Maine?" Michael waited for an answer, and when he didn't get one, he rolled his eyes. "It's all you seem to do these days," he commented, unlocking the car and getting behind the wheel.

"Leave him alone." Mark's mom, Lisa, looked at him across the top of the car, just before she got in herself. "Just because you don't have a romantic bone in your body."

Mark climbed in behind his father, pressing the 'send' button as he did so.

He wasn't about to take the bait from either of his parents, who'd both quizzed him, in their different ways, since his return. They'd both noticed Mark's uncharacteristic preoccupation, the fact that he was always on the phone, or texting, and his secretiveness. His father's interests were purely practical; his mother's more sentimental. In both cases, Mark ignored them.

As for Sarah, she was too wrapped up in her own world to take an interest in anything her brother was doing. Mark knew he bored her to death… the whole family did, she made no secret of that. And right now, that suited him fine.

It had been two weeks since he'd seen Emma and he missed her more than he even wanted to think about, so he was trying really hard not to think about that deep aching need to be with her. Still, tomorrow was Thanksgiving, and the day after that, he'd be going back to Somers Cove for a whole weekend with her. All he had to do was get through the next two days with his grandparents.

"Why can't grandma and grandpa come to us?" Sarah asked from beside him. She was sulking… definitely sulking.

"Because they want us to go to them," their father replied. "I know you don't like leaving your computer behind for more than ten minutes… but you'll just have to cope for a couple of days. We'll be back on Friday morning." He started the car, checked the mirrors, and drove into the traffic.

The Turnpike was getting busier with people trying to get home, or to relatives, for the weekend.

"I thought we'd left early enough to avoid this." Michael hated driving in traffic; he had a heavy right foot, and enough speeding tickets to prove the point.

"I don't think the weather helps," Lisa offered. It had started to snow about half an hour earlier. "You could always slow down a little…"

He turned to her… and everything seemed to happen at once. A truck on their right suddenly slewed across in front of them, Sarah screamed, Michael hit the brake, and the car started to spin…

It was the beeping that first brought Mark to his senses. Who the hell had an alarm that sounded like that? He wished they'd turn it off. His head was already pounding, without the additional noise.

He opened his eyes, and immediately closed them again. It was bright… too bright.

"Hello?" Who was that? He opened his eyes again. "You're back with us." The voice was soft, caring. A pair of green eyes were looking down at him.

"W—Where am I?" Not the most original question, he knew, but it needed asking.

"You're at Mass General." The hospital. "You're in the Emergency Room."

Mark nodded his head, then immediately regretted it. That hurt… a lot.

"Your head probably hurts," the nurse said quietly. *You don't say…* "You've had an X-ray, and there's no permanent damage. The doctor will come and explain everything very soon."

"My parents," he said. "My sister."

He felt her hand on his arm. "The doctor will be here soon," she repeated.

Fuck the pain. He had to know… He raised his head and looked around him. He was in a room by himself, attached to a monitor, which was beeping in time with his heart, he guessed.

"Tell me." He looked at the nurse, her pink scrubs making her look younger than she was. "Please."

"I'm sorry…"

The doctor walked in the door at that moment.

"My whole family…?" he whispered.

"No…" she said.

"I'll take over," the doctor announced, and the nurse stood back.

A man wearing blue scrubs stood before him. He was probably forty, maybe forty-five, with salt-and-pepper hair and dark blue eyes. "Mr Gardner," he said quietly. "Do you remember being in a road traffic accident?" Mark nodded. He didn't remember the details, but he recalled Sarah screaming and his head slamming against the window. "Okay." The doctor paused. "There's no easy way for me to tell you this," he continued, "so I'm just going to say it… I'm afraid your parents didn't survive the crash…"

"N—neither of them?" Mark was suddenly freezing cold.

"No. I'm very sorry."

"And Sarah? My sister?"

"She sustained severe injuries. She's in surgery at the moment. She suffered a head trauma… They've removed her spleen and they're trying to control the internal bleeding…"

"Will she… Will she make it?" he asked, barely able to even hear his own voice.

"They're doing everything they can."

Mark knew a white lie when he heard one.

It had been the longest week Mark had ever known. He'd been released from hospital after just a couple of days. He had three fractured ribs and severe bruising, but was otherwise unharmed. He spent all his time sitting at Sarah's bedside. She'd pulled through the surgery, but they were keeping her in an induced coma, due to the swelling on her brain. Whenever he asked how she was, what her prognosis was, if there was anything more that could be done, they told him it was just a waiting game. *Some fucking game.*

His parents' funerals were taking place the next day. Mark would go… of course he would. But Sarah? There was, of course, no way she was going to be there, and thinking about the day to come, Mark wondered if that might be for the best.

Jeremy Slater, his father's friend and lawyer had come to see him. They'd talked through his business obligations, and Jeremy had informed him that, under the terms of his parents' wills, he was now Sarah's legal guardian. He was responsible for her, and her inheritance, which she couldn't touch until she reached the age of twenty-one. Until then, it would be held in trust for her, with Mark as the sole trustee. He'd need to work out an allowance for her, take care of her, make decisions for her. It was a lot of responsibility to take on, and to get his head around.

His phone vibrated in his hand and he looked down to check the screen. He'd been inundated with calls and messages since the accident. None of them were from well-wishers… If it wasn't Jeremy, it was the press, or the funeral directors, wanting instructions, or his father's office, looking for directions from their new boss. How could he be their boss? The words in front of him blurred. Oh, God… The text was from Emma. It was the first time she'd messaged him since Saturday… Five days of silence.

He recalled reading back over the messages he'd missed from her, sitting by Sarah's bedside, once he'd been discharged from the hospital. Initially, Emma had sent a reply to his text – the one he'd sent just as his dad had started the car – but then, when his messages to her had stopped and she didn't hear back from him, her texts for the rest of that day had been filled with concern, wondering if he was okay. Of course, he hadn't picked those up straight away – he'd been unconscious. When he still hadn't replied by Thanksgiving morning, she'd started to ask what was wrong, what she'd done wrong. When he'd read those, read her hurt and confusion, he'd felt guilty and ashamed. But what could he have done? If he'd replied, he'd have had to tell her he'd lied. He'd have had to tell her who he was and, assuming she could find it in her heart to forgive him, she might have come to visit. But why? Out of pity? Or because she loved him? Did she love him? He didn't know… But he knew he didn't want her pity.

Obviously, he hadn't gone to visit her on Friday. He had still been in the hospital on Friday. And then her messages had changed again. The pain was still there, but she was also angry, and disappointed.

And then on Saturday, she'd sent the final one… and he knew there was no way back from that. He'd done far too much damage already and he knew she'd be better off without him. If he left her alone, she'd forget him soon enough.

When he'd met Emma, he was sick of being Mark Gardner – the multi-millionaire player, the heir to an empire. All he'd wanted was a normal life. He'd just wanted to be a normal guy, falling in love with a normal girl. And for a week, he'd had exactly that. And it had been the best week of his life. Now, he had a company to run; he had thousands of people depending on him; he had Sarah to take care of. He had responsibilities. And he just wanted to cry, because he knew he could never be that normal guy again.

He didn't know why Emma was contacting him after nearly a week of silence, but he blinked away his tears and read her message:

— Why, Mark?

That was all she'd written. Just two words, but there was still so much hurt in them. And he didn't have any answers. None that he could tell her, anyway.

He leant back and looked up at the ceiling. If only he hadn't started off on a lie, she'd be here with him now. She'd have heard the news and come to him. This was his fault, and he couldn't put it right. He let his head drop again and found himself staring at Sarah. He was all she had now. He had to be there for her, no matter what.

He clicked on his contacts, went to Emma's details and, even though his heart was breaking, pressed 'delete'.

Chapter Three

Present Day

Emma

"You're still doing it…" Emma looked up and across the counter. Nick was standing, staring at her.

"Doing what?"

"Re-arranging the muffins." He smiled. "You okay?"

"I'm fine."

He leant over toward her. "Nothing changes, sis. You're still an appalling liar."

She didn't reply. She wasn't sure she could trust her voice.

"What's wrong, Em? Talk to me… I'm not leaving until you do."

She knew why he was being so persistent. It was Nick who'd found her all that time ago.

"It's hard. This time of year just brings it all back." She turned away, taking a deep breath, and then she felt strong hands on her shoulders.

Nick's voice was close to her ear. "I hate seeing you like this."

"You think I'm enjoying it?"

"No." He turned her to face him, and put his arms around her. "I just wish…"

"What?" she asked. "What do you wish?"

"Well… I wish I could get my hands on him, for one thing. But, more than anything, I wish you'd realize Mark Ellis isn't the only guy out there." He took a deep breath. "You need to get over him, Em."

"I'm trying."

He leant back and looked down at her. "Really?"

"Yes, really. Most of the time I'm okay."

"No you're not."

She couldn't argue with him. He was right. She wasn't okay. She often wondered what might have happened if Nick hadn't decided to come round that night. She'd already taken more than half the bottle of pills, and drunk a third of the bottle of vodka before she sent that last text message to Mark… She'd known he wouldn't reply. He'd stopped all communication with her by then, but she'd felt she had to reach out, one last time. Would she have gone through with it? Would she have swallowed the rest of the tablets and drifted off into that peaceful oblivion she longed for, that place where the pain couldn't touch her anymore? Or would she have stopped herself just in time? She didn't know, because Nick had tried to call her, then he'd sent her a couple of text messages and, finally, when she'd failed to respond, he'd called round in person and, when she hadn't answered the door, or even yelled at him to go away, like she sometimes did, he'd broken it down and found her lying on the sofa, clutching the pills in one hand, the vodka bottle lying beside her on the floor. He'd taken her to the hospital, dealt with everything, and stayed with her for weeks afterwards, sleeping on her couch. As far as she knew, he hadn't told anyone, not even Cassie… It was their secret, and for that she was grateful. She wasn't proud of what she'd done; she just wished the pain would stop.

And she wished she didn't still long for the peace she'd come so close to finding…

"He's in my head," she whispered. "All the time."

"I know, Em. I know how this feels." She looked up at him. "I really do. But you're better than this. You're too good for him, that's for sure."

She shook her head, then buried it in his chest and sobbed while he held her.

He sighed deeply. "If he walked through that door right now," he said quietly, "would you take him back?"

She pulled back slightly. "I don't know." She sniffed and he reached over and grabbed a paper napkin from the pile on the counter, handing it to her. "I mean it's never going to happen, but I guess if he had a good reason for doing what he did, I'd think about it." Nick looked into her eyes, a dark shadow crossing his. "You've never told me what happened when you were at college," she continued before he could say anything, "but I know someone hurt you." He looked away for a moment. "Are you honestly saying that, if you could have her back, you wouldn't take the chance?"

He hesitated, then turned back to face her. "Yeah, I would. In a heartbeat."

She pushed him away. "Then stop judging me."

He pulled her back, holding onto her. "I'm not, Em. I'm not judging you at all. Like I said, I know how this feels. I—I just can't go through that again…" She could see the pain in his eyes. "I nearly lost you."

"I know. And I won't do it again." As much as she craved the silence, and the peace, she wasn't about to do that again.

"Promise?"

She looked up into his eyes. "I promise," she whispered, then she took a deep breath and released herself from his grip. "Now… You're on the wrong side of the counter," she said, trying to draw a line under their uncomfortable conversation.

"So, sue me." He smiled.

"I would, but I don't know any good lawyers."

"Haha… Make me a latte?"

"Okay." She pointed to the other side of the counter.

"I'm going." He held up his hands in surrender as he walked slowly around and sat down on a stool. "Got any plans for the weekend?" he asked.

"Yes. I have." She turned to face him.

"Good…" She could hear how happy and, maybe relieved, he was that she wasn't going to spend the weekend moping around.

"Cassie and I planned a picnic."

He snorted out a laugh. "A picnic? You have noticed it's November, right?"

"Yes. But it's not that cold. It's not as cold as last weekend."

"You keep telling yourselves that if it makes you feel better. Where are you going?"

"Jake's taking us to the hotel site."

"Sounds thrilling…"

"Well, it wasn't what Cassie originally had in mind, but he's got his client coming up for the weekend, and he needs to visit the site… and he and Cassie thought it'd make a good place for a picnic."

"Oh, okay." He took his coffee from Emma. "Who's the client?"

"Jake's still not saying."

"What's the guy gonna do? Wear a mask all weekend?"

Emma laughed. "No. Jake says he'll introduce us. But I think we'll be sworn to secrecy until the opening."

"Well, whoever he is, I hope he doesn't mind getting cold." He shook his head. "Honestly… a picnic in November."

"Oh… live a little."

He stared at her. "I will if you will."

As she locked up the coffee shop that night, Emma thought back over her conversation with Nick… This time of the year was tough. It brought back so many memories and she was glad she was going to be occupied, to keep them all at bay. But, despite her early enthusiasm for the picnic, she found she wasn't looking forward to it as much as she thought she would be. Every time she thought about it, all she could see were issues and problems…

Firstly there was the thought of spending a day with Jake and Cassie. She did this quite a lot, being as they came back to Somers Cove every weekend from their home in Portland, but deep down, she knew all it was going to do was remind her that she was alone, and they were together. She let herself into her apartment above the coffee shop, and stopped.

"What's the matter with me?" she said out loud. She felt awful. How could she be so selfish? She was pleased Cassie was back together with Jake, especially as it turned out he hadn't cheated, as Cassie had originally thought, and that it had all been a horrible misunderstanding. It seemed Jake wasn't to blame. He wasn't the villain they'd painted him for all those years. Emma even felt sorry for him… well, almost. He was a guy, after all, so he was genetically programmed to let Cassie down at some point.

"Oh my God… stop it!" She climbed the stairs. "Just stop it. You're becoming bitter."

Jake wasn't going to let Cassie down. He'd turned his life upside down for her since they'd gotten back together. He'd given up his swanky Boston apartment and bought them an amazing house in Portland. And he'd asked her to marry him the previous weekend. Emma was thrilled for them – she really was. It wasn't common knowledge yet. Jake had wanted to buy the ring in Portland during the week, so at the moment, only she and Jake's dad, Ben, knew about it. Of course, once Cassie came back to town wearing a ring, Emma gave it maybe an hour before everyone would be talking about it.

She flopped down onto the couch in her living room, not bothering to switch on the lights. If only Kate was still alive, she'd have been so proud. Cassie's mom's death had kind of been the catalyst that had brought Jake and Cassie back together. It was because of Kate's death that Cassie had returned to the town six months ago, back in May. What she hadn't realized was that Jake was going to be there, because he was in charge of constructing the new hotel complex a few miles up the coast, and had come home that same weekend to try and make things up with his dad. Of course, Jake didn't know Cassie would be there either, and neither did he know he had a daughter. It could all have ended so much worse than it did…

She sighed. They were bound to be super loved-up this weekend, what with the engagement and everything… but that was fair enough. Maybe it wouldn't be so bad after all.

Except, there was Jake's client. The mystery hotel owner, that no-one was allowed to know anything about. Part of the deal when the guy had signed the contract to build the hotel was that he and his company couldn't be identified until the opening. Jake had explained that the man was taking a risk. He'd never built a hotel before – well, neither had Jake for that matter – so he was wary of taking the chance.

In her mind, Emma pictured him as a middle-aged, stuffy businessman, more interested in finances and bottom lines than in people. As much as she wanted to see Cassie, Maddie, and Jake, she wasn't looking forward to Sunday.

Her phone rang. She checked the screen. It was Cassie, so she answered straight away, telling herself she wasn't really hoping that her friend was going to cancel their plans…

"Hi," she said, trying to sound brighter than she felt. "Where are you?" Cassie and Jake normally drove up to Somers Cove on a Friday evening.

"We're just leaving. Or we will be if Jake ever gets everything loaded into the car. How's everything with you? Have you finished work yet?"

"Everything's fine," Emma lied. "And yes, I've just finished work."

"Good." She heard Cassie take a breath and wondered what was coming… "What are you doing tomorrow night?" her friend asked.

"Nothing." *Damn.* She should've asked why before admitting she was free.

"Because I need you."

"And what do you need me for?"

"To keep me sane."

Emma smiled. "Care to elaborate?"

Again, she heard a sigh. "Jake's client's coming up to the beach house."

"Yes, I know."

"And he's staying over…"

"I know that too."

"And I've just realized that means I've got to sit through dinner tomorrow night with the two of them talking about building materials and specifications and goodness only knows what else. I'm gonna go crazy. Plus, I need to make something that's actually going to impress this guy. He's gonna be Jake's boss soon. I can't serve lasagna."

"You make a mean lasagna. So does Jake."

"I know, but I need something a bit more accomplished. This guy probably eats in high class restaurants all the time."

That was almost certainly true. Besides, Emma knew Cassie and Jake felt indebted to this man. He'd offered Jake a job when it had become impossible for him to continue working for Eldridge Construction – mainly because the boss's daughter wouldn't leave him alone. Jake was just seeing out the contract to build the hotel, then he was leaving Eldridge, and he'd be working for... well, whoever his client was. Yeah, lasagna probably wasn't going to cut it.

"So, you need my cooking expertise?" Emma asked.

"And your company."

"I won't have time to cook everything, Cassie. I'm gonna be at work all day tomorrow."

"I'm not asking you to cook it, but can you send me a recipe? Something foolproof, with easy instructions?"

"You're a great cook, Cassie, you don't need easy instructions."

"I do this weekend."

"Why?" Emma asked.

"I don't know what's wrong with me, but I'm really nervous about meeting this guy."

"Well, don't be. You've got nothing to be nervous about."

"He's a multi-millionaire, Em."

"So what? You're a successful novelist. Jake's building his hotel..."

"Hmm... I'm not sure about 'successful'."

"Your books are doing really well. That makes you a success." Emma thought for a moment. "I've got a couple of ideas I can send you through," she said. "Shall I e-mail them over?"

"Sure... or you can message me on Facebook."

"Okay."

They used Facebook to stay in touch all the time now – Cassie sent Emma pictures of Maddie and links to her books and promotions.

"Give me half an hour."

"There's no rush. I won't be starting until the morning."

"I assume he's not allergic to anything?"

"Not that Jake's mentioned, no."

"Okay, I'll come up with something."

"You're the best, Em."

"Yeah, yeah."

"And you'll come to dinner?"

"Am I being given a choice?"

"No. I know I'm going to be in a meltdown. I'm gonna need you."

"Then I'll be there."

"What would I do without you?"

Mark

He hadn't even left home yet and he was nervous as hell.

"When will you be back?" Sarah asked. She was sitting on the edge of his bed, watching him pack a small holdall.

"Sunday night… late. Don't wait up. You've got college on Monday." He turned to look at her. "What are you doing today?"

"Macy's coming over later. We're gonna go shopping."

"Okay. Just take care." He knew he was over-protective, but he couldn't help it. Ever since the accident, he'd been the same.

"Of course." He sat down beside her and put an arm around her shoulder. "I'm gonna miss you," she whispered.

"I'll be back tomorrow night," he said.

"But I won't see you until Monday night. And you've been away a lot the last couple of weeks."

"It's a busy time of year, Sarah, you know that."

"It's the worst time of year."

The weeks coming up to Thanksgiving only reminded them of the accident that had cost them their parents' lives. Sarah had recovered eventually, although she still had to be careful. She was prone to infections and suffered from bad migraines. Looking at her now, she seemed a little pale and, just for a moment, he wondered if he should cancel his plans. He mentally shook his head. He couldn't… He couldn't let Jake down again. Jake needed him to go over the plans for the new hotel and Mark had put him off so many times, simply because it meant going to Somers Cove. But Jake was a friend; he had been for nearly three years and Mark knew this weekend wasn't just about the hotel. Jake wanted him to meet his family – his daughter and the woman he was evidently going to marry, being as he'd proposed last weekend. Mark smiled to himself. He was pleased for Jake. It would be fine, and besides, Maggie was here to keep an eye on Sarah.

"I know." He rested his head against hers. "I promise I'll be here." He wouldn't leave her alone, not at Thanksgiving. No matter how busy work got.

She pulled away from him and stared up into his eyes. She was the image of their mother, probably best described as pixie-like or elfin, with short dark hair framing her delicate heart-shaped face. "Well, you'd better be here next weekend," she said.

"Why?"

"Because, brother… *I've* got an exhibition." She beamed at him.

"Really?" He was overjoyed. Sarah was studying sculpture. She was good at it too. She'd missed more than six months of high school after the accident and had been forced to drop back a year. Sometimes he wondered if she resented that – her friends moving on and eventually going to college while she was left behind – but she said she was fine, and that was when she'd really gotten into art and, especially sculpture. He was just relieved she'd found something she really enjoyed.

"It's on Saturday and Sunday, in one of the halls on campus," she explained.

"And I have to attend both days?" he asked.

"No. I thought we'd go on Saturday. But I'll need to go in on Sunday as well, in the afternoon and I'll need your help, because I've got to clear away my exhibits. I'm not sure of the times yet but I'll get more details next week."

"Well, let me know. I'll be there."

"Without fail?"

He put his hand on his heart. "Without fail."

He zipped up his bag and carried it down the stairs, Sarah following behind. Halfway down, her phone rang and she stopped to take the call.

Mark carried on, dropping his bag in the hall and going through to the kitchen.

Maggie was standing by the sink and he went over and stood beside her, leaning back against the countertop.

"I'll be back tomorrow night," he said. "But it'll be late."

"I know. You already told me twice."

"Call me if you need anything." He grabbed an apple from the bowl on the center island. "Sarah's looking a little pale…"

"I won't need anything, and Sarah's just fine."

Maggie had worked for Mark for nearly four years now, ever since Sarah came home from the hospital. She was everything he could need: a former nurse, who could cook and keep house – and she was happy to live-in. Her husband had died of a brain tumor about six or seven years ago, not long before his fiftieth birthday, and her two kids were grown up and married themselves. There was no doubt about it, as far as Mark was concerned, Maggie was perfect. She was more than perfect, because she never let him dwell on things, and she always told him how it was. When he was being an idiot, she told him. When he was wallowing in self pity and feeling sorry for himself, she told him… And he needed that.

"Sorry."

She looked up. "Don't be. Just get going, and have a good time for once in your life."

"I do have a good time… sometimes."

"Yeah, if you call those models you hang off your arm a good time."

He looked at her and grinned. "They can be."

"Hmm… save that fake smile and fake voice for them. They don't work with me."

He leant closer to her and whispered, "You get me. Every time."

"Small reward," she replied, thoughtfully. "I'd rather see you happy than be right about you being sad… Now get going."

Sarah was still sitting on the stairs talking on her phone, so he waved at her as he passed. She waved back nonchalantly, and he picked up his bag and went out the front door. He paused for a moment and looked up at the façade of the house he occasionally called home. It was enormous. There were six bedrooms, all with adjoining bathrooms, two living rooms, a sun room, a formal dining room, the huge kitchen, and Mark's office, as well as a den in the basement, plus a separate apartment on the top floor that Maggie used. It had been the family home when his parents were alive and, every time he suggested selling it, Sarah objected. She didn't want to part with her memories of their parents, she said, but that didn't make sense to Mark. They hadn't lived here for that long. They hadn't grown up here, and he often wondered whether he and Sarah really need a place like this. And anyway, were the memories that great? Whenever he thought about the house, all he remembered was that last morning, leaving the house, getting in the car, his dad criticizing him for texting Emma… and then the crash.

He opened his car, threw the bag onto the passenger seat and got in behind the wheel, running his hands over the leather surface. He smiled as he started the engine. This was good. If he was being completely honest, it was the only really good thing in his life… apart from Sarah.

His car swallowed the miles and he was within a half hour of Somers Cove before he even really allowed himself to think about the upcoming weekend.

He remembered the small town vividly. Jake had given him directions to the beach house, and Mark knew he was going to have to drive past the coffee shop to get to the lane that led down to it. Even if Emma was still there, she wouldn't be able to see him. His car had tinted windows. He'd be invisible to her. And if he saw her? Well, it'd just break his heart a little more. He shook his head. That wasn't possible. His heart had never mended. And you can't break what's already broken.

What would he really do if he saw her, he wondered? What he'd like to do is just walk right up to her and kiss her – even if half the town saw him doing it. He wanted to hold her in his arms and tell her he was sorry… so fucking sorry. Sorry for letting her down, for lying, for letting her go. He'd like to tell her what had happened… that his parents had died and that, overnight, he'd had to become Sarah's legal guardian, her carer, and her parent, as well as her brother. That he'd had to take over his father's business and become 'the boss' at a moment's notice. That he'd made difficult decisions over the last four years, but always tried to keep in mind what his father would've done, because whatever else his dad might have been, he was a damned good – and really fair – businessman. He'd like to tell her that he lay awake most nights worrying whether he was doing the right thing by Sarah and the thousands of people who worked for him; that the responsibility weighed real heavy and sometimes wore him down to breaking point. But above all, he'd like to tell her that he'd never forgiven himself for what he'd done to her, and that he missed her so much, it still hurt.

Chapter Four

Emma

"You've been a Godsend." Cassie kissed Emma on the cheek, wiping her hands on a towel.

"I've only just got here." Emma bent down and gave Maddie a hug, and a salute 'hello'. Maddie was profoundly deaf and Emma had learnt to sign, just like everyone else in the little girl's life. It wasn't an option. She wasn't as proficient as Cassie, but no-one was. Not even Jake.

"I know, but those recipes…" Cassie turned back to the stove. "They were so easy."

As Emma went over to hang her coat on the hook by the door, she had to admit, the beach house looked a picture of calm serenity. The kitchen was tidy, the living room immaculate and the table was set for four. Emma was surprised. She'd half expected to find Cassie running around panicking.

"Where are Jake and the mystery man?" she asked. "I have to say, whoever he is, he's got excellent taste in cars. Nick's probably still sitting out there admiring it. We don't get many Aston Martins around here. He said it was a DB11, not that it meant anything to me, but it's absolutely beautiful."

"Yes, I know. I'm sure it turned a few heads in town when he drove through." Cassie looked up. "I'm sure he would've done too, if he'd stopped." She smiled. "He's pretty easy on the eye himself."

"Oh, really?" Emma teased. "I didn't think you noticed things like that anymore, what with you being practically married now and everything… Speaking of which, where's the ring?"

"Being adjusted. I'll have it next weekend."

"Does that mean I've got to keep it to myself for another whole week?"

Cassie nodded.

"Shucks…" Emma grinned. "So, you never said… where are they? Jake and Mr 'easy on the eye'?" She winked.

"Upstairs in the office," Cassie replied. "They've been up there most of the afternoon, which has suited me just fine. I've been able to concentrate on the cooking."

Emma came back into the kitchen. "How did you get on with the cheesecakes?" She knew they could be a little fiddly.

"Fine." Cassie smiled across at her. "I don't have anything to make melon balls with though, so I've just sliced the melon and chopped it into cubes. That'll be okay, won't it?"

"That'll be fine. So, what's left to do?"

"The dressing for the appetizer." Cassie looked around for a moment. "And whipping the cream for the cheesecakes."

Emma tried not to let the sadness overwhelm her. She'd chosen the same menu she'd cooked for Mark Ellis the first time he'd eaten at her apartment, because she knew how easy it was. She'd cooked it in a little over an hour after work that evening; and she knew it was impressive, providing you got the presentation right. She remembered how they'd both reacted when she'd told him she was going to whip some cream, and what that had led to…

"I can do the dressing, if you want." She needed to keep focused on the here and now. "Getting the balance can be tricky," she added, and then remembered Mark's comments about the lemon… She had to stop this.

"That'd be great. The ingredients are over there." Cassie nodded in the direction of the sink.

Emma went over and started work. "I love this kitchen now," she said. "Ben did a fantastic job."

"I know."

Jake's dad had spent the whole summer fixing the place up – with Jake's help – because Cassie thought she'd have to sell the beach house – the home she'd lived in since she was six years old – after her mom had died. But once she'd got back with Jake, he'd told her to keep it, and that he'd sell his apartment in Boston instead, so they could buy somewhere together in Portland, where they needed to live, so Maddie could attend a school for deaf children.

Emma ran her hand along the wooden countertop. "What's this wood again?" she asked.

"Pecan. It's beautiful, isn't it?"

"Hmm."

"What's wrong, Em?"

Emma added a little more oregano to the bowl. "What makes you think there's something wrong?" she asked.

"The tone of your voice, and the fact that I've known you for nearly twenty years."

Emma couldn't tell Cassie the truth. Not tonight. She knew she'd break down, and Cassie had a guest. Maybe she'd talk to her tomorrow at the beach. In the meantime, she needed to find another excuse for her sadness. "I was just remembering how we sat here the night your mom died…"

"Oh."

That had been really thoughtless of her. "Sorry, Cassie. I didn't mean to remind you."

"Don't be sorry. I like to think about her too, and a lot's happened since then."

"I know, but it's only six months ago."

"Yeah. I forget that sometimes. So, what were you thinking?"

"Just about how we sat here, picking holes in everything."

Cassie laughed. "Yeah, we did, didn't we?"

"Well, the place was a bit of a mess."

"I know."

"And look at it now." Emma turned. "Your mom wouldn't know her own house." She saw Cassie's face fall. *Shit.*

"Did I do the right thing, Em?"

Emma went over to her, placing her hands on her friend's shoulders. "Yes, Cassie. She'd be so damn proud of you."

"Don't say that… you'll make me cry."

Emma sniffed. She was too emotional for this. "Well, that's gonna make two of us."

Cassie tried to laugh, but a tear fell onto her cheek and she turned around to grab a Kleenex, just as Jake came into the kitchen. There was no denying Jake was fairly easy on the eye too. He was tall, with brown hair, and the most unusual dark green eyes, that Maddie had inherited. "I didn't hear you come down the stairs," Cassie said as he walked up to them.

Emma moved away and went back to making the dressing. "Hey," she heard him say, "what's wrong? Why are you crying?"

"It's nothing," Cassie replied.

"Tell me," he urged.

"We were just talking about mom," Cassie explained.

"Oh, baby… come here." Emma turned around and saw Jake pull Cassie into his arms. He nodded to her over Cassie's shoulder and mouthed 'Hi'. She nodded back and waited until Jake released Cassie and looked down into her eyes. "Okay now?" he asked.

"I'm fine."

She wiped her eyes, took a deep breath and turned back to Emma, giving her a smile.

"The dressing's done," Emma said.

"Oh, great." Cassie looked around her. "In that case, I think we're ready – except we're missing our guest." She looked at Jake. "He's not still working, is he?"

"No, we're finished for tonight. He's just freshening up. He'll only be a minute."

"Right. Can you open the wine then?"

"Sure. And then I'll put Maddie to bed, shall I?"

Cassie leaned up and kissed him. "That'd be great." She turned back to Emma. "Do we put the dressing onto the appetizer yet?"

"No, it's probably best to let each person do their own. It's quite strong. Do you have a small jug?"

"Yeah, I think so." Cassie went to the cabinet nearest the door, reaching up to the back of the shelf. "Will this do?" She pulled out a small glass jug.

"Perfect." Emma took it from her and went back to the sink. "You could put the appetizers out now, if you want. It doesn't hurt for them to warm up a little. It enhances the flavors."

"Okay."

They were all so busy with their tasks, none of them heard the footsteps on the stairs…

Mark

He studied his reflection in the bathroom mirror. For the last four years, he'd spent as little time as possible doing this. He usually found the person looking back at him disappointing. Today was no exception. He quickly washed his hands and face, then reached for the towel on the shelf and dried him himself off, before folding it, putting it back, and flicking off the light.

Back in the guest bedroom, he looked around. He knew Jake had added this room, finishing it off just a few weeks earlier. It was a really neat little room and Mark could see how it was a great bonus to the house, as was the office he and Jake had been shut up in for most of the afternoon. Jake was really talented and Mark felt he'd made a good decision offering him a job. All he needed now was for the hotel construction to be completed and Jake to join his staff, then they could really get to work.

He had all kinds of plans for converting his existing hotels to be more energy efficient, and for building at least one more hotel along the same lines as the one Jake was currently constructing down the coast, using sustainable materials, making as little impact on the local and natural environment as possible.

He heard voices and laughter from downstairs. He'd just change his shirt and then he'd better go down to join Jake and Cassie and their other guest. He didn't know who she was; Jake had just said she was their oldest friend, and Cassie had invited her in case Jake and he wanted to talk business over dinner… it would avoid her being bored. Mark had laughed when Jake told him that, then pointed out that he'd never be so rude as to talk about work when there was a beautiful woman present. Jake had given him a look when he'd said that, and had become uncharacteristically territorial about Cassie, which had made Mark smile. Jake was a lucky man. Mark just hoped he appreciated what he had. He knew Cassie had given Jake more than one chance to make things right and, as he shrugged on a clean shirt and started to button it up, he wondered if Emma would ever let him make amends. He shook his head. No… he knew she wouldn't. Things were different for Jake and Cassie. The had a daughter, for one thing. And they'd been together for six years or something before they'd broken up. He and Emma had shared six days. He closed his eyes. The best six days of his life, but still just six days. Besides, she was probably married, or living with someone, and far away from here by now. Like Jake had said when he'd persuaded Mark to come up here, people tended not to stay in small towns like Somers Cove.

He rolled up the sleeves of his shirt, put his watch back on and, switching off the light, went out through the door.

He slowly walked down the stairs, which brought him into the living room. Maddie was sitting on the couch facing him, playing with a couple of dolls. She must've been alerted to his presence, because she looked up as he got to the bottom of the staircase. He gave her a salute and mouthed 'hello'. Jake had shown him how to do this earlier. She repeated the sign back to him, and accompanied it with the cutest smile. She was gorgeous, there was no getting away from it, but then, looking at her mother, that wasn't even remotely surprising. Yeah, Jake was a damn lucky son-of-a-bitch. And right now, he'd give all of his millions to have just a piece of that… with Emma.

He shook his head again, then noticed Maddie had tilted hers to one side, like she didn't understand. He realized she'd been watching him and that she thought he was shaking his head at her. What should he do? He didn't know how to tell her he'd been thinking to himself, so he smiled. She looked at him for a moment, then shrugged and smiled back. If only everything in life could be fixed so easily… with just a smile.

He stepped off the bottom stair onto the oak floor and started toward the kitchen.

He heard Cassie saying, "Okay."

Then he heard what sounded like a cork popping. He liked that sound. He needed a glass of wine… or two. "I'll put it on the table, shall I?" That was Jake.

"Thank you," Cassie replied to him. "Oh, hang on… what about the whipped cream?"

Whipped cream? That brought back a memory. Emma whipping cream in her small apartment and then flirting with him. God, that had got him hard. He'd made love to her not long after that. He'd taken her virginity… made her his. Well, his for a few days. She wasn't his anymore. Without a doubt she belonged to someone else now, and that thought brought a fresh chill to his cold, broken heart.

"What about it?" *That voice.* He stilled. It couldn't be…

"Should I whip it now?" That was Cassie again. He needed the other woman to speak again. Well, he thought he did.

"To be honest, that's best done right at the last minute. I don't mind doing it just before you serve the cheesecakes, while you make the coffee." It was. It was Emma. He may have only had six days with her, but he'd know her voice anywhere. He'd know her voice in a choir of thousands. Except she wasn't in a choir of thousands. She was maybe fifteen feet away. And, short of running back upstairs and hiding in the guest room, he had nowhere to go.

"Oh… okay," Cassie said.

"I'll put Maddie to bed." Jake was talking. He was also about to come into the room.

Mark was going to have to face her, take her anger, her hurt, and let her say, and do whatever she wanted, because whatever it was, he deserved it. Then, maybe – just maybe – he could explain. It was a hope.

Jake appeared. "Hey… there you are."

"Hi," Mark kept his voice quiet.

"Let me introduce you." Jake turned. "Well, you've met Cass already, obviously. Em, come on over and meet our guest."

Mark felt his palms sweating and wiped them down the sides of his jeans. Jake turned back, just as Emma entered the room, and Mark stared. It was all he could do. Not a single part of his body would work. His mouth was dust, his feet were frozen, his arms were limp, and his heart had stopped. She looked so good – even better than she had four years ago, if that were possible, which he didn't think it was. She was wearing the same blue lacy dress she'd worn on their first date, the one that seemed to be see-through, but wasn't. He knew what was beneath that illusion. He knew every inch of her – intimately. He'd spent hours exploring her. And he'd never forgotten a single second of it.

"You?" Emma spoke first.

"Yeah." Okay, so his voice was working… just.

Her eyes were filling with tears, but she blinked quickly. He wanted to go to her, but he didn't have the right. He knew that. He'd abdicated that right when he'd lied to her, when he'd left her, and when he'd hurt her.

"You?" she repeated.

He took a step forward, but she held up a hand and he stopped. The pain in her eyes took his breath away and now, more than ever, he knew he had to take a chance. He didn't care about anything else. He didn't care that he'd lied, or that he'd hurt her, or that leaving her had broken his heart and that, if he lost her again, it would kill him. He had to make it right.

He had to win her back.

Chapter Five

Emma

It couldn't be him. And yet it was. After four years of hurt and pain and longing, he was standing right in front of her, staring at her and, although she knew Jake was on her left and Cassie had just come and stood on her right, and Maddie was sitting on the couch, oblivious to everything around her, it was like there was no-one else but her and Mark in the room.

"You?" She knew she'd already said it once, but somehow saying it again seemed to make it more real.

He didn't reply this time, but took a step toward her. She held up her hand, and he stopped. Thank God. She didn't want him any closer. Well, that was a lie. She did. She wanted him right in front of her, his body pressed against hers, with his arms tight around her, holding her close and telling her it had all been a mistake and that he wanted her back. But that wasn't going to happen, because she wasn't going to let it. She wasn't going to let him get close enough to hurt her again. She saw a shadow cross his eyes, a fleeting expression of… sorrow, was it? Regret, maybe?

She turned to Jake. "Is this your client?" she asked, her voice sounding distant and faint.

"Um, yeah." His confusion was obvious. "This is Mark. Mark Gardner."

She sucked in a breath. So, not Mark Ellis, then. That meant…

She turned back to Mark. "Gardner?" she queried.

"Yes." His eyes held hers.

"Not Ellis?"

"No."

She nodded. She was struggling to take it in.

"So, you own Gardners Hotels." It wasn't a question, but he answered it anyway.

"Yes." And she noticed he at least had the decency to look embarrassed.

She stared at him for another moment. He'd lied. He'd told her he was Mark Ellis. Yeah, he'd said he worked in the hotel trade, but he'd definitely implied he worked in *a* hotel, not that his family owned dozens and dozens of them – if not hundreds – all over New England, or that he was a multi-millionaire. She felt like sliding to the floor and curling up in a ball, but she wasn't going to. Not here, not now. She could do that later.

He could have any woman he wanted. He had a reputation as a playboy – a reclusive, multi-millionaire playboy, who guarded his anonymity and privacy fiercely. He was one of America's most eligible bachelors and that air of mystery made him even more desirable, to both the press and the kind of women who pursued that kind of man. He'd obviously come to town four years ago, looking for a good time, and he'd found it with her. And she'd made it so easy for him… so damn easy. He'd never wanted to make it work, or to make it last. If he'd wanted those things, he'd have told her the truth about himself, instead of which, he'd played her.

She felt like such a fool.

She turned to Cassie. "I'm sorry," she said, her voice coming out stronger than she'd expected. "I can't stay."

"Em?" Cassie looked confused.

"I'll call you." She needed to get out of there. Now.

"Emma." She flipped her head round at the sound of Mark's voice. "Hear me out… please."

"No." She turned away from him and back to Cassie again. "I'm sorry," she repeated and, without another word, she ran for the door.

She didn't think to grab her coat from the hook; she didn't think about the fact that her phone was in her coat pocket, or that it was a long walk down the dark lane back to town, or that she was wearing high heels and a thin cocktail dress and it was a cold November evening. She didn't care. She just needed to get out of there before he saw her break. She wiped the back of her hand across her tear-filled eyes as she closed the door behind her and headed down the porch steps, along the path and out onto the lane, walking as fast as her heels would allow. Hell, her heels weren't that high. She could run... so she did.

As her feet pounded on the road, she wondered – why her? Why did she have to fall so hard for a liar? And why did he still have to make her want him so damn much. Even being in the same room as him had her aching for him, needing his touch, his kisses, his words. She sobbed out a breath and stopped for a moment to wipe her eyes on the backs of her hands again. God, this hurt so much. She put her hands over her face for a moment and lost herself to memories and tears, her whole body consumed with pain. "I'm not gonna do this again," she whispered to herself, remembering her promise to Nick and sucking in a shuddering sob. "I can't. I can't let myself go back there again." *Even if the darkness is beckoning...*

She shook her head, glanced back toward Cassie's house and took in a deep breath before she started running again.

Mark

He'd thought, while driving up here, that meeting Emma again might not end well... but this badly? Really? She wasn't even going to listen to him? She wasn't going to let him try and explain what had happened? Evidently not. She was leaving.

As the door closed behind her, he noticed her raise her hand to her eyes. Was she crying? He took a step toward the door, then stopped. She didn't want to hear his explanation, so what was the point? He thought about her crying. She'd cried when he'd left her four years ago. He remembered only too well how that had felt, driving back to Boston with the memory of her tear-stained face etched in his mind. *Fuck it.* It didn't matter if she rejected him, and it didn't matter how much that hurt; he was going after her. He stepped toward the door again.

"Mark?" Jake's voice stopped him in his tracks, and his friend moved closer, barring his way.

"I need to go."

"I already told you, Emma's one of our oldest friends. You're not going anywhere until you tell me what the hell's going on."

Mark sighed. "Remember I told you about a girl I met when I was here before?" Jake nodded. "That's her. Emma's the girl."

"Shit."

"Yeah… shit." Mark looked at him. "Can I go now?"

"No." Cassie spoke this time and Jake stood firm.

"What the…" Mark turned to her.

"I don't know what you're talking about, but I'm gonna guess you're the guy who broke her heart, about four years ago?"

"Yes." He broke her heart? He'd probably always known it deep down, but to hear it said out loud cut deep.

Cassie stared at him, her eyes narrowing. "What do you want from her?" she asked.

"The chance to make it right," he said, honestly.

He felt her eyes examining his face, like she was searching for the truth.

"She's upset and she's on her own, which means one of us needs to go after her," Mark said. "I'd like it to be me."

Cassie looked from him to Jake and back again. "Let him go, Jake," she said. Jake stepped to one side and Mark put his hand out to the door handle.

"Wait… did she come by car?" he asked, turning back.

"No. Nick – her brother – he dropped her down here. She'll be walking home," Cassie said. She moved quickly to the other side of the door and grabbed a coat from the hook. "This is hers. She'll be freezing."

"Thanks." Mark took it from her.

"You'll need a coat too."

"I'm fine." He opened the door.

"Hang on!" Cassie stopped him again. *What now?* She dashed to the coffee table, grabbed the box of Kleenex and, as she walked back to him, pulled a half dozen tissues from the top of the container, handing them to him. "Take these. You're gonna need them. Well, she is."

He smiled. "Thank you."

He let himself out and heard the door closing behind him. It was dark out here, and damn cold, and part of him regretted not taking Cassie up on the chance to get his jacket from upstairs. He ran down the porch steps and along the path, then peered down the lane. There was no sign of Emma, but she had to be along here somewhere. There was nowhere else to go, unless she'd stopped off at one of the houses, in which case, he'd never find her. Well, never was a long time… and he wasn't waiting a long time. If he didn't catch up with her, he'd go to her apartment and he'd wait there until she came home. He'd wait all damn night if he had to.

He pushed the Kleenex into his pocket, bunched up her coat into his hand and started to run. Real fast.

There were street lights at regular intervals down the lane, but the intervals were quite wide and, in between, it was pitch black. He guessed he'd gone about a third of the way down the lane before he saw her, silhouetted against the yellow lamplight ahead. He picked up his pace, knowing she'd hear his footsteps and hoping she'd stop, or at least not scream.

He pulled level with her. "Emma," he breathed.

She didn't even acknowledge his presence.

"Please?" he begged. "Please stop."

Again, she ignored him.

"Stop!" he yelled, and grabbed her arm, pulling her up beside him. She tried to back away from him, looking up into his face and shaking her head, heaving in deep breaths. "I'm not letting you go until you've heard me out," he said.

She breathed a little harder, sucking in air, then said, "I'll scream if you don't let me go."

He looked around. "Go ahead," he said. "The road's deserted. There isn't a house for a couple of hundred yards. If anyone does hear you, by the time they get here, at least you'll have heard what I've got to say." He still had hold of her arm.

She stared at him, defiantly.

"Gonna scream?" he asked. She shook her head slowly. "Gonna listen?" She didn't respond, but he took that as a yes, just on the basis that she wasn't screaming.

Without letting go – because he was scared she'd run again if he did – he took a half-step closer. "I'm sorry, Emma," he whispered. "I'm so, so sorry."

"What for?"

"For hurting you."

"Who says you hurt me?" She was angry and it was coming out as bitterness. He didn't blame her – not one bit.

"I do," he answered.

"And what makes you so sure you're right?"

"Because I know the look in your eyes," he replied. "I see it in the mirror every time I can bear to look at myself, which isn't very often." He noticed her features soften, just a fraction.

"You lied to me."

"I know. But I never meant to hurt you." She shivered and he remembered her coat. "Sorry, I brought this with me." He held it out to her and she turned and let him put it around her shoulders.

"Thank you," she muttered.

"You're welcome." He wasn't holding her now, but he wished he was. Still, at least she wasn't running. She was standing, staring at him… waiting. "I never meant to hurt you," he repeated.

"You've said that already."

"I wanted to come back," he explained. "I planned to." She didn't respond, other than to raise her eyebrows. "But, like I told you, I had to spend Thanksgiving with my family."

"I remember," she said, hugging her arms around herself.

"We were on the Turnpike…" he said and he heard her suck in a breath. She knew. He knew she did. She'd worked it out.

"Of course," she muttered. "I should've realized when Jake said your name… I mean, I read about it. I just didn't know it was you at the time."

"Obviously. I'd lied to you about who I was. Why would you have known it was me? I'd sent you a message just as I got into the car. Twenty minutes later – before you even had a chance to reply – we crashed."

"I remember the message," she whispered. "It was lunchtime, so I didn't pick it up for a while. You told me how much you were looking forward to seeing me. You said…" He heard her voice catch.

"I said how much I wanted to take you to bed, and that I wanted to be inside you."

She nodded her head. "I did send a reply, during my lunch break."

"I know. I got it. I wasn't actually conscious at the time, but I read it a couple of days later." He felt tears welling in his eyes. "You… you said you couldn't wait to see me. You said the bed would be warm, the wine would be chilled and you'd be…"

"Wet." She finished the sentence for him, her voice a barely audible whisper.

He nodded. "I was sitting by Sarah's bed when I read finally managed to read that. You'd sent other messages by then as well… less romantic ones."

"I was angry… hurt."

"You had every right to be."

"You still didn't reply though."

"I couldn't. Sarah was in a coma, our parents were dead, and I had no idea how to tell you any of it, because I'd lied to you."

"Oh, Mark." He felt her hand come up and cup his cheek, and he leant into the softness of her touch.

Chapter Six

Emma

He looked lost. "Every time I thought about sending a message, or calling you, I couldn't even work out where to begin. And there was so much to do."

"E—Excuse me? You didn't contact me, because you were *busy*?" Was he kidding?

She saw his shoulders slump. "That came out wrong."

"Then make it come out right, Mark."

"I had the funerals to arrange, the lawyers, the press – the media – to deal with. And they were fucking awful." He put his hands in his pockets and lowered his head. "They speculated about all kinds of things."

"I remember," Emma whispered, softening again. He looked at her. "Didn't they question whether you'd been driving at one stage?" she asked.

"Yeah. I wasn't." He raised his eyes to the sky. "My dad was. But I couldn't remember much of what had happened. That was half the problem. I was concussed, Sarah was in no position to make a statement, the truck driver… he'd had a heart attack and was in the ICU, but at that stage no-one knew if his heart attack had occurred before or after the crash. The other witnesses all came up with different versions of the same event. There was no-one to confirm what had actually gone on, so they made it up."

"And later?"

"Later, when I was a little better, I still couldn't remember. To this day, I still can't – not in any great detail – so they made up even more. They speculated about whether my dad was drunk, whether my parents had been arguing… It was all bullshit. I think they saw it as payback for all the stories they'd wanted to print about me and had never been able to." He stared down at her. "I guarded my private life well. I still do. They don't like it."

"Did the police ever find out what happened?" Emma asked. "In the accident, I mean…"

"Yeah. They eventually concluded the truck driver had the heart attack, lost control and swerved across our lane. My dad tried to brake, skidded, the car spun and ended up embedded under the truck. It was just an accident. One of those things. It was no-one's fault…" His voice drifted off.

"And your sister?" she asked.

"She recovered. It took her months to fully get over it, but she's okay now. Well, she has to be careful. They removed her spleen, she's prone to infections, and she gets these awful migraines from time to time…"

"I see." She let her head drop. "So that's why you were so busy."

"That wasn't all of it." She looked up at him again. "I had to take over the company, literally overnight. Before my dad died, I'd really just handled the marketing. That's what I studied at college. I mean, I always knew he wanted me to take over, and I'm sure one day, he'd have taken me through the whole business. He just never got around to it. But then, he never thought he was gonna die at fifty-three."

"I'm sorry, Mark."

She noticed his lips quirk upward, just fractionally. "That's my line."

"I mean I'm sorry you lost your parents; I'm sorry about what happened to your sister. I'm sorry for your pain."

"I know. Thank you." He looked devastated. No, he looked worse than that and she wanted, more than anything, to hold him and tell him it would all be okay… except she couldn't.

"Why did you lie to me?" she asked him. She needed to know. "Even at the end of our week together, after everything we'd done, why couldn't you tell me the truth?" She moved a little closer, looking up at him. "Didn't you know what a big deal it was for me?"

"Of course I did. It was a big deal for me too."

"Oh, really? Seriously? You weren't a virgin, Mark. And knowing who you really are, as I do now, I'm sure I wasn't your first virgin either."

She saw the pain cross his face and wanted to bite back the words, except she'd meant them – every single one.

"No, you weren't my first virgin," he replied quietly. "And obviously I wasn't a virgin myself. And I get that it being your first time made it an even bigger deal for you. That's played on my mind a lot ever since, believe me."

"Really? In that case, why the hell couldn't you just tell me the damn truth?"

"Because, just for once in my life, I wanted to be normal. I wanted to have something like Jake, you know? A life. A *real* life. It's like I told you when I first met you, I'm just an ordinary guy, or at least that's what I am underneath. I booked into the hotel here using my mom's maiden name – Ellis – because I thought I could be that ordinary guy for a week. I didn't expect to meet you. I had no idea any of that would happen, but having used a false name at the hotel, I thought it would look odd if I used my real name with you. I thought if you found out I was using one name with you and another at the hotel, you'd think I was… well, lying to you."

"You were."

"I know. It just seemed like the best idea at the time. I didn't want you to think of me as Mark Gardner. I wanted to be someone else, just for one goddamn week."

She sighed and a short silence descended. She felt like chasing this argument was getting them nowhere. She wasn't sure she'd ever understand…

"So, having lied once, and evidently felt bad about it, you thought you'd lie again… about what you did for a living?" She looked up at him.

"I didn't lie, not really."

"You told me you worked in the hotel trade."

"I do."

"Oh, come on, Mark. You implied you worked at a hotel, not that your family owns them, or that you're a millionaire." She glared at him. "What did you plan to do when you came back after Thanksgiving? Were you just gonna keep on lying?"

He shrugged. "Honestly? I hadn't thought that far ahead. I just wanted to see you again. I wanted to be with you. That was all I was thinking about. I missed you so much, I just wanted to get back here to you. I've spent my whole life in the shadows, Emma, dodging the press and photographers, never able to just live my life. The people I spend time with – with the exception of Jake – they're not interested in me, not really. They're interested in my family, my money, what I can do for them… It's been like that for as long as I can remember and I wanted something different – just for once."

"You… you think I'd have been like that? You think, if I'd known who you really were, I'd have just wanted your money, and not you?" She could feel the lump rising in her throat and the tears stinging her eyes again. "You think I'd have behaved any differently toward you because you're a millionaire, and not a guy who works in a hotel? You honestly believe that?" She looked away, her voice dropping to a whisper. "You don't know me at all, Mark."

Mark

"No! I don't think that," he said, closing the gap between them again. "That's not what I'm trying to say. I never thought you'd want my money. What I'm saying is that all the other women I've ever been with have. And I mean *all*. They never just want me, Emma. Never."

He heard her sob, "I did," just as she turned to leave.

He grabbed her and pulled her back, straight into his arms and, with one hand behind her head, holding her in place, he leant down and kissed her. He ran his tongue along her lips, but she resisted him, her muscles – her whole body – tightened against him. Her hands were pushing against his chest, and a part of his brain was telling him to stop. She didn't want this. And yet… He tried again – a last ditch attempt. He slowly, gently teased his tongue against her lips again and she opened, just a fraction, just enough, for him to delve into her, tilting his head and changing the angle of the kiss to go deeper. He heard her moan, felt her sigh. He'd broken through. He groaned loudly, and then she reached up, her coat falling to the floor as her fingers knotted into his hair. She moved closer, pressing her body tight against his and he flexed his hips into her, letting her feel the whole length of his arousal. And they were back to where they'd been four years ago. Two people whose need for each other outweighed everything else… even their own reason.

He pulled back eventually, looking down at her, but not letting her go. He had no intention of letting her go. They were both breathing hard. "I know," he whispered. "I know you weren't like that. And I'm sorry if I implied that you were." He brushed his thumb along her sensitized lips. "I'm sorry if I was rough with you just then too. I didn't mean to be. I just wanted you to understand that I want you more than anything. I always have." Her mouth opened slightly and he dipped his thumb inside. She sucked gently, not taking her eyes from his, and his cock twitched into her hip. "Nothing's changed between us, Emma. Nothing."

She released his thumb from her mouth and leant back in his arms, looking up at him. "Except you're not the man I thought you were," she whispered.

"I'm the same man, I promise. Give me a chance. Let me back in, and I'll prove it to you."

"And how are you gonna do that? You're only here until tomorrow. You'll go home again and then God knows when you'll be back. I know how that feels, Mark. I can't do it again," she sobbed. "I can't."

He pulled her close again. "Neither can I." He moved his hands, holding her face, and raising it to his. "Can I see you tomorrow? I've got to go to the site in the morning, but can I call round and see you in the afternoon? We can talk…"

"We're already spending the afternoon together," she murmured.

"We are?"

"Yes. Didn't Cassie or Jake explain?"

"No. Explain what?"

"We're all going to the hotel site. And when you've finished your business with Jake, we're having a picnic on the beach."

"A picnic? In November?" He smirked.

She smiled, just lightly. "Everyone says that."

He shrugged. "I think it sounds like a great idea."

"You do?"

He leant down closer, so his lips were almost touching hers. "You'll be there, so yeah."

"I'm not sure I will be… not now."

He felt the panic rising inside him. "Why not?"

"Because I'm not sure there's any point. I don't even know who you are."

"Yes, you do. You're the only person who's ever seen the real me. Spend tomorrow with me, please. Let me show you that I'm exactly the same man you met before. I've just got a different name, that's all." He knew he sounded desperate, but then he was. And anyway, he didn't care.

Chapter Seven

Emma

"I don't know…"

She still wasn't sure. He could hurt her again so easily and, while she didn't think she would do what she'd done before, she knew, with absolute certainty, she couldn't handle the pain again.

He was still leaning over, his lips hovering above hers. "Forgive me, Emma, please. At least try. Let me prove to you that I'm worthy of you."

He closed the gap and, rather than just kissing her, he sucked on her lower lip, then bit it gently, before covering her mouth with his. She felt his tongue twisting against hers, then heard a groan rumbling from deep in his throat, firing across every nerve in her body. "I want you," he muttered into her mouth. "I want you so fucking much." It felt like her legs were going to buckle beneath her and she clung to his shoulders for support. "Be mine again," he whispered. "Please, Emma. Please spend tomorrow with me. I promise, I'll never hurt you again… Ever."

She pulled back. "I'll think about it." He let her go, breathing heavily. "I'll let Cassie know in the morning." She bent down and picked up her coat, shrugging it on and turning away from him.

"Y—you're leaving? You're not coming back to the beach house?" He moved quickly to block her from going anywhere.

"No."

"Why?"

"Because I think it's for the best."

"For whom?"

"Everyone."

"It's not best for me, that's for sure." He sighed. "And I don't think it's best for you either, not if you're being honest with yourself." She lowered her head, but he put his finger beneath her chin and raised it again. "You said it yourself, Emma. I'm going home tomorrow and I want to spend as much time as I can with you, starting now." He brushed his fingers down her cheek. "I really don't want you to go back to your apartment and start dwelling on the past and what happened before. I want you to think about who I really am and what we can be and do together, not how much I hurt you back then. I want you to see that you can trust me and know what we can have in the future. And you can only do that if you spend time with me." He gazed into her eyes. "Say yes, Emma…"

His words were intoxicating… but then they always had been. She sighed. "Okay, I'll come back to the house," she said. "But that's all I'm promising for now."

"That's enough, baby… for now."

He'd called her 'baby', again. It sounded so good on his lips. She closed her eyes and let herself fall into him… and he caught her, just like she knew he would, holding her close in his arms. It felt good to rest there and let him make believe everything was going to be okay.

"We should be getting back," she whispered at last, pulling back from him. "I know what Cassie's cooked for dinner and it doesn't taste good burned."

He smiled. "Okay."

They started walking. After a few paces, he took her hand in his, and she let him. She wanted to slap herself for giving in to him so easily every time. His words, his looks, his kisses, his touch… all of them could break down her defenses. She just had to remind herself that they could break her heart too.

"This is yours then?" She stopped by his car, pulling her hand from his.

"Yes."

She looked over its sleek lines. "It's beautiful."

"Thank you."

She glanced at him. "Not exactly the type of car that every normal guy owns though, is it?"

He paused. "No, I guess not." He smirked. "Unless he maybe won the lottery?"

She felt her lips twitch and scolded herself, just as he placed a hand on her shoulder and turned her to face him. "If the car bothers you, I'll get rid of it. I'll buy a Ford, or something, if that helps convince you…"

She gazed up at him. "Did you choose it?" she asked.

"Yes. I bought it about a year ago. Before this I had a DB9."

"You didn't drive an Aston Martin when you came here before. You drove a Mercedes."

"Yeah. And I didn't lie about that. It was a company car. My dad insisted all the board members had one. H—he said they were the safest…" He swallowed hard. "I got rid of mine straight away, after the accident. I'm sure they are very safe cars, but I couldn't even look at it, let alone drive it."

"I'm sorry."

"Don't be."

She let out a breath. "So, this is your choice of car?" He nodded, seeming confused. "Then you shouldn't change it," she continued. "It's a part of who you are."

"Is that good, or bad?"

She studied his face for a moment. "I don't know yet, but you have very good taste in cars." His lips twitched and he leant in close to her.

"And women," he whispered. "I've got fantastic taste in women." She held his gaze for a moment, then turned and they walked up the pathway together.

He opened the screen and went to knock on the door.

"It's open," Emma said. "It's always open." She reached forward and turned the handle, and pushed. A warm hug of heat escaped, and they passed inside.

Jake and Cassie were sitting together on the couch, and Maddie was nowhere to be seen. As Mark and Emma entered, Jake got up first, followed closely by Cassie.

They looked a little awkward.

"I'll put the appetizers out," Cassie said, going into the kitchen. "I'll just need to turn the chicken back up again… Ten minutes till dinner?"

"Sounds great," Mark said.

"How about a drink?" Jake suggested.

"Hmm, please," Mark replied.

Without making eye contact with anyone, Emma removed her coat and hung it back up on the hook. Then, ignoring Mark and Jake completely, she went straight to the kitchen and sought refuge with Cassie.

∞

Mark

He watched her go and stood, feeling a little stranded, acutely aware that he was the outsider here. He might be Jake's friend, but that was a comparatively new thing. The friendships between the other three people here went back twenty years or so, to early childhood.

"Come and sit down," Jake said. "I'll get you a glass of wine."

"Thanks." Mark took a seat at one end of the couch. If he was honest, he also felt a bit shocked. Maybe the wine would help calm his nerves… something needed to.

He wanted her back. And not just because her kisses felt even better than they had before, not just because, when he'd held her in his arms, he'd felt like he'd come home. It was more than that. A lot more. He belonged to her. All he had to do was convince her that she belonged to him too.

"Mark?" He looked up. Jake was holding out a glass of red wine. He took it.

"Thanks. I need this." He took a long sip.

"I thought you might." Jake sat down at the opposite end of the sofa and looked at him. "So, it was Emma?" he said.

"Yeah."

Jake seemed to be thinking. "You told me you let her down. When we discussed you coming up here, you said it wasn't a good idea for you to meet her again, because you'd let her down."

"That's because I did."

"How?"

"I lied to her." He sipped some more wine.

"What about?" Mark stared at him. "She's a friend, Mark," Jake continued. "And, before you say anything, I know you're a friend too, but we've known Emma since… well, forever."

"I know. I lied to her about who I was. Who I am." It was clear from the expression on Jake's face that he didn't understand. "I used a false name," Mark explained. "I told her I was Mark Ellis. That was my mom's maiden name."

"Why'd you do that?"

"Because I didn't want to be Mark Gardner, just for a week. I was kinda sick of being him…"

"Sick of being a multi-millionaire?"

"Sick of having my every fucking move analyzed and scrutinized. If you haven't lived it, you can't judge it."

Jake shrugged. "Fair enough."

"I was gonna come back and see Emma after Thanksgiving, but…"

"But the accident…"

"Yeah."

"So did you contact her afterwards?"

"No." Mark let his head drop.

"Ouch."

"I know. I couldn't though. I couldn't face her. Not when I'd lied to her. And anyway, I wasn't really in a very good place, what with Sarah, work, the media… it was a fucking mess."

"What happened outside?"

"I tried to explain."

"And?"

"And she was really kind about my family. But she's still not sure about me."

Jake sighed. "That's Emma. She's one of the kindest people I know, but lying's a big deal for her." He smiled, and then looked thoughtful for a moment. "Do you want her back?" he asked.

Mark nodded. "Oh God, yes. I just hope she can forgive me for what I did to her."

Jake leant closer. "Don't give up, man," he whispered. "I didn't. Hang in there. It's worth it in the end."

Chapter Eight

Emma

"So he's 'the one'?" Cassie asked, opening the oven door and checking on the chicken, before adjusting the heat.

"Yes."

"The one who left town and never came back?"

Emma nodded. "And lied to me – evidently."

"What did he lie about?"

Emma leant back on the countertop. "He told me his name was Mark Ellis, not Mark Gardner."

"Oh… Why did he do that?"

Emma shrugged. "He says it was because he wanted to be an ordinary guy for a week. He was sick of the way the press followed his every move, and wanted to just be normal."

Cassie started setting out the appetizers. "I think that's kind of understandable," she mused.

"You do?" Emma was surprised.

"Yeah." Cassie looked up at her friend. "Don't you? I'm not saying it was right to lie to you, or that he couldn't have found a way to tell you the truth later on, but I can understand him wanting to escape and lead a normal life for a week. Having people watching you the whole time, must be horrible."

Emma thought for a moment. She had no idea what Mark's life was like, or how it felt to live like that… and Cassie was probably right, the need to escape maybe had been overwhelming at the time.

"I suppose," she said. "I still don't see why he couldn't have told me the truth though… afterwards, I mean."

"Remind me, when did this happen exactly?"

"The week Maddie was born."

"Oh, yeah."

"And then he was supposed to come back for the weekend after Thanksgiving, but he didn't turn up. At the time, I assumed… well, I just assumed he'd got what he wanted and didn't want *me* anymore. Now, of course, I know about his family and what happened to them." She looked up at Cassie. "But even so, that was four years ago…"

Cassie walked around the table and came to stand in front of her. "When I lost my mom," she said quietly, "I just wanted to shut myself away and cry, and wallow in memories, and self pity, and the horror of it all." She put a hand on Emma's arm. "I was lucky. I had Maddie and you, and Ben, and Nick… and then Jake came back. I was surrounded by love. I still am. Mark's had no-one. His sister was in the hospital, his parents had *both* been killed. From what Jake's told me, his friends were superficial; none of them were there for him. He did all of it by himself. And, unlike the rest of us, he had to do it in the eye of the media, while trying to maintain his privacy, and his sister's. And they were accusing him of all kinds of awful things, ripping apart various aspects of his personal life for the tabloids' pleasure." She sighed. "That's still going on for him. I can't even imagine how he gets through it." Emma opened her mouth to speak, but Cassie held up her hand. "I know you're going to say he's had four years – and he has. I know you're going to say four years is a long time, that he could have come back at any point in those four years and explained… and you'd be right. He could've done. But, while you're thinking that, try and remember what happened to him. Try and remember what he's been through. And… and then be the person you really are, Emma. Be the kind, forgiving, generous person you are. Don't judge him."

"You're gonna make me cry… again."

"Well, we're never short of Kleenex. Not in this house." Cassie smiled at her and grabbed a box off the countertop, holding them out.

Emma took a tissue and wiped her eyes.

"He says he wants to prove he's worthy of me."

"Then let him. Give him a chance. I did with Jake, and I've never been happier."

They were all sitting around the kitchen table. Jake sat next to Mark, with Cassie opposite him and Emma facing Mark.

"This looks really lovely," Jake said.

"Thanks." Cassie looked up at him. "I couldn't have done it without Emma."

"All I did was make the dressing."

"And supply the recipes."

They started to eat. "This is that lemon dressing, isn't it?" Mark said, looking at Emma.

"Yes." She put down her fork. "You might as well know now, this meal's gonna be kind of boring for you."

"Oh? Why?"

"Because it's exactly the same meal I cooked for you."

"You mean, that night?" His eyes penetrated hers.

"Yes."

"Then it won't be boring at all," he said. "It'll bring back the best memories."

Emma felt herself blushing.

"I take it this was a special occasion?" Cassie asked, spearing a piece of melon and popping it into her mouth.

"It was our first home-cooked meal together," Emma explained.

"Oh, so why did you give me these recipes?" Cassie inquired.

"Because I knew they were quite simple, and you asked for simple. I knew they didn't take too long, and I knew they tasted good."

"I can vouch for that," Mark added, smiling at her.

"So, did you ever cook for Emma?" Jake asked Mark. "I mean, I've eaten your cooking. I know how bad it can get."

"Thanks." Mark grinned. "I did cook for her… once."

"And she's still alive?" Jake nudged into him.

"What did he cook?" Cassie asked.

"Um… salmon, with roasted vegetables."

"Sounds nice."

"It was."

Jake added some more dressing to his dish. "What are you not telling us, Em? What did he get wrong?"

"Nothing," she whispered.

Mark rested his fork on the side of his plate. "I think what Emma's trying not to tell you, is that she's just worked out that was the evening I realized I shouldn't have lied to her."

"Oh."

Everyone looked embarrassed, but Mark continued. "We were playing a kind of game," he explained.

"Do we want to know about this?" Jake asked, trying to lighten the moment.

"Not *that* kind of game…" Mark shook his head, but kept his eyes fixed on Emma. "We were just trying to find out things about each other – you know, getting to know each other better. So, I'd asked Emma about her favorite movies and music, and her favorite flowers. And then we moved on to character traits. Emma told me the one thing she hated most in people was dishonesty." He reached forward, picked up his wine glass and took a large gulp. "And I realized I'd screwed up."

"And you went to the bathroom." Emma remembered now. That was when he'd suddenly disappeared.

"Yeah. I needed a moment to try and work out what to do. I was trying to decide whether or not to tell you the truth, when the doorbell rang."

"Yes, it did."

"It was your brother." He looked from Emma to Cassie. "Oh," he said. "Was it Cassie? Was she the friend?"

Cassie looked from Mark to Emma. "Care to explain?" she said.

Emma twisted in her seat and looked at her friend. "I'd told Mark about you. I didn't name you, I just said you were my friend, you'd left town because your boyfriend had cheated, and you were pregnant. And then, that night Nick called round with the message from your mom that you'd gone into labor." She turned back to Mark. "And you were… you were so kind."

"I didn't do anything," he replied.

"That was your idea of nothing?"

"What did he do?" Cassie asked.

"To start with, he thought you were in Portland, Oregon, so he offered to fly me there… and when I explained it was Portland, Maine, he said he'd drive me to see you."

"Did you go?" Jake asked, leaning forward. Having missed out on Cassie's pregnancy, Maddie's birth, and the first three and a half years of her life, Jake was always hungry for information about that time.

"No. Cassie's mom had said she'd call and let me know when I could visit."

"Everything was so scary at the start," Cassie explained, turning to Jake. "I just wanted to focus on Maddie."

"I understand." Jake reached across the table and covered her hand with his.

"I never did get to thank you properly for that night," Emma said, still looking at Mark. "You made everything feel like it was going to be okay, when it all seemed so bleak."

"Well, it was okay, wasn't it?"

"Yes, but it didn't look like that at the time."

"I know. And you don't need to thank me, Emma."

Cassie leant into her, just a little. "I'm glad you had someone with you," she whispered.

Emma nodded.

They'd finished their appetizers and, while Cassie prepared the chicken, Jake cleared the plates. Mark was pouring the wine, but stopped just as he was re-filling Emma's glass.

"Wait a second," he said.

"What?" She looked at him.

"If Cassie was your friend, that means Jake was the cheating boyfriend." He looked over to Jake, who was standing beside the sink, stacking the dishes. "You told me your girlfriend ran out because she was pregnant, and that she didn't tell you because you'd been an asshole back then, but you never said anything about cheating…"

"Christ almighty!" Jake said, throwing his hands up in the air. "Once and for all… I did *not* cheat."

"He didn't." Cassie joined in. "It was a misunderstanding. I got it wrong."

"So you weren't an asshole?" Mark finished pouring the wine and put the bottle down.

"Yeah, I was." Jake came and sat back down again. "But, as I explained to Cass at the time, there's a world of difference between being a selfish, irresponsible kid, and cheating. It took a while, but we worked it out."

"And now you're engaged…" Mark added.

"You know about that?" Emma asked him, surprised.

"Yeah." Mark looked across at her. "Jake told me."

She let out a sigh. "Thank goodness for that. At least there's someone I can talk to about it."

Mark leant forward. "You're gonna talk to me then?"

Emma shrugged, although she couldn't help the smile forming on her lips. "I'll think about it."

It was the end of the evening. Dinner had been a huge success and, despite the earlier awkwardness, they'd all had a great time.

"I really must go home," Emma said, leaning back in her seat. "I'm exhausted."

"Let me drive you," Mark offered. "Please?"

"I can walk."

"Like hell you can." Emma felt her lips twitching upward again. She liked his protectiveness; it made her feel safe. "I deliberately didn't drink too much so I could drive you back." He smiled. "And besides, you know you wanna try out my car." His smile became a grin.

"It's an offer you can't refuse, Em," Jake teased.

"Oh, alright then."

They all got up and made their way to the door, where Emma grabbed her coat, which Mark promptly took from her, holding it out so she could put it on, and letting his hands rest on her shoulders for a moment.

"Thank you," she murmured, leaning back into him.

"You're welcome."

As they stood on the porch, she turned to Cassie and Jake. "Thank you for a lovely evening," she said. "I'm really sorry about what happened earlier – all the drama."

"Hey… no need to be sorry." Cassie moved closer and gave her a hug. "Take care."

Jake followed suit, kissing her cheek and, before he let her go, he whispered, "He's a good guy, Em. I promise."

Emma pulled back and gave Jake a nod.

Mark took her hand and led her down the steps to his car, opening the passenger door and helping her inside. Once she was settled, he closed the door again and went round to the driver's side, lowering himself in next to her. He started the engine.

"You okay?" he asked.

She smiled. "Yes, thank you."

"Good."

He reversed out onto the lane and drove back into town.

"Do you remember telling me your favorite film?" he asked her after a minute or two.

"Yes."

"You said it was *Groundhog Day*."

"I know."

"And do you remember what you said when I asked you why you liked that film?"

"I said it was because I like Bill Murray."

"Yeah. And…?"

"And… because I liked the idea of getting a second chance at changing your life, at putting things right when you've made mistakes."

She heard him sigh. "Give me that chance, Emma. That's all I'm asking."

She turned to him. "Except this isn't a movie. This is real life. And in real life you can't keep reliving the past until you get it right. It hurts too much."

He didn't reply. Instead they drove the rest of the way in silence, then he pulled up in front of the coffee shop and turned off the engine.

"I don't want to keep reliving the past," he said, staring straight ahead through the windshield. "I want to put things right, because I made a mistake, because I hurt you. But I don't want to relive or recreate anything. I want a future… with you." He climbed out of the car and came around to her side, helping her out and closing the door again. "At least come to the beach tomorrow. Make a start. Spend some time with me… Please?"

"Okay."

He smiled. "Thank you."

He leant down and kissed her, his lips caressing hers, just gently. Her coat was open and she felt his hands come inside, resting on her waist as he pulled her closer… and then his tongue was in her mouth, searching for and finding hers. He pushed her back against the side of the car, his feet either side of hers, his body hard against her. She moaned into his mouth, her hands resting on his arms, then moving up to his shoulders, holding onto him. His hands moved up a little and she felt his thumbs brush against her hardened nipples through the thin material of her dress. She flexed her hips forward into him, feeling his long, thick erection. She wanted him… right now.

He pulled back. Even in the dim street lighting, she could see his eyes were on fire.

"I need you," he muttered, leaning down and biting on her bottom lip. "I need you so much." His eyes searched hers. "I'll take you to your door," he said, moving away from her, just a fraction.

She felt herself deflate. He must have felt it too because he moved back.

"I've gotta stop this," he explained. "If I don't, I won't be able to."

"What if I said I don't want you to?" she whispered.

His eyes widened, but then he closed them, just for a second, and took a deep breath, staring down at her.

"I'd think I was dreaming…" She pinched his arm. "Ouch! What was that for?"

"To prove you're not dreaming."

He laughed. "Okay, so I'm not dreaming. I guess I'm just in heaven then." He became serious again. "I don't want it to be like this," he murmured. "I don't want you to have any lingering doubts about me – not one. And at the moment, you still do. We both know that." He ran the backs of his fingers down her cheek. "When I take you to bed again, Emma, it's gonna because you *know* it's the right thing to do, not just because we can't keep our hands off of each other." He smirked. "Which it seems we can't."

She let out a breath and allowed her head to fall onto his chest. "Thank you," she whispered.

"What for?" He raised her face to his.

"For being sensible."

"I don't want you to have any regrets, baby. And if we went upstairs now, you'd regret it." He was right. She would. Yeah, it would be great, but she would regret it, because there was so much they needed to talk about first.

The problem was, it didn't stop her wanting him.

Mark

He'd hoped to drive to the site with Emma, but over breakfast, Jake had told him the two of them were going to leave early, in Mark's car and go up to the site. Emma and Cassie were going to prepare the picnic, and they'd follow on later in Jake's car. The plan made sense. If they had to wait for the picnic to be prepared, they'd never get everything done at the site. He knew it was sensible, he really did. He'd just hoped to be able to spend the journey with Emma.

"I'm not sure this isn't a ploy on Jake's part to have a ride in your car," Cassie said, clearing up the mess Maddie had made with her cereal.

"He's been in my car loads of times," Mark replied. "It's really not that exciting. No, it makes sense doing it this way."

Cassie looked at him. "But you'd rather have Emma's company?"

Mark smiled at her. "Do you blame me?"

"No."

"Um… I am here," Jake said.

"I meant, I don't blame Mark. Not that *I'd* want Emma's company over yours."

"Good. I'm glad to hear it." Jake checked his watch. "We should be getting ready to go."

Mark got up from the table. "Thanks for breakfast," he said. He went to turn away, then stopped. "In case I get… um, distracted, and forget to say this later, thanks for letting me stay here this weekend. It's been…" He couldn't think of the right word.

"Unexpected?" Cassie offered.

He smiled. "Yeah… unexpected."

He'd seen Cassie and Emma arrive over half an hour earlier. Cassie had driven straight past the site and down to the private beach below. He and Jake had spent the whole morning going over the building and Jake had shown him the plans for the next stage. He was impressed with everything he'd seen so far. Jake had done an astounding job and he was feeling even more enthusiastic about the upgrades to the other hotels, and the prospect of building a second one.

But right now, he just wanted to be with Emma. Walking away from her the previous night had been damn hard. It had taken all his willpower not to carry her upstairs to her apartment, take her to bed and make her his again. But he knew it was too soon and, if they'd done that, she would have regretted it and, because of that, so would he.

"Are we done here yet?" he asked. "Sorry, I don't mean to sound impatient…"

"But I'm not as interesting as Emma?"

"No." Mark laughed. "So, are we done?"

"Yeah, I guess." Jake looked around him.

Mark came over. "Listen," he said. "You've done an amazing job here. I'm really excited by what I've seen and, if there's anything we haven't covered, I'm happy for you to go ahead on your own initiative."

"What you mean is, you don't give a fuck what I do with your hotel, as long as you can go be with Emma?" Jake laughed.

"I didn't put it that way… but yeah, pretty much."

Jake put his arm around his shoulder. "C'mon then. You're not concentrating anyway."

Mark pulled him back. "I meant what I said, Jake. I'm really impressed."

"Thanks."

"And I'm glad you're coming to work with me."

"I think you'll find I'm coming to work *for* you."

"No. I got it right the first time."

Jake smiled at him. "That means a lot."

"Good. Now, can we *please* go?"

They made their way back to Mark's car, locking up the site as they went. "Whose crazy idea was a picnic on the beach in November?" Mark asked opening the car.

"Cassie's, I think," Jake replied.

"And you're gonna marry this woman?"

"Yeah." They climbed into their seats. "I love her craziness – among other things…" Jake grinned at him.

"Should I have worn more clothes?" Mark looked down at his jeans, sweater and leather jacket. He'd brought a scarf, which was in the trunk with the rest of his things, but Jake was wearing a lot more layers. "I'm not used to being at the beach at this time of year."

"Wasn't it this time of year you came here before?" Jake queried.

"I didn't spend a lot of time at the beach," Mark replied. "In fact, I didn't spend a great deal of time outside of Emma's apartment." He hadn't spent much time outside of Emma's bed, but he wasn't going to say that, even though he thought Jake had probably worked it out for himself.

"You'll be fine." Jake laughed. "You'll have Emma to keep you warm."

Mark started the engine and put the car into drive. "God, I hope so," he said.

Mark might have thought a picnic in November was crazy, but once they sat down to eat, he soon changed his mind. They settled on a large rug in the shelter of the rocks, away from the wind and Cassie laid out the dishes, which she was quick to point out, were courtesy of Emma. The food was hot, and looked delicious. Emma had made a spicy corn chowder, sticky ribs, warm potato salad, fried chicken and miniature lasagnas, baked in cupcake containers.

"You did all this work this morning?" he asked Emma.

"Cassie did help," she replied, handing out plates. "And I started the ribs cooking last night when I got home. They've been in the oven for... oh... hours and hours." She looked up at him. "I wasn't as tired as I thought, and I needed a distraction."

He smiled at her. "You did?" he said.

"Yeah." She passed him the dish of ribs and kept her eyes fixed on his as he took a bite.

"God, that's good."

She smiled.

"That'll be the secret barbecue sauce," Cassie said.

"There's a secret sauce?"

"Oh, yes."

"And you make this yourself?" He turned back to Emma.

"Yes."

"You should be cooking at the coffee shop, at the very least," Mark said. "Although, I said it before and I'll say it again, I still think you should be running the place."

"Emma does run the place," Jake replied.

He turned to her. "You do? You bought it?"

"No... I *run* it. I don't own it."

"So, you're the manager?"

"Yes. After you left, I realized I'd had enough. I was being taken advantage of. Nick had been telling me the same thing for years, but hearing it from you as well made it more real, I suppose. I guess it dawned on me that Nick kind of had to stick up for me… he's my brother. You didn't. But you still felt I was better than Mrs Adams gave me credit for. So, I called her in Florida on the Friday after you left town and told her I wanted a promotion. I was so nervous. I thought she was gonna fire me, but she didn't. She said she needed the weekend to think about it. And then she called me back early the following week and said she agreed with me."

"Why didn't you tell me?" he asked. "If this was just after I left, we were still in touch then. We were talking on the phone and texting all the time. You could've told me."

"I—I was saving it for when you came back. I was gonna surprise you."

He swore under his breath and closed his eyes. "I'm sorry, Emma," he said.

"It's okay. It's not that big a deal. It's a title, nothing more. Well, a title and a pay rise. She hasn't let me alter the menu, and I've only been able to change one supplier so far. Everything's pretty much as it was before, except I've taken on a guy called Josh. He's at senior high and he helps out on Saturdays, so I can get the paperwork done. That's one of my managerial responsibilities…" She glanced up at him. "Before Josh came on board, I was having to do that on Sundays, or in the evenings," she explained.

"And your existing staff couldn't cover the Saturdays?" he asked.

She laughed. "Only if nobody wanted to drink coffee."

He looked at her, his head tilting to one side. "I don't get it," he said.

"They won't use the damn barista machine," she told him. "They never have. I've trained them, and trained them, and they're too scared to go near it."

"They're scared… of a barista machine?" His lips quirked upward.

"I know. It's ridiculous." She let out a sigh. "Still, Josh isn't so pathetic. He works all day on Saturday; Patsy and Kathryn work until two, and I use that time to do the paperwork. Then I take over from them at two, and Josh and I cover the rest of the day. It's not perfect, but…"

He could feel her lingering disappointment, and he knelt up and crawled over to her. "You'll get there one day. I promise."

"Well, Mrs Adams was a little more receptive to the idea of selling up when I last spoke to her about it."

"Really?" Cassie twisted round to face her. "When was this? You didn't say anything to me."

"No… well, it was just a really brief conversation on Friday afternoon and I'm not reading too much into it. Besides, she got distracted."

"How?"

"Oh, that was my own fault. I made the mistake of mentioning selling home-baked cakes and cookies as one of my ideas, and she suddenly decided to get all enthusiastic about it for the first time in years. She forgot all about selling up after that. I should've just stayed on topic."

"Well then," Mark said, sitting down again, a little closer to her, "deal with the cakes and cookies thing and get back onto her. Don't let it lie for too long. And don't mention any more of your ideas to her. She'll just suck you dry." He picked up a piece of fried chicken. "You've still got your inheritance, I take it?"

"Yes." Emma nodded.

"Okay, so you can do what I suggested before and borrow whatever else you need."

Her eyes narrowed. "From you, I suppose."

He shrugged. "Well, no."

Everyone stared at him. It was Jake who spoke first. "You mean you wouldn't lend Emma the money to fulfill her dream?"

"No, I wouldn't. I'd *give* her the money. But I don't think Emma wants that, do you?"

She shook her head. "Thank you," she murmured.

Once they'd cleared away, and packed everything back into Jake's car, Maddie wanted to search the rock pools for creatures, so Jake and Cassie took her off down the beach.

"Wanna go for a walk?" Mark suggested, nodding in the other direction. Emma looked incredible. Her hair was loose and blowing in the wind. She was wearing really tight stonewashed jeans, knee length brown boots and a thick cream sweater, with a long chunky dark blue cardigan over the top, and a check scarf wrapped around her neck. She may have been bundled up against the cold, but she was beautiful… and damn sexy.

"Okay."

He took her hand and they started walking slowly along the shore.

"I've had a lovely day," Emma said.

"Me too."

"The thing is," she added. "I know you're going home, straight from here."

"Yeah, I am." He didn't want to. He really wanted to pick up where they'd left off last night. He wanted to go back to her apartment with her, take her upstairs and into her bedroom, and undress her real slowly, working his way through all those layers. Then he wanted to lower her down onto her bed, take his time rediscovering her body, touching and tasting her all over again, and then finally make slow, sweet love to her all night long. But that wasn't going to happen. "I'm coming back though," he said.

She stopped walking and turned to him.

"Please, Mark, don't say that if you don't mean it." He saw the tears in her eyes. "You said it before. Please don't get my hopes up if you're gonna let me down again."

"I'm not." He moved closer. "It wasn't my fault I couldn't come back before."

"I know." She put her hand on his chest. "And I'm sorry, Mark. I'm really sorry for what happened to your family, and for what you've been through. But you could've come back before now. That's what I'm struggling with. It keeps going round and round my head, no matter how much I try not to think it. It's been four years, and you could've come back sooner, if only you hadn't lied to me…" He heard her voice crack.

"I know. That's all completely true." He held his breath for a moment, then let it out slowly. "Emma... if you're really finding it too much of a struggle to think about forgiving me, I can leave Jake in charge of the build, and I'll get my business manager to handle everything else, and I'll never come back here again. I'll keep my distance, even though I want you more than anything. I'll stay away, if that's what you want." He paused, just briefly. "But, if you think you can try to forgive me. If you think you can let me back in and give us a chance, then I want to be in your life... and I *will* find a way to make this work."

She blinked up at him. "I don't want you to stay away, Mark. I never wanted that. That's the whole point, don't you see? Even though you lied, I still wish you'd come back and told me, I wish you'd called, or texted, and explained why you did what you did, instead of leaving me on my own for the last four years, thinking I wasn't... I wasn't good enough." She sobbed out the last few words and fell into him, weeping.

"Oh God. What did I do to you?" He wrapped his arms around her and held her tightly.

"You... you broke me," she whispered.

"Then let me make it right. Let me fix you. Please."

"How do I know you won't break me again?"

"Because my heart couldn't take it, Emma."

She looked up and he saw the confusion cross her face. "How can your heart be in danger, Mark? You weren't in love."

Had he heard her right? "And you were?" She'd spoken in the past tense, but right now he'd take it. He didn't care.

"Yes, I was. That's how I know you could break me again... so easily."

What the hell. He had to tell her. She had to know... "And that's how I know I won't. I fell in love with you the very first time I saw you, Emma. You're saying all of this in the past tense. You *loved* me. But I *still love* you. I never stopped loving you. Leaving you broke my heart. It broke me too... shattered me into so many fucking pieces. And I've been broken ever since." He pulled her in close, burying his face in her hair. "I need you back, Emma, so I can fix myself again too."

Chapter Nine

Emma

The first twenty-four hours were the hardest. But maybe that was because the memory of his words, his kisses, his touch, and that awful, tearful goodbye at the beach were still so fresh.

Realizing that he'd loved her back then – that he still loved her now – it made all the difference. She didn't want to fight him anymore. She just wanted him to fix them both and make it right again.

They'd walked and talked for the rest of the afternoon. Jake and Cassie had left them alone and, when they'd finally got back to the car, they were there, waiting for them. He'd promised to come back to her the following weekend, and she'd cried into him for ages, until he finally had to leave and had passed her over to Cassie, who'd held onto her as he drove away.

Then he'd sent her a text message, maybe ten minutes later. He said he'd pulled over at the side of the road. He needed to know she was okay. He couldn't go home knowing she was that upset. Did she need him to come back?

She'd told him she'd be alright. If he came back, he'd only have to leave again and that would just make it worse.

He'd told her he'd call when he got home… and when he did, they'd talked for two hours.

If the first twenty-four hours were hard, the rest of the week wasn't a great deal easier. Monday, Tuesday and Wednesday were particularly difficult, because Saturday still seemed so far away. By Thursday, they were able to talk about it as 'the day after tomorrow', which made it sound closer, and by Friday, it was 'tomorrow'.

"You're sure about this?" Nick asked her for about the tenth time that week.

"Yes, Nick. I'm sure."

"He hurt you, Em."

"I know. And so does he. He wants to make it right… and I want to let him."

He looked at her, lowered his head and sighed. "Okay. Just be careful."

"I will."

"I think it's gonna be for the best if I'm not around when he gets here tomorrow," he added. "I think I might be tempted to threaten the guy."

"I don't want you to threaten him."

"I know you don't. That's why I'm not gonna be here. But I'm not gonna pretend I'm not worried. I don't want to find you in pieces again… or have to try and patch you back together, Em."

"You won't. He wants it to work as much as I do."

He stared at her. "I hope you're right. I really do." He went to leave, but turned back. "Call me, if you need me?"

She nodded and watched him go, then glanced at the clock. It was just before seven and she started to close up, almost bursting with anticipation. Mark would be here tomorrow, just before lunch, and she wasn't entirely sure she could hold it together while she waited.

It was cold outside and she ran along the sidewalk to her apartment, letting herself in. She'd just closed the door when her phone rang and she pulled it from her pocket, checking the display. It was Mark and she picked up straight away, starting to climb up the stairs.

"Hi," she said, smiling. "Your timing is immaculate, as always. I've just got in from work."

"Hi." His voice sounded different to usual. There was a kind of hollowness to it.

"What's wrong, Mark?"

"Promise not to hate me…"

She felt her legs turn to jelly and buckle beneath her. She stumbled and sat on the stairs.

"W—why?"

"Just promise."

"I can't, Mark, not until you tell me why you think I'm gonna hate you."

"Because of what I'm about to do."

"Mark, stop speaking in riddles and just tell me – whatever it is."

She heard him take a breath. "I can't come up tomorrow."

She felt the lump rising in her throat and the tears pricking at her eyes, but her voice wouldn't work.

"Emma? Speak to me. Say something. Anything. Even if it's that you hate me."

"I don't hate you," she managed to mumble. "Why? Why can't you come?" Her voice gained a little of its strength, despite the crushing disappointment.

"I forgot Sarah's got an exhibition this weekend. She reminded me when I got in from work just now. I agreed to go before last weekend, before you and I even got back together."

"What's she exhibiting?"

"She's studying sculpture. This is the first time she's displayed her work – anywhere. I don't know much about it, but I guess it's kind of an honor that they'd put her work on display. I mean, I imagine they could've picked any of the students, and they seem to have picked her. I have to be there, Emma. I'm sorry… I'm so sorry."

"It's okay." It wasn't. It hurt like hell to know she wasn't going to see him tomorrow.

"No, it's not. It's not okay at all. I want to come up there and be with you, but I have to be here…" She could tell from the tone of his voice that he was feeling torn.

"Sarah needs you," she said. "I really do understand, Mark. It's just one weekend."

She heard him sigh. "God… I don't deserve you," he muttered.

"You'll come up next Saturday though, right?"

"Not on Saturday, no."

"Mark?" She sobbed out his name and the tears started to fall.

"Hey, baby. Please don't. Next week… it's Thanksgiving. Had you forgotten?"

"Um… no, b—but what difference does that make?" Now she'd started crying, she found she couldn't stop.

"I can come up on Friday morning, instead of Saturday, and I can stay over until Sunday night. We'll have three days together."

"Three days?" It sounded idyllic. It almost made up for not seeing him this weekend. Almost.

"I wish I could come before then," Mark continued, "but I can't. I mean, we've both gotta spend Thanksgiving with our families, I guess. And I obviously have to be here with Sarah on Wednesday…" Even through her own tears, she heard his voice change.

"Why Wednesday?" she asked.

"It's the anniversary of our parents' deaths."

She felt awful. "I'm sorry, Mark. I should've thought… So the anniversary is the 22nd?"

"No, they died on the 26th. I know it's a bit odd, but even from that first year, we've always remembered them more on the day before Thanksgiving, rather than the actual day it happened. I guess it's that holiday atmosphere thing that brings it all back. The 26th is really just a random day. For us, it's always been about that Wednesday…" His voice drifted to silence.

"This is a tough time of year for you," she said.

"Yeah… I'm really gonna need you this week."

"I'm here, Mark."

"I know. Thanks, baby."

"Call me, anytime."

It was Tuesday night. Emma was in bed, and it was getting late. Not only that, she was getting tired. Mark hadn't called her since that morning; a call which had been very brief, because he'd had a meeting to get to.

She knew he was busy and pre-occupied, and that he'd be thinking about tomorrow, but he'd only sent one text message all day, and hadn't responded to her answer. His language had changed too. Yesterday he'd forgotten to call all day, but he'd apologized in the evening and they'd talked for twenty minutes, although he'd been less romantic and playful. Sure, he'd still said he loved her at the end of the call, but it was like a cursory sign-off, like something he needed to say before he could move onto whatever else he was doing. She hated to admit it, and she knew it had only been a couple of days, but it was starting to feel like he was cooling off toward her.

She swallowed down the threatening tears and told herself he was just busy. That's all it was. She was overreacting. She picked up her phone and tapped out a message:

—Just off to sleep. Talk in the morning. E xx

That didn't sound too demanding, or clinging. She pressed 'send'. He replied immediately.

— Sorry. I'll call early. Sleep well. M x

She read the message and didn't bother to swallow down her tears. He was obviously available if he could reply that fast. He could've called. Or at least he could've explained why he hadn't called. He could've said he missed her, or he wanted her, or anything that would make her feel a little less like he'd forgotten she even existed.

She put the phone down on the nightstand, switched off the light and turned over. It took her hours to get off to sleep.

Her alarm woke her at ten after six and she immediately checked her phone. 'Early' to Mark meant before six am… before either of them needed to be up. There was nothing; no missed call, no message. She threw the phone onto the bed and headed for the shower.

As she walked through from the bathroom, back to her bedroom wrapped in a large gray fluffy towel, her wet hair dripping over her shoulders, she heard her phone ringing and ran to pick it up.

"Hi," she said, connecting the call and throwing herself on the bed at the same time.

"Hi." His voice was aloof… again.

She hadn't expected happiness, or good cheer. Not today. She took a breath and remembered today wasn't about her.

"How are you?" she asked. It was a dumb question, really, but she didn't know what else to say.

"Okay."

"What are your plans for the day?"

"Oh… We'll do what we usually do, I guess," he replied. "Sarah likes to go for a walk down by the river. There's a particular spot our mom used to take her to."

"Just her… not you?"

"There's a ten year age gap, Emma. By the time Sarah was old enough to remember going there, I was in senior high."

"Yes, of course."

"Sorry, can you hold on a second."

She heard him talking in muffled tones to someone; presumably he'd covered the mouthpiece of the phone, but then as he uncovered it, she heard him say, "I'll be there. Just give me a minute."

He sounded harassed.

"You're busy," she said. "I'll let you go."

"No, it's fine. I feel like we haven't spoken in ages."

"That's because we haven't."

"I'm sorry."

"It's okay, Mark. I understand."

She heard a crashing sound in the distance. "Sorry," he said. "I'm gonna have to go. I'll try and call you back later."

"Okay. I…" She was going to say that she couldn't wait to see him on Friday, but he was already gone.

He didn't call, or text all day. In a way, she wasn't that surprised. It had to be an awful day for him and Sarah. She wished she could be there for him, but she'd probably only feel like she was intruding.

While she was eating dinner, she sent him a message:

— *Hope you're okay. Call later if you need to. E xx*

He didn't call. He didn't text either.

Emma spent the following day with Nick and their parents. She didn't enjoy it one bit. Not only did her mother moan at her constantly – about everything and anything – but Mark didn't call. He sent her a very quick text. He didn't mention her message at all. He just wished her happy Thanksgiving, and told her he'd see her the next day. He added 'love you', like he usually did, but she was really starting to wonder.

"What's wrong?" Nick asked her as they slowly drifted down Main Street. He was walking her home, having left his car at her place.

"Nothing."

He stopped and took hold of her arm, pulling her back. "Cut it out, Emma," he said. "Something's wrong."

"It's Mark."

"What's he done?" She could see the dark anger in Nick's eyes.

"He didn't come up last weekend."

"Yeah, I know, you told me. But that was because he forgot his sister's exhibition."

"And he's been really weird all week," Emma continued.

"Define 'weird'."

"Distant, aloof. It's like I don't exist. Last week, he called me three or four times a day, and sent me text messages in between. This week, I've had two calls and maybe four text messages all week. And they've all been really remote, like I'm getting in the way of his life."

"Has he given you an explanation?" Nick asked.

"No. I haven't asked for one. Yesterday was the anniversary of his parents' death. I didn't want to add to his problems."

Nick looked up at the dark clear sky above them for a moment, then lowered his eyes to hers. "Do you trust him?" he asked.

She thought for a moment. "Yes," she whispered.

"A little more conviction would be good, Em." He sighed. "Look, if you're sure about this guy, then give him some time. This has gotta be a tough week for him. Talk to him when he gets here tomorrow... tell him how you feel."

She looked up at him. "Why are you being so understanding? I thought you'd be the first person in line telling me to walk away from him."

"Ordinarily, I would." He smirked. "Well, ordinarily, I'd be having a quiet word with him myself. But if you're really serious about him, then you need to try and work it out... not give up at the first hurdle."

"I'll talk to him," Emma said. "He's driving up tomorrow morning."

"Okay. And call me if you need to," Nick reiterated. "You know where I am."

She woke the next morning to the sound of her phone ringing, and grabbed it from the nightstand, checking the screen. It was Mark. She let out a sigh, waiting for a moment before she clicked the 'connect' button.

"Hi," she said quietly.

"Hello."

"How are you?" she asked. Like a lot of their phone calls over the last week, she felt as if she was making polite conversation, but she didn't know what to say to him.

"I've been better."

"What's wrong?" Was he ill?

"There's no easy way to say this, Emma…" She felt her blood run cold.

"S—say what?"

"I'm not gonna make it today."

"W—why?" Was he with someone else? Was that it? Was that why his calls had lessened, why his tone had changed? He wouldn't, would he? Not after all those things he'd said to her before he went home… a lifetime ago now.

"I can't get away. I'm sorry."

He was *sorry*? The ice in her veins turned to fire in an instant. She was nobody's doormat. Well, not this time, anyway. She wasn't going to let him do this to her again. "Do you know what? Don't bother, Mark," she snapped. "Just don't bother."

"Emma? Let me explain…"

"No! I don't need to hear your excuses. You've hardly called me all week; you've barely texted me either, and when you have, it's felt like I'm an inconvenience to you…" She paused for a moment and took a breath. "I get that it's been a hard week for you, I really do. And I've been here for you. Except you didn't want me – or need me – not once. You said you'd need me; you asked me to help you through it, but when

113

it came down to it, you didn't need me at all… and I think that tells me everything I need to know." She felt her voice catching, and stopped it, just in time. "Do you know what I really wish, Mark? I wish you'd just be straight. I wish you'd just tell me you don't want me anymore. I wish you'd admit that you made a mistake, that a long-distance relationship doesn't work for you. I wish you'd be honest. Oh except, I forgot… You've never been any good at that, have you?"

She hung up the call, threw the phone down on the bed and sobbed, her heart breaking all over again.

Mark

He stared at the phone for a full minute. He felt sick… truly sick. He was sure he'd heard her crying as she'd hung up, and that just made him feel worse. What had he done to her? Again.

He put the phone down carefully on his nightstand, although every instinct in his body was yelling at him to hurl it across the room, and then he put his head in his hands.

God, he'd had a fucking awful week. He'd only got through it by remembering he'd be seeing Emma again today. And now… now she'd hung up on him in tears. He thought back to what she'd just said. Had she ended it? Or had she accused him of ending it? He wasn't sure, but either way, she was talking like it was over, and whatever she thought, that was the last thing he wanted, or needed.

Last weekend had been bad enough. Sarah's supposed 'exhibition' had turned out to be a small display of her whole class's work, not just hers. When he'd asked her about it, she'd said he must've misunderstood and, to be honest, he couldn't remember their conversation that clearly, so he accepted what she said, and spent the whole weekend resenting the fact that he'd given up his time with Emma for nothing.

On the Sunday evening, he'd sat Sarah down and told her he'd met someone. He'd explained he needed Sarah's understanding, because he was going to be away a lot more at the weekends, and when he wasn't away, Emma was going to be with them, in Boston, because his spare time was going to revolve around Emma from now on.

She'd hugged him and told him how pleased she was that he'd finally found someone he wanted to spend time with. He knew she'd always felt a bit uncomfortable about his lifestyle and had done his best to keep that from her, but he wanted her involvement with Emma, because he hoped she'd be a part of his life for a very, very long time. Well, he was hoping for forever, but he didn't say that to Sarah.

Then, during the night on Sunday, she'd been ill. She'd come into his room and woken him and he'd spent most of the night sitting up with her. Sarah being unwell was always a worry and, on Monday, he'd found it hard to concentrate. He'd even forgotten to call Emma. He remembered now feeling guilty for neglecting her.

Sarah's illness had worsened during the week. She'd refused to see a doctor, becoming almost hysterical with fear they'd want to admit her to hospital – something that always filled her with dread. So Maggie and Mark had taken it in turns to look after her; although Maggie had told him on Wednesday morning that she wasn't convinced Sarah was as sick as she was making out, and she did manage to rally sufficiently to go down to the river, although the trip exhausted her and she went straight to bed when they got home, insisting he stay with her all evening. Maggie had brought their supper up on a tray and, when she came to clear away, she'd asked him to come outside with her, and she'd told him, once more, that she wasn't convinced about Sarah's illness. She'd checked again and Sarah had no temperature. Sure, she'd been sick on Sunday night, but since then it had just been tiredness and nausea, nothing to panic about. Mark had accused her of not caring for Sarah and they'd had a fight about it. He'd apologized almost straight away – he knew he was in the wrong. Maggie always did her job, but he hated the way she judged Sarah sometimes. When he'd gone back in, Sarah had been playing a game on his phone, but then she'd wanted him to read to her and he had, even though he'd wanted to go to his own room and call Emma… He hadn't spoken to her, or heard from her all day and he'd needed to. It had been such a damn awful day.

They'd spent Thanksgiving together. Maggie's family were busy, so she was spending the day with Mark and Sarah, who seemed to be getting a little better. She'd stopped complaining about feeling sick quite so much, anyway. Over breakfast, he'd explained that he'd be going up to Somers Cove the next day to visit Emma. Sarah had reacted badly, asking him how he could think of leaving her on her own, when she wasn't well, and especially on the anniversary of their parents' death – which would fall on the Sunday. He'd pointed out that they didn't normally do anything on the day itself, but Sarah had burst into tears and fled from the room.

"You've got your own life. You've gotta go," Maggie had said to him.

He'd looked at her across the kitchen table. "I can't, can I?"

Maggie had just shaken her head and started clearing away.

A knocking on the door brought him back to reality.

"Come in," he called, pulling the comforter up a little.

It was Maggie, and she was carrying a steaming cup of coffee.

"What's this?" he asked. "You don't normally bring me coffee in bed."

"No, and I'm not setting a trend either, so don't get used to it. I just figured you could use a cup."

She put it down beside him. "Thanks, Maggie," he said. "I'm sorry it's been such a horrible week."

She ignored his apology. "Have you decided what you're doing today?" she asked.

He felt his shoulders slump.

"You're not gonna go are you?" He could hear the disappointment in her voice.

"How can I?"

"It's easy. You pack a bag and get in your car, and leave Sarah with me."

"You've got tomorrow off." Maggie had booked the Saturday off to spend with her family, as they hadn't been able to spend Thanksgiving together.

"I can cancel that, if I have to."

"No, it's fine. I've already told Emma I'm not going."

"Well, more fool you."

"Maggie, you saw what Sarah was like. She needs me."

"And this young lady of yours doesn't?" She walked to the door, resting her hand on the handle. "Think about what you're doing, Mark," she said. "You've given up a lot for your sister. Don't give up your happiness too." She moved silently through the door and pulled it closed behind her.

Mark stared at the space where she'd been standing for a long while. He didn't agree with everything Maggie had said, but she had hit one raw note… Emma needed him just as much as Sarah did; and he'd let her down – again.

He grabbed his phone and looked up her details, connecting the call. It rang five times and went to her voicemail. He didn't want to leave a message. He tried again, with the same result. She didn't want to talk to him – that much was clear – so he went onto his message app, and typed…

— Emma. I'm sorry. Really sorry. I know I've hurt you, but please let me explain. Call me… please. I love you. M xx

Typing that, putting some genuine affection into it, made him realize how abrupt and cool his messages had been over the last few days. He'd had to type them out quickly, between working and caring for Sarah, but they'd been hurried and casual, not the romantic messages he usually sent her. It was no wonder she'd reacted the way she did when he'd cancelled the weekend. What must she think of him?

He waited for her to call – or even just text back. He waited a full hour, but heard nothing. He went and had a shower, got dressed and checked his phone again. Still nothing. Okay… He started typing again:

— You're not gonna call. I get it. That's okay. It just means this is gonna be a really long message. Because I'm gonna

explain, whether you want to hear it or not. I'm sorry I can't come up there today. I really am. I've missed you so much and there's nothing I want more than to be with you. I don't care what you say, or think, I did need you this week. I still do. I always need you, more than I'll ever be able to tell you. But Sarah's ill. She's been ill all week and I can't leave her. I think I told you she's vulnerable to infections. I'm sorry if the way I've been this week has made you feel I don't want you. Nothing could be further from the truth. Whatever you believe of me, I'm not giving up, Emma. I told you I'd make this work, and I will. I want to see you so much. Is it possible for you to come here? Can you come down tomorrow? Even if you can't, please call me, or just answer this. Please, don't give up on us. I love you, Emma. M xxx

He re-read the message, making sure there was nothing that could be misunderstood, then pressed send.

It was lunchtime before he heard anything. She didn't call, she replied to his message.

—I'm sorry to hear Sarah's unwell. I hope she gets better soon. I'm not sure how I can come to you tomorrow. I don't finish work until 7, and I don't have a car. Even if I did, I wouldn't get to you until after 10 and I have to be back on Sunday evening. I hear what you're saying, Mark... but I'm sorry, I just don't see how we can make this work. E x

Sarah was looking at him across the table.

"Who's that?" she asked.

"Emma."

"Oh? Is something wrong?"

He looked up at her. "Why?"

"You've gone a bit pale, that's all."

"No. Everything's fine. Or it will be." He got up from the table. "Excuse me."

He went out of the kitchen, across the wide hallway and into his study, closing the door behind him. He didn't want to be distracted.

He sat at his desk and stared at his phone for a moment, re-reading her message, then he started typing…

— We can make it work. It's out of season… the coffee shop's quiet. Can't your staff cope without you for a couple of hours? You've got Josh now. You could finish at 2 or 3, maybe? And I'll send a car for you. I told you, Emma… I need you and I'm NOT giving up. I love you. M xxx

Her reply came through straight away this time.

— I'll talk to Patsy and Kathryn and see what they say. I'm not making any promises. E x

— Thank you. I need to speak with you. If I phone later, just after 7, will you take my call? Please? M xxx

— Yes. x

— I love you. xx

He waited. He knew she wouldn't say 'I love you' back to him. She wasn't ready for that yet, especially not after the last week, but that didn't stop him from staring at his phone for nearly half an hour, and hoping. Because hope was pretty much all he had left.

Chapter Ten

Emma

"Hi." She was sitting in the living room, curled up on the couch, waiting for his call, and answered on the first ring.

"Emma, I—"

"I didn't know Sarah was sick," she interrupted. "I'm sorry."

"Why the hell are you saying sorry?" He sounded surprised.

"Because I should have let you explain, rather than assuming the worst about you."

"Why? Why should you? Christ, I've let you down so much these last few days." Now he was sounding upset.

"Mark? Are you okay?"

"No."

"Tell me what's wrong?" she urged.

"I—I've been thinking… all afternoon. When you said you couldn't see how we could make this work, I've realized you meant us, not this weekend, didn't you?"

She couldn't lie to him. "Yes." She heard him suck in a breath.

"I thought so." There was a pause, and then he whispered, "I came too fucking close to losing you – again."

"It's just really hard being so far away from you – and then, when we don't even talk, it's doubly difficult. No, that's not true… it's impossible."

"I know. That's my fault. I got sidetracked. I won't let it happen again. I promise."

"Don't make promises, Mark. Please. It's not fair."

"But I mean every word, Emma." Now he sounded offended.

She sighed. "I'm sure you do, when you say them. But when we're apart, I kind of slip into the background. I don't know… I guess it's like I'm out of sight, out of mind."

"You really believe that?"

"Yes. I do."

"You're so wrong…"

"Am I? Can you honestly say you were thinking about me this week?"

"Yes, I was." There was a definite hurt tone to his voice. But she was hurting too.

"So, why didn't you return my message on Wednesday, or call me? If I was in your thoughts, why couldn't you just take a few minutes to do that?"

"What message? I didn't get any messages from you, apart from the ones where you were replying to me…"

"But I sent you a message on Wednesday evening. I thought you might be feeling low, and you hadn't called, so I sent a message. I told you to phone me, if you needed to talk. You didn't call. You didn't even reply."

"Because I didn't get your message, Emma. Sarah was upset on Wednesday night. She wanted me to sit with her."

Emma didn't understand why he'd have received all her other messages and not that one. It didn't make sense, but she didn't want to labor the point.

"It's understandable that Sarah would be upset, but don't you see?" she said instead. "That's exactly why I don't want you to make me any promises. You've got other responsibilities. You've got Sarah, and your business, all the people who work for you… I understand that, really I do. I understand that sometimes other things have to take priority."

"*Nothing* takes priority over you."

"Except it does, Mark. This week has proved that. I just need you to be honest, with yourself as well as with me. That way, when this happens again, I won't feel so let down."

"It's not going to happen again. I'll—"

"Please, Mark," she interrupted. She had to say it; she had to tell him. "I know you've had an awful week, but it's been hell for me too. You shut me out and you didn't tell me why. It felt like you were rejecting me, like I didn't matter to you anymore. I know why now, but I didn't then, and I was sitting here on my own, wondering what you were doing – maybe who you were doing it with – and what I'd done wrong, why you wouldn't let me in. It b—brought back all the f— feelings I had before, when we broke up last time." She couldn't fight back the tears any longer. "You made me feel like I'm not g—good enough… again," she wept. "I don't want to feel like that ever again. I can't. You have no idea what it was like for me back then, and I'm not about to tell you… but I can't go back there. It's easier for me to just accept that I'm not always in your thoughts, that I'm not always gonna be top of your list…" She let out a loud sob, even though she'd tried to hold it in.

"Emma? Oh God. Please, please don't cry. I—I can't… I can't hold you." She heard the stuttering emotion in his voice. "I don't want you to feel like that. It's so far from the truth. You are top of my list. Hell, there isn't even a fucking list. It's just you. I screwed up, and I'm sorry. I just got wrapped up with Sarah and work, and the anniversary. It all got on top of me."

"I know," she whispered. Why couldn't he see? He was quoting her a damn list…

"And I really am sorry, Emma."

"I know," she repeated, finally managing to choke back her tears. "Can we let it drop now, Mark? Please? I know you're sorry. Let's just leave it there. I don't want to keep raking over it. It won't get us anywhere and I hate going over and over things like this, especially when you're not here. I need you to hold me, and you can't."

"I know. I need to hold you too. I just want you to know how sorry I am for not calling, and for being so offhand with you… And that I'll do my best to make sure it doesn't happen again."

She smiled, just slightly. "That sounds a little more realistic."

"And I'm sorry if I made you feel anything other than loved this week, because you are. I love you so much, baby."

She wanted more than anything to say it back to him, but she needed to tell him to his face, not over the phone.

"And I wasn't with anyone else," he whispered. "I've either been working, or I've been with Sarah. There's no-one but you, Emma. I promise." She heard him suck in a breath. "Tell me you believe me?"

"I believe you," she replied immediately.

He sighed. "Good. Because you know I'd never lie to you again, don't you?"

She nodded her head.

"Don't you?" he repeated, sounding worried.

"Yes. Sorry, I was nodding my head."

He laughed. "I wish I was there."

"So do I, Mark. I really do." She heard him sigh again.

A moment's silence descended, while they both breathed in their relief and recovered from the threatening storm. "Where are you?" he asked eventually, his voice a little calmer.

Strange question. "In my apartment." Where else would she be?

"No, I mean where exactly."

"Oh. I'm sitting on the couch."

"Does your apartment still look the same?" he asked.

"Yes. I haven't changed anything."

"Okay. Then tell me precisely where you're sitting, and what you're wearing."

"I'm sitting near the window, with my legs tucked up under me, and I'm still wearing my work clothes; my black pants and white blouse… Why?"

"Because I'm just trying to picture you, that's why."

"That's not fair. I can't picture you."

"Yeah, you can. I'm sitting on my bed, propped up against the pillows. I'm wearing jeans and a black t-shirt."

"But I don't know what your bedroom looks like. I've never seen it. You could send me a picture…"

"I could. Or you could see it first hand, if you come visit tomorrow…" He hesitated. "Can you?" he asked. She could hear the need in his voice. "Did you speak to Patsy and Kathryn?"

"Yes. They're happy to cover for me and Patsy can lock up. So, I can come… if you can work out how to get me there."

"I wish I could drive up and get you, but Maggie's not gonna be here, so I can't leave Sarah by herself, not for that long, not at the moment."

"Who's Maggie?" She'd never heard him mention that name before.

"She's a kind of housekeeper, nurse and cook, rolled into one."

"Does Sarah need a full-time nurse then?" Emma didn't think she was *that* sick – not all the time.

"No. But it's been useful to have a qualified nurse on hand sometimes. I took her on when Sarah came out of the hospital and Maggie nursed her and cooked our meals, then once Sarah was well enough to go back to school, Maggie dropped her off and picked her up. Now she's more of a housekeeper than anything else, really."

Emma had never known anyone who had a housekeeper, or a cook.

"I'll send Anthony to pick you up," he added.

"I'm guessing he's your driver?"

"Yeah."

Mark had a driver too. He lived in a completely different world. She didn't even have a car, let alone someone else to drive it for her.

"What time should he get to you?" Mark asked.

"Two o'clock. I can't leave before then. I've still got to do all the week's paperwork."

"Two it is. You should be back here just after five."

She felt a little nervous at the prospect of spending three hours in a car with a man she'd never even met.

"Oh, okay."

"What's wrong?"

"Nothing." Now she felt pathetic for letting him hear her uncertainty.

"Emma? Tell me."

"It's nothing, honestly. I'm just being silly."

"Is it because I'm not coming to get you?" he asked. "I would if I could… honestly."

"It's not that exactly."

There were a few seconds' silence. "Is it because you don't know Anthony?" he asked. She nodded her head, but didn't say anything, feeling even more foolish now. "Talk to me, baby," he said.

"Yes," she whispered.

"He's a really nice guy, honest." Mark sounded reassuring.

"I'm sure he is, but I don't know him. And you want me to spend three hours with him… on my own."

"You don't have to spend any time with him at all. You can sit in the back, with the partition up and act like he's not there. He won't be offended."

"I couldn't do that." Emma was horrified. "I couldn't ignore someone who'd been kind enough to drive all that way to pick me up."

"Emma, he's being paid to come and pick you up. I mean, sure, he *is* kind; you'll like him. But driving people around… it's his job." She heard the smile in his voice.

"Even so, I couldn't ignore him."

"Then sit up front with him. He's dying to meet you."

"He is? How does he even know I exist?"

"Because I've told him about you. I've told Maggie about you too."

"You have?" She was stunned.

"Of course." There was a pause. "I may not have been talking *to* you that much, but I've talked *about* you all the time. Whenever I could. Maggie didn't give me any choice. She noticed something was different straight away. She said I was… how did she put it? Oh yeah… I was being annoyingly distracted."

Emma couldn't help but laugh. "Really?"

"Yeah. When I got back here, after that weekend at Jake and Cassie's, I was incapable of thinking straight, let alone making a decision, or holding a conversation. I nearly drove Maggie insane, I think."

"And Sarah?"

"She didn't seem to notice."

"I meant, have you told her about me?"

"Oh… Yes."

"And?"

"And she's really pleased. I don't think she liked the way I lived my life before, so I think she's kinda relieved I've found someone special." Emma felt herself blushing.

"I feel like I've got a lot to live up to. You seem to have built me up beyond expectation to everyone."

"No. I've just told them the truth about you." He paused again. "And I've told them all that they need to get used to having you around, because I'm not letting you go."

She couldn't help but smile, even though there were tears rolling down her cheeks. But, at least these were happy tears.

Mark

He knocked on Sarah's bedroom door at just after ten the next morning.

"Come in…" he heard her call and opened the door.

She was sitting up in bed, her laptop in front of her. He walked over and sat down on the chair by the window.

"How are you feeling?" he asked.

"A lot better, thank you," she replied, not looking up.

"Good." He looked at her, but she continued to concentrate on her computer. "You gonna get up any time today?"

"Yes. I said I'm feeling better. I'm just finishing this."

He assumed she was doing some college work.

"Okay." He got up. "Just so you know, Emma's coming to visit."

Sarah's head shot up. That had got her attention.

"When?" she asked.

"I'm sending Anthony to collect her this afternoon—"

"You're sending Anthony?" she queried, closing her laptop and moving it to one side.

"Yes."

"Can't she drive?"

"Yes, she can, but she doesn't have a car."

"She doesn't?"

"No."

"It's a long way to come for a visit."

"Emma's staying over, Sarah."

"Oh… but, Mark." He saw her bottom lip quiver. "I mean, tomorrow's the anniversary…"

"Yeah, I know it is, but we don't normally do anything then, do we?"

She shrugged, but he knew she was upset. He went across to her. "I've already explained, Emma's important to me. She's part of my life now. I need you to understand that."

"I do… but it's a special day for us."

"Sarah, we've never done anything on that date before now. Why would we start this year?"

"I'm not suggesting we would. But we've also never shared it with anyone else."

"No. I've usually been at work, and you've been at school. That's how *special* it's been. We're only gonna be together tomorrow because it's a Sunday." She glared at him. "And Emma's not just anyone. I didn't see her last weekend because of your exhibition. I pulled out of going up there yesterday because you're not well. I'm not cancelling on her again… not even for you."

She folded her arms across her chest. "Fine," she muttered. He noticed a shadow cross her eyes. "I assume you're going to one of your hotels tonight then?"

He wasn't surprised she'd make that assumption. He'd never brought a woman into their home before.

He went across to her. "No. We're gonna stay here. I told you, Emma's different. Besides, I'm not gonna leave you on your own. You're not completely well yet, and Maggie won't be back until late."

He softened his voice; he needed her to understand. "I meant what I said, Sarah. Emma's important."

"More important than me?"

"It's not a contest. I love you, you know that… but I love Emma too."

"Y—you love her?" She looked shocked.

"Yes. I do."

"I… I didn't know."

"Well, you do now. So… you'll welcome her?" he asked.

She smiled, although it didn't touch her eyes, and then she nodded her head. He guessed it might take her a while to get used to the idea, and that was only fair. She wasn't used to sharing him.

"Thank you," he said gently. "I appreciate it." He leant over and messed her short hair with his hand. "And if you could try and get up before lunch, that'd be great too."

"Hmm… I'm not making any promises on that."

It was just before five and Mark had been pacing his study floor since four-thirty, which he knew was ridiculous. Emma had sent a text message at ten after two, saying they were just leaving, so he knew they couldn't possibly arrive until after five… probably nearer five-thirty. That didn't stop him pacing impatiently though.

Sarah had spent most of the afternoon in her room, although – much to his relief – she'd been fine over lunch and had talked about Emma's visit with more enthusiasm than she'd shown in the morning. Her absence during the last few hours had enabled him to catch up on some work, and that had taken his mind off of Emma's impending arrival. He wasn't worried, or nervous; he was just impatient – hence the pacing.

His phone buzzed on his desk and he went over and checked the screen. It was a message from Emma.

— **We're evidently about ten minutes away. You can put the coffee on now ;) xx**

He smirked and tapped out a reply.

— **I can think of better things to do when you get here ;) We'll drink coffee later. Much later. M xx**

There was a delay of a few minutes.

— I'm sorry, Mark. I'm not sure I'm ready for that. Should I get Anthony to turn around and take me home? E

What the fuck?

— NO. I was kidding, Emma. Just get here. We'll talk. I love you. M xxx

Again there was a delay. He didn't like it.

— Tell me you haven't turned around. M xxx

— No. We're just pulling up outside your house. E x

He dropped the phone onto his desk and went to the window. Sure enough, the familiar sedan was already parked by the curb out the front of his house.

He stood and watched Anthony come around and help Emma from the front of the car. She'd obviously chosen to sit with him, rather than on her own in the back. Although he was now more worried than he'd been all day, Mark couldn't help but smile as he took in her long legs, encased in tight jeans, the way her hair hung loose over her shoulders and the beautiful smile that danced on her lips as she talked to Anthony, and nodded. He dragged himself away and went to the front door.

As he opened it, she glanced up from the sidewalk.

"Hey," he said. She didn't reply, but looked up at him for a moment. He held out a hand and she climbed the steps to him, letting him pull her into the house and close the door. Then they stood and stared at each other. "You're really here," he murmured.

She nodded, and he pulled her close, holding her in his arms and burying his face in her hair.

"Tell me you're really here, Emma."

"I'm really here."

He pulled back again, staring into her eyes. "God, I've missed you so much." Leaning down, he kissed her, his tongue finding hers, his hands roaming over her back while hers rested on his shoulders, clinging to him. He felt her breasts heaving into his chest, her gentle moan filling his mouth, and his whole body shuddered. He'd never needed anything more than he needed her... A quiet cough broke into the moment and Emma jumped away from him in an instant. He turned and saw Sarah standing on the bottom stair, looking at them. *Damn.*

"Sarah," he said. "This is my girlfriend, Emma." He glanced down at Emma and saw the look of surprise on her face. "Emma," he continued, not batting an eyelid, "this is my sister, Sarah."

Sarah took the last step down and walked toward them, holding out her hand. He noticed she'd changed out of the jeans she'd been wearing at lunch and was now in a designer dress she'd bought a couple of months before. It was very elegant and very, very expensive – so expensive, he'd had to top up her allowance for her to buy it. He wasn't sure why she'd put it on, unless of course she wanted to create a good impression, which he thought was kind of sweet.

Emma took Sarah's hand and his sister smiled. "It's lovely to meet you," she said. "Mark's told me so much about you." He had? He'd talked to Maggie and Anthony a lot more than Sarah; she hadn't seemed very interested. "I hope you had a pleasant journey?"

"Um… yes, thank you," Emma replied. She sounded a little unsure of herself.

"I'm gonna take Emma upstairs," Mark said. "I'll just show her where the bedroom is."

"Okay," Sarah smiled up at him. "I guess we're ordering in tonight?"

"Yeah." He looked at Emma. "Is that okay with you? Maggie's not here and you've eaten just about the only dish I can safely be trusted to cook."

Emma grinned. "You should've said. I'd have cooked."

"Not a chance," he replied. "You've been at work."

"I've been sitting in your very luxurious car all afternoon, that's not work."

"Either way, you're not here to cook. We'll order in."

Sarah moved forward again. "Mark's right. Guests here don't do the cooking." She turned to Mark. "I'll get the menus and meet you in the kitchen. You won't be long, will you?"

"No, I guess not." He knew he and Emma had a lot to talk about, and he needed some time alone with her, but that didn't look like it was going to be possible now.

He took Emma's hand.

"Wait," she said. "What about my bag? I left it in the car."

"Leave that," Sarah said dismissively.

"Yeah, it's fine," Mark told her. "Anthony will bring it in, if he hasn't already."

"Oh, okay."

They started off up the stairs.

"See you in a minute," Sarah called after them.

"Yeah," Mark replied over his shoulder.

He squeezed Emma's hand and led her up to the top of the stairs, where they turned, went along a landing and up another flight.

"How much further?" Emma asked, looking up. There were still another two floors above them.

He pulled her to a stop. "That kinda depends," he said, looking down at her.

"On what?" She bit her bottom lip, seemingly doubtful.

"On where you want to sleep," he replied, feeling worried about this for the first time. "My room's at the end of the corridor here." He nodded in the direction of his bedroom. "Or there's a guest room one flight up. I got Maggie to make it up for you before she left, just in case. You choose, baby." Although he'd thought it only fair to give her the choice, he was wishing he hadn't now, because after that text message, he was afraid she'd choose the guest room, and he really didn't want to spend the night without her.

She hesitated for a long while, then replied, "I want to sleep with you, Mark," in a whispered voice. He grinned. He couldn't help it. He took a step toward his room, but she pulled him back. "The only thing is, you might not want to sleep with me…"

Was she insane? He'd thought of little else for four years. "Why the hell not?"

"Because there's a very strong chance that all I'll want to do is sleep." She lowered her eyes. "Like I said in the message, I'm not sure I'm ready. I know things got kinda heated between us when we were back home, when you said we couldn't keep our hands off each other. I honestly thought I was ready then, Mark. But this last week…" Her voice trailed off and she left the rest of her sentence unspoken.

He was overwhelmed with relief. "I know. We've got things to say, things to work out between us. I understand." He paused, just for a moment. "I'll wait, Emma. I'll wait as long as it takes. I'll be happy just to fall asleep with you in my arms and wake up beside you." She looked up at him. "Just sleep in my bed… with me," he whispered. "That's enough." She nodded and he smiled down at her, pulling her past two closed doors to a third at the end of the hallway, which he opened, allowing her to pass through, flicking on the light switch as she did so. The room was bathed in a soft glow from the two lamps placed on the nightstands either side of the bed.

He closed the door behind him and pulled her into his arms, placing one hand on her cheek and looking into her eyes.

"I meant everything I said. I'll wait for you," he said firmly.

Her eyes dropped and her cheeks flushed.

"It—It's not that I don't want to," she murmured. "I do. But…"

"I screwed up this week, didn't I? I made you unsure about me again… even more than you already were." He leant closer. "I know it feels like we took a backward step, but don't worry. We'll work it out. We'll talk it through."

She nodded, bringing her hands up and resting them on his biceps. "I think you must be a mind reader." She smiled up at him. "I—It's just, I can't go from where we've been these last few days, to… to falling into bed together, Mark."

He brushed his thumb along her lip. "I know. I get it, and it's fine. And I was genuinely kidding with that message, Emma. I'm sorry. That was insensitive of me. You never have to do anything you don't want, you know that, right?" She nodded. He leant down a little closer. "I love you, baby," he murmured.

She looked up into his eyes. "I love you too."

He felt his breath catch in his throat and his heart flip over in his chest. "Y—you do?"

She nodded. "Of course I do. I never stopped either."

"But… at the beach, you said it all in the past tense, like you didn't feel that way anymore."

"I was still angry with you then."

"And you're not angry with me now? After everything that's happened this week?"

"I'm hurt… I'm not angry. But it's only because I love you that you can hurt me."

"I don't mean to."

"I know."

He let his forehead rest on hers, their noses touching. "God… I love you so damn much," he murmured.

"Then tell me you can make this work."

"I can. I can make this work. Nothing's gonna come between us, Emma. I promise."

He tilted his head and covered her mouth with his, gently kissing away her pain, his tongue finding hers as she moved her hands up his arms and around his neck. Although he knew she wasn't ready, he could feel the longing in her kiss and deepened his own.

"Mark?" Sarah's voice came from behind him, followed by a sharp knock on the door. Emma jumped, pulled out of his arms, and moved away from him, further into the room.

"What?" he said. His voice was more abrupt than he'd expected, but why the hell couldn't Sarah just wait?

"Are you coming down?" she asked through the closed door.

Mark let out a long sigh. "Yeah. We'll be there in a minute."

He looked over at Emma. "You okay?" he asked.

She nodded her head. He moved closer, but she looked unsure.

"I'm sorry," she whispered. "I can't. I've kind of lost the momentum."

He pulled her into a hug, and moved them to the other side of the room, well away from the door.

"It's okay," he murmured. "And I'm the one who's sorry. She's my sister."

She shrugged. "It can't be helped."

"I wish it could. But we can pick this up later." Emma let out a sigh. "What's wrong?" he asked.

"Please don't take this the wrong way, but will Sarah let us? I mean, she interrupted our kiss downstairs. You said we'd be down soon… and she followed us. For all we know, she's still out there." She glanced toward the door.

He kissed her, just gently. "It'll be fine. I guess she's just feeling a bit left out. We'll have dinner together and she'll probably go to bed, or attach herself to her laptop, like she usually does… and we can talk. We can talk all night, if you want to."

"And if we end up wanting to do something other than talk? I'm not saying we will, but if we do…?" He saw the glint in her eye.

"Then we can do that too." He smiled.

"Has Sarah done this before? Played gooseberry like this, I mean?" Emma asked. "When you've brought other women here?"

"I've never brought a woman here before, Emma."

"Not one?"

"No." He shook his head, smiling down at her. "Remember me? The privacy freak? There's no way I'd have let a casual date come here. I never let them get that close."

She was staring at him. "So where did you take them?" she asked.

"I own a *lot* of hotels, baby."

"Oh, I see."

"This is a first for me." He brushed his lips softly over hers. "And I like it. A lot."

"Even with the interruptions?"

"Yeah… I mean, obviously I'd rather not have the interruptions, but I like having you here. And I really can't wait to wake up next to you tomorrow."

She nuzzled into him. "Neither can I."

"Just before we go downstairs… Were you okay with me calling you my girlfriend?" he asked. "You looked kinda shocked."

"No," she murmured. "I liked it."

"Hmmm… I liked it too. Very much."

They spread the Chinese take-out over the informal kitchen table, which was set in the middle of the enormous space, in front of the island unit. Emma was looking self-conscious and uneasy, and Mark sat beside her, as close as he could.

He had opened a bottle of wine and hoped that might settle her nerves a little.

As they helped themselves to the food, Sarah leant across the table.

"I've set up a movie downstairs," she announced, looking at him.

"You have?" He was surprised. They hadn't watched a movie together in ages. "Um... I'm not sure..." He glanced at Emma, but she was looking down at her hands in her lap.

"I've chosen *Saving Private Ryan*, just for you."

"Oh. That's... that's really sweet of you, Sarah." He loved the movie, but it was nearly three hours long. Even if they started watching it straight after dinner – which they wouldn't – it'd be gone ten before it finished. He was going to have to tell Sarah that they couldn't, not tonight. It was more important for him to spend the evening with Emma. She needed him.

"I thought we could make some popcorn and the three of us could watch it together," Sarah added, her enthusiasm more than obvious. He knew she was trying to include Emma, to make her feel welcome, and he appreciated it. He didn't want to seem ungrateful but he felt like the evening was slipping away from him. He was going to have to disappoint one of them, and it was going to have to be Sarah.

"Emma's tired..." he started to say.

"I think that sounds lovely." Emma spoke at exactly the same time.

"You do?" He turned to her. She looked up at him and he noticed the slight shrug of her shoulders. She didn't mean it. She was just saying it to help him out. He reached over and covered her hands with one of his, giving them a squeeze, letting her know he understood, and was grateful.

Sarah made the popcorn while Mark and Emma cleared the table.

"I'm sorry," he whispered, pulling her into a hug. "This is *not* what I had in mind for this evening."

"I know." She pressed her hand against his cheek. "But it seemed unfair to say no. She's just trying to make me feel welcome."

"Yeah, she is." He kissed her cheek. "Thank you."

Downstairs in the den, Sarah had put the lights on, but left them really dim, perfect for watching a movie and they all placed their popcorn bowls on the low table in the centre of the U-shaped sofa that faced the big screen on the far wall. Sarah sat in one corner, and Mark took the other, Emma went to sit beside him, but he grabbed her and pulled her down, sitting her between his legs and back against his chest.

"Comfortable?" he asked. She nodded her head. "I figure you can turn yourself around and hide against me for the first twenty minutes," he murmured, and she chuckled.

"Shall I start it?" Sarah suggested.

"Sure, go ahead."

Mark held onto Emma as the credits started to roll…

They were probably half way through the movie when he felt her breathing change and knew she was asleep. He wasn't that surprised. She'd have been up early, and he guessed it had probably been an emotional week for her, knowing she'd been worried about what was going on between them. He just wished she'd fallen asleep naked in his arms in bed, not watching a movie in front of his sister. He didn't want to wake her, and it wasn't hurting anyone for her to sleep where she was, so he sat out the rest of the movie, although he'd never enjoyed it less.

As soon as it finished, Sarah turned it off.

"She's been asleep for ages," she commented.

"I know. I did say she was tired." He carefully slid out from under Emma, mindful of not waking her, then got to his feet and bent down, lifting her into his arms.

"Don't lock up," he said to Sarah. "Maggie's coming back late. Thanks for doing this. I know Emma appreciated it… and so did I."

Sarah shrugged. "That's okay." She got up and followed him up the stairs, turning out the lights. "I'm just going to get a drink," she announced as they passed the kitchen.

"Okay. Goodnight, Sarah. See you in the morning."

He turned and climbed the two flights of stairs to his room, opening the door and going inside before flicking on the lights and carrying Emma over to the bed. He lay her down, her sweater riding up a little to reveal a strip of soft, naked flesh.

Now, all he had to do was undress her…

Chapter Eleven

Emma

Emma woke slowly, the pale morning sun teasing her from sleep. She felt strange and she glanced around the room, just for a moment, uncertain where she was… and then she remembered. Mark. She had to admit, his bedding was certainly luxuriously soft and she turned over, stretching, and came up against his warm, hard chest. She smiled and snuggled into him, as he instinctively brought his arms around her.

"Good morning," he mumbled, sleepily.

"Hello." She nestled down a little further, savoring the comforting feeling of his skin against hers. She gazed up at him. She'd forgotten how gorgeous he looked first thing in the morning. "Just out of interest," she added, "how did I end up naked?"

He opened his eyes. "I undressed you."

"And I didn't wake up?"

He shook his head. "No. You were out for the count."

"Sorry."

"Don't be. I had a great time." He grinned.

"Um… doing what?"

He rolled her onto her back and looked down at her. "Just undressing you. I wasn't going to touch you, not without your permission. Besides, sleeping beauty, I'd like to think that if I'd done anything, you might have at least shown enough interest to wake up from your slumber."

"Yeah, I think I probably would." She smiled.

He kissed her gently on her lips. "I need the bathroom," he whispered. "Do you want to come shower with me?"

She wasn't sure how to answer him. A part of her wanted to. She wanted him more than she was ready to admit; but at the same time, they hadn't had a chance to talk yet and she knew, deep down, that if they showered together, they'd end up having sex and then the talking would probably never happen.

"We don't have to do anything," Mark added. "We can just shower."

"Seriously? You actually believe that the two of us could get in the shower, completely naked, and not touch each other?"

"Well… no, probably not."

"No, neither do I."

He paused, just for a moment. "In which case, I guess I'd better go by myself."

He pulled back the comforter and Emma's eyes automatically roamed down his chiseled chest and taut abs to his long, thick erection. She sucked in a breath and, without even thinking, bit on her bottom lip. She was instantly wet for him, her nipples hardened and she could feel that familiar tingling deep inside… that longing to feel him.

He reached over and, using his thumb, pulled her lip free.

"That feeling you've got – that need – it's entirely mutual, in case you hadn't noticed," he whispered.

Her eyes shot up to his. "I'm sorry," she murmured.

"Hey, it's okay. Just because you turn me on, doesn't mean I have to do anything about it. I told you… I'll wait."

Mark's shower room was probably as big as her bedroom, but then his bedroom was nearly as large as her apartment. He lived on a much grander scale than she did, in every way.

After she'd showered, she wrapped herself in a fluffy white towel and came back out into the bedroom. Mark had made the bed and was lying on top of it, wearing jeans and a white button down shirt.

"I made you coffee," he said, nodding to the nightstand.

"Oh, thank you."

She perched on the edge of the bed.

"What's wrong?" he asked her.

"Nothing. What makes you think there's anything wrong?"

"Well, you seem uncomfortable." She felt his hands on her shoulders and then he pulled her back down onto the bed.

"My hair's wet. I'll soak the bedding."

"I don't care." He lay down beside her, raising himself up on one elbow. "Talk to me, Emma."

"There's so much to say. I don't know where to start."

"Just say the first thing that comes into your head."

"Your house is enormous."

He smiled, then laughed. "Seriously? That's what's going through your head?"

She nodded. "At the moment, yes."

He looked around the room. "I've never really liked this place," he said wistfully. "I think it's a bit… ostentatious. I keep suggesting to Sarah that we should move, but she likes it here."

Emma could feel the relief washing over her. "So, this isn't your choice then?"

"No. This was my parents' choice. It was their house."

She nodded her head. "So it's not like the car?"

He smiled. "No. I wouldn't choose this as a home."

She turned onto her side so they were facing each other, then she moved a little closer. "I'm so relieved," she said, honestly, and he leant over and kissed her.

"Don't you like it either?" he asked.

"It's not that I don't like it," Emma qualified, feeling guilty and ungracious. "I just don't feel like I could ever belong somewhere like this."

Mark reached across and ran a finger down her cheek. "Hey, it's okay. I feel like that most of the time too. Still, it's not about where we are, is it?" he asked. She thought she detected a little doubt in his voice.

"No," she reassured him.

"I'm much more comfortable in your apartment than I am here."
He seemed to think for a moment. "This is one of the things I was trying
to escape when I came to Somers Cove four years ago," he said. "I was
sick of it all."

Emma looked around the room. "I think there are a lot of people
who'd find that odd," she remarked.

"It's like I said to Jake, until you've lived this kind of life, you can't
judge it. I spent almost all my time holed up here, trying to dodge the
press, not able to just hang out with my friends... not that I really had
any true friends back then; I just had people who wanted to be with me
because of who I was and what I had. I always knew that if I didn't have
the money, I wouldn't see them for dust."

"That's horrible. No matter how bad it's been for me, I've always
had Cassie and Nick..."

"How bad was it?" he asked.

Emma felt her skin tingle. "What do you mean?"

"Before we met the first time... what was your life like? We never
really talked about it."

"It was lonely." It was a simple but honest answer.

He moved closer and put his arm around her. "And after? After I left
you? When you worked out I wasn't coming back... what was it like
then?" His eyes pierced hers.

She shook her head.

"Tell me, Emma. I want to know."

"Worse. It was much worse."

"In what way? Tell me about it."

She felt tears welling in her eyes. "No. I—I can't."

"Why not?"

"I just can't. Please, Mark, don't make me. Please leave it. It's in the
past now. It doesn't matter anymore."

He stared at her for a long moment. "Okay," he said, but she knew
he'd ask her again one day, and she wondered how long she could avoid
telling him the truth.

"Emma… this is Maggie." Mark made the introduction and Emma held out her hand to an attractive woman, probably in her early-fifties, with short, neat blonde hair and a friendly smile. She was a little smaller than Emma, but not much, and she wiped her hands on a towel before shaking Emma's.

"It's lovely to meet you at last," she said.

The kitchen was magnificent, with shiny white cabinets, gray marble countertops and an oak floor. The table at which they'd eaten the previous evening was laid for four, for lunch. There were double doors leading from the hallway and at one end of the kitchen, an archway led through to a more formal dining area, with a large rectangular table and eight chairs… It was Emma's idea of heaven and right now it was filled with delicious smells.

"What are you cooking?" Emma asked.

"Roast lamb. It's one of Mark's favorites. It'll be ready in about an hour."

Emma glanced at him across the kitchen island. "I didn't know roast lamb was a favorite of yours."

He came and stood behind her, putting his arms around her. "That's because you always cooked me so many amazing things, I never had the chance to tell you." He kissed her shoulder through her thin sweater. "Speaking of which, what do I have to do to get you to share that barbecue sauce recipe with Maggie?" he teased.

"Make me a coffee and ask nicely?" She tilted her head back and looked up at him.

"The coffee I can do now," he whispered. "The asking nicely will have to follow later, when we're on our own." He winked at her and Emma smiled and nestled into him.

"Barbecue sauce?" Maggie queried.

"Yeah," Mark replied, looking up. "Emma made the most amazing ribs I've ever eaten and, evidently, the secret to them is in the barbecue sauce."

"Well, that and the slow cooking," Emma added.

Maggie put the towel down on the countertop and came and sat at the island unit, patting the seat beside her. "Come here," she said to Emma. "I need to hear all about this."

While Mark watched on, Emma spent the next half hour explaining the secrets of her slow cooked ribs to Maggie, who asked questions and seemed genuinely interested, even to the point of getting out a large scrapbook from one of the kitchen drawers and making notes in it. Emma enjoyed herself, relaxing properly for the first time since she'd arrived.

Once Emma had finished explaining, Maggie got up and went to check on the lamb, just as Mark's phone rang and he excused himself, leaving the room to take the call.

Maggie turned back toward her. "Do you always cook a roast lunch on a Sunday?" Emma asked. She wanted to know Mark's habits.

"No, not always. It depends what Mark's got planned. Quite often I just make them a snack at lunchtime and a more substantial meal in the evening… or they'll have brunch, and then nothing at lunchtime. It varies."

Emma nodded, and Maggie came and sat down again.

"I hope you don't mind me saying this," she began, "but you're good for him."

"I am?" Emma was surprised.

"Yes. He's happier… much happier than I've ever seen him."

"That's probably because Sarah's better. It's not just because of me."

"Don't you be so sure of that," Maggie said, leaning a little closer. "Sarah's been ill before and she'll be ill again, I have no doubt." Emma thought she sensed something in Maggie's voice, but she wasn't sure what it was. "But when he couldn't come visit you, he was devastated."

"Who was devastated?" Sarah's voice broke into their conversation and Emma tensed. She'd been enjoying herself talking with Maggie, but Sarah's presence cast an instant shadow.

"No-one you know," Maggie said, getting to her feet. "Nice of you to put in an appearance, just before lunch is served," she added.

"It's Sunday." Sarah yawned expansively. "They were invented to spend in bed, doing nothing."

"Not for all of us, they weren't," Maggie countered.

Sarah came further into the room and Emma noticed she was wearing another designer outfit, different to yesterday's one, but almost certainly as expensive. She felt a little underdressed in her jeans and sweater.

"I hope you slept well," Sarah said to her.

"Oh... yes, thanks," Emma replied. For some reason, that felt like an awkward question for Mark's sister to be asking her, when she'd just spent the night with him. "I'm sorry I fell asleep during the movie. I was obviously more tired than I thought I was."

"Don't worry about it." Sarah poured herself a glass of orange juice from the refrigerator. "Mark and I enjoyed the movie anyway, but then we always enjoy doing things like that together. Speaking of Mark... where is he?"

"He had to take a phone call," Emma replied. "I don't know where he went though."

"He'll be in his study," Sarah said, leaning back against the countertop and eying Emma over the top of her glass.

Emma wished at that moment she could go and join him, rather than being scrutinized, like an exhibit at a museum.

"Sorry about that," Mark's voice whispered across her frayed nerves and she turned and smiled at him as he walked through the double doors toward her, putting his arms around her and leaning down to kiss the top of her head. "You okay?" he asked. She nodded. She was okay, now he was there.

"What are we going to do this afternoon?" Sarah's voice once again cut into their moment.

"This afternoon?" Mark queried.

"Yes, Mark." Emma saw what looked like tears in Sarah's eyes as she looked pointedly at her brother. "This afternoon. Don't tell me you've forgotten what today is."

There was a brief pause before Mark spoke. "We've been through this already, Sarah," he said patiently. "I know it's the anniversary, but we've never done anything before – not today. That's what Wednesday was all about." Sarah blinked and a tear fell onto her cheek. "Oh..." Mark said, going around the island unit to her and pulling her into his arms. "I'm sorry." He sounded conciliatory, but his tone wasn't quite the same as when he spoke to Emma.

"We can't just let the day go by and not do anything," Sarah mumbled, her head against his chest.

Emma saw Mark's shoulders rise and fall as he sighed.

"What did you want to do?" Emma asked, trying to help out. Sarah glanced across at her, although the look she gave was anything but friendly. Emma understood it straight away. She was the intruder. "If you guys want to do something together, I'm sure I can entertain myself for the afternoon." She wasn't. She had no idea what she'd do, but Sarah was putting Mark in an impossible situation – again.

"No," Mark said firmly. "Whatever we do, we'll do together—"

"Mark," Emma cut in. "It's fine. I get that Sarah wants to be with you today." He looked at her and she knew he was struggling, so she smiled at him, putting as much affection into it as she could muster. "I can stay here with Maggie. She can tell me all your secrets and how to make your favorite meals." She tried her hardest to sound more cheerful than she felt.

Mark's shoulders dropped, as though he'd accepted that their day was falling apart before him and there was nothing he could do about it. "What do you want to do?" he asked, turning back to Sarah.

"I—I'd like to go visit their graves," she whispered.

"Really?" He seemed surprised. "You've never wanted to before."

"I know, but I want to today. Just you and me. Emma's fine with it, aren't you?" Sarah looked at Emma, smiling. "And we won't be gone for long."

"Sure," Emma said, shrugging her shoulders. She looked across to where Maggie was standing, her arms folded, and a look of thunder in her eyes. "I can stay here with you, can't I?"

"Of course you can." Maggie's face softened. "We'll make brownies…"

"Sounds like fun." Emma felt slightly better already.

"I always add chopped hazelnuts," Maggie explained, mixing them into the dark chocolatey batter.

"Is that something Mark likes?" Emma asked.

"No, I like them." Maggie smiled. "I like the texture. Mark doesn't tend to eat many of these, but I can't resist." She winked. Mark had certainly eaten plenty of the roast lamb, but then Emma didn't blame him; it had been delicious. He and Sarah had left fairly soon after lunch and he'd promised they'd only be gone for an hour and a half.

"I know the feeling," Emma agreed. "I've been known to add marshmallows to mine. I love that added goo."

"You can never have too much goo, not when it comes to a brownie." Maggie poured the mixture into the baking pan, scraping out the bowl, then transferred it to the hot oven. "We've got forty minutes," she said. "Time for coffee…"

"I'll clear away while you make it," Emma said.

"Oh, I *really* like you." Maggie grinned across at her.

"You're not the only one." Mark was standing by the double doors, watching them, a broad smile on his face.

Emma turned to him, feeling a sense of relief wash over her. She'd had a lovely time with Maggie, but she was glad Mark was back.

He walked across the room and pulled Emma into his arms. "Everything okay?" he asked, looking down at her.

"Hmm… Maggie's been making brownies and we've been talking about you," she teased.

"Nothing good, I'm sure," he replied.

"No, nothing at all." She rested her hands on his chest.

"Just as I thought," he smirked and held her a little tighter. "Thank you for being so understanding today."

"Is Sarah alright?"

"Yeah. She's out in the hallway. Her phone rang just as we got back… one of her college friends, I guess."

"Oh, I see."

"So, how long until these brownies are ready?" he asked.

"I don't know. About half an hour, I guess." She looked up at him. "But I wanted to have a talk with you."

"Oh, okay. Do you want to go upstairs? Or we can go into my office?"

Emma smiled. "It's not that kind of talk," she said. "I've been thinking while you've been out and I need your advice... well, I think I do."

He looked intrigued. "You do?"

"Yes." Emma took his hand and led him over to the island unit, sitting on a stool. Mark sat next to her. "Do you remember me telling you about Mrs Adams agreeing to let me stock homemade cakes and cookies?"

"Yeah..." He seemed confused.

"Well, I've been trying to source them," Emma continued, "but I'm having so much trouble getting hold of the genuine article. I can find companies who claim to supply 'homemade' goods, but they're not. They're factory made products which have been finished by hand and branded as homemade. And that's not what I want. I'd be no better off than I am now. I'd make them myself, but I'm already working twelve hours a day. I can't do it... So, I wondered if you had any ideas."

"Have you thought about using someone more local?" Mark suggested, taking her hands in his.

"There aren't any catering suppliers local to Somers Cove."

"I'm not suggesting a catering supplier. Is there any reason why you couldn't use cookies and cakes baked by the local housewives?"

Emma stared at him. She thought it through for a minute. "I suppose not." Even as she began to agree that it might work, the problems started to surface. "But how would I decide who to use? The women in the town probably all think they make the best cakes, and if I chose one of them over the others, I'd alienate half the town."

Mark smiled. "Hold a competition," he suggested. "Get them to all bake the same thing – like brownies, for example. You can have a blind tasting in front of the whole town, then you can't be accused of favoritism."

Emma thought for a moment. Mark's idea was a sound one. She could sample the cakes and choose the best ones, and get those women to agree to supply to her on a regular basis. She'd have to explain her requirements in advance so they knew what they were getting into. "Do you know, I think you might have something there," she said.

"There's one condition to you using the idea," Mark added, a smile forming on his lips.

"What's that?"

"Maggie's not allowed to enter."

"Why can't I enter?" Maggie asked from the other side of the kitchen. "I think it sounds like a great idea."

"I know," Mark agreed, "but if you won, I can see you'd end up moving up to Somers Cove and baking for Emma full-time, and then where would I be?"

Emma finished packing up her holdall and Mark carried it downstairs for her.

"Are you sure about this?" she said as they reached the bottom step. "I can go by myself. I was fine with Anthony on the way here."

"I know." He turned to her and put the bag down on the floor. "But I feel like I've hardly seen you all weekend. I want to spend some time with you, on our own, with no chance of anyone interrupting us. If that has to be in the back of a car for three hours, then so be it."

"But by the time you get back here again, it's going to be…"

"About two in the morning." He finished her sentence and leant down to kiss her gently. "And I don't care. I'm coming with you." He kissed her again, his tongue delving into her mouth this time. When they broke free, Emma turned and saw Sarah standing by the entrance to the kitchen, watching them.

"We'll be leaving in a minute," Mark said to his sister.

"We?" Sarah queried.

"Yeah. I'm going with Emma."

"When are you coming back?"

"Tonight. I'm coming straight home again." He turned back to Emma again. "I've just gotta go see Maggie. I'll be right back and then we can leave."

Emma nodded, wishing she could find a reason to go with him, rather than staying with Sarah on her own, but she'd already said goodbye to Maggie.

"He's really busy, you know," Sarah said, as soon as Mark was out of earshot. "This is a crazy time of year for him."

"Yes, I know," Emma replied.

"I'm not sure he should be doing this. He's going to be very tired tomorrow. Work is important to him."

Emma took a deep breath. "I understand that. I offered to go by myself, but he insisted."

"That's because he's so kind and generous. But that's Mark for you. He's like that with everyone he meets," Sarah commented.

Emma felt the dismissive tone, the implication that she was nothing special, no different to 'everyone' else in Mark's life. "I'm sure he is," she said, determined not to let Sarah see she was affected by her comment.

"Of course, because he's so generous, we always have to be mindful of him getting too friendly with the type of people who are only interested in him for his money," Sarah added, looking Emma up and down.

Emma felt tears pricking behind her eyes.

"Excuse me." Emma turned at the sound of a male voice and saw Anthony standing behind her. Part of her was grateful for his interruption. She was afraid she'd been about to cry in front of Sarah.

"Yes?" Sarah said.

"I've come to collect Emma's bag."

"Miss Woods' bag," Sarah corrected.

Emma was aware of the tension and picked up her bag, handing it to Anthony. "Thank you, Anthony," she said quietly.

"You're welcome," he replied, smiling kindly. "I'll be waiting out front, whenever you're ready."

"You shouldn't call him Anthony," Sarah said as he walked away.

"What should I call him?" Emma hadn't realized there was a protocol for addressing Mark's employees, and felt herself flush.

"His surname is Mathis."

"So I call him Mathis?" It seemed odd, but if those were the rules…

Sarah nodded, smiling.

"Right…" Mark came back into the hallway at that moment and saw Anthony taking Emma's bag out through the front door. "Ah, great. Anthony's got your bag, has he?" Emma nodded, wondering why Mark called his driver Anthony, not Mathis, and why this surname rule didn't seem to apply to Maggie. She was so confused. "We'd better be going then." He turned to Sarah. "Don't wait up," he said. "I'll see you tomorrow night."

"Okay." She sounded really miserable. "I'll probably go to bed soon anyway. I've got a headache coming on." She looked up at Mark, and Emma half expected him to change his mind and say he couldn't come with her after all. He went over to his sister, standing in front of her, and Emma held her breath.

"Oh, poor you. I guess that's the stress of going to see the graves for the first time. Still, Maggie's here," he said, sounding sympathetic. "She'll look after you. And there are painkillers in your bathroom cabinet. Take a couple and get some sleep. You'll probably feel a lot better in the morning." He kissed her forehead, then turned back to Emma, holding out his hand. "C'mon," he said to her, smiling. "Let's go."

Emma let out her breath and moved forward, putting her hand in his and feeling his fingers grip hers.

She couldn't help but relish that small moment of triumph, even though she knew it was petty.

The back of the limo was even more luxurious than the front. It was dark, with blackened windows and dark gray leather seats, although there were lights along the edge of the carpeted floor, which gave a soft glow to the space.

"Would you like a glass of wine?" Mark offered once they'd got under way.

"I'd love one." Emma sank bank into the comfortable seat, and watched Mark retrieve a bottle of red wine and two glasses from the cabinet in front of his seat, handing her one while he poured.

"Cheers," he said, placing the bottle back into the cabinet.

"Cheers," she replied, and they clinked glasses.

"And I'm really sorry for the way this weekend turned out." He sat back next to her. "It wasn't what I had in mind at all."

"It's fine, Mark. It was always going to be a difficult time, what with the anniversary and everything." She tried to sound more understanding than she felt, considering how hostile Sarah had been just before she'd left. "This is very nice," Emma whispered, looking around the car's interior.

"You don't need to whisper," Mark said, speaking normally. "Anthony can't hear a thing."

As Mark spoke, she suddenly recalled that she'd never heard him call his driver by anything other than his first name and it dawned on her that maybe Sarah had been trying to cause trouble, perhaps wanting to show Emma up, to have her call him Mathis and have Mark correct her; possibly even think badly of her for being formal with his staff…

"You're sure?" she asked, not wanting to reveal her misgivings about his sister.

"I'm absolutely positive." He smiled and took her glass from her, placing it on the cabinet shelf. "He can't see anything either," he added, moving closer and pulling her into his arms.

"Wait!" she cried, pushing him back.

"What's wrong?"

"What about people on the outside?" she asked, looking through the windows at the passing cars. "We're lit up in here. Won't they be able to see?"

He smiled. "No. The windows are specially tinted. No-one can see anything. Trust me." He leant down, moving in to kiss her.

"You've done this before then, have you?" She pulled away a little, looking up into his eyes.

"No." He cradled her cheek in his hand, fixing her with a stare. "I've never kissed another woman in here… or done anything else, for that matter." He smirked. "I was always able to show a lot more self control around them, and wait till we got to our destination. You're different. I struggle with controlling anything when I'm around you." His voice dropped to a whisper and he covered her mouth with his. She responded, opening up to him, running her hands up his arms and resting them on his firm biceps, while he lifted her onto his lap, so she was straddling him, her legs either side of his. "You feel good," he murmured into her mouth.

"So do you," she muttered back, fisting his hair with her hands. He groaned and she felt his hands come around behind her, resting on her ass and pulling her closer still, so she could feel his erection pressing into her. She leant back, breaking the kiss. "I'm sorry," she whispered. "I can't. Not here…"

"Hey, it's okay." He brought one hand up, cupping her face tenderly. "I'm okay with just kissing, if that's what you want. I'm happy just to be with you, and have you to myself." She looked down at him and nodded. "But I can't help the fact that I'm hard," he added, and lifted her off of his lap, laying her down on the wide seat, and moving on top of her, his weight on his elbows. "You do that to me. All the time." He grinned and leant down to kiss her again.

By the time they got back to Somers Cove, Emma was already regretting her decision. She was breathless and tingling with anticipation, and needed the release she knew only Mark could give her. But they still hadn't really talked and she didn't want their first time after four years to be in the back of a car – even if it was a very nice car.

As they pulled into the town, Mark sat up and helped her straighten her clothes.

"Can I come see you next weekend?" he asked. "I don't feel like we got anywhere near enough time to ourselves at my place."

"I'd love you to," she replied, relieved he didn't want her to go back to Boston again too soon.

"Who knows," he added, "without interruptions, we might even get to have a conversation." He smiled.

"Just a conversation?" She smiled back.

"We can do anything you want, baby… whenever and wherever you want. And if you still don't wanna do anything, other than talk and kiss and hug, then that's fine too. I'll drive up on Saturday—"

"Don't. Don't confirm anything right now," Emma interrupted, her voice dropping to a whisper. She rested her hand on his chest. "Let me know for sure later in the week." She stared at him. "I couldn't stand to be disappointed again."

He ran his fingers down her cheek. "I'll be here," he said with certainty. "I won't let you down."

She wanted so much to believe him… but she knew that only time, and the coming week, would tell.

Mark

After the previous weekend, Mark couldn't wait for Saturday to come around again. In between work, he spent the week texting and calling Emma, their messages much more playful and full of love. He felt like they'd already recaptured something of what they'd lost in that awful week; he also knew that whatever they'd lost was entirely down to him and he had a lot of work to do to make it up to Emma. Sure, she'd dropped a hint that she might be ready for more before she got out of the car, but he still felt like she was holding something back… like she was scared of completely committing to him, for fear he'd hurt her again. He wouldn't. He'd never hurt her again. He just needed to find a way to prove that to her and reassure her he meant everything he said. He loved her so much… he just wished they could have some time together, so he could show her that.

As the week progressed, the memories of the previous weekend became more distant, with a few exceptions, which remained crystal clear. He remembered waking up with Emma in his arms and the feeling of her naked body next to his; he remembered kissing her for almost three hours on the way back to Somers Cove, although he still wasn't sure how he'd managed not to make love to her. And, more than anything, he remembered the tone of her voice and the expression on her face when she'd refused to tell him what had happened to her after he'd left her four years ago. She was hiding something, and it was something she didn't want to revisit. And if he was being completely honest with himself, that was eating away at him. It scared him. It also made him even more determined not to get it wrong again, because he never wanted to see pain like that on Emma's face again. Ever.

"I'm gonna try and get to you around three tomorrow," he told Emma when he called her on Friday evening after work.

"Okay. For a minute there I was afraid you were going to say you couldn't make it."

"No, baby. You know I'll move heaven and earth to be with you. I'm not gonna let you down again." He meant it. He was so haunted by that look…

"I'm afraid you'll have to watch me working for a few hours."

"That's no hardship." He smiled. "I love watching you. I'd come up earlier and watch you all day, but I've gotta take Sarah shopping in the morning."

"That sounds like fun." He could hear her grin.

"Actually it sounds like my idea of hell."

"What are you shopping for?" Emma asked.

"A party dress, I believe."

"And Sarah can't do this by herself because…?"

"Because she's said she wants another opinion."

"And her friends can't give her that?"

"Evidently not. I'd like to think it's because I have such impeccable taste, but in reality, I think it's because it's two of her friends who are giving the party. All I know for sure is I got roped in to shopping. She caught me off guard and, before I knew it, I'd agreed. I'd rather be doing pretty much anything than standing around in a boutique while Sarah tries on endless dresses." He'd rather be watching Emma, he knew that.

"Well, I guess it's just one morning," she said, with a slightly wistful tone to her voice.

"I'll take you out for dinner on Saturday night," he offered.

"Why don't I cook?" she suggested. "It's more private. Now I know what a privacy freak you are…"

"It's okay when we're up there," he said. "We've eaten out before, if you recall."

"Yes, but you were Mark Ellis then."

He hesitated for a moment. "I'd still be Mark Ellis," he replied. "At least to everyone else."

"I'm sorry?" He could hear her confusion.

"I've thought this through and, if we ate out while I'm up there, I'd book the restaurant as Mark Ellis. I think it's best if I don't use my real name, Emma… I'm sorry. I know you don't like this kind of deception, but it's as much for your protection as mine. If the press found out about us, they'd make your life a misery."

There was a pause before she spoke again. "Does that mean we can never be open about our relationship?"

He smiled, just a little. She'd acknowledged they were in a relationship. That felt good. It had a ring of permanence about it which felt reassuring. "Never's a long time, baby. We'll go public one day, but not until I know for sure I can protect you from the media attention. Until then, we have to keep it between us – well, us and our families. I won't let the press get near you. They can do so much damage and I'm not gonna let them get close enough to do that to you."

"Oh, okay." He could hear her disappointment.

"I'm sorry."

"It's okay. I know you're just trying to protect me."

"Of course I am. I'll always protect you. I love you."

They were on the third shop, and probably the thirtieth dress. Mark checked his watch again. It was already twelve-thirty. There was no way he was going to make it to Somers Cove by three. Not even if he left now… and that didn't look likely. He pulled his phone from his back pocket and typed out a message to Emma.

— *Hi. Sorry. Still in Boston. Still dress shopping. Not sure when I'll be leaving but I'll keep you updated. I'll get there as soon as I can. I love you. M xxx*

Emma's reply came through almost immediately. He knew she'd still be doing the paperwork at this time of day, so he wasn't surprised she was able to respond quickly.

— *Okay. E x*

That was abrupt.

— *Is everything alright? M xxx*

— *Just busy. E x*

Why didn't that feel reassuring?

Sarah came out of the dressing room, wearing a pink and white dress that looked, frankly, horrible. Mark was tempted to tell her it looked great, in the hope she'd buy it and they could get out of there, but he remembered his conversation with Emma about honesty in situations like this and shook his head. She shrugged and ducked straight back into the dressing room.

He glanced down at his phone again. Emma's reply was so out of character, especially considering how playful – even flirty – she'd been in her texts all week. He couldn't leave it there.

— *Something's wrong. Talk to me. M xxx*

He waited for her to reply. It took a few minutes.

— *I can't. You're not here. E x*

— *Can I call? M xx*

— *There's no point. Anyway, I'm working. x*

Why was she shutting him out?

— *Don't do this, Emma. M xxx*

He waited a moment, and then his phone rang. He answered straight away.

"Don't do what?" she said by way of greeting. She sounded angry. "I'm not the one who's gonna be late. I'm not the one who's cutting short our time together – again. I'm not the one going back on everything he's said – again. I'm not—"

"Wait a second," he interrupted. "I'm not going back on anything. I'm still coming up there."

"Really?" He could hear the doubt – and the hurt – in her voice.

"Yeah, really. I know I'm gonna be late, but I can't help that."

"Can't you, Mark?"

"No."

A short silence followed. He wasn't sure what to say to her… he just knew he'd rather say it to her face. In the end, he didn't need to worry; Emma broke the silence.

"Remember, you told me there wasn't a list?" she said quietly. "Remember, you told me it was just me? Think about it, Mark. Think about how last weekend turned out, and what happened the week before that, and how this all feels from my perspective. And then maybe make use of the time it takes you to drive up here to work out why I'm not thrilled that you're gonna be late…" And she hung up, although he was fairly sure he heard a sob before the line went dead.

He stared at his phone for a moment, but it didn't take much longer than that moment to reach a decision.

"Sarah?" he called out.

"Hang on. I'm just coming." He heard her voice from behind the curtain and started pacing up and down until she appeared, this time wearing a pale blue dress that was far too young for her. She looked like she was about fourteen. What on earth was she thinking?

"No," he said bluntly. "You can't possibly wear that."

She looked down at herself. "I did wonder, but I like the color."

"How much longer is this going to take?" he asked.

"I don't know. As long as it takes, I guess."

"Well, we're going to have to give it up for today. Get dressed—"

"Why?" she interrupted. "There are still two more shops to try."

"No, Sarah. I should've left over an hour ago. I can't spend any more time on this right now."

She folded her arms across her chest. "Well, I'm sorry. I didn't realize I was holding you up. I thought you were happy to help me choose my dress. This party's important to me, Mark…" Her voice had become a whisper.

He closed the gap between them. "I know it is, Sarah, but I can't spend the whole day on it. I've got plans. I told you—"

"I'm not asking you to spend all day. But it's a Christmas Eve party and everyone's going all out. I want to make sure I get the right dress."

He looked at her, taking in what she'd just said. "Christmas Eve?" he repeated.

She nodded.

"Then why the hell are we shopping now? Christmas is still ages away yet."

"You're never here these days," Sarah replied, sulkily. "I thought if we didn't do it now, I might not get the chance…"

"That's not true, Sarah. I was here last weekend—"

"With Emma," she interrupted again.

"Only for part of the time," he qualified, resisting the urge to tell her that she'd kept him and Emma apart for most of their brief time together. "And I'll be here next weekend too."

She looked up, a slight smile forming on her face. "You're not seeing Emma next weekend then?"

"Yes, of course I am. I was gonna invite her to come down again. But that means I've got most of Saturday free. She won't get here until five, so I can spend the whole day shopping with you, if you want. I just can't do any more today."

Her smile faded. "Why don't we just finish up here. I've only got three more dresses to try on, then we could have some lunch and you can leave. You'll be away by three at the latest…"

"No, Sarah. We can come back next Saturday." He was adamant. He needed to get to Emma. Her tone had him more than worried. "Get dressed. Please, Sarah."

"O-kay." She flounced back into the dressing room.

"And if you could hurry it up a little, that'd be great," Mark called after her.

Despite his best efforts, it was just before two o'clock by the time he finally got into his car. Sarah had taken ages to dress – or it felt like ages to Mark, but then he was impatient to leave, so it probably hadn't been that long. He'd driven her home, through heavy traffic and picked up his bag, which he'd left packed in his room.

He sat behind the wheel of his car, with the engine running and pulled out his phone, typing out a message to Emma:

— *Hi. Just leaving. Should be with you by five. I know you're busy, but please text me back. Please tell me you still love me like I love you. M xxx*

He only had to wait a minute, although it seemed like a lifetime…

— Of course I still love you. I'm a little mad at you, that's all. Just get here, please. E xx

— Please don't be mad at me. I'll make it up to you. And I'll get there as soon as I can. M xxx

He went to put his phone away but it beeped again and he checked the screen. It was another message from Emma and he smiled when he read it.

— Okay. Please take care. E xx

He threw the phone onto the passenger seat, selected drive and pulled out into the traffic.

He parked up behind the coffee shop, grabbing his bag from the trunk, and walked around the front, opening the door and walking in. Emma was wiping down one of the tables and she looked up as soon as she heard the door. He took a quick glance around the coffee shop, but it was deserted. There were no customers and the other servers were also nowhere to be seen. They were completely alone.

Then his eyes locked with hers and he knew from the look on her face and the sparkle in her eyes that they didn't need any words. He walked straight up to her, dropped his bag, put one hand behind her head, the other in the small of her back, and pulled her close, kissing her, really hard. He felt all of her love and longing in that kiss and returned it with his own, knowing she'd understand what he meant, without him needing to say anything.

It was a full five minutes before he finally pulled away and looked down at her.

"Hello," he said simply.

"Hi." She was breathless, panting. He liked that.

"I've been wanting to do that so much, all week."

"Me too." She smiled, and then he leant down and kissed her again, more gently this time.

"Where is everyone?" he asked eventually.

"It's been really quiet today," she explained, still resting against him, her head on his chest, her arms around his waist.

"Don't you have a guy who works here on Saturdays now?" he asked.

"Yeah, but I sent him home around an hour ago. There was no point in both of us working when there are so few customers." She pulled back and took his hand, he picked up his bag and she led him across to the counter, where he sat down on the stool he'd always sat on before… four long years ago.

"Latte?" she offered, staring at him, like she couldn't quite believe he was there.

"I'd love one." He watched her prepare it, and one for herself, and she stood opposite, running her finger around the rim of her mug and leaning on the counter, their faces just inches apart.

"I'm sorry for the phone call," she said quietly.

"Don't be," he replied. "You were upset… angry. You had every right to be. I understand."

She looked up at him. "Do you?"

"Yeah. I get that for you it probably does feel like there's a list of priorities in my life and that, when we're not together, it might seem like I'm pre-occupied with other things, and you fall down the list." He leant forward even further, so their lips were almost touching. "But," he added, "you're in my thoughts, all the time. Every. Single. Second. You're right, I do have responsibilities. I have the business, and all the people who work for me. I've got Sarah and Maggie and all of that… and a lot of the time it can be really full-on, but you're always there Emma. You're right at the top, I promise. And I'm sorry… I'm really sorry if I don't always make you feel like that."

"I wish we could be together more often," Emma whispered. "Then it wouldn't be so hard. You'd be able to hold me and kiss me, and remind me I'm still in your head… somewhere—"

"Hey, don't say it like that," he interrupted. "I promise you, you *are* in my head. But, more importantly, you completely fill my heart."

She gave him a shy smile. "That's such a lovely thing to say."

"It's the truth."

"Even so… Being apart so much, it's kinda hard to remember that sometimes."

He ran his fingers down her cheek, and she leant into the touch.

"I know," he said. "I know it's tough, and I feel the same. I want us to be together all the time. We're still finding out about each other, getting to know each other again, and spending so much time apart isn't making that very easy. But I'm not gonna give up on us just because it's hard."

"I don't want to give up either, I really don't." He looked into her eyes and saw the love he felt reflected in them.

"I know I keep saying this, but we can make this work. I know we can." She lowered her forehead to his and he let it rest there for a moment. "Still mad at me?" he asked her.

"No. I stopped being mad at you when you walked in the door. I just want to enjoy the weekend now. I don't want to waste any more time arguing, or apologizing, or feeling awkward around each other because of something that's already happened, that we can't change. I just want to be with you, Mark… by ourselves."

"Sounds like heaven," he murmured and he kissed her again.

He spent the next hour or so watching her working, drinking coffee, and snatching as many kisses as he could.

At closing time, Emma switched everything off, said goodnight to Noah and led Mark out through the front of the shop, locking up behind them. He took her hand as they walked to her apartment and she let them in, leading the way up the stairs. Emma turned on the lights as she went into the main room, going over to the kitchen and checking on whatever was in the oven

He put his bag down in the hallway and followed her.

"Dinner smells good," he said. "I've missed your cooking."

"I can't think why when you've got Maggie."

"Maggie isn't you," he replied, leaning against the breakfast bar. "So, what is it that smells so delicious."

"I made beef and vegetables in a red wine sauce," Emma replied. "When I got your message that you were gonna be late, I thought this would be easier. It can cook almost indefinitely, you see. So, it's been slowly bubbling away since lunchtime. I've only got to slice the bread and we can eat." She was rambling a little, like she was nervous all of a sudden. "I'll just set the table first," she said, selecting the cutlery from the drawer.

He shrugged off his jacket, leaving it over one of the stools by the breakfast bar, then came and stood in front of her, blocking her way to the living room. "Why are you so tense?" he asked.

"Who said I'm tense?" She tried to smile, but it didn't work.

"Me." He took the knives and forks from her hand and put them down on the countertop beside her. "You're on edge."

"I'm… I'm nervous." Well, at least she'd admitted it. Now he just needed to know why.

"Of me?" he asked, even though that idea troubled him. "Or of what might happen?"

"Not of you." *Thank God for that.*

He took a half step closer, so their bodies were almost touching. "Nothing has to happen if you don't want it to. We can take this at whatever pace you want, Emma."

"That's just the problem." She sighed and looked up into his eyes. "I know we should probably talk, and there are things we need to work out, things I want to ask you, but… well, if I'm honest, I'd rather… I mean, I just… Oh, I don't know what I want."

"Now, *that* wasn't honest at all," he whispered. "Because I think you know exactly what you want… don't you?"

He brought his hands up, either side of her face, cupping her cheeks, as he leant down and kissed her. His tongue found hers at once, and she pushed her fingers up into his hair, fisting it. Even as she caught her breath, he changed the angle of his head, taking her deeper and, moving his hands down to her waist, he lifted her onto the countertop, sweeping the cutlery onto the floor. He spread her legs as wide as they'd part, pulling her forward to the edge of the surface, and he stood close, nestled against her, so his cock was hard against her core. Within moments, her hands were fumbling with his shirt buttons as she worked her way down from the top to the bottom, undoing them one by one. Once it was open, she rested her hands on his bare chest and, as he felt the contact of her skin against his, he groaned into her mouth. He felt around her waist, pulling her blouse from her pants, then brought his hands to the front, to the tiny buttons that held it together. They were too damn small. He'd be there all night…

"Fuck it," he mouthed into her and yanked hard, ripping it open. Buttons popped everywhere, then he pulled the blouse from her shoulders and down her arms, dropping it on the countertop behind her.

Still not breaking the contact of their mouths, he unclipped her bra, pulling it off and releasing her, his hands covering her full breasts, tweaking her erect nipples between his thumbs and forefingers.

Her moans matched his and he felt her reach in between them, finding his belt buckle and tugging at it.

Something in his head told him to stop. It was like an alarm bell, telling him this was all wrong – all really wrong. He broke the kiss and pulled back, breathing hard. "Wait," he said, taking a step away, even as she reached out to him again. "Stop. We've gotta stop…"

"What's wrong?" she looked crushed, disappointed, and confused, like she didn't understand what was going on. Of course she didn't.

"I'm not gonna fuck you on your kitchen countertop," he said quickly.

"You're not?" She still looked bewildered. He needed to explain… fast.

"No, I'm not—"

"Oh." She didn't give him a chance to say any more, but started to climb down, moving her arms across her chest to cover her nakedness. She was embarrassed now, and he was in danger of fucking this up… royally.

He stopped her, pushing her back onto the wide surface and holding her in place, his hands on her thighs, his body firmly between her legs. "Wait, Emma. Please. Please listen to me… I—I've dreamt about this moment for the last four years," he whispered gently. "I've thought of, and dreamt of, nothing else other than making love to you again. And in my dreams, I've taken you, really gently, really slowly… on your bed. I've tasted you. I've touched you. I've explored every single inch of you.

I've buried myself so deep inside you and felt how wet and tight you are. I've made you come, and scream my name, over and over. And that dream – that thought – has been the only thing that's kept me sane, kept me hoping, for the last four years, even when my life was at its darkest." He let out a long sigh. "So I'm damned if I'm gonna fuck you on your kitchen countertop." A slow smile started to form on her lips. "We're gonna do this," he continued, "and we're gonna do it right, just like in my dreams… And if you thought for one second that I stopped just then because I don't want you, you need to think again, because you're about as far from the mark as you can get." He ran the backs of his fingers down her cheek. "I want you so much, I'm struggling to keep it together right now… okay?"

She nodded.

"So, can I take you to your bedroom? And can I please make love to you?"

She nodded again.

He picked her up and she wrapped her legs around his waist, her arms around his shoulders. Christ, that felt good. He really liked her clinging onto him like that and he held her closer.

As he started toward the bedroom, he let out a chuckle. "Oh, and just so you know," he murmured, "tomorrow, I *am* gonna fuck you on your kitchen countertop, really hard. Really, really hard…"

She giggled into his chest and nodded her head. "Hmm… I'd like that."

"I thought you might."

"You still taste incredible," he whispered, licking her juices from his lips and tasting her again. She'd come even harder than he'd imagined and he could see from the look in her eyes that she still hadn't calmed fully. He crawled up her body and raised himself above her. "I love it when you come on my tongue. I always did. And I love the fact that you're shaved, just like you used to be. But, now I really just wanna be inside you…" He paused. "Do I still need a condom?" he asked. "I am clean…" He left the sentence hanging.

She nodded her head.

"Okay." He didn't ask any more. He really didn't want to know anything about her sex life while they'd been apart. The thought of her with another man filled his whole body with an unfamiliar feeling. It wasn't one he liked. He wiped the thought before he could dwell on it and leant over the edge of the bed, grabbing his jeans and pulling a condom from his pocket. He knelt back up between her legs and noticed she was watching as he tore the packet and slowly rolled the condom over his length. Christ, now she was biting her lip as well. Whatever thoughts and feelings had been in his head a moment ago, he couldn't think of anything now but being inside her again.

He smiled down at her, then lowered himself and, fisting his erection, guided himself to her entrance. She was so damned tight and he let out a long sigh as she took his whole length. They didn't need words, their locked eyes said everything that needed to be said. He'd joined them, made them whole again. Together, they were complete… they were one, and that was what they both needed. He moved inside her, so slowly and tenderly, taking her body with his and finally claiming her back entirely.

He ground into her, savoring this moment, cherishing the sight of her beneath him, her body surrendered to his. Her hands roamed over his chest and shoulders and she brought her legs up, allowing him to go deeper. He lengthened his strokes and, at the same time, leant down and sucked on her hardened nipples, one at a time, while she moaned loudly.

It didn't take long before he felt the beginning of her orgasm – that familiar tightening and rippling right at her core. He was close and, as she threw back her head and the first shattering wave of pleasure crashed over her, she screamed his name and he thrust hard into her one last time, exploding deep inside and howling out his own release.

He fell onto her, just for a moment, before he turned them both so they were on their sides, facing each other.

"I love you," she whispered.

"I love you more," he replied, kissing her tenderly. "And I'm so happy we found each other again."

"Hmm… me too." She snuggled into him and he held her tight.

"I hope you're okay with staying in bed for the next twenty-four hours," he said, running his fingertips down her spine. She shuddered at his touch, and looked up at him and smiled.

"Oh, I'm fine with it."

Later, they sat naked on the bed, eating the beef, which had held up surprisingly well, with a glass of red wine each.

"So, was that your idea of waiting for me to be ready?" she asked, looking across at him.

He grinned. "I've never been very good at waiting when it comes to you," he replied. "But, be honest, you wanted me to make love to you, didn't you?"

"Of course I did. I still do…"

He stared at her for a moment, then turned and put his dish down on the nightstand, moving toward her.

"You do? You want more?"

She nodded her head, her eyes sparkling, a sexy smile forming on her lips. How the hell had he forgotten that insatiable need in her? He took her bowl and put it with his.

"Good." He moved his hand down between her legs, which she parted instinctively. "We've got four years to make up for, baby. It's gonna be a long night…"

Chapter Twelve

Emma

Emma felt a little sorry that this weekend would be spent at Mark's place. They'd had such a spectacular time at her apartment… well, in her bedroom, really, being as they hadn't left it for the whole time Mark was there, other than to go to the bathroom, or to the kitchen to get food or drinks. Except for that time on Sunday morning, when she'd got up to make them breakfast, and Mark had appeared behind her, and kept his promise to fuck her really hard on the kitchen countertop. She closed her eyes, shuddering slightly at the memory. Yeah, apart from that, the rest of the time, they'd stayed in bed, making love, holding each other and – occasionally – sleeping in each other's arms. It was exhausting and exhilarating in equal measure and she wished they could repeat the whole experience this weekend, but he'd asked her to go to Boston again. And she had to admit, she wasn't really looking forward to it. Not only would they not get as much privacy, with Sarah's constant interruptions, but there was no way they could even begin to hope to spend as much time in bed, and she was really sorry about that, because she wanted nothing more than to feel Mark deep inside her… all the time.

"You'll be here by five, right?" Mark asked on Friday evening when he called.

"I'll do my best to get away by two. The rest is down to Anthony. I don't suppose…" She hesitated, slightly nervous about asking him.

"You don't suppose what?"

"I don't suppose you could ride up here with him… and we could travel back together?" She wondered if she sounded as desperate for him as she felt.

"Oh God," he breathed, "that's an amazing idea. I wish I could, but I'm sorry, I can't. I've gotta take Sarah shopping again."

"Again?" Emma couldn't hide her disappointment, or her frustration that, once again, Sarah seemed to be getting in the way. She knew it was petty of her, but it seemed Sarah was there at every turn.

"Yeah, I cut short her shopping trip last weekend so I could get away and come up to see you… Your call kinda scared me."

He hadn't told her that before and she felt a little ashamed of her thoughts now. He'd put her first after all. "I'm sorry." She found herself saying the words without even thinking about it.

"You've got nothing to be sorry for. After you called, I realized pretty much right away that I needed to get to you; I didn't need the journey up there to work it out. So I told Sarah we could continue the shopping trip this weekend. I told her she could have my undivided attention until you get here, and then I'm all yours, baby, and you're all mine." His voice dropped as he said those last few words and she felt the heat build within her.

"I can't wait," she breathed.

"Neither can I. All I've been able to think about all week is being back inside you again."

"Oh… God yes."

"I wanna feel you underneath me." A lot of their calls had been like this during the week and his voice, his words made every nerve in her body sing with anticipation. It was like the perfect torture. "I'm gonna to make you come so hard, baby."

"Please, Mark… Please."

"I'm so hard for you," he whispered.

"And I'm so wet. I need you."

"I know. I need you too."

"I can't take much more of this." She genuinely couldn't. She was close to insanity.

"Text me tomorrow when you're on your way," he said. "I'll make sure I'm back before you get here. And I don't care what happens, I'm taking you to bed."

She smiled. "I'm gonna hold you to that."

The journey seemed to have taken a lot longer this time, even though she knew it hadn't. She knew it was because she was strung out with nervous excitement.

As Anthony pulled the car up outside the house, Mark opened the door and she looked up and saw him standing there, wearing jeans and a white button-down shirt. God, he looked good. She wanted to leap from the car and run to him, but she waited for Anthony to come around and open the door. Then she ran up the steps and threw herself into Mark's arms, letting him carry her into the house as he closed the door.

He kissed her deeply and, not breaking the kiss, he started to walk. She wrapped her legs around his waist and he picked up the pace, carrying her up the two flights of stairs, along the corridor and through the open door of his bedroom, which he kicked closed behind them before taking her across to the bed and lowering her onto the soft mattress.

He stood and looked down at her, pulling his shirt off over his head.

"Hello," he said, speaking for the first time. He undid his jeans, lowering them and his trunks and she sucked in a breath, seeing his hard arousal.

"Hello," she replied.

"You've got far too many clothes on," he whispered and held out his hand. She took it and let him pull her back to her feet. He removed her jacket, pushing it off her shoulders and letting it drop to the floor, then took the hem of her sweater and pulled it over her head.

"Fuck," he mouthed. "You look good." He reached around behind her and undid the clasp of her bra, freeing her breasts, before leaning down and slowly licking across each extended nipple, in turn.

Then he knelt down, undid the fastener and zipper of her jeans, and slowly lowered them and her panties to her ankles.

"Kick off your shoes," he told her, and she did. He held up his hand for her to take while he helped her to step out of her jeans, then he stood up again.

"That's better," he said, smiling. "I much prefer you naked."

"So do I."

He claimed her mouth with his, kissing her deeply and moving her backwards to the bed, laying her down and settling between her legs, parting them with his own.

He didn't hesitate for a moment, but entered her in one swift, deep movement and they both let out a moan of satisfaction as he began to move, slowly to start with, but quickly building the speed and intensity of his strokes. They'd both needed this so much, a week's worth of delayed gratification poured out of them. She matched his rhythm with her own, bucking her hips up into him, wanting more of him. He felt incredible, and she could sense he was close already…

"Wait!" she cried, as reality dawned on her from somewhere in the depths of her consciousness. He stilled instantly and looked down at her, concern etched on his face. "Condom, Mark. You're not wearing a condom…"

"Fuck!" He pulled out of her and leant over to the nightstand, grabbing a foil packet, tearing it open and rolling the condom down over his length.

He entered her again and they rediscovered their rhythm instantly. He took her harder and faster, until the familiar tingling started deep inside. She was going to come soon…

"I'm close, Emma," he muttered.

She brought her legs up around him, wanting him as deep as possible and, as he plunged into her again, she exploded around him, her body arching off the bed. She felt him swell inside her and heard him cry out her name, even through the sound of her own blissful moans.

"I really needed that," he said, lying by her side and holding her close.

"Hmm… So did I." She ran her fingers up and down his back. She wasn't sure how it was possible to forget how good he felt from one weekend to the next, but somehow she'd seemed to, because he felt better and better every time they touched. "We—We weren't too noisy, were we?" she asked. "Will Sarah have heard us?"

He smiled. "No, not unless she's capable of hearing us from downtown… and I doubt even you were *that* loud." He smirked.

She leant back and looked into his eyes. "Isn't she here then?"

"No." She noticed a shadow cross his face.

"What's wrong?" she asked.

"Oh, it's just that I took Sarah out this morning to buy her dress and… well, she found one quite quickly – probably by about ten-thirty – but then she insisted we go look for shoes. I was okay with it. I mean, I'd told her she could have my attention all day…"

"And?" Emma prompted.

"And, we'd been looking at shoes for about half an hour, when we ran into a couple of her friends… and she just dumped me and went off with them."

Emma laughed. "Oh dear." She ran her fingers through his hair. "Try not to feel left out…"

"I'm not. You're missing the point, baby," he said, looking at her.

"I am?"

"Yeah. By the time she left me standing on the street corner, it was eleven o'clock. Anthony had left to pick you up about twenty minutes earlier. If I'd known Sarah was gonna do that, I'd have come with him to get you, and let her get on with it."

"Oh, I see." Now Emma understood the look in his eyes and she felt a little irritated herself, especially when she thought about all the things they could've been doing together in the back of the car… for three whole hours.

"Hmm…" He pulled her closer so she could feel his arousal again. "You're thinking pretty much what I'm thinking, aren't you?"

"That kinda depends what you're thinking."

He kissed her, nipping gently at her bottom lip. "I'm thinking that I could've stripped you naked in the back of the car… spread you out on the back seat and tasted you… and then, maybe, I could've sat back and let you take me…"

She gasped just thinking about it.

"You like that idea?" he asked and she nodded. "You wanna take me?" She nodded again.

He grinned and rolled over onto his back.

"Well, don't let me stop you, baby."

Later, while they were dressing, Mark came over and kissed her, really softly.

"What was that for?" she asked, pulling her jeans back on.

"Because we're together, so I can." He smirked. "It's so great having you here, and being able to do this."

"Without interruptions," Emma added.

"Yeah… without interruptions." He buttoned up his shirt. "I've been thinking all week about how we can spend more time together."

"You have?" She looked up at him.

"Of course I have. One day at the weekend – which is basically all we get – isn't enough for me."

"It's not enough for me either."

He leant over and kissed her. "Somehow I didn't think it was." He grinned. She felt herself blushing. "Hey, don't be embarrassed," he said. "I love the fact that you like sex so much…"

"With you," she added.

"With me." He nodded his approval.

"I've been going insane all week, needing you so much," she admitted.

"Me too. I haven't been able to think of anything except being naked with you, being inside you… all week long."

"We'd better stop this, or we'll end up back in bed again."

"I don't have a problem with that," he smirked.

"No, neither do I, but you said Sarah might be home soon, and I don't want to be interrupted."

"No." He looked at her, his eyes on fire. "And we've got all night," he whispered.

"Oh, God… yes." She felt her whole body tingle with the anticipation of it.

They stared at each other for a moment.

"So, did you reach any conclusions?" Emma asked eventually.

"What about?"

"How we can spend more time together."

"Oh… No, not yet. It's tough. I mean, I don't have to live here."

"You don't?"

"No. I could work from anywhere, really. I hardly spend any time in the office as it is. I'm always out visiting one hotel or another, or I'm in meetings. It really wouldn't matter where I was based."

"So you could move?" She couldn't help but let the hope rise.

"I could. But I've got Sarah to think about. I can't uproot her from college. She had enough problems at high school after the accident, and she's settled there now."

"I understand that, but couldn't she get her own place here? Or maybe live with friends, like most students do when they're her age?"

"She could, but I don't think she's ready yet. Maybe she could look at it in her sophomore year…"

Emma felt that hope slide away again, replaced by the familiar sense of resentfulness toward Sarah, the way she was so dismissive of Emma, and the level of control she seemed to be able to exert over Mark… She shook herself internally. She shouldn't feel like that. She had a good relationship with Nick and she'd hate for Mark to interfere with that, which meant she had no right to do the same between him and Sarah. She'd just have to bide her time. Sarah would get used to her being there eventually, and then things would calm down…

The three of them sat together in the smaller of the two living rooms while Maggie put the finishing touches to their evening meal. Emma felt more comfortable in here than in the larger, more formal space Mark had shown her earlier, and she suspected he felt the same, although she'd really rather be out in the kitchen with Maggie.

Mark was sitting beside her on the couch, holding her hand in his, and Sarah was on one of the two chairs opposite.

"So, you got everything you needed in the end?" Mark asked her.

"Yes, thanks. I found a fantastic bag as well, with Macy's help."

"I'm sure your friends were of much more use than I'd have been." He smiled across at her, but squeezed Emma's hand.

"Very probably." Sarah smiled back. "I'll show you everything sometime next week, when we're alone again."

Emma felt a little excluded by that comment, and wondered if Sarah was doing it on purpose.

"You could show us now," Mark said. "I'm sure Emma—"

Whatever he was going to say was interrupted by his phone ringing. He checked the screen.

"Sorry, ladies," he said. "It's Jake. I'd better take it. Back in a minute." He gave Emma's hand another quick squeeze and got up, answering his phone with a "Hi," as he left the room.

Alone with Sarah, Emma was unsure what to say, but she needn't have worried, Sarah started to speak almost the moment Mark had gone.

"I suppose you know how those two met?" she asked, her eyes narrowing, just fractionally.

Emma thought for a moment. "No, I don't think I do, now I come to think about it."

Sarah smiled. "Oh. I thought you'd know." There was something in her tone that made Emma uncomfortable, but she didn't get the chance to dwell on it. "Well," Sarah continued. "It was about three years ago, I suppose. Mark went to a charity ball with his girlfriend. She was a model, and incredibly beautiful, of course…" Sarah glanced down at her nails, then back up at Emma again. "Anyway, she had to leave early for some reason and he ended up at the bar, drowning his sorrows with Jake. They hit it off and have been friends ever since. Jake's gorgeous, isn't he? He's just perfect, don't you think?" Sarah's eyes pierced hers.

"He's been a friend of mine for as long as I can remember," Emma replied, trying to smile. "And he's far from perfect. Like everyone, he's got his faults."

"But don't you think he's just divine?" Sarah was pushing the point, although Emma didn't really understand why.

"I've never thought about him that way," she said. "Besides, he's been dating my best friend for years now, so I wouldn't think of him like that…"

Sarah's eyes narrowed again, just as they heard Maggie calling them to dinner.

Mark met them in the hallway and put his arm around Emma's shoulders, leading her into the kitchen.

Over dinner, Sarah dominated the conversation, talking about her afternoon in town and what she'd done with her friends. Emma had to admit, she wasn't very interested. She was thinking more about her earlier talk with Sarah and why she'd so obviously been trying to get her to comment about Jake's looks, and why she'd made such a point of telling her about Mark being at an event with his girlfriend, who'd been a model… That image made her feel uncomfortable and she zoned out the small talk between Sarah and Mark while she pictured him in the arms of a tall, thin beautiful woman…

"Oh, Mark!" Sarah cried out loudly, just as Maggie was clearing the plates.

"What?" he said, seemingly surprised by her outburst.

"I forgot to tell you… You'll never guess who I saw this afternoon?"

He shook his head and took a sip of wine. "No, who?"

It seemed to Emma that Sarah was building up to something.

"Nicole," she said, grinning.

Emma looked at Mark and saw the color had drained from his face. Who the hell was Nicole, she wondered.

Sarah seemed oblivious to her brother's discomfort and carried on, "She was Christmas shopping and we bumped into each other. We ended up going for coffee, and had quite a long chat about how much fun we all used to have together. She asked how you are and said if you want to catch up, she'd really love to see you again sometime. I thought that was so sweet of her and I said I'd pass the message along… So, I have." She picked up her glass of coke and took a long gulp, before replacing it on the table.

"I—I need the bathroom," Emma managed to say. "Please excuse me." She stood up from her seat and just about managed to avoid actually running from the kitchen. She didn't know where any of the other bathrooms were, she was just looking to escape, so she ran up the two flights of stairs to Mark's bedroom, bolting inside, closing the door behind her and leaning back against it. She didn't need the bathroom anyway. What she needed was Mark. She needed him to tell her what the hell was going on; who Nicole was and why she wanted to see him… and what he was going to do about it.

She stood there for all of two minutes before she felt the door being pushed behind her.

"Emma?" It was Mark's voice. "Can I come in?"

She moved away from the door and he opened it, coming inside and closing it again.

"You okay?" he asked. "Sorry I've been so long… I tried the bathroom downstairs and the other one on this floor and you weren't in either of them, so I guessed you'd be in here."

She looked up at him. "Who's Nicole?" she asked.

He sighed, took her hand and led her to the bed, sitting them both down and keeping her hand tightly in his.

"She was the first woman I went out with after we broke up."

"Did you sleep with her?" Emma asked, although she already knew the answer to her question.

"Yes. We dated for a few weeks just over three years ago…"

Three years? "Does that mean you waited a whole year before dating anyone?"

"Nearly, yes." He turned to her and held her gaze. "I told you on the beach that day… I never stopped loving you. I never got over you, not really."

"But you still dated other women?"

"Yeah… I needed someone, or something, I suppose, even if it couldn't be you. Surely you understand that?"

He seemed to be implying she must have felt the same, but she hadn't. She didn't. Still, she had other questions to ask and didn't want to get sidetracked.

"And why does she want to meet up with you now?"

"I've got no idea. The last I heard, she was engaged to some big shot financier. And before you ask, I don't follow her life. She's a catwalk model and her engagement made the gossip columns. It was Sarah who told me about it." He turned toward her, putting his arms around her. "I don't give a damn what she's doing or what she wants, baby… I'm not gonna meet up with her."

"Then why would she be asking that?" Her voice gave away her insecurity and she knew it.

"I don't know. But you've got nothing to worry about, I promise."

She looked up into his face. "I know you have a bit of a reputation, but how much of that is true? I mean, is it all tabloid trash, or… or were there really a lot of women?" she asked.

"Since you?" he queried and she nodded her head in confirmation. "Yeah, there were quite a lot. Nicole was the only one I really dated though. The rest were little more than one night stands. After I broke up with her, I realized I didn't really want a relationship, if I couldn't have one with you, so I just had casual sex from then on. And, before you say anything, I don't expect you to like any of that. I don't expect you to like the idea of me with Nicole, or with anyone else for that matter, even if it was casual and meant nothing. But I guess that's the same for both of us, isn't it?"

"What do you mean?" she asked, confused.

"Well, I don't like the idea of you being with other guys while we were apart, but it was four years… and that's a long time, and we didn't know we'd ever get back together, and it's in the past, so—"

"But I wasn't with any other guys, Mark."

"You mean you didn't sleep with anyone else?"

"I mean I didn't even date anyone else."

She saw the moment of realization slowly dawn on his face. "No one?" he asked.

She shook her head. "No."

He leant back, just a little. "You mean… You mean you were alone, all that time?"

She felt tears building behind her eyes, stinging and threatening. "Yes."

He held her tight, hugging her to him. "Oh God, Emma… I'm sorry," he murmured into her hair. "I'm so, so sorry."

The sincerity and emotion in his voice were heartbreaking and she pulled back, looking up into his face. He must've realized she didn't understand why he was apologizing like that.

"I really broke you, didn't I?" he whispered.

Although it was a question, she knew she didn't need to reply, which was just as well, because she couldn't.

She settled into the back seat of the limo and Mark climbed in beside her.

It had been another horrible weekend, really. Yes, they'd had great sex yesterday afternoon, but then Sarah had come home and everything had gone downhill from there…

Mark had sat on the bed holding her for what felt like hours the previous evening and then he'd gone downstairs, just briefly to say goodnight to Sarah and Maggie, and he'd returned to her. They'd gone to bed, but they hadn't made love. Emma wasn't really sure why, but when he'd touched her, she'd pulled away, and asked him to just hold her. He hadn't argued, or even questioned her decision. He'd just held her real close until she eventually fell asleep.

This morning, she'd woken up in his arms. He was hard, but he hadn't touched her. Instead he'd asked her, really softly, if she wanted to make love. She'd told him she did, but she couldn't and, again, he was kind and understanding, holding her and kissing her so tenderly, it almost hurt. They'd stayed in bed for hours, just lying in each others arms like that. It was kind of comforting, but less than satisfying.

He was riding back to Somers Cove with her again and she hoped that, away from his home – and his sister – they could be themselves once more.

Once they were on the freeway, he pulled her across the wide seat and onto his lap, holding her tight.

"I'm sorry it's been such a shitty weekend," he murmured. "It started so well…"

She nuzzled into him. "Yes, it did. And I'm sorry I've been so distant."

"I do understand, Emma… really."

"Do you?"

"Yeah." He leant back, forcing her to look at him. "You're feeling… insecure?" he guessed. She nodded. "You do know you've got no need to, don't you? None of them meant a damn thing to me. It was just sex. It was…"

"Please," she interrupted, shaking her head and holding him tighter, "I don't want to hear about it. Not any of it. I can't handle hearing details, or knowing what went on. I can't…"

"I'm sorry."

She wanted to change the subject, and find out the truth about something else that Sarah had mentioned. "Can I ask a question?"

"Sure."

"How did you meet Jake?" she asked.

"Has he never told you?"

"No."

"Oh… Well, we met at a charity function."

"When?"

"About three years ago, I guess."

"And?" she prompted.

"You want the detail?"

"About this, yes."

"I—I'd gone to this event with… someone…" He hesitated.

"Nicole?" she asked.

"No. This was just after I broke up with Nicole. I went to the event with another model, I think… or she might have been an actress, I can't remember now."

"How can you not remember your own girlfriend?"

He looked at her. "Because she wasn't my girlfriend. She was just a model, or an actress, or whatever… and I asked her to accompany me to that one event. That was our one and only date." He looked into her eyes. "And before you ask, I didn't sleep with her." He paused for a moment. "Whatever made you think she was my girlfriend?"

Emma didn't want to admit she'd already heard the story from a Sarah, so she shrugged and said, "I just assumed, I guess."

He held her closer. "Well, you assumed wrong. You're the only woman I've ever called my girlfriend."

"What about Nicole?" She'd asked the question before she'd even thought it through, and let her head drop, dreading his answer.

"No. I dated her, I slept with her." She tensed and curled in on herself. "But I didn't love her, Emma. She was never my girlfriend." He reached down and raised her face to his. "That's only ever been you." He kissed her just gently, his lips caressing hers.

"What happened?" Emma asked him eventually.

"When?"

"At the event… when you met Jake?"

"Oh…" He smiled. "My date abandoned me when she realized I wasn't very good company, which I wasn't, because I didn't want to be there… I wanted to be with you. And she went and found some more interesting and famous people to spend the evening with. I ended up at the bar, sitting next to Jake, and we drowned our sorrows together."

"Sorrows?"

"Yeah. He told me all about Cassie and how he'd lost her, and I told him almost nothing about you, because I didn't know him then, so I was wary of opening up. Then we both got blind drunk, wallowing in self pity over the women we'd loved and lost."

She remembered Sarah's version of the story. "So you weren't upset about your model friend abandoning you?" she asked.

He chuckled. "Hell no. It was all about you, Emma. All of it."

Mark

He looked into her eyes and couldn't fail to see the confusion there. That wasn't a surprise. After all, she'd just found out that he'd spent the last three years sleeping around, so why wouldn't she be confused that he was still drowning his sorrows over her after such a long time?

"I know it had been a year or more," he explained, keeping a firm hold on her, even though she was still tense in his arms. "But I still missed you every single minute of the day, and knowing it was all my own fault just made it worse. Jake felt the same. He felt responsible for what had happened with Cassie. We were just a couple of miserable, lonely guys, feeling sorry for ourselves, and each other, and getting very, very drunk."

"And that's all there was to it?" She seemed to expect something more.

"Yeah. Anthony drove us both back to my place. Jake crashed out somewhere. I don't think I even made it to my room. I was barely able to stand, let alone make it up two flights of stairs. And then the next morning, Maggie filled us with bacon and eggs, and black coffee, until the world seemed like a slightly less abhorrent place to be. Jake stayed for the whole day, we hung out together, and we've been friends ever since. We never really talked about that night again," he admitted. "We were neither of us at our best, but I guess we always knew somehow, without ever needing to say it, that we'd be there for each other. I'd never had that in a friend before. I value it – and him – probably more than he'll ever know."

He held her close. Her muscles were still rigid. They had been since he'd mentioned sleeping with Nicole. Even as he thought that, he recalled their conversation of yesterday and his realization that she'd been alone all the time they'd been apart. He was willing to admit a part of him was pleased about that. He liked the idea that she was still his and only his. But at the same time, he hated the thought of her being alone and lonely, and knowing it was his fault. And he was still haunted by the knowledge that she was keeping something back from him about that time, by the look of pain he'd seen in her eyes. On the whole, he knew he'd rather live with the thought of her having been with other men, than ever have to see that look again.

She shifted slightly on his lap, and he placed his finger beneath her chin, raising her face to his and staring into her eyes, just as his lips met hers. He kissed her deeply, his tongue exploring her mouth, brushing against her lips, the contact making her gasp out her pleasure. He took his time, holding her, caressing her cheeks, her neck, her back, her legs, letting her feel his arousal, but not putting any pressure on her to do anything. He knew they'd taken a backward step this weekend; he knew he had to regain her trust, and he'd do whatever it took. She moaned, just softly, into his mouth and he increased the intensity just a fraction. He wanted her to feel the depth of his love for her, even if she wasn't ready for them to make love again yet.

He broke the kiss after a long while and looked into her eyes once more.

"I love you," he whispered, "and I want you to understand you have nothing at all to fear from my past. Absolutely nothing. None of them mattered to me. I was too broken to give a fuck… You are the only person who's ever meant anything to me, Emma."

"Can we just forget about it?" she murmured, still a little breathless from their kiss.

What did she mean? "Forget about what?" He felt sick with fear.

"The past, the women… Nicole. All of it."

"Sure." His relief was palpable, and he hugged her closer still.

"I'd just rather we got in with our lives," she explained. "I don't want to dwell on the past."

"If that's what you want, then that's fine with me." It was. He had no desire to revisit his past either. He wished he could feel reassured that Emma's reasoning was that she wanted to focus on their future and not that she wanted to hide her own past – her own secret – from him. But he wasn't going to push it. Not now.

"It's about us, isn't it?"

He recognized the slight hint of doubt in her voice and replied quickly, "Of course it is, baby. Nothing else matters. None of it." He kissed her again, putting everything he had into the connection, because it was all he could give her until she said otherwise.

He rolled her onto her back, along the seat, and lowered himself on top of her, holding her in place with his body and taking her mouth. Her hands fisted in his hair, her breathing became more ragged, her breasts heaved into his chest and finally, she parted her legs, letting him nestle between them, and bringing them around behind him, clasping him to her completely. She wanted him, he knew she did, but he wasn't going to do anything about it. She was going to have to tell him. It was going to have to come from her this time, so they both knew she meant it.

Anthony pulled the car up at the front of the coffee shop. It was late – gone eleven – and Main Street was deserted. Mark sat up and helped Emma to sit too, straightening her clothes a little.

"Sorry," he murmured, looking across at her.

"Don't be. I liked it." He smiled, and a part of him felt like he was winning her back.

"I'll walk you to your door," he said.

She nodded and he climbed out of the car, going around to her side and opening the door. She took his offered hand and he pulled her to her feet.

Anthony popped the trunk from inside the car and Mark retrieved Emma's bag, carrying it across the sidewalk to her front door.

"Are we okay?" he asked dropping the bag and holding her in his arms.

"Yes…" He was relieved by her answer, but sensed she wanted to say something more.

"What is it?" he asked.

"I—I know it's really late, b—but could you come up… just for a while?"

He smiled. "Of course I can. Just hang on a minute." He let her go and went back to the car, tapping once on the window. Anthony wound it down and Mark bent over, keeping one hand on the roof of the car. "I'm just going upstairs with Emma for a while," he said. "I won't be long…"

Anthony nodded, smiled just slightly, but said nothing and, as Mark stood, he wound the window back up again.

Mark returned to Emma, picked up her bag and waited while she opened the door. She walked ahead of him up the staircase and he put her bag down by the bedroom door. When he turned back, she was right behind him.

"Will you take me to bed, please?" she whispered.

His heart swelled in his chest, but he had to be sure. "Why?" he asked her. She looked down, seemingly ashamed, or embarrassed. He raised her face to his. "Hey, there's nothing I want more than to go to bed with you, but I need to know why you're asking me." She looked confused. "Is it because you think it's what I want? Or because of what's happened over the weekend… with all the revelations about Nicole and my past?" He saw and felt her flinch just slightly at the mention of Nicole's name. "Or is it because you're feeling insecure," he continued, "and you want some reassurance? Because you don't need reassurance, baby. I love *you* and nothing's gonna change that. My past means nothing. It doesn't matter. And while I want to make love to you more than anything, I don't want to do it if it's not right for you… so please don't do this just because you think it's what I want."

She moved a little closer, so their bodies were touching. "I'm asking because it's what *I* want," she whispered. "It's also what I need; it's what *we* need… both of us. This is who we are. You told me you could fix us, so fix us." She stared into his eyes. "Put us back together. Please, Mark."

The raw emotion in her voice cut through him and he lifted her into his arms. "It's okay, Emma… I'll make it right again," he murmured into her hair, and he turned, carrying her into her bedroom, and putting her down beside the bed. Without a word, and without taking his eyes from hers, he slowly removed her clothes, dropping them onto the floor, until she stood before him, naked, staring up at him in the moonlight. He quickly undressed and moved her back toward the bed, lying them both down. He kept their eyes locked, as he gently caressed her body, running his fingers lightly across her skin, until she was breathing hard, panting and arching her back off the bed.

"Please, Mark…" she whimpered.

"It's okay, baby," he reassured her, and he moved between her parted thighs, palming his cock and running the tip along her wet, sensitive folds to her entrance. He pushed inside, just gently and he heard her suck in a breath, her head rocking back on the pillow. She was soaking… and tight. "You feel so good," he told her, pushing in a little further, taking her slowly, deliberately, feeling every inch of her surrounding him. She looked up at him.

"I love you," she mouthed.

"I love you." He was all the way inside her, joining them back together.

"Take me," she muttered.

Part of him was reluctant to move, but he wanted her, and she wanted him, and she was right… they both needed this. So, he pulled out, almost all the way, then plunged back deep inside her again, hearing her gasp as he buried himself to the hilt. He took her slowly, deeply and tenderly, putting all of his love into every movement, every look, every sigh, groan, touch and kiss… and he felt her love being returned to him. This was like nothing else they'd ever done. He'd joined them physically, and maybe he was fixing them, putting them back together, but it wasn't all him. There was something in Emma's eyes, something more than the sparkle. It told him this was different for her too… that the connection was more complete than it had ever been before.

He was moving at a slow steady pace, taking her with him as she matched his thrusts with her own… and, after a while, he felt the beginnings of her orgasm. He saw it too, saw the change in her face, the expression in her eyes, felt the tight fluttering deep inside her.

"I'll have to pull out," he murmured reluctantly.

She shook her head. "No. Stay…"

"I don't have a condom, baby. I…" He stilled for a second, his own release getting close. "I wasn't expecting anything to happen."

"I know," she whispered.

"So," he breathed, struggling to keep his composure as her inner muscles tightened around him. "So, I have to pull out. Real soon." He didn't want to, but…

She shook her head again.

"Emma, what are you saying?"

"I want you to come inside me."

Had he heard that right? His cock certainly had. He almost came and he stilled again, regaining control.

"We've taken a risk already, baby," he said. "Not just tonight, but yesterday too, when I forgot the condom."

"I know," she replied, her hips still grinding into him. She was close. It was almost too much for him. "But I need this, Mark. Please. Fill me… now."

He couldn't hold back any longer. Her words pushed him over the edge and he groaned as he plunged into her one last time, letting go deep inside and filling her, just as she clamped around him, crying out his name.

It took a lifetime, maybe longer, for him to realize he'd collapsed down onto her, and he raised himself up, looking down into her smiling face.

"Are you okay?"

"Yes." She nodded her head, and brought her hands up onto his biceps, resting them there. "Thank you," she murmured.

He turned them onto their sides, facing each other, still joined. "I should've pulled out, Emma…" He'd never done that before. Ever.

She caressed his cheek with her fingertips. "It'll be fine. My period's due next week."

"When next week?"

"Thursday, I think…"

"You think?"

She smiled. "Don't panic. I'm fairly sure it's Thursday. I can't be certain without looking at my calendar. You did just kinda fry my brain."

Now it was his turn to smile. "Sorry."

"Don't be. I liked it."

He nuzzled into her. "Hmm, me too." He paused. "It's definitely due next week though, right?"

"Yes." She chuckled. "Stop worrying."

"I'm not," he lied, "but we're not gonna make a habit of that. Okay?"

"Okay. I just wanted all of you. Just this once. It mattered." The emotion in her voice took his breath away. She was right. Regardless of what the consequences were, it had mattered.

"I know," he managed to say eventually. "I wanted it too, and it felt sensational." He smiled. She looked like she wanted to say something.

"You've got a question, haven't you?" he asked.

She nodded. "I'm just not sure if I should ask it, if it's too soon…"

"Ask it anyway," he said.

She swallowed hard and looked up at him, gorgeously nervous. "Do you want to have kids? Not now, obviously, but one day in the future… With me, I mean."

He grinned. "Yeah, one day." He kissed her gently. "And definitely only with you." He heard her sigh. "Please don't feel nervous about asking me things like that," he said. "Or about talking to me about anything. I'm yours. I want us to share everything. All of it. I don't want there to be anything we can't talk about."

She looked away and he knew she still wasn't ready to tell him about whatever it was that had happened when they broke up. And he knew he'd just have to wait, be patient and give her time.

"Can I ask you something else?" she asked out of the blue, turning back to him.

"Of course."

"Can you stay the night… please?"

He heard the hope in her voice and hated himself for having to crush it. "I'm sorry, baby. I can't. I've got a meeting at eight."

She smiled, trying to put a brave face on it. "That's okay. I just thought I'd ask…"

"There's nothing I'd like more, you know that, don't you?" She nodded. "But I can't."

"I—I guess you're gonna have to go," she said reluctantly.

"In a minute, yes." He held her closer. "We can pick this up again at the weekend."

"Well, I'll have my period by then…"

"And does that bother you?"

"How do you mean? I have one every month. I have done since I was twelve. I'm kinda used to them now."

He smiled, shaking his head. "I mean how do you feel about making love when you've got your period?"

"Oh… Um. I've never really thought about it. But, I don't think I like the idea. What about you?"

"I'm okay with it, but if you don't want to, that's fine. We'll just have to hug and kiss… a lot."

She nodded. "Will you come here?"

"Yeah, if that's okay. I think we need some time alone, don't you?"

She nodded again and he kissed her.

"I've got no plans for Saturday, so I could drive up Friday night, if you like?"

"Are you sure? It'll be really late by the time you get here and what will you do on Saturday?"

"Watch you work." He grinned at her. "And if I get too frustrated not being able to kiss you, I'll go down to the beach house and see Jake and Cassie."

Emma nodded her approval. "And we'll get to spend two nights together?"

"Maybe three." He saw her eyes light up. "I'm not making any promises, but I'll try and clear my Monday morning, so I can stay Sunday night too."

"Really?"

"I'll do my best."

She sighed. "I'm normally as regular as clockwork, almost right down to the hour… but I wish my period would be late, just for once."

"Hey, it doesn't matter if we can't make love. I'm happy just to be with you."

He held her in his arms for as long as he could, until it was time for him to leave.

He sat in the back of the car, staring blindly out the window. Normally, when he was on his own, he'd sit up front with Anthony, but he wanted some time to himself to think.

He wished more than anything that someone would cut him and Emma some slack. They had barely any time together as it was, and it seemed there was a conspiracy to screw up what little they did get. One thing was for sure, he'd have to find the time to speak to Sarah. She needed to learn some tact – and fast. Obviously meeting up with Nicole was unfortunate, but Sarah could have waited and told Mark about it when they were on their own, after Emma had gone home. She didn't need to blurt it out in front of her. He was sure she didn't mean any harm, but it had ruined the whole damn weekend.

Maybe in a way though, Sarah had done them a favor. They'd gotten the past out in the open; Emma knew about the women he'd slept with; he knew she'd been alone… and a lot more broken than she seemed to want to admit. Plus neither of them wanted to dwell on it, and that felt good. It felt like they could move forward more positively, especially after they'd made love in her bed. There had been something very, very special about that. It had felt cathartic, like a homecoming, in all kinds of ways. He felt they'd really turned a corner after tonight… like they were in a whole new emotional place now.

Of course, not using a condom and coming inside Emma had been a risk, but he didn't think it would be a problem. She seemed fairly convinced the dates were okay… and if they weren't, well then they'd work it out. He'd be there for her, no matter what.

It wasn't until Wednesday that Mark got the chance to speak to Sarah, over dinner. She apologized profusely.

"I had no idea Emma would be so upset by what I said," she added.

"Of course she was gonna be upset." Mark found it hard to believe Sarah wouldn't realize. "No-one wants to hear about their boyfriend's ex."

"Oh. Okay. I didn't think she'd be that sensitive."

Maggie moved nearer the table. "It's not about *Emma* being sensitive, Sarah. It's about you being insensitive to other people."

Mark thought that was maybe a little out of line, but he didn't say anything. He didn't need to fight with Maggie at the moment. He was too tired.

"Let's just forget about it," he said, trying to keep the peace. "I'm going up there at the weekend… and, just so you both know, I'm leaving on Friday night and staying there until Monday morning."

"What about work?" Sarah asked.

"I've cleared my diary." It had taken some doing, but he'd finally rearranged the last appointment that day and had called Emma to confirm his plans. She'd thanked him, and then she'd cried, and that had made him feel bad. Did she really feel she had to be grateful to him for his time? He needed to talk that through with her.

"Good for you," Maggie said. "You and Emma could do with spending a few days together."

He smiled. "Yeah, we could. Oh, and I'm gonna invite Emma here for Christmas as well."

"You are?" Sarah was surprised.

"Yeah."

"What about her own family?"

"They're not that close. She might want to be with her brother, I guess, but I'm gonna ask anyway."

"That'll be lovely," Maggie said. "I'm looking forward to it already."

He'd planned to wait until the weekend to ask Emma about the holidays, but the next day, he found her the perfect present and couldn't resist calling her a little earlier than usual that evening, to find out what her plans were.

"So…" he said, feeling nervous all of a sudden. The necklace was lying in its box on the bed beside him. It looked incredible. It was a long eighteen carat white gold chain with what appeared at first glance to be twelve pebbles set into it at regular intervals. It was only when you studied it that you realized that four of the 'pebbles' were blue topaz, four were cultured pearls, and four were icy white diamonds. It looked like an understated, everyday piece of jewelry, that Mark knew Emma would probably pair with jeans and a sweater… and which she never needed to know had cost him just under sixty thousand dollars. "I was wondering," he continued. "Do you have any plans for next weekend?"

"Um… you're coming here, aren't you?" She sounded doubtful, bordering on scared.

"Yes," he said quickly. "I meant the following weekend."

"You mean Christmas?" she asked.

"Yeah."

"My parents are going away," she replied, sounding really pleased at the prospect, "so Cassie and Jake have invited Nick and I down to the beach house. I'm gonna help Cassie with the cooking and we're planning a long walk on the beach after lunch. Probably followed by games to keep Maddie entertained, and lots of drinking and talking into the early hours, I imagine…"

For a moment, Mark contemplated changing his plans and joining them. It sounded idyllic, and really relaxing. But he couldn't leave Sarah.

"And how would you feel if I asked you to duck out of that, and maybe take a couple of days off work?" he asked.

"Why?"

"Because I'd really like you to come here for the holidays. I was wondering if you could come down here on Christmas Eve, maybe… and stay for a few days?"

There was just a moment's hesitation before Emma replied, "I'll have to check with Josh, but he's been asking for some extra work over the holidays. I can't see it being a problem."

"And what about your brother, and Jake and Cassie?"

"Oh, they won't mind if I'm not there."

"I'm sure they will."

"Well, maybe. But they'll understand." He could hear her smiling. "So you'll come?"

There was another hesitation before she said really quietly, "Oh, God… I hope so."

He laughed out loud.

Chapter Thirteen

Emma

Mark called her again the next morning, really early. They'd talked for over an hour the night before, and he'd called her again as she was going off to sleep, just to say goodnight. When she'd heard his voice, she'd burst into tears, yet again. She seemed to be doing that a lot lately. She'd done it when he'd told her he could stay until Monday morning, and he'd done his best to comfort her, even though she couldn't explain why she was feeling so tearful – other than missing him, of course.

Although their last weekend together had been horrible, thanks mainly to Sarah – again – she felt they'd made a real emotional connection, and she wanted more of that. And judging by Mark's calls and messages, so did he. He was even more affectionate and loving than he'd been before and, although she missed him desperately, his words brought her more comfort than she would have believed possible, in the absence of his touch.

She was really looking forward to their weekend now. The thought of a few days with him was heavenly. She wanted to have some time to talk to him, face-to-face, to find out how he'd feel about her taking the birth control pill. She'd never even contemplated using it before – well, she'd never needed to – but she'd really felt the difference when he'd made love to her without a condom and she wanted it to be like that every time, without the worry of getting pregnant. Speaking of which… She had to tell him, but decided to try and make light of it:

"We're still in luck," she explained over the phone, taking a breath and crossing her fingers.

"I'm sorry. How do you mean?"

"My period hasn't arrived. We might get to make love when you get here tonight, assuming you're not too tired."

"I won't be. But… it hasn't arrived?" He sounded worried.

"No…" His worry was contagious and re-doubled her own.

"Why didn't you say something before? I thought you were regular as clockwork. Down to the hour, you said."

"I am… normally."

"And, I'm guessing that hour would have, or should have been sometime yesterday?" Now she could really hear the worry.

"Yes. For the last ten years or so, I've had a regular cycle, so I usually start on the twenty-sixth day, around lunchtime."

"Ten years?" His voice had dropped to a whisper.

"Yes."

"And you didn't mention that your period hadn't started when we spoke last night because…?"

"I was going to, but then we started talking about Christmas, and I forgot. And then, when you called the second time, I was crying…" She stopped, wondering whether the reason for her feeling so emotional and tearful might be staring her in the face.

There was a short silence. Was he thinking the same thing? "And the twenty-sixth day was yesterday?" he clarified.

"Yes."

"And it chooses this month, after the one time I decided not to use a condom, to break that routine?"

"So it would seem. And it wasn't your decision, Mark. I asked you to come inside me."

"It's my responsibility," he said.

She swallowed hard and decided to voice her worst fear. "It doesn't have to be…"

"I'm gonna pretend I didn't hear that."

"I'm serious, Mark. I was the one who suggested we forget the condom. This is down to me. You don't have to—"

"Emma," he interrupted, "we made that decision together. We'll deal with the consequences together, if there are any. I love you."

"I love you too."

"Then stop assuming I'll leave you, just because you might be pregnant."

"I'm not… but we only just got back together and, I know you said you were okay with having kids, but that was in the future, not right now. I just don't want you to feel obligated."

"I'm not obligated. But I am committed. And that means I'll be here, no matter what happens."

"Thank you."

"Don't thank me." She heard him sigh. "Are you okay?" he asked.

"Nervous, I guess."

"That's understandable. But I'm sure it's fine." He sounded more reassuring now. "It's only a day late, after all."

"Yeah."

"Do you want to take a test?" he asked.

"No. I don't think so… I know I'm scared, but I'm sure the timing's out. I'm sure it was too late in my cycle."

"Okay."

She wanted to lighten the mood, for both their sakes. "Of course, in an ideal world, my period will start on Monday morning, just after you leave… and after we've had a weekend filled with sex."

"I love your optimism."

"What about? A weekend filled with sex? Don't you like the sound of that then?"

"God, yes. I can't think of anything better than a whole weekend spent with my cock deep inside you." She squirmed, hearing his words.

"Really? There's nothing better than that?"

"Can't think of anything, no."

"So a weekend sounds like long enough to you, does it?"

He chuckled. "Oh, I see what you mean. No it doesn't, but it'll do to be starting off with."

"I love you."

"I love you too, Emma. So much. And don't be scared."

Her phone beeped during the busy breakfast rush. While she was frothing the milk for a latte, she quickly checked to see who had messaged her and was surprised to see it was Mark, considering they hadn't spoken that long ago.

— ***Please call me when you pick this up. M xxx***

Emma looked around the coffee shop, and checked the clock on the wall. It was busy, but she knew from experience that in about an hour, the place would be much quieter. Whatever it was Mark had to tell her, it was going to have to wait a little longer.

It was just before nine when she left Patsy on her own, went through to the kitchen and out the back, connecting the call to Mark as she went.

"Hi." He sounded weird, kind of distant.

"Sorry I couldn't call back straight away, I was in the middle of breakfast service. Um…Where are you?" she asked.

"In the car."

"Going where?"

"I'm on my way up to Manchester… in Vermont."

"Vermont?" She already knew what was coming before he said another word and she leant back against the wall for support.

"Yeah. I'm sorry, Emma."

"You're not gonna make it tonight?"

"I'm not gonna make it this weekend."

"Why?" She heard the break in her own voice, and two lone tears fell onto her cheeks.

"Please," he murmured. "Please don't get upset. I promise, if I could be there, I would. Hang on…" There was a pause, then his voice came back on the line. "Sorry, I needed to change lanes. I'm so sorry to do this to you, again," he continued. "There's been a fire at the hotel up there."

She stood up straight. "A fire?" she echoed.

"Yeah. I don't know much detail yet. The manager was injured."

"Oh God… Badly?" she asked.

"I'm not sure. He's in the hospital. The police called me about an hour ago, and I just ran out of the house. I've called my business manager, and she's driving up there separately. To be honest, it's a fucking nightmare. We don't know the cause of the fire yet… it could be anything from a wiring problem to arson."

Emma gasped. "Arson?"

"It's highly unlikely, but the fire investigators are looking into it."

"Oh my God."

"I know." He took a deep breath. "And then there's the business side of it… The place is booked solid for the holidays, and we've gotta do damage assessment, deal with the insurance, and get all the guests into alternate accommodation, and re-book future guests into other sites, or refund them. I'm trying real hard not to think about what it's gonna cost, and the press are gonna be all over it, especially if it's arson, or negligence of some kind…" She heard him sigh.

"Should you be going then?" she asked. "If the press are going to be there, I mean."

He let out a slight laugh. "Normally, I'd say no, and I'd let Becky deal with it."

"Who's Becky?" she asked.

"My business manager. But I can't do that, not when one of my employees is injured. It wouldn't feel right."

"Are you gonna be okay?" she asked. "Is there anything I can do? I mean, I know there probably isn't, but…" She didn't know what else to say.

"Hey… Thanks for offering," he replied, and she could tell he was touched. She wondered how often people thought to offer help to him. Maybe never? "I really appreciate the thought. And I'm sorry about the weekend."

"Mark… It doesn't matter. We've got Christmas to look forward to. Just please drive carefully. I'm sure you're speeding. Please don't."

"I'll be okay, I promise." She sensed a pause. "I know we only spoke a few hours ago, but is… is there any sign of you know what yet?" he asked.

"You know what?" She didn't know what he was talking about.

"Your period."

"Oh… No. Not yet. But don't worry about that. You've got more important things to think about."

"Nothing's more important than you, Emma." She felt a warm glow inside at his words. "Listen… I don't want you to worry if you don't hear from me for the next few hours," he said. "I've got no idea what I'm gonna find up there."

"It's fine."

"I'll call you when I can, baby."

"Okay. Take care."

"You too. I love you."

"I love you."

She waited until the line had gone dead before hanging up and going back inside. It was hard not to feel disappointed, but she was more concerned about Mark than anything. He'd sounded worried, and she didn't blame him.

It was late morning when her phone beeped. She was cleaning down the tables and put down her cloth, pulling her phone from her back pocket. She read the message and smiled.

— Hi. Arrived safely. Thought you'd want to know, as you sounded so concerned about me. I like that, by the way ;) I'm sorry about the weekend. I had such amazing plans for us. I love you. M xxx

She replied immediately.

— Thanks for letting me know. Don't worry about the weekend. The plans can keep. Hope everything's okay. Take care of yourself. I love you too. E xxx

She returned her phone to her pocket, but it beeped again straight away and she pulled it back out.

— Forgot to say. Keep me posted about the late arrival. M xxx

She smiled and shook her head, but didn't reply. She knew he'd be busy.

She didn't hear from Mark again until early Saturday morning. He called at just after six.

"I'm sorry if I've woken you," he said.

"You haven't," she lied.

"Yeah, I believe you. You sound sleepy… and real sexy. God, I wish I was there with you."

"Have you had any sleep at all?" she asked.

"A couple of hours," he replied. "I was gonna call you last night. I meant to, but it was nearly two am by the time I finished. It was a lot worse than we thought, Emma. The place is a mess."

"How's the manager?" she asked.

"He's gonna be okay, thank God. I went to see him yesterday afternoon. It was mainly smoke inhalation. He's got minor burns to his face and hands. He stayed inside to make sure people got out."

"Seriously?"

"Yeah…"

"And no-one else was hurt?"

"No. Thanks to Kyle."

"Kyle?"

"The manager."

"Oh, I see. Do they know what the cause was yet?" she asked.

"No, but they have at least ruled out arson."

"And the wiring?"

"That seems okay too. There are a couple more tests they need to do, but it's looking like an accident."

"That's a relief."

"Yeah. I'm gonna get all the hotels checked out now though, just to be on the safe side."

She could hear his worry. "So how did it start?"

"It was definitely in the kitchen, but that part of the building has been destroyed, so we're not sure if it's human error… you know, like someone just left something switched on, or whether there was something faulty."

"Will the insurance pay up?"

"It had damn well better," he replied. "The premiums are high enough, and we've got cover for every eventuality, so I don't see why not, although I'm sure they'll try and find some wriggle room if they can."

"Well, I know a good lawyer…" she said, although she was sure he probably had a team of lawyers all of his own.

"Yeah. Hopefully I won't need one, but I'll bear that in mind." He sounded really tired.

"So, what have you got to do today?" she asked.

He sighed deeply. "So much, I can't even think straight." She heard something odd in his voice.

"What's wrong, Mark?" she asked.

"Oh, it's nothing."

"It's clearly something. Tell me."

"It's just… I don't know. Normally in situations like this, Becky's so on the ball. She's better than another right hand, you know?"

"Kind of, I guess." Emma didn't really. She'd never had anyone she could rely on like that, except Mark… and Nick. "But she's not on the ball at the moment?" she queried.

"Well, she is and she isn't. There's definitely something wrong with her, and I don't need it right now."

"What's wrong with her? Is she ill?"

"That's just it. I'm not sure. I mean, I know she was having trouble with her husband, but this seems like something different. Something more."

"So, what makes you think there's something the matter?"

"She's just being kinda weird…"

"That's not real helpful."

He chuckled. "I'm sorry. This isn't your problem."

"I want to help, if I can. Maybe try talking to her? If you need her to step up a bit more, you can't just leave it, can you? Besides, she might appreciate having someone to talk to, if she's really got problems, I mean."

"Yeah, I know."

"Let me know if I can help at all. I can't really speak to her… I don't know her, but I'll listen to you, if it helps."

"It helps just knowing you're there, baby."

"I'm always here for you."

"Thank you for saying that. Oh, and just so you know, I'm probably gonna turn my phone off today. The press have gotten hold of the story already. My PR people are holding them off at the moment, but I don't need the distraction of my phone ringing every five minutes."

"The press have your phone number?"

"There's one reporter who does… a guy who's slightly less dishonest than most of them, but the interruptions would come from my PR guys. I'm sorry, baby, but I'm gonna need the peace."

"That's fine, Mark. I understand."

"I'll turn it back on every couple of hours and check for messages from you. So, if you need me, send a text and I'll pick it up."

"I'm okay, Mark, really."

"I know, but I want you to keep me informed."

"And I will. I promise."

"So, it's two days late now," he said, but she noticed there was no worry in his voice this time. She couldn't pinpoint his emotion, but he definitely didn't sound worried anymore. Maybe he was just too tired to register his emotions properly.

"Yes." She wanted to tell him that she'd had a dream during the night, a dream in which she and Mark were sitting down by the ocean and he was cradling a baby… their beautiful baby boy. She also wanted to tell him that, when she'd woken up, she'd felt so full of hope, it was almost overwhelming. But she didn't. No matter how much she was starting to warm to the idea of having his baby, she was absolutely certain the last thing he needed right now, on top of everything else, was for her to be pregnant…

That night, Emma sat at the breakfast bar with her laptop. She decided that, rather than focusing on missing Mark – which she was – she'd spend the time working out the logistics of the cake competition he'd suggested.

She initially reasoned, like Mark, that the best thing was for every entrant to cook the same thing, so the taste testing was as impartial as possible, and decided that she'd ask everyone to cook brownies, because they were such a favorite in the coffee shop, but then she wondered about adding in a second cake, or cookie of each entrant's choice, so she could see how versatile they all were.

She set about designing a poster to put up in the coffee shop and had just put in the finishing touches, when her computer pinged. She'd opened her Facebook page earlier to catch up with Cassie's latest book reviews, and news of a signing she was doing – and the 'ping' meant she had a message from someone. She knew it couldn't be Mark; he wasn't on Facebook. She checked, and felt her heart sink. It was her mother, wondering why she hadn't responded to the posting she'd put on Emma's wall a couple of days earlier. The honest reason was that Emma couldn't be bothered. She hated the fact that her mother only did this to demonstrate to her own friends how 'in touch' she was with her daughter, when in reality, they rarely spoke. She tapped out a reply, telling her mom that she'd been really busy and hadn't seen the posting.

While waiting for her mother to respond – which she was bound to – Emma went onto Google, and idly typed in Mark's name. She wondered how close to him the press had managed to get in the last twenty-four hours, and how that was affecting him.

She drummed her fingernails on the breakfast bar while she waited for the results to come up, and then stopped abruptly, her blood turning to ice. She couldn't quite believe what she was seeing…

There were three 'news' items. They all featured the same photograph and a similar headline, and none of them were about the fire. Without even realizing what she was doing, she absently clicked on the first picture and waited for an eternity, while her browser took her off to the website of a tabloid newspaper.

The headline splashed across the screen in big bold letters.

'Multi-Millionaire Mark finds love at last!'

And beneath, was a picture clearly showing a smiling Mark, sitting in a restaurant, with a blonde woman next to him. The woman's face was obscured by the cocktail glass she was holding, but it was clear they were intimate.

Although she wanted to close the window, and her computer, Emma found herself scrolling down the page, reading about how Mark Gardner, multi-millionaire son of the late Michael and Lisa Gardner, and one of America's most eligible bachelors, had finally come out of his self-imposed exile, for the love of this mystery woman… And how did they know it was love? Because nothing less would have dragged renowned recluse Mark Gardner into the limelight.

Emma couldn't help herself. She went back to the search engine and clicked on the next news article. It showed the same picture, with a similar headline, and this time the article said that Mark Gardner had frequently been seen around Boston in the last few days, on the arm of this mystery woman, and had left a high-class restaurant with her on Thursday night in his Aston Martin, declining to comment on where they were headed.

Emma slammed her laptop shut.

Thursday night? He'd called her early. There was nothing to say he couldn't have then gone out with this woman, whoever she was…

Tears fell down her cheeks, landing on the countertop. She didn't bother to wipe them away, but picked up her phone and looked up his details, waiting for the call to connect. It didn't. It went straight to voicemail and she heard him saying he wasn't available, but if she wanted to leave her name and number, he'd call her back. Very businesslike.

She hung up. She didn't want to leave a message. She wanted to speak to him. She wanted to know what was going on, where he'd really been on Thursday, and why it seemed like he was lying to her again.

Mark

Everything was turning out to be so much more complicated than he'd imagined it would be.

The only saving grace so far, was that Kyle was going to be okay and the hospital expected to be releasing him on Monday at the latest. He wouldn't be fit to return to work for a while, but that wasn't a problem, being as there wasn't much of a hotel for him to work in at the moment.

He'd spent all of Saturday afternoon in a meeting with Becky going through their insurance documents. While they were covered and they knew the insurance was going to pay up, it would take time, which meant they had to find alternate employment for the fifty-seven people who worked at that hotel, and make arrangements for all the guests who were booked in there for the next six months.

Later, back at the hotel he was staying at with Becky – which was another of his, roughly fifteen miles from the one that had burned down – he'd called Jake and asked him to come up and help look over the site. He needed to know whether it was worth trying to salvage anything, or whether they should start from scratch and rebuild. Jake agreed to travel up on Monday morning, which was a relief. It'd be good to have his opinion, because to Mark, the hotel looked like a wreck.

And just to top it all off, he'd taken Emma's advice and had managed to find what he thought would be a few minutes to talk with Becky over dinner on Saturday night… and then, in a way, he'd wished he hadn't. To start with, Becky had denied there was anything wrong, but then she'd broken down – much to Mark's embarrassment – and, when she'd pulled herself together again, she'd told him that things had gotten worse with her husband. She'd not gone into detail, but he'd sat up with her, talking things through until the early hours. He'd offered to find her somewhere else to live, so she could move out of the marital home; he'd offered to help her get a divorce, if that was what she wanted; he'd offered her every kind of practical support and advice he could think of, but she seemed incapable of making a decision. He found it exasperating, and he fell into bed, exhausted, at just after one-thirty. Just before falling asleep, he checked his messages again. He hadn't done this for a few hours, because of talking to Becky. There were about twenty missed calls and messages, but only one he cared about, which was from Emma. She hadn't left a message though, so he guessed it couldn't be important, and he couldn't return the call at this time of the morning. He'd try her when he woke up. Tomorrow – well today – was Sunday. At least she wouldn't be at work, and they could talk.

The next morning, he woke feeling unrefreshed and – if anything – even more tired than when he'd put his head on the pillow six hours before.

The first thing he did, after visiting the bathroom, was to check his phone again.

There were no further calls from Emma's number, but he had more text messages than he wanted to think about. He sat down on the edge of the bed and started going through them, one by one. He'd only reached the third one, when his entire world started to crumble. It was from the reporter he'd told Emma about – the one who was slightly more honest than most – asking for confirmation of a story that had just hit the internet. He checked the time of the message and saw it had come in at ten o'clock the previous evening. Why the hell hadn't he checked his messages properly last night? And what the hell was this damn story? The guy had sent Mark a link, so he clicked on it... and that crumbling feeling turned into an avalanche.

His face, his name, and a totally fictitious story about him were all over the internet. *Fuck.* How the hell had that happened? He looked closely at the picture. It was definitely him, and the 'mystery woman' was Nicole. And the picture was three years old, so the bullshit in the articles about him being out with her on Thursday night was just that... bullshit. Even as he thought that, his skin started to crawl. *Emma...*

She'd called him. He checked his phone again. Her call was timed at eleven-fifteen. What if...? What if she'd seen this? Oh, God. He pulled up her details, connected the call and waited. It went straight to voicemail. He waited for her recorded message to finish, and then the beep, and then started to talk.

"Emma," he said. "I don't know if you've seen the shit that's all over the Internet about me, but please, baby... please believe me, it's not true. I promise, it's not true. Just call me when you pick this up. I'm gonna be in a meeting but I'll keep my phone on. Call me. I love you."

He ended the call and sat, waiting. He didn't know how long she'd take to reply. She could've gone out… she could still be asleep, or in the shower. He went back to the article on the Internet and studied the picture again. He remembered the photograph. It was one that had been taken by Sarah – although he couldn't remember whether it was on her phone or Nicole's – when he'd taken them both out to dinner one night. He remembered that Sarah had asked one of the waiters to take a picture of all three of them together on her own phone. The thought slowly dawned on him… what if the guy had taken some pictures of his own? What if he'd sold them to the tabloids? But did that make sense? Why wait three years to sell them? Mark's name had been far more newsworthy back then, when the accident that had killed his parents was still fairly fresh in people's minds. Still, if it wasn't the waiter, who else could it be?

He went back to the message from the reporter, knowing he needed to try and crush these rumors before they got out of hand. He tapped out a reply, curt and to the point, saying he had no idea where the picture had come from, and there was no truth to the story. He asked the guy to print that… and nothing else. He wasn't sure it would work, but at the moment, there was little else he could do.

He checked his phone again. There was still nothing from Emma, so he started going through the rest of his messages, most of which were from his PR people. Some were about the fire, some about the 'news' item. They wanted to know how they should handle it. He sent messages back regarding the fire and told them to do nothing about the other matter. He'd deal with it.

There was also a message from Becky. She didn't mention their conversation of the previous evening, but told him she'd heard from the insurance company and they were sending someone down that morning to look at the fire damage. He'd be there at ten o'clock.

Mark checked the time. That gave him an hour to get showered and dressed and drive over to the hotel… and hopefully hear from Emma.

Chapter Fourteen

Emma

Emma had cried herself to sleep, although sleep had only caught up with her at around five in the morning; until then she'd driven herself nearly insane, wondering what Mark was doing, and with whom.

It was ten-thirty when she woke up with a start, and for a second, she forgot the horror of the night before… but her sore, itching eyes soon reminded her, and she felt her heart sink.

She reached across to the nightstand and looked at her phone. There was a missed call from Mark, and he'd left a message. She called her voicemail and put the phone to her ear, listening to his words and, just for a moment, allowing his voice to soothe her. He said the story wasn't true and he sounded so sincere. But then she remembered the picture, the woman leaning in to him, the fact that he'd guarded his privacy so jealously, refusing to let them have a public relationship, and yet he'd allowed this photograph to be plastered all over the Internet. And she couldn't help but remember his earlier lies, the ones right at the beginning, the ones he'd admitted to. He was good at this – and she knew it.

He wanted her to call him back, but her first instinct was to turn off her phone and hide, and she was about to do that, her thumb hovering over the button on the side of the device, when she changed her mind. She wanted to hear him for herself, not a recorded message that he could easily have rehearsed…

She called him, before she lost her nerve. He picked up after just one ring.

"Hi," he said. His voice was soft, but she resolved not to soften with it.

"Hello."

"Okay," he said, warily. "I'm gonna guess from your tone that you've seen the stories on the Internet?"

"Yes. I saw them last night."

There was a moment's silence. "I'm sorry," he said. She felt sick and cold.

"Why are you sorry, Mark?"

"I'm sorry you had to see that, that's all. But there's no truth in any of it. Sorry, can you just hang on." There was a pause, she heard another man's voice, although she couldn't hear what he was saying, and then she heard Mark say, "No, that's not acceptable. I want it dealt with before then." The other man spoke again, and Mark replied, "Of course I can afford it, but that's not the point, is it? I don't pay insurance premiums to cover things like this myself. Surely there's some way to expedite the claim?" There was a pause, and then she heard Mark come back on the line again. "Hi," he said. "I'm sorry about this."

"You're obviously busy," she said. "We can talk later."

"No," he replied quickly. "We'll talk now. This is important."

"I can wait, Mark," she told him quietly.

"You don't have to."

She let out a breath. "Is it a real picture?" she asked. "I know they can do clever things with computers. I mean, do you even know this woman?"

There was a pause and she wondered if he was there still, but then he said, "Yes, the picture's real."

"Who is she, Mark?"

"Nicole."

Emma wasn't sure whether she felt angry, disappointed, sad, heartbroken, or too numb to feel anything at all. "So you did meet up with her," she cried, tears falling down her cheeks. "You told me you wouldn't, but you did. How could you?"

"I didn't," he said. "I promise, I didn't. It's an old picture, Emma, from when she and I were together before. I haven't seen her since then. The photograph is from an evening I spent with her and Sarah. Please, you've gotta believe me… Hang on."

What now?

She heard some background noises and then the sound changed. It seemed windy, like Mark was outside.

"What's going on, Mark?" she asked.

"I'm just going out to my car. I'm not gonna talk to you about this in front of Becky and an insurance assessor, and there are too many people here to have a private conversation in the parking lot."

She waited. She could hear voices, men calling out to each other, then the clunk of a car door and all the other sounds disappeared.

"Does all of this have anything to do with me not having sex with you last weekend?" she asked.

"What?" He almost shouted. "What the hell are you talking about?"

"Did you decide to meet up with Nicole last week because I wouldn't have sex with you?" She spelt it out.

"Firstly, I *didn't* meet up with Nicole," he said, his voice a little harsh. "I've just told you, I haven't seen her for three years. And secondly, you did have sex with me. We made love when we got back to your place… and it was incredible. But even if we hadn't, I still wouldn't have met up with Nicole, or anyone else for that matter." He stopped and she heard him sigh. "I'm sorry," he said again. "I didn't mean for that to come out quite like that…"

"How did you mean for it to come out?" she asked.

"I didn't mean to sound like I'm mad at you. I'm not. What I'm trying to say is, that you decide, Emma. You decide when we have sex. It's your choice. Every time. If you say no, it doesn't happen. It's that simple."

"And does that leave you frustrated?"

"No. I leaves me wanting you, and needing you, and accepting that, for whatever reason, the timing doesn't work for you. I love you, Emma. It's gotta be right for you if it's gonna work." He paused. "I—I know I can be a bit full-on and intense where sex is concerned… I get that. I've never been like that with anyone else. That's one of the reasons I always knew you were different. I've never wanted anyone like I want you. I can't get enough of you and, before you say anything, I know you feel the same. I can see it in your eyes." She wasn't about to deny it. "I can't help that you turn me on," he continued. "But I do get that, although you like sex, sometimes you might just want to kiss, and hug, or go to sleep, or watch a movie, or go for a walk, or do something other than make love with me… and that's absolutely fine. I don't mind. I honestly don't. I know it doesn't mean you don't love me; it just means you're not in the mood for sex. As long as we can still be together, nothing else matters. I love making love with you, Emma, I really do. But I love you so much more."

"Tell me I can believe in you," she murmured. "Tell me I can trust you." Even as she said it, she knew it was a dumb thing to say. Of course he was going to tell her she could trust him, but she wanted to hear him say it and know he meant it.

"You can believe in me, Emma. I already told you, I'll never lie to you again – not ever – not after last time. I learned my lesson on that one, and it was a damn hard lesson. A four year penance." He paused. "As for trusting me… well, I'm not sure."

"What?" The tears welled in her eyes again. "W—What are you telling me, Mark?"

"Just this… I'll know you trust me when you tell me whatever it is you're hiding from me."

"What are you talking about?"

"I'm talking about the thing you won't tell me. The thing that happened to you when we broke up before. I know there's something, and I know you're not ready to tell me. And when you do, I'll know you trust me."

She couldn't. He didn't know what he was asking. "I—I can't."

"I know."

"I don't mean I can't trust you. I mean I can't tell you."

"They're the same thing."

"No, they're not."

"They are to me, Emma."

She sniffed and wiped her eyes on the back of her hand.

"Don't cry, baby," he said softly.

"How can I not cry? I feel like my life's falling apart."

"It isn't. I promise, it isn't."

"But I can't tell you about that, which means in your eyes I'll never trust you. And in my eyes, I do."

There was a pause. "I'm so glad you said that," he murmured.

"But, I feel like we've already got so many things going against us right now… Is this thing from my past gonna come between us too?"

"No, of course not. If you really can't tell me, then I'll have to deal with that. But I wish you'd try. Whatever it is, we can work it out together."

It was a nice idea… except she didn't think she was strong enough to work it out herself yet. She started to sob, really hard.

"Please, baby…" She could hear the hurt in his voice. "Please."

"Mark," she wept.

"I know. I'm sorry I'm not there. If I was, I'd hold you in my arms and kiss away your tears. These stories about me, they're not true." She wasn't even thinking about that at the moment.

"And the other thing?" she cried. "The thing I can't tell you about?"

"Hey, stop worrying about that. I've known about it for a while, haven't I? Has it stopped me loving you? Has it changed anything about how I feel for you? No. And one day, when you're ready, you will tell me. I know you will."

She stuttered out a deep breath.

"Why—Why is this happening to us?"

"I don't know. I've spent the last few hours trying to think how they could've gotten hold of that picture. I do remember Sarah taking some photos on Nicole's phone, and the waiter taking some too, on Sarah's. I don't think I've got a chance in hell of tracking down the waiter – I can't even remember what he looked like now, but I'm wondering if Nicole's behind this…"

"Why?"

"You heard what Sarah said. Nicole wanted to meet up with me. What if there's more to it? What if this is some kind of revenge, or something?"

"Revenge? What for?"

"I broke up with her. She wasn't exactly happy about it at the time."

"But that was three years ago, Mark. Why wait until now?"

"I don't know. I'm gonna try calling her later——"

"You're gonna do what?" Emma interrupted.

"I'm gonna call her."

"You're still in contact with her?"

"No, but like I said, she's a catwalk model. She's not exactly untraceable."

Emma thought about it for a moment. "I'm not convinced," she said quietly. "It doesn't add up to me that she'd wait three years to do this."

"I know, but what else have I got?"

"You could try asking Sarah. She might remember more about the waiter, maybe?"

"I doubt it. I dated Nicole about a year after the accident. Sarah hadn't been out of the hospital for that long. She was still quite ill and didn't really connect much with people. That's why I took her out with us that night – just to get her out of the house."

"So, you think Nicole's your best hope then?" she asked.

"Yeah, but please don't worry about it. You are worrying, aren't you?"

"Yes, of course I am. I don't want you calling your ex."

"She doesn't mean anything to me. I love you, Emma. No-one else. I'll speak to her later and, as soon as I know anything, I'll call you."

"Okay."

"How are you?"

"Tired. I didn't sleep much… And emotionally drained, I guess."

"I'm so sorry about all this."

"I know."

She believed him. She really did. She also felt the faith he was placing in her, allowing her to keep her secret from him and not blaming her for doing it, or pushing her to tell him.

"And what about the late arrival?" he asked.

"Still no sign yet…" she hadn't dreamt about the baby last night; she hadn't dreamt at all. But that hope was still there – deep inside her. She placed her hand on her belly. She knew the dates were probably wrong, and the chances were against it happening, but that didn't seem to stop the hope from building every time she thought about it… Even as she tried to reason that she couldn't be pregnant, she also kept wondering if that was why she was so tired and emotional.

"Do something for me?" he asked, interrupting her train of thought. "Get a test. Please. I'm going insane here." Insane with fear? Or insane with hope? No, he'd be worried, not hopeful.

"With everything else you've got to think about, *that's* what's driving you insane?" She tried to keep her voice light and calm.

"Yeah, of course it is. It's about you. Get a test, Emma. Please."

"Okay. I'll get one and do it in the morning." She wanted to change the subject, just in case he told her how much he hated the idea of her being pregnant right now. "When are you going back to Boston?" she asked him.

"Tomorrow night. I've got Jake coming up here in the morning to inspect the damage and advise me on what's best to do about it. Once he's finished, I'll deal with the last few things and drive back home again. Becky's gonna stay a couple more days, but I don't need to be here as well. I'm better off in the office."

"And Christmas?" she asked.

"What about it?"

"Should we cancel it?"

"Cancel Christmas? Who are you, Ebenezer Scrooge?" She laughed.

"I just meant cancel our arrangements, not the whole holiday."

"No. I still wanna see you."

"But will you be around?" She didn't want to spend the holidays with Sarah, that was for sure.

"I'll make sure I'm around."

"I—I really wish you could come back here, instead of going to Boston. I need you."

"I need you too. I could really use a hug right now."

"Oh… Are you okay?"

"Yeah. I'm fine. Just missing you. I'll see you soon… I promise. It's less than a week till Christmas Eve and then we'll be together. I love you, Emma."

"I love you too."

She heard his sigh. "Thank you for saying that," he said. "I don't think I've ever needed to hear you say it more."

"I love you," she repeated.

Mark

Mark woke up early and, bleary-eyed, looked around. Although the hotel room was luxurious, he couldn't deny that, right now, he'd sell his soul to be in Emma's tiny apartment, curled up next to her, with his arms tight around her soft, naked body.

He turned over and checked the time on his phone. It was six-thirty. He was probably safe to call her. He smiled, wondering if she'd taken the pregnancy test yet. He hoped so… he really hoped so. The waiting was making him a little crazy. Weirdly, what had started as nervous fear that she might be pregnant, and what they'd do about it, considering the current geographical distance between them and the comparative newness of their relationship, had – over the last forty-eight hours – become a hope. He had no idea where that hope had come from and, although he knew it was unlikely she was pregnant, the hope remained. It had even grown, and he found he wanted her to tell him the test was positive almost as much as he wanted to see her and hold her in his arms again… and he wanted that as much as he wanted to take his next breath.

He called her, putting the phone to his ear and smiling in anticipation. It rang four times, then went to voicemail. That was odd. She knew he'd be calling her. He waited for the recorded message to finish, then spoke:

"Hi, baby," he said softly. "Call me when you get this. Love you."

He ended the call and, turning onto his other side, went to his message app. At least today he only had thirty messages to go through. He quickly scrolled down, ignoring most of them and stopping when he saw one from Emma, timed at six am. She'd been up early, even by her standards.

He clicked on the message and read:

— **You're off the hook. Test's negative. Just as well, really. I can't do this anymore, Mark. I'm sorry. It's over. Emma.**

What. The. Fuck.

He sat bolt upright and read it again, just to make sure he'd understood.

She was ending it with him? By text. By fucking text?

His phone rang. It was Becky. He ignored it and went to Emma's details, calling her up again. The call went to voicemail for a second time, after the same four rings. He waited impatiently for the recorded message to finish.

"Why, Emma? Please call me. Please tell me why. Oh, and just so you know, it's not over. It's nowhere near over."

He didn't know what else to say.

Becky had left a message, causing his phone to beep three times. He ignored that too and went back to his text app, going to Emma's message. He didn't want to read her words again, but he tapped out a reply:

— **I'm guessing you're ignoring my calls. Please tell me why you think we're over, Emma? I love you and I'm not walking away from you. Ever. M xxx**

He waited, sitting on the bed for twenty minutes before his phone beeped again. He glanced at the screen. It was a message from Emma. He almost didn't want to read it, but he had to:

— **I can't be lied to, not again. Like you said, you've got no idea what it was like for me before, and I'm not going to tell you, especially not now. But I will tell you, I can't go back there. I can't, Mark. I'm truly sorry, but I have to do this for myself. It really is over. Emma**

He read the message twice, then replied.

— It's not over, Emma. I haven't lied to you. I promise. Tell me what it is you think I've done. M xxx

She replied immediately.

— Google yourself, Mark. Then tell me how I'm supposed to feel. And then leave me alone. Please.

He went to a browser and did exactly as she'd suggested, typing in his own name, and waiting for the page to come up… and at that moment, he would have been willing to swear his heart stopped beating.

The picture was of him with Nicole again, this time at a charity function they'd attended at one of his hotels while they were dating. Again, he remembered Sarah being there as well. He'd used the event as an excuse to spoil her, buy her a party dress and take her out. She'd seemed to enjoy it, not that it mattered now. The picture showed his face fairly clearly, although Nicole's was obscured, enabling her to maintain the label of 'mystery woman'. The reason her face was obscured was because they were kissing… *Great.* But even that wasn't the worst part. No, the worst part was the headline that ran above the picture…

'New Year Wedding and Spring Baby for Mark and Mystery Woman'

Could this get any worse? Maybe it could – he had no idea.

He read the beginning of the article. It said he'd been seeing this woman for months, and that a source 'close to the couple' had told the reporter that Mark and his fiancée were 'overjoyed' at the news she was pregnant, that the baby was due sometime in the spring, although they were being coy about the precise date, and that they were getting married early in the New Year at a secret location. He groaned as he read the last line, promising 'further updates' in the near future. There was gonna be more of this?

He went back to the picture. He remembered the event well. He'd taken so much care that night, mainly because he'd had Sarah with him, but also because of his need to protect his own identity. No press had been allowed inside the hotel and he'd deliberately arrived early, and used the staff entrance, leaving by the same route and making a point of avoiding the photographers outside. And now it seemed it was all for nothing.

All the years of guarding his privacy had been blown to smithereens, and his life was being shot to pieces at the same time, and so was Emma's. God, what must she be going through?

He called her number, but got her voicemail… again. This was beyond frustrating. He hung up without leaving a message, but typed out a text instead.

— *I need to speak to you. Take my call. Please. M xxx*

Her reply was almost immediate.

— *No. We have nothing to talk about.*

— *Yes. We do. Take the damn call.*

— *No. And don't talk to me like that.*

That was a mistake. A big one. He was being a dick and he needed to calm down. He took a deep breath.

— *Forgive me. I'm sorry. Please just look at the picture online. It's not recent. Look at my hair. It's different. These are old pictures. I promise. xxx*

There was a delay. And then his phone rang. He didn't bother to check the screen, he picked up straight away.

"Emma?"

"Is it old news too?" He could hear her tears, the emotion thickening her voice.

"What do you mean?"

"Was she pregnant? Were you engaged?"

"Hell, no… on both counts," he said. "I've never been engaged. Ever. And I've always been real careful about using protection. Except with you the other night. That was the first time I've ever done that… well, other than when I've temporarily forgotten the condom before, with you. It seems you do that to me."

She didn't say anything for what felt like forever, but he could hear her breathing, and the occasional sniffle.

"Are you okay?" he asked her eventually.

"No." She paused and he let her. "It… Oh, God… It's been so awful, Mark."

"Tell me, baby."

"I—I woke up early. I—I'd bought the pregnancy test." He closed his eyes, only now remembering the beginning of her message, which had been overshadowed by its ending. "I wanted to give myself plenty of time. I did the test and… and you have to wait three minutes. So while I was waiting, I went into the kitchen to make a coffee, and I was checking my emails, and I stupidly went online to look at the weather report, but I was so tired, I ended up refreshing the page with the news stories about you… and this came up. I was so upset, I couldn't even think straight. I wanted to call you, but it was so early—"

"It would've been okay. I wouldn't have minded."

"I know, but like I said, I wasn't thinking properly. And I saw the word 'baby' on the screen and remembered the pregnancy test, and I went back through to the bathroom…" She seemed to run out of words.

"And it said you weren't pregnant?"

"Yes."

He paused. "And?"

"And what?"

"And how do you feel about that?"

"I don't know." He thought she probably did though.

"Shall I tell you how I feel?" he asked.

She didn't reply.

"I feel kinda disappointed," he said.

"You do?"

"Yeah. I don't know why, but I'd started to hope you might be."

He heard her whimper, and then she let out a gut-wrenching sob.

"Oh, Emma… You wanted it too, didn't you?" He pictured her waiting for the result, maybe crossing her fingers, impatient to know… and then seeing the story about him on the Internet. What must that have felt like to her? Especially when the test was negative. "Emma. I'm sorry." Why was Nicole doing this to them? He knew now that he needed to take a long time to calm down before speaking to her, because right now, he was incapable of being even vaguely polite. Emma was hurting… badly. Her continued sobs brought him back to reality. "Please don't cry." His words sounded so ineffectual, so helpless. There was nothing he could do for her, not from where he was.

"I—I'm sorry," she whispered eventually.

"What the hell are you sorry for?"

"I'm sorry for telling you about the pregnancy test in the way I did. If I'd known you wanted it too, I'd have told you more kindly than that."

"Hey, don't worry about that."

"And I'm sorry for saying we're over."

"So we're not?" There was silence. "Are you shaking your head?" he asked her.

"Yes."

"Tell me we're not over," he urged her. "Tell me properly."

"We're not over. I'm sorry."

Thank fuck for that. He let out the breath he'd been holding. "Don't be sorry. Just do something for me?" he asked. She didn't answer, so he carried on. "Don't look at the Internet for the next few days? I still don't know what Nicole's playing at, or what she's gonna hit us with next, but I don't want you seeing any more of it."

"Have you been able to contact her yet?" she asked.

"No. I haven't managed to get hold of her number. I've got Becky working on it. For now, just avoid the Internet. None of what they're saying is true, so just ignore it. Don't even look at it. And believe in me, Emma, I'm never gonna hurt you."

"Okay." Her voice was so weak, so broken, he wanted to hold her and make her feel stronger again.

"Do one more thing for me?" he asked.

"Hmm?"

"Don't ever dump me again. You scared the shit out of me."

"I won't, I promise. I'm sorry."

"Please stop saying sorry. I don't want you to be sorry. I just don't want to go through that… ever again."

Mark hung up his phone and stared at it. He'd been speaking to various people all morning, but that call had him more concerned than any of the others… well, except for his conversation with Emma, of course. Maggie had been worried, but not upset. She'd told him there were maybe twenty or thirty reporters outside the front of the house, and that Sarah had gone into a complete meltdown. Some of them were there about the fire; but most of them wanted details about the 'other story' as Maggie had put it. Mark asked if Sarah knew about the story to do with Nicole and Maggie'd told him she hadn't done, until the reporters had turned up. And now she was really distressed by the whole thing. He'd told Maggie they should both stay inside and he'd promised to get back as soon as he could and deal with everything. Maggie had tried to tell him she could cope, but he knew she had to be concerned about Sarah, or she wouldn't have called him. He knew where his responsibilities lay. He put his phone into his back pocket just as Jake's BMW pulled onto the hotel site. He hoped his friend might actually bring him some good news… He could do with some.

He watched Jake climb out of his car and stop, looking at where the front of the hotel had once been. The rear was still fairly intact, if smoke damaged, but that still meant over half the hotel had been destroyed.

"Jeez, man," Jake said, as Mark walked toward him. "You like to do things properly, don't you?"

"I didn't do this," Mark replied. "Not personally."

Jake turned to him. "You okay?" he asked. "You look like shit."

"Thanks."

"No, seriously," Jake added. "Are you okay?"

Mark looked at him and saw the concern in his friend's eyes. "I take it you've seen the stories on the Internet?"

"I hadn't, not until this morning."

"Has Cassie seen them?"

"Yeah. It was Cassie who showed them to me over breakfast."

"Did Emma tell her then?"

"No… Shit. Does Emma know as well?"

"Oh yeah… Emma knows."

They both leant back on Jake's car. "And?"

"And it's been a fucking nightmare…"

"Wanna talk about it?"

Mark turned to Jake, resting his elbow on the top of the car. "She broke up with me."

"Oh, man…" He could hear the sympathy in Jake's voice.

"It's okay. We're back on. But it was a real scary moment. Well, a real scary half hour, I guess."

"You need to go see her," Jake suggested.

"I wish I could." Mark nodded in the direction of the damaged building. "I've got this to deal with… and I've just had a call from Maggie. The house is under siege."

"Under siege?"

"Yeah. The press. There are about thirty reporters camped outside. So I'm driving back there as soon as we're finished here. I was gonna hang on here until tonight but Sarah's not handling having all the reporters there. I think it's probably reminded her of when mom and dad died. I've gotta get back to her."

"And Emma?" Jake said.

"She's coming down on Christmas Eve."

"Yeah, I know she is, but she's all alone up there, Mark."

He sighed. "I can't be in two places at once. We're talking on the phone. She's okay."

"Is she?"

Mark looked at him. "Do you know something I don't?" he asked.

"I doubt it." Jake paused. "But I know Em's not as strong as she likes people to believe she is. She never has been. And I know if it was Cass, I'd wanna be with her."

"I do. Of course I want to be with Emma. But I've just had a fucking hotel burn down on me. My name's all over the Internet, and my sister's having some kind of breakdown, thanks to the fucking press…"

"Okay. Calm down."

"Sorry."

Jake pushed himself off the car, stepped away and then turned back. "I'm taking some time off, starting tomorrow and we're going up to Somers Cove until after the holidays. We'll check in with Emma and make sure she's okay, if that helps."

"Yeah, it does. Let me know, will you?"

"I will. But you guys need some time together, away from everything and everyone else."

"I know we do. It's just real hard at the moment."

Jake stepped closer. "No, it isn't. You love her, so just make the fucking time for her, Mark."

Chapter Fifteen

Emma

"I'm sorry I didn't call you last night," Mark said. It was early and his voice was kind of quiet and distant. It reminded Emma of how he'd been that week before Thanksgiving.

"Well, I guessed you'd probably get home late, so I didn't worry about it."

"Oh, it wasn't late. I got back here around four in the afternoon, I guess, but it was chaos."

"But, I thought you weren't leaving Manchester until last night?" she queried.

"No, there was a change of plan," he explained, sighing. "I had a call from Maggie yesterday morning. The press had taken up residence outside the house, and Sarah had cracked up over the whole thing." Sarah? He'd gone home early… for *Sarah?* "She's better now I'm back, and I called the police and got them to move the reporters on, so it's not such a problem now."

"Couldn't Sarah have done that herself?" Emma asked. "Or Maggie?"

"I guess, but they're not as used to all this as I am. Anyway… How are you?"

"I'm fine." She didn't see the point in saying anything else. It wasn't like he was going to drop everything and come to *her* aid, was it?

"And you haven't looked at the Internet today?"

"No. You asked me not to." She paused for a moment. "I'd like to know what's going on though. Has anything new been put up?"

"Yeah." He sighed again. "There are two new pictures."

"Of you and Nicole again?"

"Yes. But they've really just re-hashed the same story from yesterday, except they've added a date for the birth of this supposed baby, which is in May, evidently."

"Mark," she said tentatively. "I've been thinking. Why don't we go public with our relationship?"

"Are you kidding?" He raised his voice. Was he angry?

"No…" Why would she be kidding? "It would refute the stories in the press and you wouldn't have to keep hiding away anymore—"

"Christ, Emma…" he interrupted. "Don't I have enough to think about at the moment?" That hurt. Why wouldn't he want people to know about them? And surely it would help, wouldn't it?

"What's wrong?" she asked, feeling afraid of his response.

He huffed out a breath. "There's no way we can go public with all of this going on. How the hell could I keep you safe from them when you're up there and I'm down here?"

Oh… He was only concerned for her. She felt guilty now for doubting him.

"I'm sorry," she said. "I didn't think about it like that."

"I'm not gonna let them get to you Emma. When we go public, it'll be when we're together." She thought they already were, but decided not to say anything. He was obviously stressed.

"How are you getting on with contacting Nicole?" She changed the subject.

"Becky's managed to track down her number. I've called her about a dozen times, I guess… and I've sent her a few messages too. She hasn't replied though."

"Well, maybe she's gone away for the holidays. Or she's just not got her phone with her."

"She never went anywhere without her phone, and she never turned the damn thing off, either. I'll just have to keep trying."

Emma really didn't like the idea of him contacting Nicole, but she knew it was pointless bringing that up again, especially with the mood Mark was in today.

"I still don't really understand why she'd be doing this," Emma said instead.

"Neither do I. But I can't see who else it can be."

"How… I mean why did you break up with her?" she asked.

"She'd become too demanding, too possessive."

"Oh? In what way?"

"She kept wanting me to spend more and more time away from home, away from Sarah. It was like she was jealous of my relationship with her, which was ridiculous. It wasn't that long after the accident and Sarah wasn't all that well still; she was just settling back into high school. It was a tough time for her. Nicole wasn't being very understanding about everything, so I ended it. But then it was never that serious for me anyway."

Emma felt a surge of empathy for Nicole. "Was it serious for her though?" she asked.

"I've got no idea. She never said she loved me, or anything like that. To be honest, Emma, I don't really care. I just want all this to stop, which means I need to get hold of her."

"And if it's not her?"

"It has to be. There's no-one else. It can't be the waiter, can it? The pictures were taken at more than one place. No, it's got to be her." He sounded really frustrated.

"Can I say something?" she asked.

"Sure."

"I mean, can I say something without you biting my head off?"

"Of course. I'm not gonna bite your head off, Emma."

"Really? Because, if I'm being honest, you're starting to sound like you did in that week before Thanksgiving. That's what I wanted to say. You're being distant, remote and moody again. I don't like it. It scares me…" She stopped speaking and waited. A long silence followed. "Are you still there?" she asked.

"Yeah."

"I shouldn't have said anything."

"No," he said quickly. "No, you're right. I'm being grouchy, I know I am. I'm just so tired, that's all. I know I'm not being myself, but it's got nothing to do with you, honestly."

"It's got everything to do with me, Mark."

"What I mean is, it's not your fault."

"What you mean is, the list has gotten even longer, right?"

Again there was a long silence. "Yeah, I guess."

"It's okay." It wasn't, but telling him that wasn't going to help.

"No, it's not. I want to be with you Emma. I want to be on your couch, with you curled up in my arms."

"Hmm… that sounds good."

"I miss you so much."

"I miss you too."

"It's only four days until you come down here," he said. "I know there'll be interruptions, and work's gonna get in the way a bit, but I'll make the time to be with you, I promise."

"I know."

"And I'll stop being such a grump… and maybe, if we're really lucky, some Hollywood A-lister can do something scandalous with a hooker in the next couple of days and that'll wipe me off the headlines, and I can get at least part of my life back on track."

"Fingers crossed." She smiled, feeling just a little more hopeful.

Maddie threw herself into Emma's arms and hugged her, then leant back and, with her right hand, made brushing motions in little circles up her chest a couple of times, then she made the same hand into a 'C' shape and swept it around in front of her.

Emma put Maddie down on the floor and returned the sign, saying, "Happy Christmas," at the same time. Then she looked up at Jake and Cassie who were standing watching their daughter.

"Can I take it someone's a little excited about the holidays?" she asked.

"Oh, just a little," Jake replied. "I don't think we'll be getting much sleep at all on Christmas Eve."

Cassie came over and hugged Emma. "You okay?" she asked, looking into Emma's eyes.

"I'm better than I was," she replied.

Cassie looked around the coffee shop. "It's quiet in here," she said. "We could talk, if you want?"

Emma nodded. "You know... I'd really like that." She could already feel tears forming behind her eyes.

Jake stepped forward. "How about if I take Maddie to the store and we'll get in some supplies and go back to the beach house." He looked at Cassie. "Call me when you're done and I'll come get you."

She leant up and kissed him. "Thank you," she said.

"Anytime." He looked at Emma. "Are you really okay?" he asked.

She found she couldn't reply, but she nodded her head.

He stared at her for a moment, then crouched down in front of Maddie. He raised both his hands to shoulder level, touching his fingers to his thumbs and then shook his hands back and forth, twisting them at the wrist. "Come to the store?" he said.

Maddie nodded her head and clasped his hand in hers. He stood and turned to Cassie.

"She's only being so agreeable because she knows she'll get candy." They started walking toward the door.

"Not too much, Jake."

"Yeah, I know. She'll be bouncing off the walls."

"Yeah... and I'll make you catch her." Cassie smiled as he got to the door.

"Jake!" Emma called after him.

"Yeah?" He stopped and turned back. She went across to him.

"You saw Mark yesterday, didn't you?"

"Yes," he replied. "I drove up to Manchester to look at his hotel."

"And?"

"The place is gonna need rebuilding..."

"No," Emma smiled at him. "I meant how's Mark?"

"Oh... He's tired, stressed, feeling the strain." He moved closer to her. "And he's missing you."

Emma felt herself blush.

"He said that?"

"Yeah… but he didn't need to."

Maddie pulled on Jake's hand. "You'd better get going," Emma told him.

"Don't worry about him, Em. He's fine."

"Thanks, Jake." She turned back to Cassie as the door closed behind them.

"He's good with her, isn't he?" Emma said to her friend.

"He still spoils her, but I guess that's to be expected. They've got a lot of time to make up for. He's bought her so much for Christmas, it's ridiculous."

"Well, I guess it's like her birthday. It's the first one for him."

"Yeah, I know. I'm just gonna make sure it's him that has to get up at four am on Christmas Day, when she's so wired she can't wait to see if Santa's been… and I'm gonna stay in bed."

"Of course you are." Emma didn't believe a word of that. She knew Cassie was loving them being a family.

"Shall we sit and talk?" Cassie suggested.

"Yeah. I'll get Josh to make us a coffee." Emma went and asked him for two lattes and led Cassie over to a table on the far side of the shop, away from the counter and the only other couple in the place, who were concentrating on each other and unlikely to listen in anyway.

They waited until Josh had brought them over their coffees and, once he'd gone, Cassie spoke first:

"I wanted to call as soon as I saw the stories, but I wasn't sure what to say."

"They're not true." Emma felt the need to defend Mark.

"I know. I know he wouldn't cheat on you for one thing, but when do the tabloids ever print anything that's true?" Emma felt Cassie scrutinizing her. "Doesn't mean it didn't hurt to read it though, right?"

"Yeah, it hurt." Emma took a breath. "The timing sucked, what with the fire and everything."

"Were you due to see him last weekend?"

"Yes. He was coming here on Friday, but he couldn't because he had to go to Manchester. Then the first story broke on Saturday night, but

227

the second one was even worse, really, because that was when I found out I wasn't pregnant—"

"I'm sorry… Did you say 'pregnant'?"

Emma stopped. "Yes, but I probably shouldn't have said that bit."

"Like hell you shouldn't. You thought you were pregnant? Are you late?"

"I was. My period started earlier today. But I thought I might be, so I took a test yesterday morning, and while I was waiting for the result, I read the second article… the one that said Mark and his mystery woman were expecting a baby and getting married. The test was negative. I was so disappointed…"

"You were? You wanted to be pregnant?"

"Yeah. It turns out we both did. It wouldn't have been planned, or intentional, but when we realized it was a possibility, we both started to want it."

"I'm sorry, Em."

"The timing was just really bad. Reading the article about Mark, and his supposed baby, and then getting the negative result, I realized I couldn't handle any more of it… So, I broke up with Mark."

"Oh, Em…"

"It's okay. He called me, and we're back together."

"But?"

"But… It's just so awful, Cassie. He's in Boston; I'm here. I feel like there's a million miles between us sometimes."

"He should be here with you."

"He's busy. There's the fire to deal with, and the press were camped outside his house, so he had to go back there, because Sarah couldn't handle it." She found her voice had slipped into a slightly mocking tone as she said the last few words.

"Oh."

Emma looked up into Cassie's eyes and knew her friend understood. She tried to sit up straight and square her shoulders. "Still," she said, "it's only a couple more days until I go there for the holidays."

"It'll be easier when you can see him," Cassie acknowledged.

"It'd be easier if they'd stop printing all this crap about Mark," Emma added.

"As long as you know it's crap."

"Yeah. I don't look at it any more. Mark told me not to."

"It would be good to know who's behind it," Cassie said. "The press must be getting their information from somewhere. They can't be making up all of it."

"The woman in the pictures is an ex-girlfriend of Mark's," Emma admitted.

"Oh? I didn't know that."

"Yeah. They dated about three years ago, for a few weeks."

"So they're real pictures?"

"They're real. Mark remembers them being taken. He thinks the ex-girlfriend – Nicole – is behind it all."

"Really?" Cassie seemed surprised. "Does that add up?"

Emma shrugged. "I don't know. But he can't think of anyone else…"

"Why would she do it?" Cassie asked.

"Mark broke off the relationship. He thinks she's looking for revenge."

"After three years? Why wait?"

"I wondered that. She saw Sarah a couple of weeks ago in Boston, and said she wanted to meet up with Mark. Sarah implied she wanted to get back together with him…" Emma's voice faded.

"Sounds a bit far-fetched to me. I mean, if she really wanted to meet up with Mark, why not just go to his office? Or his house? I know he's reclusive, but he's not impossible to get hold of. And surely, she'd realize that exposing him, and pissing him off like this isn't likely to make him want her back… *If* that's what she's looking for."

"I agree with everything you're saying. The problem is, Mark can't think of anyone else. There was a waiter at one of the restaurants, who took some pictures, but it can't be him, because he wasn't at the other places."

"Who was?" Emma looked at Cassie.

"What do you mean?"

"Was there anyone apart from this Nicole – and Mark – who was present at all the places where the photographs were taken?" she asked.

"Only Sarah…"

Cassie stared at her. "Sarah," she repeated slowly.

"She wouldn't," Emma said.

"Wouldn't she? You've told me already how difficult she is…"

"Yeah, but this is hurting Mark. She wouldn't do that to him. And I don't think she'd know how to manipulate the press like this. She's only a kid."

"She's nineteen, Em. She's not a kid. She's a young woman, who's jealously protective of her relationship with her brother, and who sees you as a threat to that."

Emma thought about what Cassie was saying. Parts of it made perfect sense. Sarah didn't like her, that much was obvious, and Mark had told her she'd been at all the places where the pictures were taken… but surely she wouldn't do this? She wouldn't expose Mark to the press like this – not even to hurt Emma.

"You need to speak to him, Em," Cassie said.

Emma looked up at her.

"How can I?" She knew, without even thinking about it, that Mark would take Sarah's side.

"I don't know, but you're going to have to."

"You really think it could be her?"

Cassie nodded. "Yeah, I do." She stared at Emma. "And if you're being honest with yourself, so do you."

Mark

Mark sat in his study at home, waiting for the call to connect to Emma.

He'd worked from home for the day, because Sarah was too scared to let him leave the house. Maggie had tried to reason that she was being silly, and that Mark had responsibilities, but Mark had seen the look in Sarah's eyes and he couldn't leave her.

"Hi." Emma picked up on the fourth ring.

"Hello. Are you okay?" There was something about her voice that made him nervous.

"No."

He quickly tapped his own name into a search engine on his laptop and checked the latest news reports, but nothing had been updated since he'd last looked. It couldn't be that then.

"What's wrong?" he asked her. She didn't reply. "Emma, you're scaring me. Tell me what's wrong."

"I don't even know where to start," she said.

He sat forward. "Okay, now you're really scaring me. Just tell me."

"I've been thinking... well, thinking and talking things over with Cassie."

"Right." He'd had a text message from Jake earlier in the afternoon to say he'd seen Emma at the coffee shop, she seemed okay, maybe a bit quiet, and was going to have a talk with Cassie. He'd felt relieved at the time, knowing Emma had her friend to talk to... Now he wasn't feeling so sure.

"We were talking through what's been going on... the stories on the Internet, the photographs and who might have taken them."

"Yeah..."

"And we wondered..." Her voice faded.

"Tell me, Emma."

"We wondered if it could be Sarah." She blurted out the words, although he felt like asking her to repeat them. Had she really just accused his sister?

He took a deep breath and tried to stay calm.

"Why? Why would Sarah do this?" he asked.

"She hates me," Emma said, although her statement sounded more like a question. "And she was there at all the places the pictures were taken. You've already told me that."

"She hates you?" he repeated, ignoring the second part of her answer.

"Yes."

"That's bullshit, Emma."

"No it's not."

"She likes you. She's told me she likes you."

"She's horrible to me, Mark."

"When has she ever been horrible to you?" He could feel his anger building, but fought it down.

"All the damn time. Whenever you're not in the room, she makes snide comments. She's careful not to let you hear them, but they're there, Mark."

"Sometimes she says things that are a bit… I don't know… a bit juvenile, I guess. You shouldn't be so sensitive. You're overreacting, Emma."

"I'm not."

"Yeah, you are. She's a kid. You're twenty-six years old. You're the grown-up here. Well, I thought you were."

"And what exactly does that mean?" He heard the anger in her voice now.

"It means you're the one behaving like a child right now. I don't know where you got this dumb idea from – Cassie, I'm guessing – but Sarah wouldn't hurt me like that. She's just not capable of it. I know her and I know she couldn't do it. She wouldn't know how… Whatever you think about her, she's just not that mean."

He heard Emma suck in a deep breath. "She's not a kid, Mark. She's nineteen years old. She's a young woman. And has it occurred to you that she's scared?"

"Yeah, it has. She's damn scared right now. She's scared because the house was surrounded by reporters, and I wasn't here. Do you actually think she'd bring that down on herself? She knows what it was like after the accident, Emma. She's not gonna put either of us through that again."

"Maybe she didn't realize it would get this bad."

"Or maybe she didn't do it." He breathed deeply, trying to calm down. He knew he was letting his tiredness and anger get the better of him and he didn't want to fight with Emma, even if she was being unreasonable and irrational.

There was a moment's silence. "I wasn't meaning that she was scared about the situation, I meant that she's scared of losing you," Emma said quietly.

What was she talking about now? "Losing me? When's she gonna lose me?"

"Well, maybe she thinks us getting together means she'll see less of you? You can't be with both of us, can you?"

"Are you asking me to choose between you?"

"No, of course I'm not! But I think Sarah might be."

"That's ridiculous."

"Is it?"

"Yeah. I explained to her about you; that I'd be spending my spare time with you. She was fine about it."

"Are you sure about that? You don't think it's odd that she's tried to keep us apart so much?"

"She hasn't, Emma." God, this had to be the most exasperating conversation ever. Why was Emma so determined to blame Sarah for everything?

"Yes, she has. There was her exhibition, then she was ill, and then that shopping trip you didn't need to go on… and when I'm at your place, she's always interrupting us."

"For Christ's sake," he exploded. "I'd promised her I'd go to the exhibition. What did you want me to do, go back on my word to her? She couldn't help being ill, it happens sometimes with her. I explained that to you. And the shopping trip was just a misunderstanding. Jeez, Emma… Have you heard yourself? You're accusing Sarah of being jealous of us, but it sounds like you're envious of my relationship with her…" He fell silent, remembering a conversation he'd had when he broke up with Nicole. This felt alarmingly similar. Except he wasn't breaking up with Emma, and he'd never loved Nicole, or cared about her that much. Not like he did about Emma.

"I'm not, Mark." Emma's voice was chillingly quiet. "I understand that you love your sister."

"Really? Is that why you're accusing her of this?"

"I'm not accusing her. I'm asking you to consider it as a possibility and maybe look into it."

"No, Emma. I don't need to, because I know Sarah isn't responsible for this."

Again, there was a long sigh. "Is there…? I mean… can you drive up here?"

That threw him, and he took a moment before replying. "When?"

"Now. I know it's gone seven, but you'd be here by not long after ten. You could stay over. We could talk things through. I hate the fact that we do everything over the phone. I need to talk to you face-to-face."

"I can't. You know I can't. Not at the moment."

"Why?"

"Because Sarah's still real scared; because I've got a business to run; because I've got a hotel that just burned down and now needs rebuilding… Do I need to go on?"

"No, I guess not," she whispered. "I'm at the bottom of the list – again."

He didn't have an answer to that.

"You're coming down in a couple of days, Emma." He said more softly. He knew he'd been harsh with her. But just because he was angry with her, didn't mean loved her any less. "We can spend some time together then. I'm sure whatever it is, it can wait."

"No, it can't. I can't."

What the fuck? "What does that mean?"

"It means I need you now, Mark. I'm scared too. I've never had a boyfriend before, let alone one like you, whose name hits the tabloids and all hell breaks loose, turning my life upside down; I've never thought I might be pregnant before; I've never had to deal with anything like this. I just need you here to hold me and kiss me, and tell me you can fix it, and it'll all be alright. Is that really too much to ask?"

It wasn't. He knew it wasn't. But, as much as he loved her, he couldn't get around the fact that she'd just accused Sarah of being behind the nightmare their lives had become, with no evidence, other than her obvious and illogical dislike of his sister.

"I can't. I'm sorry."

"Why not?"

"I've already explained."

"Because Sarah needs you?" That sounded a little sarcastic to Mark and he felt the irritation rise again.

"Amongst other things, yes," he barked.

"*I* need you, Mark. You promised to protect me." He couldn't deny that, but it didn't alter how he felt.

"I know, but I have to protect Sarah too. She's had it hard for the last four years, Emma. She lost a lot when our parents died. I'm all she's got."

"I understand that." He heard the emotion building in her voice. "But what if she's the one who's doing this to you?"

"She isn't."

"Why won't you even consider it? Maybe she needs help of some kind. Why won't you just look into it?"

"Because I know it's not her. She wouldn't do this."

He heard her sigh. "You're not gonna come, are you? You're not gonna put me at the top of the list…"

What was it with Emma and her fucking list? Why was she being so unreasonable? Couldn't she see it was impossible for him to leave right now? After Sarah's reaction to the idea of him going to work for the day, he didn't want to think what she'd do if he suddenly announced he was driving up to Somers Cove for the night.

The silence stretched.

"Fine… let's just forget it then, Mark," she said eventually. *What?* His breath caught in his throat and his skin prickled.

"What do you mean?" he whispered.

"If you can't do this one thing for me, there's really no point…"

"No point?" Was she breaking up with him? His anger evaporated in an instant and was replaced by overwhelming panic that gripped his whole body.

"Yes, no point."

"Emma? Don't do this. Don't make this into something it isn't."

"What is it then, Mark?"

"It's a disagreement, that's all. We—"

"You really think that's all this is?" she interrupted. "A disagreement?"

"Yes. Why? What is it to you?" He felt cold and scared, right to the pit of his stomach.

"It's a lot more than a disagreement. You won't even think about what I've said. You're dismissing me and everything I'm saying about your sister. But I think I could ignore that. I really do. What I can't ignore… what I can't forgive, is that you won't put me first, just this once. I've been on my own throughout all of this… all those stories, the pictures, the things they said about you, the pregnancy test, all of it. I thought you needed to stay in Manchester to work, but then you told me you went home early – for Sarah. You knew how hard it was for me; I told you I needed you, I told you how difficult it was for me, but you didn't come back here because *I* was hurting, did you?" He heard the crack in her voice which brought a lump to his throat. "And I *was* hurting," she continued, before he could speak, "so much. And now, you still won't come up here, even though I've asked you – again – and told you how much I need you. So, yes, it's a lot more than a damn disagreement. I'm sick of coming second, or third, or wherever the hell you decide to put me on your list. If you can't, or won't do this for me, then we're through."

"You really want me to choose between you and Sarah?" That's what she was asking. She was really going to put him in that position?

"No."

"That's what you're saying, Emma." He ran his fingers through his hair, unable to believe this was happening.

"You can take it that way, if you want. But that's *not* what I'm saying. The bottom line is, I'm just asking for you to spend one night here with me, that's all… just one night, Mark."

"And in doing that, you're also asking me to turn my back on Sarah when *she* needs me. Dress it up however you like, that's asking me to choose."

"Okay then, choose!" she yelled.

"I can't."

There was a brief pause. "You just did." He heard the tears behind her voice, and then a sob as the connection between them ended…

Chapter Sixteen

Emma

It was over.

He wouldn't put her first, not even when she'd said how much she needed him and asked him for just one night. He'd still put Sarah above her, and that was what hurt the most. Even if Sarah wasn't responsible for all the lies being told about Mark, he'd still put her first, and he always would. She knew that now.

She clambered off the bed, where she'd been sitting to take the call, and wandered through the apartment. It was dark; she hadn't gotten around to putting the lights on, and now she didn't really want to. She didn't want to see the reality of her empty life. She'd been lonely and alone before… she remembered it well. But even back then, she hadn't felt this sense of rejection and abandonment. He'd told her he loved her; he'd made her believe in him… and yet she still wasn't enough. When it came down to it, she still wasn't enough.

Her phone was still in her hand. Should she call him back? Should she beg him to forgive her, ask him to try again? What would be the point? He'd still always find something, or someone, who needed his attention more than she did.

She felt her legs give way and crumpled to the floor by the breakfast bar.

She couldn't do this by herself. She knew she couldn't. She needed help.

She called up Cassie's details on her phone, through the blur of her tears, and waited while it rang… once, then twice.

"Hi, Emma."

"Hi."

"Oh, God. What's wrong?"

"Everything."

"Emma? Tell me what's happened?"

"Mark and I broke up. For good this time."

"You asked him about Sarah?"

"Yeah…"

"And?"

"And he wouldn't hear a word against her. I asked him to come and see me tonight. He said no, because Sarah needed him. He put her first, Cassie. Again."

Cassie didn't reply. And then the realization dawned on Emma.

"I—I know this is difficult for you," she said, gulping down her tears.

"For me?" Cassie sounded surprised.

"Yeah. Mark and Jake are friends. And Mark's gonna be Jake's boss soon. You're bound to feel loyal to him, I guess. Your futures depend on him… And you've got Maddie to think about." Oh God… Was she going to lose Cassie and Jake as well? She curled in on herself, pulling her legs up and wrapping her free arm around them, like she was protecting herself from the blast of a storm.

"Emma. You're my oldest friend, apart from Jake. My loyalty lies with you. Look, Jake's out right now, but the minute he gets back, I'll come over and see you. Maddie's in bed already, and I can't leave her…"

"No. I'm fine," Emma lied. "I just need to think. I'll be okay."

"Emma?"

"Please, Cassie. I don't want to see anyone. I just wanna be by myself…" She ended the call and dropped her phone on the floor. It felt like she was being stretched to breaking point, like she was a piece of elastic, just about to snap in two… for good.

She closed her eyes, lay flat on her back and tried to breathe, to suck some air into her lungs and gain some peace, to escape the whirlwind of loss that was sweeping over her. She fought hard to relax each part of her body, talking herself through it as she struggled against the tempest of emotions. "Feet," she whispered. "Legs… arms… back… shoulders… neck." She lay there on the floor, trying to become weightless, to become nothing. It should have been easy. She *was* nothing.

He didn't want her. Well, not enough, anyway. He was the only man she'd ever loved; the only man she was ever going to love… and he didn't want her. She stuttered in a breath. The peace she needed wasn't there. It was out of reach, in the distance, beyond her grasp.

She curled up again covering her face with her hands, and let the tears roll over her, sobbing until she thought she had nothing left, but then another memory or thought of Mark would enter her head, and a new wave of tears would overwhelm her.

She was vaguely aware of the sound of a key turning in the front door, and then of footsteps pounding on the stairs.

"Emma?" It was Nick's voice. He was kneeling beside her in an instant. "Em?" There was a hint of desperation in his voice. "Em, look at me."

She didn't want to uncurl herself and face reality.

"Emma. Please." She felt his hands on her wrists, pulling them away, and she stiffened against him. "Don't fight me," he said, pulling harder. She wasn't strong enough and he forced her hands down. "Fuck," he whispered as she opened her eyes. He looked so scared. "Please, Em," he said, "please tell me you haven't taken anything."

She shook her head.

"Promise?"

"Promise," she murmured, and he heaved out a sigh of relief, then pulled her up into his arms and got to his feet, carrying her over to the couch.

"Why are you here?" she asked, her voice a hoarse whisper.

"Cassie called me," he explained. "She said you and Mark split up. She was worried about you… She said Jake's out and Maddie's in bed already, or she'd have come herself, but you told her you didn't want to see anyone…" His voice wavered and he stared down at her, taking her hands in his. "Thank God I still have a key to this place." Emma had given him one when he'd stayed with her before. "I doubt you'd have let me in if I'd just knocked…"

She shook her head. "No, probably not."

He smiled, just lightly. "In which case, I'd have been paying for another new front door, Em. You know I'd have broken it down again, don't you?"

"Yeah, I know."

He sighed. "Well, I'm here now," he said. "I'm not going anywhere, other than to get us both a coffee. And then you're gonna tell me what that dumb son-of-a-bitch has done this time…"

An hour later, Emma was still lying on the couch, Nick was sitting beside her on the floor. They'd both drunk two coffees each and Emma had told him everything… all of it. He'd raised an eyebrow when she'd told him about the pregnancy test, but other than that, he hadn't reacted at all.

When she'd finished, he looked at her.

"And it's really over?" he asked.

She nodded and he shrugged.

"What?" she asked.

"I still think you'd take him back."

"Maybe I would. I love him, Nick. But he won't be coming back. Not this time. I accused his precious sister."

"It sounds like you had good reason. Based on what you've told me, she's the perfect candidate. I'd suspect her in your shoes, and I'm a lawyer."

"Well, Mark doesn't agree." She started to sob again and Nick moved closer, hugging her. "I wanted one goddamn night, Nick, that's all. He'd got the police involved to get rid of the reporters; they weren't a threat to Sarah anymore. Why couldn't he just come up here and talk it through with me?"

"I don't know."

"Well, I do." She sniffed and pulled away from him. "I'm not enough. I'm not good enough. I wasn't then and I'm not now. He never loved me… well, not enough to make it work, anyway." She sobbed again.

He knelt up in front of her. "You can cut that out, right now," he said, sternly. "He's the one who's not good enough for you."

"You have to say that; you're my brother."

"I don't have to say anything, Em." He sat back on his heels. "Well, that's not strictly true. I have to say one thing…"

"What's that?" she asked.

"Can you find some sheets and a spare pillow?"

"Why?"

"Because I'm sleeping on your couch tonight."

"You don't have to, Nick."

He looked into her eyes. "Yeah, I think I do." He sighed. "I know you made me a promise, but right now I'm not sure I can trust you to keep it… which means I'm staying."

She gulped down her tears. "Thank you," she muttered.

And as he pulled her into his arms again, they both sighed out a breath of relief, because deep down, they both knew he was right.

Mark

He'd sat at his desk, paced the floor, tried to work, flicked through a dozen or more TV channels, paced a bit more… and spent two hours generally trying to avoid thinking.

It wasn't working, so he took a deep breath and sat down in the armchair by the window, staring out at the street.

Emma was his life. Whatever she thought, with her damn list, she was everything. The pain, the utter agony of not having her in his life was too much bear. How the hell was he supposed to live without her? That thought was like a physical wound… a raw, rasping gash in his soul.

And yet, however he looked at it, he couldn't forget her words. She'd broken up with him… over Sarah.

There was no getting away from it. Emma had been jealous and childish and hurtful. She'd forced him into a corner, with her words and accusations. It was his job to protect Sarah. She had no-one else in her life to look out for her. He had to keep her safe, even if it meant breaking his own heart to do it.

He took another deep breath.

Emma's accusations were beyond ludicrous and he couldn't help but wonder whether she'd realize that, once she'd calmed down and thought it through. He wondered if she'd call, or text, and maybe ask if they could talk. He was still feeling upset, and a little mad, but he'd talk, if she wanted to. He didn't want it to be over. That was the last thing he wanted. He wondered if maybe he should call her. What would he say though? Whatever he said, it would feel like a betrayal of Sarah. And that felt wrong, because he knew she was innocent of everything Emma was accusing her of. Sarah would never willingly or knowingly hurt him. She knew how he felt about Emma; he'd told her and she'd understood, he knew she had. She'd been pleased for him, for crying out loud. Not only that, she'd never risk bringing the press into their lives again. It was just like he'd said to Emma, Sarah remembered what it had been like before. She would never put either of them through that torture again. Why the hell couldn't Emma have some faith, and just believe in him?

And therein lay the answer. She didn't believe in him. She didn't trust him, that was for sure, not enough, anyway. Not enough to tell him her secret… The one that had given her that hurt, scared look in her eyes.

He wondered how her eyes looked right about now. Filled with tears, hurt, confusion, he imagined, just like his own. He shook his head and got up, swallowing the lump in his throat and running his fingers through his hair.

God, he loved her…

He dumped the block of cheese on the countertop and rummaged deeper into the refrigerator. He wasn't remotely hungry. He didn't really even know what he was doing.

"What are you looking for?" Maggie's voice made him jump.

"I don't know."

"Are you hungry?" she asked.

"No."

"Then leave the refrigerator alone." She came over, picked up the cheese, opened the door wider so she could reach in around him, and put it back on the shelf. "Sit down," she said. "I'll make you a coffee. You look like you need one."

He followed her instructions, like he had no free will of his own. Maybe he hadn't any more.

Maggie put ground coffee in the machine, filled it up with water, and switched it on, and then came and stood in front of him, the kitchen island separating them.

"Gonna tell me what's wrong now?" she asked.

"Emma."

"What about her?"

"We broke up."

He looked up in time to see Maggie let out a sigh and close her eyes, just for a moment. "Well, that's a damn shame," she said. "I really liked her."

"Yeah, so did I."

"Oh, you did a helluva lot more than *like* her."

He looked at her. "Yeah."

"So, what did you do wrong?"

"What the hell makes you think I did anything wrong?" This wasn't his fault.

"Just the fact that she loved you. Probably still does. Maybe always will. I don't see her breaking up with you for no reason. So, what did you do wrong?"

"I didn't do anything wrong."

"Oh, really?"

"Yeah… really."

"So, you're telling me it was *her* fault."

"Yes."

Maggie shrugged. "Okay then, what did *she* do wrong?"

"She accused Sarah of being behind these stories in the press, and then laid into her about being… well, basically a bitch to her behind my back. It was pretty ugly."

He noticed an odd expression cross Maggie's face. "And that's why you broke up?"

"Well, yeah… kind of. I mean, she wanted me to go up there for the night and I said no."

"Why?"

"Because Sarah needs me here, of course."

"Sarah's got me, and Anthony's still here. Nothing's gonna happen to her. To be honest, I was surprised you came back here from Vermont. I half expected you to go to Emma's first."

"Why? You called me, Maggie. You told me Sarah had gone into a meltdown about the reporters outside. Of course I was gonna come back here."

"I called you to let you know about your sister, and about what was going on. I did *not* tell you to come rushing back here. *You* decided to do that, Mark, so don't go blaming me. And I did nothing to stop you from going to see Emma first. It must've been really hard on her, reading all that crap about you in the news."

"Yeah, it was" He softened a little, remembering Emma's tears, and how she'd told him earlier how hurt she'd been… and how he'd done nothing. "Especially with the pregnancy and—" he whispered. He hadn't meant to say that out loud. He looked up at Maggie.

"She's pregnant?"

"No. But we thought she might be."

"At the same time as all this was happening?" Maggie waved her hand toward the front of the house, where the reporters had been camped out.

Mark nodded.

"And you still came back here?" She leant across the kitchen island, glaring at him. "What's wrong with you?"

He'd never seen Maggie this angry before. "She wasn't pregnant, Maggie."

"And that makes it okay that you just left her up there by herself, does it?"

"No," he murmured. "But what else could I do? I had the situation in Manchester to deal with. Emma understood that."

"I'm sure she did. She's a very understanding young woman. But how did she feel… about not being pregnant, if you don't mind me asking?" Maggie was staring at him still.

He closed his eyes. "Disappointed… like me." When he opened his eyes again, the anger had left Maggie's face. "She took a test," he told her. "We both wanted it to be positive. It wasn't."

"I'm sorry." Her voice was quiet now, more understanding. "But don't you see? She did that on her own, Mark. And at the same time, those vultures were printing all that garbage about you. Can you even begin to imagine how that felt for her?"

"Yes. She broke up with me then as well. She said she couldn't handle it."

"I'm not surprised. The poor thing. She's not used to how you live your life. She's not used to any of this. She needed you and you weren't there for her – again."

"How could I be? I was up in Manchester, dealing with the fire."

Maggie closed her eyes and huffed out a breath. "Sounds to me like there's always a reason not to be with Emma."

"That's not fair, Maggie. It's not true either."

"Isn't it? Think about it. Try real hard to think about how it must feel to her. Because it sounds to me like you had a list of priorities, and you just expected Emma to put up with accepting her place – wherever you decided that was at any given moment."

His mouth dropped open. Emma had said the same thing. "What is it with you women and your damn lists?"

"Oh. Did Emma tell you she felt like she was on a list too then?"

"Yes." He felt a little embarrassed that Maggie had seen through him so easily.

She stared at him, but didn't say a word.

"I didn't mean for it to feel like that," he said eventually.

"Well, I'm sure that'll help her feel a lot better… one day." Her sarcasm wasn't lost on him.

"Christ, Maggie. I feel like shit too, you know."

"She needed you, Mark."

"Maybe she did, but not as much as Sarah does."

"You honestly believe that? You honestly think Emma didn't need you more?" She looked at him, pityingly, like he'd lost the use of his brain. "You didn't really know her at all, did you?" She didn't wait for him to answer. "I was constantly amazed by how kind and patient Emma was."

"With me?"

"No. With Sarah. Some of the things she's been doing over the last few weeks… they made me want to give that sister of yours a good slap."

Mark suddenly felt really sick.

"Such as?" he asked slowly.

"Such as playing you and Emma off against each other," Maggie explained. "Take the anniversary of your parents' death. You were right… you've never done anything before on that day, but because Emma was here, Sarah decided to make a big thing of it, and she made Emma feel so damn awkward that she felt she had to exclude herself from what you were doing."

"She did that to help me out, to avoid me having to…" he sighed, "to choose between them." He let his head fall into his hands.

"Yeah, because Sarah had put you in the position of *having* to choose in the first place. It was Emma who got you out of it."

He remembered now. She had. She didn't want him to feel like he had to make that choice. It wasn't Emma who'd made him choose; it was Sarah. His stomach churned, feeling heavier.

"And then Anthony told me Sarah had been making snide comments to Emma."

"What kind of comments?"

"Oh, just spiteful little things, like telling her she was no different to everyone else in your life, pointing out that a lot of people are just interested in you for your money… things like that. Anthony said Emma was close to tears, which isn't surprising, really."

"When was this?" Mark asked.

Maggie thought for a moment. "It was that same day. The weekend after Thanksgiving, when you were gonna go home with her. Anthony said he'd just gone into the hall to pick up Emma's bag and he overheard what they were saying."

"Emma never mentioned it to me."

"She wouldn't. And do you remember Sarah saying she had a headache that night?"

Mark nodded slowly.

"Well, if she had a headache, I'm Julia Roberts. Once you'd gone, she called up her friend, Macy and they talked for over an hour, and then she went upstairs and had her music blasting so loud, I had to go up and hammer on her door to get her to turn it down."

"Then why did she say she had a headache?"

"To get you to stay here, of course. Why can't you see it?"

"See what?"

"She doesn't want to lose you."

He felt like a lead weight had hit his stomach. "Emma said exactly that," he whispered.

"Then maybe you should've damn well listened to her, before you broke her heart."

"I broke *her* heart?"

"Yes." Maggie nodded.

"She broke up with *me*, Maggie."

She turned toward the coffee machine. "You really believe that?"

"Yes. She told me it was over. She was the one doing the breaking, not me."

Maggie turned back. "Maybe because you gave her no choice." She came back to him, walked around the island unit and stood right in front of him. "Your sister did so many things to make Emma feel out of place here, from her cruel remarks to wearing those expensive designer outfits…"

"What was wrong with her wearing nice clothes?"

"Mark," she said, still looking at him like he was stupid, "Sarah never wears anything like that around the house normally. She wanted to remind Emma that you're different to her; that you've got money, and she doesn't."

"Sarah wouldn't do that."

Maggie sighed loudly. "Keep kidding yourself if it makes you feel better. But you've always been blind when it comes to Sarah. Truth of the matter is, Emma took a lot from her, and you did nothing to protect her. Nothing. And whatever you think, Emma needed your protection more than Sarah ever will. She's a lovely girl, but she's… she's vulnerable, Mark."

He suddenly felt a chill down his spine. "What do you mean?"

"Exactly what I'm saying. Remember… I was a nurse before I came here. I've seen people like Emma many times. Behind that façade, I don't think she's anything like as strong as she'd have people believe."

The words were too familiar not to ring bells. "Jake said that too."

"And he's known her some time?"

"All his life."

"Then maybe you should've paid more attention to him while you had the chance."

"The thing is, Maggie, whatever else Sarah may or may not have done, I know she wouldn't do this thing with the press. She wouldn't expose me – or herself – to them like this."

"Maybe not. But she did everything else Emma tried to tell you about. And you weren't even prepared to go there and comfort her… to give her one night of your time. How do you think that made her feel?"

He put his head in his hands. He knew exactly how it would've made her feel. She'd already told him, more than once. It would have made her feel like she wasn't good enough, like she wasn't important enough, like she was right at the bottom of his list. She'd only asked for one night. She'd told him she was scared and she needed him, and he'd done nothing. She just wanted him to be there for her, to listen, to hold her, and make her feel like she mattered, to do what he'd promised and fix them. To put them back together and make it right again. And after everything she'd been through on her own, he'd given her nothing. "Oh God…" he whispered.

"What's happening?" Sarah's voice broke into his thoughts.

"Nothing," Maggie replied, turning and fetching two cups from the cabinet.

"I'm not falling for that," Sarah said. "Mark?" She turned to him.

"Emma broke up with me," he told her, looking up.

"Oh no." She came over and put her arm around his shoulder. "I'm so sorry."

He glanced at Maggie and raised an eyebrow. Why couldn't everyone see? Sarah wasn't the person she was being painted. Maggie didn't respond.

"Thanks," he said to Sarah.

"Did she give you a reason?" Sarah asked.

"Yeah, but it's complicated." He didn't want to explain and have Sarah feeling guilty, or responsible in anyway. This wasn't her fault.

"Oh… Poor Mark. Are you okay?"

He looked at her. Emma was wrong about Sarah. She cared about him far too much to do anything to hurt him. "No," he said.

"And there's nothing you can do?"

"No. I really don't think there's any way back. Not this time." He knew the truth of that statement even as he said it. Emma had forgiven him countless times already. There were only so many times he could ask that of her.

And even if she could, how was he supposed to choose between her and Sarah?

Sarah's face fell. "I'm really sorry, Mark."

He put an arm around her and gave her a quick hug, then released her.

She sat next to him, settling quickly. "Can I have a hot chocolate, Maggie?" she asked, a smile forming on her lips.

Chapter Seventeen

Emma

"It's been a lovely day," Emma said to Cassie as she hugged her goodbye. She meant it too. She'd enjoyed herself, much to her own surprise.

As Christmases went, it had been a good one. Maddie had been as bright as a button; they'd walked on the beach; played games; drunk far too much; eaten even more, and she'd only thought about Mark maybe every other minute of the day.

"Are you sure you'll be okay walking home?" Cassie asked.

"We'll have to be," Nick replied. "We've all had too much to drink for any of us to drive. I'll walk down tomorrow and get the car, if that's okay."

"That's fine," Jake said as he gave Emma a hug. "Are you okay?" he whispered in her ear. She nodded, just once. "Seriously?" he added.

"Yes."

"Is that why Nick's staying with you?"

"Please don't, Jake," she murmured, and he pulled back, although she noticed the dark shadow across his eyes.

"I haven't spoken to him, in case you're wondering," Jake said.

"I wasn't," Emma lied. She'd been thinking that thought all day, but hadn't known how to ask.

"I'm due to see him in the second week of January to talk through the plan for the Manchester hotel, but other than that, well, I feel kinda awkward."

Emma put her hand on his arm. "But that's wrong," she said. "You'd normally call him, so call him. You're his friend."

"Yeah, and you're mine."

"I know. But I've got Cassie and Nick and you."

"And?"

"And he's got you, Jake. You're it. When it comes down to it, you're the only friend Mark's got. Please don't abandon him."

"I—I'm not. I'm just not sure what I'd say to him, because at the moment, I just wanna punch him."

"Well, don't. I won't thank you. In fact, I'll be damn mad at you. He probably needs a friend right now, Jake." She felt like she was going to cry. "I hate the idea of him being on his own. Please be there for him, Jake."

He took her hand from his arm and held it in his. "I will. Don't worry, Em."

She walked home side by side with Nick. It was a cold night, the stars were shining bright, and the moon lit their way down the lane.

"That was a kind thing you did back there," he said out of the blue.

"Sorry?"

"Asking Jake to look out for Mark. That was kind."

"I meant it. I don't like the idea of him being on his own."

"He's got his sister, Em."

"Hmm. Like I said, I don't like the idea of him being on his own."

"You really don't like her, do you?" Nick asked.

"I don't trust her."

"You don't like her."

"No. I think she's manipulative… bordering on evil."

"Wow. That's quite something, considering she's only nineteen."

"Yeah. I hate to think what she'll be capable of in a few years' time."

"Starting to think you're better off out of there?" he asked.

"No. I just wish Mark could see her for what she is."

"She's his sister. I'm not sure that's ever gonna happen."

She felt the truth of his words, like a nail in her coffin. Mark would always be blinded to Sarah's faults, no matter what they were. They walked on in silence.

"Are you planning on staying much longer?" she asked him as she unlocked the door.

He looked down at her. "Trying to get rid of me?" he mocked.

"No. I'm just asking. You do have a life, Nick."

She climbed the stairs ahead of him and switched on the light.

"It's been rumored," he replied. He sat down at the breakfast bar. "I'll leave when I'm completely convinced you're okay."

"I'm better than I was."

"I know." He caught her eye. "You're not there yet though. I'm not deaf, Emma."

"Sorry?"

"I can hear you crying at night."

"I can't help it. It was only a matter of days ago, I thought I had everything. I had Mark, and – while it wasn't perfect – we were so in love, or at least I thought we were. Hell, I even thought I might be pregnant with his child, and he told me wanted that too. He said he was disappointed when the test was negative. I—I thought we had a future together. I was looking forward to spending a few days with him, talking things out. He told me he loved me. I loved him. I had it all. And now I've got nothing…"

"You've got me. You've got Cassie and Jake."

"I know. But it's not the same."

He came around the breakfast bar and put his hands on her shoulders. "I know, Em. I really do. I know how much this hurts. I'm not criticizing you for crying. I'm just saying you're not ready for me to leave yet."

She rested her forehead on his chest. "No," she whispered. "No, I'm not."

"You need to find something to do," Nick suggested over breakfast the next morning.

"You don't think working twelve hours a day is enough?" She glanced up at him over the top of her coffee cup.

"You've still got too much time to think."

She couldn't deny it. All she did was think about Mark. If she wasn't wondering how he was and what he was doing, she was thinking about what they'd done together, remembering how he felt and his words, the sound of his voice, his breath on her skin, and then their last conversation…

"Well, I suppose I could… I could do something with the competition," she said, thinking out loud.

"What competition?"

"It was an idea Mark gave me." She paused, but Nick didn't react at all. "Do you remember, Mrs Adams told me I could start selling home-baked cakes and cookies in the shop?"

"Yeah. I remember you mentioning it."

"Well, Mark suggested I get the local housewives involved and that I run a competition to find the best bakers."

Nick nodded slowly. "Sounds like a good idea. Especially at this time of year, when the town's so quiet and there's nothing going on. It'll give everyone something to look forward to."

"Yes, it will."

"Well, why don't we start working on it at lunchtime."

"I already put together a poster."

"Okay… well, put it up in the coffee shop and see what happens."

By the time Nick came in at lunchtime, Emma had already had nine people come in asking for more details, and to register their names for the competition. There was a real buzz in the town; everyone was talking about it.

"It's gone so much better than I thought." Emma smiled at him.

He leant across the counter. "It's good to see you smile again," he said. "And I don't know why you're surprised. I heard Louisa Cooper mentioning the competition to Mary Westcombe outside the store. And you know what Mary's like. I imagine it was all around the town by nine am."

Emma nodded. "That explains a lot." She wiped down the counter quickly. "I've decided to hold the competition on the first Saturday after New Year, starting at noon, I think. I figure it's gonna take a while to get through the tastings, then we've got to make the decision and then the announcement as to who's gonna be supplying the shop… and then we need to wind down before we have to close."

"The first Saturday in January? That's quite soon."

"Well, I want to keep the excitement going. People seem really interested. I figure if I make it too far away, they'll get bored, and maybe forget about it."

"Hmm, maybe." He leant across and lowered his voice. "Can I be a judge?" he asked. "You know I've got really good taste in cake."

"No."

"Damn." He smiled. "Who's gonna judge then?"

"Me, obviously, with Patsy and Kathryn."

"How are you gonna compare though, being as everyone's gonna bake something different?"

"Because they're not. Everyone's gotta bake brownies, so we can judge them fairly. And then they can bake one other cake or cookie of their choice, so I can see how versatile they are."

"And you're gonna choose one person to supply the shop?"

"No, I think I'll end up choosing more than one. We need a lot of cakes; I doubt if one person could handle it."

"This is a really great idea, sis."

She looked down at the cloth, clasped in her hands. "I can't claim any credit. It was Mark's idea, not mine."

"Hey…" Nick took her hands in his. "He might have given you the idea, but you're the one making it work."

She smiled, just slightly and wished Mark could be there to see what she'd achieved.

Mark

Mark was glad when Christmas was over. He'd thought it had been bad four years ago, after his parents had died and he'd broken up with Emma the first time, but that was nothing compared to what he was going through now. He'd had no idea it was possible to miss someone as much as he was missing Emma, or to hurt like this. He felt as though a part of himself had been physically removed and, rather than the pain lessening with the passing of each day, he felt as though it was just getting progressively worse. He shut himself away in his bedroom a lot, and kept looking at the necklace he'd bought Emma for Christmas. He'd originally thought about taking it back to the store, but he couldn't bring himself to do it. If that was all he had left of her, he'd keep it.

It was New Year's Eve. Maggie had cooked a lovely meal and they'd all sat together. Mark had originally planned to visit Emma for New Year, so this wasn't what he'd had in mind at all.

"You need to cheer up," Sarah said to him. "You're never going to get over her if you just mope around."

Mark looked at her for a moment. Her eyes were filled with concern. "I'm not moping. I've been working."

"Well, you need to go out," Sarah replied. "You were never short of company before. I'm sure you can find someone to spend an evening with."

Mark shuddered at the thought. "I can't—" he muttered.

"Sarah!" Maggie protested, speaking at the same time.

"What?"

"You're being insensitive."

"Am I?" She looked surprised and shrugged her shoulders, getting down from the table and leaving the room.

"She doesn't mean it," Mark said, defending Sarah.

"Really?" Maggie got up and started to clear the dishes.

"Yeah, really. She just doesn't understand how this feels. She's never been in this position."

"And that excuses her saying things like that, does it? I've never broken my leg, but I can feel sympathetic toward someone who has."

Maggie carried the dishes to the kitchen sink and came back again. "How are you, really?" she asked.

He looked up at her. "I feel like my life has stopped," he replied. "And like it's never gonna start again."

"Can't you go and see Emma? Talk things through with her?" Maggie suggested, sitting down next to him.

"I've thought about it, every day. Well, every minute of every day."

"And?"

"And every time I think about it, I play out the scene in my head. I'd be asking her to forgive me… again. She's already forgiven me so many times, Maggie."

"Maybe she'd be willing to do it again. You won't know if you don't ask."

"I know. But even if she did, there would still be the problem of Sarah. Emma suspects Sarah of being behind the reports in the press. She clearly doesn't like her very much and I'd feel like I was being forced to choose between them. I know we'd just end up fighting again every time something came up. Every time Sarah wanted me to do something, I'd end up feeling guilty because of Emma and vice-versa."

"So you're just gonna give up? Because of Sarah?"

"No. If I'm giving up at all, it's because of Emma."

"You still think it's her fault?"

"Not entirely, no. I got a lot of things wrong… but she's wrong about this. She's wrong about Sarah. I know she is. And it would always come between us. Of course, it'd be easier if Nicole would reply to my damn messages."

"Why? So you could crow at Emma and prove you're right?"

"No. So I can find out why the hell Nicole chose to do it in the first place."

Maggie sighed. "I guess you should be grateful the stories have stopped."

"I am. Although I feel sorry for that Pittsburgh running back."

"Why? If he chooses to take three women to bed at the same time, *and* he's dumb enough to let them take pictures, he's only got himself to blame."

There was no doubt about it, the story had knocked Mark's headlines off the front pages and no-one was very interested in him anymore. He welcomed the peace, if nothing else.

Mark had decided against seeing in the New Year, and went to bed early, but found he couldn't sleep and, shortly before midnight, he put on some jeans and a t-shirt, and crept out the back of the house onto the decking, standing alone, oblivious to the cold, staring up at the star-filled sky.

"Happy New Year, baby," he whispered to the darkness. "I miss you." Everything blurred and he struggled to swallow down the lump in his throat, before he gave up, collapsed to his knees and choked out, "I really fucking miss you, Emma."

He didn't know how long he knelt there, but eventually he went back upstairs, grateful that no-one had seen him crying to himself in the moonlight.

The following day, Mark was sitting in his bedroom, looking at Emma's necklace, again when his phone beeped. Every time it had done that for the last ten days, he'd got his hopes up that it might be Emma, but having spent an hour or so out on the deck the previous night, crying quietly to himself, he really needed this to be her. He hoped that maybe she missed him too, that she might ask him to drive up there and see her, so they could talk and, despite everything he'd said to Maggie the previous evening, he knew that if she did, he wouldn't say no to her again. He still wasn't sure they could work it out, but he'd go see her, if she asked.

He held his breath, and checked the screen.

It was a message from Jake. He was disappointed, and relieved, and kinda scared at the same time. He hadn't heard from Jake since he'd split up with Emma and was worried that his friend was mad at him, and maybe that he'd even pull out of the job Mark had offered him. He opened the text message and read it:

— *Hi. Sorry I've been out of touch. Let me know how you are. J*

He smiled. It didn't sound like Jake was mad. He thought carefully about how to reply, knowing he needed to ask the question that had been plaguing him the most.

— *I feel like shit, but thanks for asking. Have you seen Emma? How is she? M*

Jake's reply took a few minutes to come through.

— *Sorry, I feel awkward answering questions about Em. But I know you're worried. Nick's staying with her. I'm here if you need to talk. J*

That reply worried Mark. Nick was staying with Emma? Why? That suggested things were bad, but he knew he couldn't ask any more of Jake, and he knew he probably didn't have the right to inquire about Emma anyway.

He slowly tapped out a response.

— *It's okay. I understand. Yeah, I'm worried. Thanks for being there. I appreciate it. M*

Jake's reply was much quicker this time.

— *Call me if you need me. Anytime. J*

Mark's screen blurred as he read the words. He needed Jake, but nowhere near as much as he needed Emma.

That first week of January slipped by and Mark reached Friday afternoon and found himself working from home and dreading the weekend. With the holidays over, he felt like the weekends held nothing for him now. There were no visits to Emma to look forward to and she wouldn't be coming to see him either. Those two days stretched before him like a dreary eternity. The only star on his horizon was a meeting with Jake that was scheduled for the following week, to discuss the hotel in Manchester. Maybe then he'd be able to find out why Nick was staying with Emma, because that thought was still bothering him.

His phone rang at just after four in the afternoon and he sat up straight at his desk.

It was Nicole's number.

"About fucking time," he muttered under his breath as he connected the call.

"Nicole," he said, trying to keep his voice calm.

"Mark?" Her voice hadn't changed at all, even though it had been more than three years since he'd last spoken to her. "You've been calling me?" she added.

"Yeah. I needed to talk to you about these press reports."

"What press reports?"

Seriously? She was gonna play dumb?

"You know what press reports, Nicole. The ones you've been feeding the tabloids."

"I've got no idea what you're talking about, Mark." She sounded genuinely surprised, but then he remembered how she'd always been able to turn on her charms whenever she wanted something from him. She'd been good at that.

"Are you for real?"

"If you mean am I telling the truth, then yes. What are these press reports about?"

"They're about us?"

"Us? What do you mean 'us'?"

She was good, he'd give her that. "Oh, come on, Nicole. Cut the crap. You know perfectly well what I mean."

"Mark. I really don't."

For the first time, he started to feel a little uncertain.

"Are you anywhere near a computer?" he asked her.

"Yes. Wait a moment… my laptop's in front of me," she replied. "What am I looking for?"

"Just Google my name," he told her.

"Okay, hold on."

He waited, listening while she tapped on the keyboard.

"What the hell is this, Mark?" she said suddenly.

"That's what I'd like to know."

"Oh, my God… They're saying I'm pregnant with your child? Seriously? And that we're getting married?"

"Yeah."

"Where the hell did they get this from?"

"You… you mean it didn't come from you?" he stammered out.

"Of course it damn well didn't." She sounded really angry now. "Why the hell would I do this? I've just got married, Mark. I've been on an island in the Pacific for just under a month, on my honeymoon. There was no wifi, which is why I didn't pick up your messages until today. So why –and how – the hell would I be telling the press a pack of lies about us?"

He felt cold and clammy, and pushed his fingers through his hair. "You recognize the pictures though, right?"

"Yes, of course I do." She was talking to him as though he was being stupid. Why was everyone doing that lately? "But why would I do any of this? Christ, Mark… what if Callum sees this?"

"Who's Callum?"

"My husband."

"Oh…"

"Is that all you can say… 'oh'?"

"This isn't my fault, Nicole."

"Well it's not mine either. What am I supposed to tell him, if he sees them?"

Mark thought for a moment. He really did believe her now. She was sounding truly fearful of her husband finding out about the images and the stories. "If you want my advice, I'd tell him about them, rather than waiting for him to find out."

"And what should I tell him, Mark?"

"The truth?"

"Which is?"

"That none of this is real. That we dated for a while, but haven't seen each other for three years, and that he's got nothing to worry about, that the press have made all this up, and that we're both victims…"

"They may have made up the stories, Mark, but who gave them the photographs?"

"I assumed you had."

"No." She was adamant.

"But they were taken when we were together…"

"Obviously."

"And we were real careful to avoid the press."

"Wait a minute," Nicole said. He heard her clicking on her keyboard again. "Mark," she said after a minute or two, "all these pictures were taken by Sarah… on her phone."

Sarah… It seemed as though his head was spinning, while his whole body became damp with sweat and he felt bile rising in his throat. This couldn't be right. It couldn't be.

"Can I ask you something?" Nicole said. She sounded a little calmer now.

"Yeah." He barely recognized his own voice. It sounded like an echo in his head.

"Are you with someone? Are you seeing someone, I mean."

"I was. It ended."

"I see," she replied slowly. "And did these news items have anything to do with that?"

"Partly…"

"So what was the other reason? If you don't mind me asking…" It was like she already knew the answer.

"My ex-girl—" He was finding it hard to say. This was Emma he was talking about; she was never meant to be an ex- anything. "My… my ex-girlfriend, she thought Sarah was behind all this."

"And don't tell me? You sided with Sarah?" She paused, but before he could reply, continued, "I don't know why I'm even asking that question; you always sided with Sarah, so why change now?" He heard her sigh. "Well, I guess at least Sarah got what she wanted."

"What do you mean, Nicole?"

"Well, unless Sarah had a personality transplant in the last three years, she wouldn't have wanted you to be with this woman."

"How do you know that?"

"Because she didn't want you to be with me either. She spent the whole time we were together being an absolute bitch to me, Mark."

"Oh, really? Well, if Sarah's such a bitch, why did you go out for coffee with her a couple of weeks before Christmas? Why did you give her the message about meeting up with me?"

"What are you talking about?" She sounded incredulous again. "I haven't seen your sister since we broke up. Why are you being so stupid… and blind? If I saw Sarah, I'd cross the road to avoid her… Hell, I'd leave *town* to avoid her. But I already told you, I've been away on my honeymoon for just under a month. I got married two weeks before Christmas, so I certainly wasn't out shopping, or drinking coffee with your sister." She paused and took a breath. "Mark, she was the whole problem in our relationship – as far as I was concerned, anyway – so, there's no way I'd have anything to do with her… I remember, when you broke up with me, you accused me of being jealous of your sister and your relationship with her, but that wasn't true at all. I just wanted to spend some time alone with you – other than when we were in bed – which I didn't think was that much to ask, considering we were supposed to be dating. Even so, you wanted to include her in pretty much everything we did. I went along with it, to an extent, because I wanted to be with you, and because I understood she was still struggling after the accident. But it didn't matter how hard I tried to get on with her, Sarah never liked me. She did everything she could to make me feel like I wasn't good enough for you." He heard her let out a half-laugh. "You know, there was one thing I was always grateful to you for, and that was that you never took me to your home. Whenever we were actually alone, you always insisted that we went to one of your hotels. The very idea of being with Sarah, on her home ground, so to speak, would have been absolutely terrifying."

"Terrifying?" He found that hard to believe.

"Yes, Mark," she reiterated. "Your sister could be damn terrifying when she wanted to be. And she was only sixteen then… I can't imagine how evil she's become in the last three years."

Mark was struggling to take in her words. Sarah? Terrifying? Evil? Not the Sarah he knew. He realized Nicole was still talking:

"She was snide, sarcastic, rude, and over-protective of you, but worse than that, she seemed to be able to find my weaknesses and exploit them. She knew how worried I was about putting on weight, because of my job… and she'd just constantly pick on me for eating the wrong things, or she'd tell me I was looking heavy that day, or that my clothes seemed a little tight. She knew the things that made me more self-conscious and she picked away at them. Anyone who wasn't completely confident in themselves would really suffer at her hands…"

Mark remembered how Nicole had been such a bore when it came to food, barely eating when they went out, and constantly worrying about her weight. It was another of the many things he loved about Emma. Her love of cooking and enjoyment of tastes and food were a revelation.

"Was it really that bad?" he asked.

"Yes, Mark. It was. And if you've just ended a relationship because of Sarah… well, more fool you, because she's not worth it. All I can say is, I hope this woman didn't matter to you—"

"She did," Mark interrupted. "She really did."

"Then I'm truly sorry for you, because you're a nice guy." He heard the sincerity in her voice and it took him by surprise. "But I'm even sorrier for your ex-girlfriend. Being with you isn't always easy, Mark. Your privacy thing is kinda tough to handle, your constant fear of press attention could be incredibly stifling. Did she meet Sarah, this ex of yours?"

"Yeah. Emma came to stay a couple of times."

"Really? She came to stay at your house? She's braver than I was." Mark tried to remember Maggie's words about all the things Sarah had said and done to Emma, but Nicole was still talking…

"… and I'll bet having all this crap come out in the news would've been real hard on her." Mark heard something that sounded like sympathy in Nicole's voice. "Is Emma a model, or an actress or something?" she asked.

"No. She works in a coffee shop, in a small town in Maine."

He waited for the judgmental comment, but it didn't come. "Then that just makes it even harder for her," Nicole said. "She wouldn't be used to this kind of lifestyle." There was a pause before Nicole spoke again. "I can imagine Sarah latched onto her weakness real fast."

"What weakness?" Nicole didn't even know Emma. What was she talking about?

"She works in a coffee shop. You're a multi-millionaire. There's probably a huge difference in your lifestyles."

"So what if there is? What does that matter?"

"It doesn't. But I can just picture Emma coming to your place, and I can imagine Sarah probably doing something like… I don't know… getting dressed up in some expensive outfit, the like of which Emma would never be able to afford."

Mark turned cold. "She did," he whispered.

"And I can just see Sarah making all kinds of bitchy comments to Emma behind your back, undermining her, making her feel inadequate. She probably turned to you for help… for protection, hoping you'd look out for her and put her first and, I have no doubt at all, that when it came down to it, you put Sarah right up there instead. And now I guess you're gonna defend her, like you always did. You're gonna tell me I've got her all wrong and that poor little Sarah's had it tough. Well? Go on then…"

"I'm sorry," he murmured. He didn't know what else to say. He had nothing left. He was starting to wonder how much his view of Nicole had been clouded by Sarah's comments. She was certainly kinder and more sympathetic than he remembered. He'd misjudged her. "I'm so sorry, Nicole."

"You're apologizing to the wrong person, Mark."

"I know." He felt numb. "Are… are you gonna be okay?" he asked.

"Me?" She seemed surprised by his question.

"Yeah. With your husband… the news stories…"

"Oh. I'll go and speak to him now. You're right; it's better to tell him than let him find out. Not that you can really tell the pictures are of me, but I think I'd better tell him anyway, just to be on the safe side."

"And the stories are complete crap anyway."

"Well… except the part about me being pregnant."

"Really?"

"We only found out a couple of days before the wedding…"

"Congratulations… to both of you." He meant it. He was pleased for her, and her husband.

"Thank you." She hesitated. "I hope you find a way to work it out with Emma, Mark," she said. "You deserve to be happy."

He couldn't reply. He had no words left. And he didn't feel like he deserved happiness at all. He ended the call and put the phone down on his desk, holding his head in his hands.

Emma had been right. She'd been right about all of it. Everything she'd said about Sarah was true.

He needed to think about that some more, but he'd do that later. Right now, none of that felt like it mattered. What mattered most to him was a mixture of memories: there was Emma's face when she'd told him he'd broken her four years ago; the crack in her voice when she'd asked him to fix them; to put them back together; and the look in her eyes when she'd refused to tell him how bad it had really been; that secret she'd refused to tell, the one that had haunted him; and the knowledge that she needed Nick to stay with her. He'd broken her back then, just by leaving her. This time, by his lack of faith, by not putting her first, by not trusting her *and* by leaving her, he knew there was every chance he'd destroyed her.

Chapter Eighteen

Emma

"Are you absolutely sure about this?" Nick asked for probably the third time that evening.

"Yes."

"Let me stay for dinner at least."

"Is that because you want something to eat, or because you think I need your company."

"Both." He smiled across the breakfast bar at her.

"Okay. But I'm really feeling a lot better, honestly. The competition's tomorrow. It's been a good distraction for me."

"And that's why you still cry in your room at night, is it?"

"I'm gonna be crying for a long time to come, Nick. I'm not gonna get over him in just a couple of weeks. But you can't sleep on my couch forever, and I promise, I won't do anything stupid."

He stared at her. "You really promise?"

"Yeah."

He nodded. "Okay."

She pulled a large pan from the cabinet. "Pasta okay?" she asked. "It needs to be something quick, I've got a lot to do before tomorrow."

"Pasta's fine."

Emma started to chop a small onion. "Can I ask you a question?" she said.

"Sure."

"Why are you alone?"

"Sorry?"

"It's not a hard question, Nick. Nor is it a trick one. You're kind; you're a good looking man. You've got a great job. Okay, you live in a trailer, but that's not the end of the world. I don't understand why you don't have anyone in your life. To my knowledge, you never have had… not since before college, anyway."

"That would be out of choice, Em."

"Yes, but why?"

"Do we really have to talk about this?" He looked pained.

"Yes, we do."

"Why?"

"Because you never talk about it."

"So?" He stared at her.

"And… and because I feel like it's a secret between us. You know everything about me, Nick." She put the knife down on the chopping board. "Even Mark doesn't know what happened with the sleeping pills. I never told him. I couldn't. But you know it all, and yet I feel I know so little about you." She felt tears prick behind her eyes.

He reached across and took her hand. "Hey… It's okay," he said quietly. "I'll tell you." He took a deep breath. "There was a girl, when I was at college. We dated for a while…"

"And?"

"And I fell in love with her." He looked away for a moment, and when he turned back Emma noticed his eyes were a darker gray than usual.

"What happened?"

"We broke up. Badly. I guess I've just never gotten over her…" His voice faded.

Emma sighed. "Maybe we're just no good at love, you and I."

He shook his head. "Don't give up, Em. You should never give up on love."

"Why not? You have…"

He looked up at her. "Oh no I haven't. I've never given up."

Emma woke early on Saturday.

There were going to be fifteen entrants in the competition and a part of her was dreading tasting her way through that many brownies and cakes. Still, at least it was a blind tasting, so she couldn't be accused of bias toward one person or another. She'd have no idea who'd baked what. Noah was going to be in charge of receiving all the baked goods and ensuring none of the judges found out who had cooked what.

She also expected that a lot of the townsfolk would pack into the coffee shop and, with her, Patsy and Kathryn all doing the tastings, she'd managed to rope Cassie into helping Josh with serving the customers.

She poured some cereal into a bowl and added some cold milk, then sat at the breakfast bar and twirled a spoon in her hand.

This was a big deal for her and she had to admit she was nervous, to the point where she'd lost her appetite. She pushed the bowl away and put her head in her hands, thinking for a moment of the other thing that was on her mind… well, the other thing apart from Mark, obviously, because he was constantly in her head, no matter what else was going on… No, the other thing that she couldn't stop thinking about was the conversation that she'd had with Mrs Adams between Christmas and New Year… the conversation she'd told no-one about yet, not even Nick. It was the kind of thing she'd have liked to share with Mark, if only she could.

Mrs Adams had finally agreed to sell the shop, and what was more, Emma actually thought she might be able to afford it. With her savings and a small loan from the bank, she really thought it might be possible. The thing she wasn't sure about was how she would afford to pay for the upgrades she wanted to do. She didn't know whether to try and borrow the extra money and do them straight away, or wait a while, save up some cash, and get everything done at a later stage. She really needed to talk to someone about that, and Mark would have been the obvious choice. Except Mark wasn't here.

Thoughts like that brought it home to her how much she missed him, not that she really needed the reminder. She missed him every waking moment of the day; and most of her sleeping ones too. When she woke in the morning – every morning – just for a second, she'd forget that he wasn't in her life anymore, and then she'd remember again, the pain cutting just a little deeper. During the course of the day, there would be reminders of him. Over Christmas, *Groundhog Day* had been on the television and she'd cried all the way through it; if she heard a track by Coldplay, she found it hard to keep it together, and she was haunted by memories of his kisses, his touch, the way he felt when he was deep inside her… his voice, his arms around her, the way he'd made her feel safe and loved, and wanted. Until he didn't want her, or love her, that is. Until he didn't listen to her, and didn't want to hear what she had to say. Until he put her so far down his list, there was no way back.

She really wished she could explain to him that he'd been wrong. Not necessarily about Sarah… that didn't matter. But he'd been wrong about her. She'd never expected him to choose between her and his sister. All she'd wanted was for him to listen to her, to accept the possibility that Sarah might not be the person he believed her to be, and – if she needed it – to maybe get her some help. Emma would have been more than happy to help him support Sarah through whatever her problems were… and to be there for him while he worked it all out.

Except, as it turned out, he didn't need her.

Mark

He got up early on Saturday. He didn't wake early, because he hadn't slept.

After he'd finished his call with Nicole, he'd decided to spend the night thinking over what he now knew. Apart from anything else, the sadness and confusion he'd felt at the end of that phone call had soon turned to raw, blind rage… mainly with himself, but also with Sarah, and he knew it was unwise to confront her while he was in that frame of mind.

He'd pleaded a bad headache the night before and gone straight to bed, where he'd tossed and turned all night, going over everything Nicole had said to him. He wondered if he knew his sister at all. He'd thought, since the accident, that they'd become close but, listening to Nicole, he'd realized he had no idea who Sarah even was. And hearing the kind of person she'd become, he knew he didn't want to.

Knowing the effect she'd had on Nicole, he wondered how Emma had coped with it. Emma wasn't anything like as strong as Nicole had been… and, rather than protecting her, he'd brought her into the lion's den, and often left her alone with Sarah. And she hadn't said a single word of complaint to him… not one.

He thought about some of the comments he'd heard Sarah make himself, like her assertion that he should try and get over Emma by going out with other women. And to think, he'd made excuses for her to Maggie, who'd also been right, it would seem. God, how had he been so blind?

The question he kept asking himself, over and over was, 'how could she do this?'. How could his own sister have tried to wreak so much havoc in his life? How could she have gone out of her way to make him so unhappy? How could she knowingly break him away from the only woman he'd ever loved? He had no idea how she'd manipulated the press, but he intended to find out.

Even though it was still not yet eight o'clock and Sarah rarely got up before ten at the weekends, he showered, dressed, and went along to her room, knocking once on the door before entering. She could moan all she wanted about her privacy. As far as he was concerned, she'd relinquished her right to that when she'd ridden roughshod over his life – and Emma's.

The room was in darkness, the drapes drawn across the wide windows. Mark went over and pulled them back, exposing the room to the stark early morning sunlight.

Sarah blinked awake, then pulled the comforter up over her head. "What the hell, Mark?" she cried out. "What are you doing?"

"I need to talk to you," he said, sternly. "So I suggest you wake up. Now."

Slowly, she lowered the comforter again and looked over at him, wincing against the brightness.

"What's the matter?" she asked. He'd never spoken to her with that tone of voice before.

"Why?" he asked her simply.

"Why what?"

"Why did you send the press those photographs?" He noticed the color drain from her face and knew he was right.

"I—I don't know what you're talking about," she stammered.

"Bullshit, Sarah."

Her bottom lip started to quiver, but he wasn't falling for that. "Why are you being like this?" she asked.

"Because you're responsible for everything that's happened to me – and to Emma – in the last couple of weeks. You broke us up. You broke her heart… and mine. *You* did that, Sarah. Why?"

Sarah sat forward a little "Did Emma tell you this?" she asked, ignoring his question. "She's never liked me, not since the first time she came here."

"I haven't spoken to Emma, not recently, anyway. But I have spoken to Nicole."

"N—Nicole?"

"Yes. Oddly, she says she couldn't have met you in town before Christmas, because she was getting married at the time, which I guess means you made that up." He glared at her. "And she told me you were more than unpleasant to her while we were dating, and that the photographs the press have been printing were all taken by you." He took a step closer to her bed. "Show me your phone, Sarah. And your laptop. Now."

"No."

"That really wasn't a request."

"I'm nineteen. Not nine. You can't give me orders."

"If you're gonna start messing with my life like this, I think you'll find I can. Hand them over."

"No." She glowered at him.

"Why not?"

"Because they're private."

"If you've got nothing to hide, then you won't mind showing them to me."

A tear fell onto her cheek. "I've done nothing wrong," she whimpered.

"Then show me your goddamn phone, Sarah."

"No." She started to sob.

He still wasn't moved, but turned away and sat down on the chair by the window.

"Do you have any idea what you've done?" he asked her.

"I haven't done anything."

He stared at her for a moment, before continuing, "I've never told you this, but I knew Emma before the accident." She looked up at him, her mouth open just slightly. "Yeah, you never knew that, did you? We were together back then, very briefly."

"She was another one of your flings?"

His eyes narrowed. "No. Emma was always different. I was gonna go and see her after Thanksgiving. I couldn't – obviously – and later, I realized I had to choose between staying here and looking after the business, and you… or being with her. I chose you, Sarah. I gave her up back then to be with you."

"And for the business, Mark. It wasn't just about me."

"It was mainly about you. I worked out real early on after mom and dad died, that I can run the business from pretty much anywhere in New England, but you were always rooted in Boston… by hospital appointments, school, friends, memories, this house. If I was going to care for you, I had to stay here. I never thought I'd get the chance to be with Emma again, but I did – purely by accident – and I took that chance, because I love her. I always did. I always will. I know how lucky I was that she gave me a second chance. I know I didn't really deserve it, but she let me back into her life… and I blew it again, because I put you first."

"And why shouldn't you put me first? I'm your sister."

"Then why the fuck can't you act like my sister?" he bellowed at her, and she flinched.

"Don't shout at me," she whimpered.

"Why not? You've wrecked my life…"

"I haven't. Emma did that. She broke up with you."

He stood up. "Be real careful, Sarah." His voice was quiet now. Quiet and menacing. "Don't even think about trying to blame her for what you've done."

"I keep telling you, I haven't done anything."

"Then show me your phone," he persisted.

"No. You've got no right—"

"I've got every goddamn right."

"I've told you it's private."

"Yeah. I had a private life once," he said sarcastically. "I went to great lengths to protect my privacy from the outside world, and then you came along and exposed me to public scrutiny."

"I did no such thing," she countered.

They stared at each other for what seemed like ages.

"Fine," he said eventually. "If you insist on denying it, I'll put in a call to the damn reporters. I'm sure they'll love to hear from me in person. I'll pay them… I'll pay them a lot of money, Sarah, to tell me where they got their information from."

"It doesn't matter how much you offer them, they won't tell you."

"How do you know?"

"Because they promise anonymity."

"Do they, Sarah?" He didn't move, his demeanor calm as he realized he'd caught her out. "And how do you know that?"

"E—Everyone knows that." She was stuttering again.

"Do they?"

"Yes."

He moved closer to the bed, so he was alongside her, then he leant over, so his face was just a few inches from hers.

"I don't believe a single fucking word you've said." He was just whispering now.

"It's the truth."

274

"You don't know the meaning of the word." He stood upright. "I'm going."

"Where?" She pushed the covers down and knelt up, moving across the bed toward him. "Where are you going?"

"I'm gonna drive up to Emma's and I'm gonna see if I can persuade her to let me back into her life."

"Why?"

He tilted his head to one side. "I've already told you. I love her. I want her back."

"And what about me?"

"What about you?"

"What am I supposed to do."

"Do you want an honest answer to that?" She didn't reply, so he told her anyway. "I really don't care anymore, Sarah."

She shot off the bed and stood in front of him. "You never did!" she yelled at the top of her voice. "You've never cared about me. Ever."

"I've done nothing but care for you since mom and dad died," he countered, keeping his voice calm, despite the storm she was trying to create.

"Seriously, Mark? Is that what you call caring for me? You've slept around with every model in town; you've stayed out all night; you've worked all the hours God sends. You never have any time for me. I lost everything when mom and dad died. Everything!"

He took a step closer to her. "Firstly, I did not sleep around with every model in town. That's a huge exaggeration. I slept with quite a few women in the past… but that's my business, Sarah, not yours. I work damn hard because I have to. Unlike you, I have to work to keep dad's company going. I wasn't given a choice in what I do for a living. And we both lost a helluva lot when they died. We both lost our parents, but I also lost my freedom, my right to choose my own career… and I lost Emma."

"Emma, Emma, Emma," she mocked, smirking. "God, I'd have loved to have seen her face when she saw those pictures of you with Nicole, and even more so when she read the bit about Nicole being pregnant. That was priceless. I only had to hint at it and the reporter leapt all over it."

The temptation to hit her was so strong, Mark had to clasp his hands together behind his back and grip them tightly.

"It *was* you…" He knew already, but to hear her boasting like that took him by surprise.

"Of course it was me."

"Do you have any idea of the damage you've done?"

"It was a few reporters. So what? They've gone now, haven't they?"

"Yeah, and I know why. Because since Emma and I broke up, you've stopped feeding them bullshit." He took a breath, clenched his fists and tried real hard to calm himself. "Emma thought she was pregnant," he murmured. "She found out she wasn't the same day that story broke." Sarah's face was impassive. "That really hurt her."

"Why?"

"Why? Are you really so insensitive to other people's pain? Why do you think? She wanted to have my baby… and I wanted it too."

Sarah laughed. "How do you even know it would have been yours?"

He stepped closer and saw the flicker of fear in her eyes. "I'm not even going to justify that degrading comment with an answer." He paused, calming slightly, before continuing, "And then to make matters worse, you faked a goddamn breakdown to get me back here, so I wouldn't go visit Emma. I should've been with her."

"Why? Why should you have been with her? You've known her for all of five minutes. What right has she got to have all your attention?"

"The right of loving me, that's what. She gave me everything… everything! She gave me all she had, and more – and I threw it back in her face." He moved right up close to her. "For you."

"Because I'm your sister…" Her voice softened. "I love you too, Mark."

"You've got a damn weird way of showing it. You were such a bitch to her as well. Every time she came here, you were at her the whole time."

"How do you know that? I suppose she came running to you, telling tales, did she?"

"No. Maggie told me. And Nicole said you did the same thing to her too."

"Well, Emma was here the whole time… or you were there; or you were on the phone, or texting each other. Christ, even on the anniversary of mom and dad's death, she couldn't just leave us be…"

"But she did. She let us go out by ourselves. She stayed here with Maggie."

"Not that anniversary… the real one."

"What are you talking about? I didn't see Emma that day. I didn't even hear from her." Mark had a vague recollection of Emma saying she'd sent a text… a text he didn't receive. He stared at Sarah.

"She couldn't even let us spend a quiet evening together," Sarah continued. "She had to interfere."

"She… she said there was a message," he whispered.

Sarah looked up at him. "Of course there was. I mean, God forbid she'd actually leave you alone for five minutes."

"And you deleted it?" He remembered going to speak with Maggie and coming back into Sarah's room to find her playing on his phone.

"We needed some time alone," she was saying.

"We'd had the whole goddamn day alone. *I* needed Emma."

Sarah looked up at him, disbelief and anger etched on her face, a face he felt he hardly knew. He couldn't stay here any longer. He wasn't a violent man and he'd never even contemplated hitting a woman before, but Sarah was pushing him to his limits.

He unclasped his hands at last and shook out his aching arms.

"God, I've got a headache," she murmured, collapsing back on the edge of the bed. "All this shouting and drama is really bad for me."

"Maybe you should try telling that to someone who actually gives a fuck," he said, turning away from her, toward the door.

"Where are you going?" she asked, a note of panic in her voice.

"I told you. I'm gonna go and see Emma."

"You know she's only after your money, don't you? I was just trying to protect you."

"Bullshit, Sarah," he yelled. "Emma's never been interested in my money." He opened the door.

"You're just going to leave me here... like this?"

He turned back and looked at her sitting on the edge of the bed, staring across at him. "Yes. I don't wanna be in the same house as you, Sarah. I'm gonna go and see Emma. Whatever happens with her, when I come back to town, I'll stay at one of the hotels. I'm not gonna tell you which one and I'm not coming back here. I can't even bear to look at you."

"But... Mark?" she whimpered.

"Oh, just leave it, Sarah."

He opened the door and heard her sob, just as he crossed the threshold and closed it behind him.

He quickly packed a bag and went downstairs to the kitchen, where Maggie was making coffee.

"I need you to watch Sarah for me," he announced.

Maggie looked at the bag in his hand. "Are you going somewhere?"

"Yeah."

"Well, that's okay. I usually watch over Sarah when you're not here."

"No," he said quietly, "this is different."

"Why?"

"Because I'm not coming back."

Maggie dropped the cup she was holding and it shattered on the floor.

"N—Not ever?" She bent and started gathering the pieces, putting them on the countertop.

"I don't know. Ever's a long time, Maggie. But I'm not coming back here for a good long while. I'm taking enough clothes for a few days. Can you pack up the rest for me?"

"All off it?"

He nodded. "I'm not sure where I'm gonna be yet, but I'll let you know, and maybe you can get Anthony to drop all my things to me?"

"Um... sure. Am I allowed to know why?"

He put his bag down and sat at the kitchen island. "Yeah, I think you're entitled."

Maggie came and sat beside him. "What's happened?" she asked.

"Emma was right," he said quietly.

"About what?"

"Everything." He looked across at Maggie. "Sarah was behind the stories being leaked to the press. She gave them the pictures. She fed them the bullshit, she faked her little meltdown to get me back here, so I wouldn't go visit Emma…"

Maggie's face had paled. "Has she admitted it?" she asked, her voice little more than a whisper.

"Yeah, eventually."

"Oh, dear God." Maggie put her hand on his arm. "I knew… I knew she didn't like Emma, but to do this… it's evil."

"I know."

"What are you going to do?"

"I'm gonna go and see Emma. I'm gonna beg her to give me another chance. I'm not sure she will, but I have to try."

Maggie smiled. "I hope she does, for both your sakes."

"So do I."

"And… and you're not coming back?"

"Not any time soon, no."

"You're gonna stay up in Maine?"

"I don't know what I'm gonna do. It kinda depends on Emma, really. I'll have to come back to town for work, and when I do, I'll stay at one of the hotels – probably the Central – but I haven't decided on that yet. I can't see Sarah though, not at the moment, Maggie, and I don't want her knowing where I am."

"I understand."

He sighed. "I think I need to look into getting her some help."

Maggie shifted in her seat. "I've still got some contacts. I could make some calls."

"Would you?" He looked at her. "I'm not washing my hands of her. I just can't have her in my life right now. But I'll pay for her treatment and do whatever I can to help her get better."

"And then?" Maggie asked.

"We'll see." He took Maggie's hand in his. "Are you gonna be okay with her?" he asked.

"Of course I am. I'm used to her."

"Yeah. I thought I was too."

"Well, she and I don't have that emotional connection you two do. It makes it easier."

Mark nodded. "I'll call you," he said. "And if anything happens, or you need anything, I want you to call me."

"Okay. And you'll let me know?"

He tilted his head to one side. "What about?"

"You and Emma, of course."

He got up and looked down at her. "Yeah, I'll let you know. Wish me luck."

"You don't need luck. Just be honest with her. Tell her how you feel. Let her see how much she means to you… and let love do the rest."

He really hoped that would be enough.

Chapter Nineteen

Emma

Five tastings in, and Emma had already found two cakes she wanted to stock. She was a bit sick of brownies already, but the red velvet cake, and the lemon muffins with poppy seeds had been mouthwateringly good. As for the brownies themselves, so far she hadn't found any to match Maggie's and was seriously wondering whether she could have them trucked in from Boston every day.

As plate number six was placed before them, she noticed they seemed to contain some kind of nuts and she couldn't help but remember Maggie saying how she liked the texture of nuts in her brownies, and how Mark had told Maggie she couldn't enter the contest, or bake for Emma.

God, she wished he was here.

She sucked in a sharp breath, picked up the brownie and took a bite. It wasn't bad. It was moist, nutty, rich with chocolate and had just the right amount of goo. She had to give it a mark out of ten… and she awarded this particular brownie a nine: the highest score of the day so far.

As she laid down her score sheet and pen, she looked around the coffee shop. It was filled to bursting. All the tables and booths were occupied; people were even standing around, looking on, while she, Patsy, and Kathryn sat in front of the counter, tasting the contents of each plate that Noah brought out to them. It was a fairly slow process, but everyone seemed to be taking an interest, and drinking lots of coffee, which was keeping Josh and Cassie busy.

Nick was standing over by the door, leaning against the wall, his arms folded across his chest, watching her, making sure she was okay. Every so often, she'd glance in his direction and, when she could see him through the throng of heads, he'd just raise an eyebrow, and she'd nod, or smile. They understood each other.

Of course, she wouldn't go so far as to say she was enjoying herself. That wasn't something she'd really done since the last time she was with Mark; not even Christmas Day had been completely happy. But she'd definitely had worse days… She'd had much worse days.

If only he could have been here to see this, so he could see her making a success of his idea, and so she could tell him she was going to be able to buy the coffee shop herself real soon, and maybe ask his advice. Then everything would be just perfect…

But that was just a dream.

And besides, it would never work. Because there would always be something else more important for him to do, other than be with her. And there would always be Sarah…

She sighed as Noah brought out a dark chocolate fudge cake. *Oh good, more chocolate.*

Mark

It was just before two by the time Mark pulled up behind the coffee shop. He parked in his usual space around the back, but left his bag in the car. He wasn't taking anything for granted and didn't want Emma to think he was.

He locked his car and walked slowly around to the front of the shops. Main Street was quiet, which wasn't surprising for early January. At this time on a Saturday, he assumed Emma might still be up in her apartment, doing the paperwork, so he thought the best idea was to go straight past the coffee shop, and try her apartment first. With any luck, she'd be there and he could talk to her in private. If she wasn't up there and was already working downstairs… well, he'd just have to take his chances, hope that maybe she'd be willing to take a break, go upstairs and speak to him, or even just speak to him in front of whoever was in the coffee shop. There wouldn't be that many people around, even on a Saturday lunchtime, not in early January, but even if there were a few customers, he didn't care.

As he approached the coffee shop, he could hear the noise coming from inside, and then, looking in through the window, he saw the place was positively heaving with people. Not only were all the tables filled, but people were standing as well, their backs to the window, facing the counter. He couldn't see what was going on, but then a poster in the window caught his eye.

He read it through quickly and smiled. The competition. She'd done it. And it was today… and from the looks of it, she'd made a huge success of it too. He felt really proud of her.

He couldn't see Emma, but he knew she'd be in there. Then a man in a red check shirt moved to one side and he noticed Jake and Maddie sitting in one of the booths.

This wasn't what he'd had in mind at all, but he wasn't going to wait. He wanted to see Emma; and he wanted to see her as soon as possible.

He went to the door and pushed it open. The noise level shot up, and he felt the warmth of the gathered people, and smelt the familiar aroma of ground coffee beans. He stepped inside and closed the door. He still couldn't see Emma and took another step forward, just as a hand came down on his shoulder.

"Outside. Now," a low voice said in his ear, and he turned and found Nick glaring at him. The grip on his shoulder was strong and, while he felt fairly confident he could have shaken it off, he wasn't sure that was a good idea. Nick was Emma's brother, after all.

He turned, opened the door and went back out into the icy air, with Nick right behind him.

"What the fuck are you doing here?" There was a more than unfriendly edge to Nick's voice. He might be Emma's brother, and he might even be staying with her, but his attitude made Mark defensive.

"I've come to see Emma," Mark replied, testily.

"I think I worked that out for myself."

"Then why ask the fucking question?" Mark looked at him.

"Because I want an explanation."

"I owe Emma that… and more. I wasn't aware I owed anything to you."

Nick continued to glare at him, unflinching. "You hurt her."

"I know."

"I'm not sure I should let you go anywhere near her. She can't handle being hurt again."

"I'm not gonna hurt her again."

"Oh, really? I think you've said that before. And I don't think you understand. I *really* mean it. She can't handle it." He sighed and Mark saw his shoulders drop. "You've got no fucking idea, have you?"

"About what?" Mark was getting fed up now.

"About Emma." Nick ran his hands down his face. And then he shook his head slowly from side to side. "She'd kill me if she knew I was talking to you about this, but I think you need to know what you've done to her." He took a couple of steps. "Walk with me," he said, over his shoulder. "I know what this town's like. There's less chance of being overheard if we walk."

Mark fell into step next to him and they walked in silence for a minute or so before Nick spoke again.

"Before I can even think about letting you go in there to speak to her, you need to fully understand how vulnerable she is." He glanced at Mark. "You need to know how damaging you and your actions have been."

"I've hurt her. I know that. I know it's been bad for her." Mark didn't need to have salt rubbed into the wound. "But, trust me, I know how she's been feeling, because I've been there myself these last few weeks."

"No you haven't. You've got no fucking clue what she's been through. I'm gonna tell you this because I think, deep down, you're probably a decent guy, and if you really knew what had gone on before, if you'd understood the consequences of your behavior, you'd have done things differently this time around." Mark felt a cold fear grip his spine as Nick looked up at the pale blue sky for a moment, before turning back to him. "You've got a little sister, right?" Mark nodded, but didn't say anything. He didn't know where Nick was going with this and he want to tell him what Sarah had done, not yet. "Okay," Nick continued. "And, from what I've gathered from Em, you're real close to her." This time Nick didn't wait for confirmation. "So, let me ask you this… Have you ever had to break down a door, and find your little sister half way through a bottle of sleeping pills?"

Mark stopped in his tracks, frozen… numbed. "What?" he whispered.

Nick turned and stepped back in front of Mark. "Yeah. She did that. She was having trouble sleeping, and Doc Cooper gave her some pills to help. She took half the bottle, straight down, with a vodka chaser."

Mark felt like his throat was closing over, like he'd never breathe normally again. "When?" he managed to say. "Was this when we just broke up… before Christmas, I mean?"

Nick shook his head and looked down at the ground. "No. It was four years ago, when you broke her heart the first time."

The pain stabbed into Mark's chest, like a knife. And then a thought, a distant memory crossed his mind.

"When *exactly* was this?" he asked. "What day, I mean."

Nick seemed to think for a moment. "It was the week after Thanksgiving. The following Thursday, I think. I can't be sure… I lost track of the days around then."

Mark sighed. "Oh God. She sent me a message," he whispered.

"She did?" Nick was surprised. "What did she say?"

"She just asked me why…"

Nick took a step closer, a dark shadow crossing his face. "And it didn't occur to you, when you got that message, that she could be in trouble? You didn't think to reply, to find out what was wrong?"

Mark shook his head.

"You asshole," Nick hissed. "You're the only person who could've stopped her, and you did nothing."

"I'm sorry. I didn't know."

"Too wrapped up in your own world, as usual." Nick hurled the accusation.

"I guess," Mark whispered. "When I read that message, I was sitting at Sarah's bedside. She was still unconscious after the accident; my parents' funeral was gonna be the following day, but she didn't wake up in time, so I went to that by myself. I had lawyers, businessmen, accountants… you name it, they were hassling me, and then there was the press…" His voice faded.

"Shit. I'm sorry," Nick said. Mark looked up and saw Nick's expression had altered. The anger in his eyes had been replaced with genuine sympathy.

"Don't be," Mark replied. "You're right. I should've done something. If I'd known, I'd have called her. Hell, I'd have come back to her. I'd have done whatever she needed me to do… I just didn't realize."

"I get that now."

They stood for a moment. "So, *that* was her secret," Mark said, breaking the silence.

"What's that?" Nick asked.

Mark looked at him. "Her secret. I knew there was something from before, but she wouldn't tell me. She wouldn't trust me with knowing it."

"Of course she wouldn't. She's ashamed of it. No-one knows about it, not even Cassie. I took her to the hospital that night, got her treated, brought her back home again and stayed with her until I knew she was okay. It took weeks. We agreed to tell no-one and she… she promised me she'd never do it again. And I believed her."

"Why do I sense there's more…?"

"Because there is. When you two split up before Christmas, Emma was in a bad way. She broke down completely, and she called Cassie for help, but then she felt kinda awkward talking to her about it…"

"Why? Cassie's her friend." Mark was confused.

"The way Emma explained it to me, she felt she was putting Cassie in a difficult position because you and Jake are friends, and because Jake's gonna be working for you soon."

"But none of that matters. She needed Cassie. She needed someone."

"I know, but Emma hung up on her… Cassie was worried about her, but Jake was out and Maddie was already in bed, so she called me, and told me what had happened. She knew I'd still be at work. She said that Emma had begged her not to go round there. Knowing Emma's track record, that scared the shit out of me, so I ran straight over to her place."

"And?"

"I found her curled up on the floor in the kitchen. She was a mess."

"She hadn't… She hadn't taken more pills? Please tell me she hadn't…" His eyes were stinging, blurring, but he didn't care.

Nick shook his head. "No, but I'm fairly sure she was going to."

"How do you know?"

"Because I suggested I should stay. I told her I didn't trust her to keep her promise, and all she said was 'thank you'."

"So that's why you've been staying with her? I wondered…" Mark's voice faded.

Nick nodded. "How did you know I was staying there?" he asked.

"Jake told me," Mark explained. "I needed to know she was okay, but all he would tell me was that you were staying with her. I knew things must be bad, but I had no idea it would be this bad…"

Nick started walking again and Mark followed, catching up quickly.

"How is she now?" he asked.

"Well, she's not better, if that's what you're asking. I moved back into my own place last night, but she still cries herself to sleep. She still blames herself…"

"She what?"

"She blames herself. She thinks she wasn't good enough for you."

It was Mark's turn to run his hands down his face. "Christ. She's too damn good for me."

"Yeah, I told her that too." Nick stopped again and turned to him. "Do have have any idea what you did to her?"

"I broke her… again."

"Yeah, you did. The thing is, how many times do you think you can do that before she can't be fixed at all… before she's in too many pieces for anyone to put her back together again – even me."

"I'm not gonna break her again. Not now."

"She thought that the last time. She trusted you."

"I know. And I let her down. I won't do that again."

"You've said that before."

"I was blinded before," Mark admitted.

"What by?"

"By my sister." Nick raised an eyebrow. "Emma was right. Sarah was behind all the press stories."

"You finally worked it out then."

"Um… Yeah." How did Nick know?

"It didn't take a genius to see that your sister was the only one with a motive, and the opportunity to do it. Cassie and Emma got to the bottom of it over a cup of coffee… But like you said, you were blind to it."

"Well, I'm not blind anymore."

Nick glanced back in the direction of the coffee shop. "I know you wanna go back in there," he said. "But the thing is, if you do, and you manage to persuade Emma to give you another chance, I'm gonna be living in fear. I'll be living in fear that you'll do this to her again, and that, if that happens, I might not get to her in time. So… I need you to give me a good reason why I should let you walk in there and put *my* sister at risk, when she's never done a damn thing to hurt you."

"Because I love her," Mark said simply.

"Not good enough. You've said that before. Didn't stop you hurting her, did it?"

Mark shook his head. He couldn't deny that.

"I'll never hurt her again."

Nick looked at him. "You're a bit fucking repetitive, aren't you? I remember Emma crying that over and over in the night, that you'd said you'd never hurt her… and yet you had." Nick paused for a moment. "Try telling me something different, and fucking mean it."

Mark put his hands in his pockets and felt his car keys lying there. "I'm gonna hazard a guess, either because Emma's told you, or because you know about the press stories, that you know who I really am."

Nick frowned at him. "Yeah, I know you're Mark Gardner… and I'm not impressed."

"You're not meant to be."

"Then what's your point?"

"My point is, that I'd give up everything I've got – all of it – if I could have Emma back in my life, because if she's not with me, I'm nothing anyway. I can't live without her, Nick… and, if you're being honest, you know it's the same for her too. We've never really had the chance to be together – not properly – but you know as well as I do, if I'm *really* with her, I'll keep her safe. I can keep her safer than anyone, and not because I'm a millionaire, but because I love her more than anyone else ever could. I'll never hurt her; I'll never let anyone else hurt her… and I'll never let her hurt herself. Ever again."

Nick let out a long breath, then turned back in the direction they'd come, walking slowly toward the coffee shop.

"Okay," he said eventually, "I'll let you go in there."

"Thank you."

"Don't thank me. I still don't trust you. I'm doing this because I know you make Emma happy, and if she's willing to try again with you, I'll back off. But if she isn't, if she doesn't want anything more to do with you, then you need to leave her alone for good and never come back here." Nick turned and looked at Mark. "I'm giving you one shot at this. Get it right, for fuck's sake, because I can't watch her go through this again."

"You won't have to."

They continued walking in silence for a while.

"Would you really have stopped me seeing her?" Mark asked just as they got to the coffee shop.

Nick looked at him, a slight smile forming on his face. "What do you think?" he asked, opening the door and allowing Mark to pass through ahead of him.

"Yes?" Mark guessed, turning to him.

"Hell, yes." Nick took up his position by the door, folding his arms across his chest. "One chance," he murmured, just loud enough for Mark to hear.

Mark nodded, and turned away. He still felt numbed, shocked. He was finding it hard to process everything Nick had told him. At least he now understood why Emma had kept her secret from him… he didn't blame her for that. He wished she had told him, but he understood why she hadn't. And he wanted, more than anything, to prove to her that she could feel safe with him, and that she was more than good enough. She always had been.

Mark caught Jake's eye and went over to his friend, sitting down opposite him. He gave Maddie a 'hello' salute and a smile, which she returned.

"Didn't expect to see you here," Jake said to him.

"No, but then there's a lot gone on lately that's kinda unexpected."

He briefly filled Jake in on what Sarah had done, and told him he wouldn't be going home for a while.

"What are you gonna do?" Jake asked him.

"To start with, I'm gonna do whatever it takes to get Emma back."

"Be careful, Mark," Jake warned. "She can't take much more."

"I know. I've just spoken to Nick. He's filled me in on what's been going on with Emma…" He held Jake's gaze for a moment. "And I'm even more grateful for your support now, knowing what I do. I know Emma's your friend. It can't have been easy contacting me."

"You don't owe me your thanks, Mark. You owe Emma."

"I do?"

"Yeah. I wasn't sure I wanted to see you again after what you did to her… well, unless it was to punch you, really fucking hard. I was seriously thinking about walking away from the job, and from you, for good. You hurt my friend – badly."

"I know I did." Mark sighed. "So, what changed your mind?" he asked.

"Emma. She told me I'm all you've got, and that I needed to step up and be there for you. She told me she's got Cass, and Nick and me, but you haven't got anyone. She said she hated the thought of you being on your own, and I needed to be your friend as well as hers."

"She said that?" Mark felt a glimmer of hope. She still cared.

"Yeah. Don't read too much into it, Mark. That's just Em being Em. She's got a heart of gold."

"I know. And I managed to break it. Twice." He looked around the crowded coffee shop. "Where is she?" he asked.

"Over by the counter. She's tasting cakes for this competition,"

Mark smiled. "I'm real glad she made this work," he said.

"How did you know about it?"

"We talked about it when she was last in Boston…" He wasn't going to take any credit for coming up with the idea. Even he hadn't realized she could make an event like this out of it. He stood up.

"Why don't you wait for things to die down a bit?" Jake suggested.

"Because I'm done waiting for her."

Mark slowly worked his way through the crowd of people, until he made it to the front. Emma was sitting behind a table, flanked by Patsy and Kathryn and he saw her, maybe five seconds before she looked up and saw him. She was writing something on a piece of paper and, as she put her pen down, she glanced up. Her eyes locked with his, like a magnet, and she froze.

He smiled and, even from where he was standing, he saw the tears filling her eyes. He wanted to go to her, pull her to her feet and hold her, but he didn't know how she'd react, and if she reacted badly, then doing that in front of almost the whole town would be horrible… for both of them. So, he stood his ground, keeping his eyes fixed on hers.

She turned away and, with a shaking hand, picked up a brownie from the plate in front of her, taking a tiny bite from it. She chewed for a while, then swallowed and made another note on the sheet in front of her, before leaning over to Patsy and whispering something in her ear. Patsy nodded her head and Emma stood, saying they were just going to take a break for a few minutes. She turned and left quickly, heading in the direction of the ladies' room.

Mark didn't hesitate, not even for a second. Even though he knew everyone would be watching, he followed her.

Chapter Twenty

Emma

She wanted to run, but she knew people would be watching. She knew they'd have seen Mark and, although no-one knew who he really was, a few people had seen him around the coffee shop before Christmas, and knew he and Emma had been together. The last thing she needed was to be the subject of gossip.

"Emma!" She heard him call out to her in a loud whisper.

She ignored him and headed for the ladies' room.

"Please."

She managed to get her hand on the door when he caught her arm and turned her around. She looked up into his eyes, her own a blur of tears, and felt her heart twist inside her, strangling her emotions into a mixture of pain and love which caught in her throat, choking her.

"Please, Emma," he said. "Just hear me out."

She shook her head. Her voice wasn't going to work, not yet.

"I know I don't have the right to ask," he continued. "You owe me nothing, but please, please, just listen to what I've got to say."

She didn't respond at all. She couldn't, because she didn't know what she wanted. There was a part of her that wanted to tell him to leave, to get out and never come back. But there was a part of her that needed him so much, she ached.

"You were right," he said eventually, clearly taking her silence as an acceptance. "It was Sarah. I—I spoke to Nicole yesterday, and she confirmed everything you'd said. She told me how awful Sarah was to her too, and that the photographs were on Sarah's phone…" He closed his eyes just briefly, and sighed. "I confronted Sarah this morning. She denied it to start with, but then she admitted all of it. I've left, Emma. I'm not going back. I can't be around her. I don't want to see her, not at the moment, and not for a long time… maybe never. I want you, Emma. I want us."

She heaved in a breath. "It's a bit late to be telling me all that," she whispered. "I knew it was Sarah, but you wouldn't listen to me. I needed you to trust me… and you wouldn't."

"It was hard, Emma. She's my sister. It was hard for me to believe she'd do that to me."

"I know that. I told you that. I said, didn't I? I said that I knew she was your sister and you love her…"

He let out a half laugh. "I'm not sure I do."

"Yeah, you do. I know you, Mark. You couldn't stop loving her…"

"Maybe. But I don't like her very much. Not at the moment."

"I always understood your loyalty to her, Mark. What I didn't get was that you wouldn't even listen to me. You wouldn't give me a chance. All I was trying to tell you, if you'd have let me, was that you needed to speak with Sarah, maybe try and find out how she really felt about you having a close girlfriend, rather than the casual ones you'd had before… maybe check with Nicole how Sarah had been with her, being as she was the only other woman you'd dated for a length of time. I wasn't asking you to turn your back on her, *or* to make a choice between me and her. I just wanted you to have a little faith in me. I wish you'd trusted me and shown me some support, when I needed you most. But like I said, most importantly, I just wanted one night of your time, that's all. Just one night. Only you couldn't give me that, could you? You assumed I was the one with the problem and that Sarah was perfect. You put her first, Mark, and me last… and I needed you. I needed you so much."

"Do you still need me?" he asked.

She opened her mouth to speak, just as the sound of laughter from the coffee shop interrupted her. "I don't have time for this right now," she said, swallowing down the rising lump in her throat, and she turned and went into the ladies' room.

She sat in the stall for a full five minutes, just trying to calm her nerves, then came out, washed her hands, and checked her reflection in the mirror. She looked pale, but that couldn't be helped.

She opened the door and gasped. Mark was standing waiting for her, leaning against the wall opposite, his arms folded across his chest. As she came out, he pushed himself upright.

"I spoke to Nick," he said, stepping nearer to her. "Well, he spoke to me."

"When?"

"Just now, when I first got here. Don't be mad at him, Emma…"

"Why would I be?"

"He told me… about the sleeping pills."

She let her head drop into her hands, covering her face, and then sensed Mark's body close to hers, felt his hands on her wrists, pulling them away. "Look at me," he said and waited. She kept her head low. "Look at me, Emma. Please." She slowly raised her face to his and saw there his pain and confusion, his love and compassion, and the tears brimming in his eyes.

"Why didn't you tell me?" he asked. "Why couldn't *you* show that faith and trust in *me*?"

"You think I want to talk about that?"

"No, but… well, I wish you had. I wish I'd known."

"Why? Would you have treated me better?"

She saw in his eyes how much that had hurt him and part of her regretted it. "Yes," he said honestly. "I'd have tried harder. I'd have put you first… every time. I'd have come back here after the fire, not gone to Boston."

"You should have done all of that anyway, Mark."

"I know. I know I messed up. I got it wrong the first time by lying to you, and I got it wrong the second time by not listening to you and by not trusting your judgement, and by being blinded by Sarah's fucking games… and both times, I fucked up by not putting you first. But I won't let any of that happen again. I'll do whatever it takes to win you back, Emma. I'll fight for you, and for us, because I still love you and I know you still love me…"

"How?"

"Because I know how much you're hurting. If you didn't love me, it wouldn't hurt like this."

She couldn't deny that.

"And I know we're meant to be together. We're right for each other. You know that just as well as I do. You know I can make you happy and keep you safe. You just have to let me. I'm not giving up on us, Emma."

She stared up into his eyes. "God," she whispered. "I really wish I could believe you."

"You can."

"The problem is, Mark, I've heard it all before… too many times."

She shook her head just once, then turned and walked back into the coffee shop, resuming her seat at the tasting table, trying to look as composed as she could.

A few minutes later, out of the corner of her eye, she saw Mark make his way slowly through the crowd toward the front door, and blinked back her tears. So much for all his words. Nothing had changed… He'd given up on them already.

Mark

He stepped back outside through the door and felt the cold hit him, sucking the air from his lungs, just for a moment.

Emma's words rung in his ears. 'I've heard it all before…' That was true… it was so true. And it was those words which, as she'd turned her back on him, had given him the inkling of an idea.

"Giving up already?"

He swung around. Nick was glowering at him.

"No. I'm not giving up at all," he replied.

"Just walking out on her again then?"

"No."

"Then what the fuck are you doing? I gave you one chance—"

"I know," Mark interrupted. "I'm trying to take it."

"By leaving?"

"I'm not leaving." Mark took a couple of steps to the edge of the sidewalk, turned and looked up and down the store fronts, until he saw what he needed. He stepped back to Nick. "I need ten minutes," he said, "and I'll be back. Just keep an eye on her for me, make sure she's okay, and make sure she doesn't leave… or none of this is gonna work."

"You're not making any sense."

"It'll make sense to Emma. Trust me."

Nick's eyes narrowed, but he nodded his head and stepped back inside the coffee shop.

Ten minutes later, Mark stood back outside the front door once more.

In one arm he held the most enormous bouquet of yellow flowers and, nestled in among the various buds and blossoms, were a few daffodils. The lady in the shop had explained it was early in the season, but she'd just gotten hold of some that weekend. Mark didn't care. There were daffodils: that was all that mattered.

He took a moment to catch his breath and still his nerves. He had one shot at getting this right, and he had to do it in front nearly the whole town. He'd never gone public with his identity before, and he was about to go as public as it could get… hell, he was about to put his heart out there, and his nerves were killing him.

Still, she was worth it.

If they were going to make a go of it, they needed a fresh start… and this was definitely going to be that. At least he hoped it was.

He opened the door and let the warmth envelop him once more.

The noise level was lower. Everyone seemed to be listening and his arrival, together with the size of bouquet he was carrying caused a few heads to turn. Nick's was among them. He looked at the flowers, then at Mark, then he shrugged. It wasn't an inspiring reaction.

He entered as quietly as he could and listened. Although he couldn't see her through the crowd, Emma was talking, she was saying how good the bakes had been…

"So, all that remains now is for the other two judges and myself to make our decision. We'll do that as quickly as we can. And, if you all want to enjoy some more coffee, and sample the rest of the cakes, which Noah's just going to bring out, we'll get back to you as soon as we can."

Mark edged forward as she was speaking, nudging his way through the crowd, so by the time she'd finished her speech, he was standing at the front and, as she turned and looked up, their eyes met for the second time. Her mouth opened and, yet again, he saw tears forming.

He stepped forward, knowing the whole crowd would now be watching him as he stood before her. He knew, as he looked down at her, that she would remember exactly what he'd said to her four years ago, word for word. Emma was that kind of woman. She would always remember every detail, every moment of their time together. So, he had to get this right, or it would all be for nothing.

He held out his hand to her. "My name's Mark." He paused, looking into her eyes and willing her to take his hand, to see the point in all this. "Mark Gardner," he added.

He heard a collective gasp from behind him as those nearest heard his name, and then a low humming whisper as word spread throughout the coffee shop. He didn't care. He just looked at Emma, imploring her to shake his hand. Finally, he saw her eyes soften. He knew it was pity and good manners, but he didn't care.

He felt her hand in his, soft and delicate. "Emma Woods," she whispered. She got it… thank God.

"It's a real pleasure to meet you," he murmured back, taking another step closer. "I… I know you think you don't know me. I know you've got doubts about me, and I've just walked in here off the street, and back into your life, but would you like to have dinner with me tonight?"

Emma stared at him, and he knew she was remembering. There was just a flicker of heat in her eyes and he leant in a little further. "I'm not sure," he heard her say.

"You know I'm not a madman, or an ax murderer, or a serial killer, but I guess you're still gonna find it hard to trust me…" He paused. "You can, I promise." He smirked. "But then you've heard all this before, haven't you?" He looked into her eyes.

"Yes."

"Deep down, I'm really just an ordinary guy."

"Are you?" She looked doubtful. He'd adjusted the script to fit the circumstances, but she'd just taken them way off track with that one simple question… But that was okay. He could still bring it back.

"Yeah. I am. Have dinner with me and I'll prove it to you, unless you've got other plans, that is?"

He thought, just for a second, that he saw the corners of her mouth twitch upward.

"I don't have any other plans," she said quietly.

"Then you've got no reason not to have dinner with me…"

"Why, Mark?"

Oh… Fuck the script.

"Because I love you. Because I need you. And because you know I'll keep you safe." He put the flowers down on the table beside him, took a step closer and reached forward, touching her face gently with his fingertips. "And while safe can be boring, there's nothing I want more than to protect you – from everything – because being safe with you is anything but boring. Just let me love you again Emma, please."

She nodded her head and let out a sob at the same time, and he caught her in his arms, holding her close, while the people around them burst into spontaneous applause.

Chapter Twenty-one

Emma

Emma slipped on her high-heeled black shoes, then sat on the edge of the bed.

She'd felt sorry for Mark, standing there holding out his hand, in front of more than half the town, waiting for her to respond. And, really, it was kind of sweet, the way he'd introduced himself, using the same words he'd done four years ago. And if she was being honest, a small part of her had fallen for him all over again right then, even though she wasn't going to let him see that.

She got to her feet, and left the room, switching off the light and going through into the kitchen. She knew it must've been a big deal for him to do all of that so openly, with so many strangers looking on, and she appreciated how embarrassing he must have found it, with everyone watching while he said those words to her, and then to have them all clapping at the end. She'd found it mortifying, and she knew everyone in the room… So what must Mark have felt like?

She checked her watch. He was due in five minutes, so she grabbed her coat and shrugged it on, doing it up and wrapping her big cream scarf around her neck.

She'd found it hard to focus on the end of the contest after everything that had happened with Mark. Patsy had taken over really and, between them, they'd managed to reach a decision, choosing Andrea Mitchell, Heather Bennett, and Miranda Ross as the three winners, who would supply the coffee shop with various cakes and cookies. And while that was all taking place, Mark had sat with Jake and Maddie, watching Emma the whole time. Even when she was busy going through the scores with Patsy and Kathryn, and when she was making the final announcements, she'd been aware of his eyes on her. They hadn't left her once.

And then he'd helped with the clear up, talking with Jake and Cassie, just like old times. Nick had stayed too, she knew to keep and eye on her and make sure Mark didn't step out of line. She could sense Nick's distrust of Mark, but she couldn't blame him for that.

Mark had left once the coffee shop closed, and had gone to check in at the hotel, promising to be back in half an hour to take her to dinner.

The doorbell rang and she jumped, feeling nervous. Her hands were shaking as she grabbed her purse from the kitchen countertop, casting an eye over Mark's beautiful bouquet of flowers sitting in their vase, before she flicked off the light and walked down the stairs.

When she opened the door, he was standing there, staring down at her. He looked gorgeous, but then he always did.

He was wearing black jeans, a cream sweater, and a dark gray top coat.

"Hi," he murmured.

"Hello."

She stepped out and closed the door, locking it behind her, then turned and saw he was holding out his hand. She looked up at him. "Take it, Emma," he whispered. "You've got the rest of me already." She put her hand in his and felt his warm fingers clasping hers. "Thank you," he said, and they started down the street together.

Fernando's was a little busier than the last time they'd eaten there, but Elaine found them a quiet table and made a fuss of them as she took their coats. It became clear the news had traveled fast.

Before they sat down, Emma felt Mark's eyes roaming over her body. She'd worn a red turtleneck sweater dress that came down to her mid-thigh and was very, very fitted. It contrasted with her dark hair, which she'd left loose around her shoulders… and her high heels made her legs seem longer than they really were. She felt herself blushing under his gaze.

This time, they both chose the Tagliatelle alle Vongole and Mark selected a bottle of Sancerre to go with it.

"How are you?" he asked Emma, once Elaine had opened the wine and poured it, then left it in an ice bucket beside them.

"Tired."

"The competition went really well," he told her. "You put a lot of work into that. And you made a huge success of it." He was grinning at her and she couldn't help but feel a little proud of her achievement.

"Thank you. I think it was worth it in the end." She took a sip of wine. "What's happening with your hotel?" she asked.

"We're going to rebuild from scratch. Jake and I are meeting next week, then he'll be getting the plans drawn up as quickly as he can."

"And Kyle?"

He looked at her, evidently surprised. "You remembered his name?"

"Of course. How is he?"

"He's okay. He's hoping to be fit enough to return to work in the next month or so. I'll just need to find him a slot… somewhere."

"And what about all the other employees."

"Becky moved them all around, so they've got temporary employment until the new hotel's built."

"How long will it take?"

He shrugged. "I don't know yet. I'm waiting on Jake for that."

She nodded.

"And how's Becky?"

"She's okay. We haven't really talked much more, but she's been a little better."

They both took a drink of wine and stared at each other. The silence was in danger of becoming awkward, when Elaine appeared with their food.

"It needs more garlic," Mark whispered, after a couple of mouthfuls, leaning forward so no-one could overhear him.

Emma nodded. "I always make my Vongole with more chili than this, and I add just a dash of lemon juice before I serve it."

He smiled. "Yeah, but that's because you're addicted to lemons."

She smiled back. "I'm not addicted. I just think they add something to certain dishes. And anything with seafood in can only benefit from a splash of lemon."

"And a good kick of chopped chili."

"Exactly."

They continued to eat and make small talk, passing up both coffee and dessert, just like they had before.

Elaine brought them the check and, after Mark had paid, using his credit card this time, he helped Emma into her coat, letting his hands rest on her shoulders for just a little longer than necessary. She wrapped her scarf around her neck again, while Mark shrugged on his own coat and then they were back out on the street.

"Thank you for a lovely meal," she said, as they walked slowly down the sidewalk, hand in hand.

"Even if there wasn't enough garlic, and it needed more chili and a splash of lemon." He smiled down at her.

She looked up at him. "Even then."

"Thank you for agreeing to come out with me," he replied.

She took a deep breath. "The thing is, Mark, we've been acting almost like strangers all evening, talking about this and that, but we haven't talked about the one thing we really need to."

"I know." He stopped and pulled her back.

"You assumed Sarah was right, and I was wrong. You said some really horrible things to me."

"I know, and I'm sorry. I'm sorry for all of it."

"You're good at saying sorry."

"I've needed to be."

"The problem is, I'm not sure I can face a future like that." She looked up into his eyes and was surprised to see him smile back at her.

"I'm relieved you're even thinking about a future with me, Emma," he said gently and took a small step, so he was even closer to her. "I'm not gonna be making any of those mistakes again. I'm gonna get it right this time."

"I want to believe you, Mark, I really do. But you're asking so much of me."

"I'm not asking anything of you, baby. Well, except maybe a little patience while I try and work out a few things over the next couple of days." He moved a little closer still. "And your forgiveness for all the mistakes I've made." He rested his forehead against hers. "And the hope that we can have a future together. So I guess I am asking quite a lot, but I know being together is the right thing for us."

"How?"

"Because being away from you is just all fucking wrong, that's how."

She didn't reply, because she wasn't sure what to say. His words were so heartfelt and sounded so convincing… but she'd been here before with him.

He moved back and they carried on walking. "Can I come and see you in the morning before I leave?"

She turned to him. "You're leaving again? Already?"

"I have to. I've got meetings early on Monday, and Jake's coming to Boston on Tuesday to discuss the plans for the Manchester hotel… and, like I said, I've got a few things I need to work out. But I'm coming back, Emma. So, can I come and see you tomorrow morning?" he repeated.

"I guess so."

"I know you've got no reason to believe me, but I promise, I'm coming back."

They reached her apartment door and she looked up into his eyes. "I'm not gonna hold my breath waiting for you, Mark. Not this time. You've made me that promise before. And you've let me down – too many times."

He stepped closer. She could feel the heat from his body.

"I know. I've got no right to ask you to wait for me. But I'm not gonna let you down. I'm not gonna let you go either. I've come too close to losing you… for good, it seems. It's not gonna happen again."

By mid-afternoon on Sunday, Emma was starting to wonder if the whole thing had been a dream.

Mark had called round in the morning and they'd had a coffee together. He'd told her again that he was coming back, that he loved her, he wanted her in his life and he wasn't going to let her down and, once again, she desperately wanted to believe him, but the memory of all the hurt was still too raw.

He'd driven off just before ten and she'd spent the morning going through the paperwork she hadn't done on Saturday, before making herself an omelette for lunch and sitting in front of the television for an hour, pretending to watch whatever was on.

Her phone beeped. It was in the kitchen and she got up and went over to the countertop, checking the screen. It was a message from Mark.

—Just got to the hotel. Sorry I'm late. Traffic really bad on freeway. Hope you're okay. Can I call later? I love you. M xx

She felt the tears burning behind her eyes. His message was just like the ones he used to send.

She waited, thinking for a moment, then tapped out a reply.

— Glad you arrived safely. Thanks for letting me know. I'm okay. I'm here all day. E

She wasn't ready to put kisses on her message yet, or 'I love you', so she pressed 'send'.

His response was immediate.

— You're there, but can I call? M xx

— Yes. E

— Thank you. I'll call this evening. I love you, Emma. M xx

— I know. E

But she still wasn't sure if love was enough.

He'd phoned on Sunday evening, and again on Monday morning. He texted frequently throughout the day, then called again that night. On Tuesday and Wednesday, it was the same. It was just how it had been before. His messages, his calls, his voice… they were all filled with love for her. Still, she half expected it to all come tumbling down again.

On Thursday morning, Emma woke early. She'd had a strange dream, in which Sarah had set the whole town against her, spreading rumors and gossip. Oddly, Mark wasn't in the dream at all, and Emma was having to battle Sarah all by herself, without him. It was terrifying.

She woke, startled and fearful, about twenty minutes before her alarm went off and decided to make herself a coffee while waiting for Mark's call. Except he didn't call. Eventually, she gave up waiting and went for her shower. And when she came out, there was no message, no missed call, no text. She sat on the edge of her bed and held her phone in her hands.

After just a couple of days, she'd already come to rely on hearing from him. Was he going back to his old ways again already? She bit back the lump in her throat and blinked away the tears that threatened to fall. She'd told herself not to build up her hopes, because all that happened was he let her down, and she ended up feeling despondent again.

By lunchtime, she still hadn't heard anything. She'd checked her phone regularly. She'd thought about calling him, but whatever was going on between them, it had to come from him… and he knew that. He needed to rebuild the trust. She thought about calling Nick, but she knew he'd worry; he'd probably come over and sit with her and be angry with Mark, and she wasn't in the mood for that either.

Luckily the coffee shop was fairly busy, which took her mind off her disappointment. She was fixing a couple of lattes when she heard the door open and close. Patsy was in the kitchen, but whoever it was would take a seat and she'd get to them in a minute…

"Hi." She heard his familiar voice behind her and flipped around, spilling milk on the floor.

"Shit!" She grabbed a cloth. "Sorry." She looked up and murmured, "Hi."

He smiled, leaning over the counter. "Do you need a hand?"

"No. I've got it." She wiped the spilt milk and stood up, looking straight into his eyes. "You're here," she said, feeling a little stupid for stating the obvious.

"Yeah. I told you I'd come back."

"But… but it's Thursday."

"I know." He looked around. "And you're busy." He leant back again. "I'll go and check in at the hotel, and come back in a little while."

"But you've only just got here."

He smiled across at her and winked. "I'm not going anywhere, Emma, other than to the hotel. I'll check in, I've got a few calls to make and then I'll come back."

He walked across to the door and turned just as he was about to leave, smiling at her. She couldn't help but smile back.

Mark came back around four in the afternoon, when the coffee shop had quietened down a little. He sat in a booth; Emma made him a coffee and came to sit opposite him, leaving Josh in charge. Since New Year, he'd started working two evenings a week, after school, as well as Saturdays.

"You didn't call," she said quietly.

"When?" Mark looked up at her.

"This morning."

"No. I'm sorry. I had some things to deal with at the office, and then I was driving… and, besides, I wanted to surprise you. I know you didn't think I'd come back again."

"Do you blame me?"

"No." He took a sip of coffee, reaching over and taking her hand in his. "I've spoken to Maggie," he said. Emma felt her heart sink. Had he driven all the way out here to tell her he was going back to see Sarah after all? Was she falling down the list already?

"And?" she prompted, trying to get the better of her nerves. It was already dawning on her that she needed to give him the benefit of the doubt and hear him out, before jumping to conclusions. She'd made that mistake before.

"And Maggie's found Sarah a therapist. I know she needs help and I've agreed with Maggie that I'll pay for it. I'll make sure she gets whatever help is available."

"Are you going to go back there?"

"No. I can't. I'm not sure I'll ever be a part of her life again, not in the same way, anyway. I can't even think about her at the moment without getting madder than hell." He took a breath. "She's gonna stay on at the house in Boston for now, although I'm thinking of selling it and buying somewhere smaller. She doesn't need that big place just for herself. I've moved all my things to the hotel where I've been living… Well, Anthony and Maggie did that for me."

"You didn't even go back to move your things?" She was shocked.

He shook his head. "No. I can't bear to be near Sarah. I don't want to see her, or speak to her."

Emma placed her other hand over his. "Give it some time, Mark."

"Are you serious?"

"Yes. Try and forgive her."

"Why the hell should I do that?" He was incredulous. "She hurt you… She hurt me. I can't forgive her."

"Try. I'm not saying you'll be able to do it right away, but don't rule it out. She's all the family you've got left, Mark. Maybe once she's had some therapy, once she's better, you'll be able to understand why she did it…"

He stared at her. "Nick and I were both so damn right about you."

She tilted her head to one side. "What does that mean?"

"You're too damn good… for me, and for Sarah."

She shook her head, lowering it and looking at their clasped hands.

"How have you been getting on, living in a hotel?" she asked him, changing the subject.

He smiled. "I probably shouldn't say this, considering I own the place… but I hate it."

Emma giggled. "No, you probably shouldn't say that. Why do you hate it?"

"It's so impersonal. I don't feel like I belong there."

"So, what are you going to do? Buy another place in Boston?"

"No, not yet anyway. I think I told you once, I don't really have to live there."

"Yes, I remember you saying. But isn't that were your office is?"

"Yeah, but I work from home quite a lot. And I travel around to the hotels. I probably only go into the office one or two days a week, and I don't always need to do that. I just go in sometimes to remind them what I look like."

"So where are you going to live?"

"I've found a place… Well, I think I have. I wanted to ask your opinion about it."

"You did?" She was surprised.

"Yeah." He glanced around the coffee shop. "Look… It's real quiet in here now. Can you sneak off early. I'm sure Josh can handle things and lock up for you, and I can drive us down to see this house. I'm really in two minds about it… especially the kitchen."

"The kitchen?"

"Yes. I'm not sure about it at all. I could do with an expert's view."

"I'm not an expert."

"Well, you know a darn sight more than I do."

She smirked. "When it comes to cooking, that's not hard."

"Fair point." He squeezed her hand. "So, will you come?"

"We'll be back tonight, won't we?"

"Yeah. It might be late, but I'll make sure to get you back."

"Okay, let me go and speak to Josh…"

"Where are we going?" Emma asked. They'd only driven about ten miles out of town before Mark turned off the highway into a private, tree-lined lane that seemed to lead to nowhere.

"We're going to see the house."

"It's here?"

"Where did you think it was?"

"A lot nearer to Boston."

He glanced across at her. "No. It's here. Nearer to you…" Just at that moment, the lane bent round and Emma gasped as the house came into view. Overlooking the ocean, it was a beautiful classical house, with an idyllic beach frontage.

Mark parked the car and climbed out, coming round to open Emma's door and help her to her feet.

"What do you think?" he asked her.

"I think it's incredible."

"It's pretty amazing, isn't it?" His eyes were shining. "Wanna come see inside?"

She nodded her head. He took her hand and led her to the main entrance, pulling a key from his pocket.

"You've got a key?" she said.

"Yeah. The realtor let me have it."

He opened the door and let Emma go inside ahead of him. He flicked on the light switch and, again, she gasped. They were standing in a huge hallway, with oak floors and white walls. She glanced to her right, through double doors, into what seemed to be a living room, although there was no furniture.

"Does no-one live here?" she asked.

"No… The current owner moved out about two months ago." He took her hand. "Come see the kitchen…"

He led her into the enormous living area, and through to the kitchen, which was larger than Emma's whole apartment. The cabinets were off-white; the countertops black granite. There was an eight-burner stove and a built in double-width refrigerator, with wine cooler. In the center of the room was a huge island unit, and the whole of one wall was made of folding glass doors that looked out over the garden and the sea beyond. At the far end of the kitchen was a further set of double doors, which led through to another space that Emma assumed would be used as a more formal dining room.

"What exactly weren't you sure about?" she asked.

He came and stood in front of her.

"Whether it's good enough…"

"Of course it's good enough. It's spectacular."

"Okay. There's something else I want you to see. Just come with me a minute…" He led her back into the entrance hall, pointing out two further rooms, one of which he said was already set up as a home cinema, and the other, he was thinking of using as his office, although he'd not reached any firm decisions yet. Then he took her up the wide stairway. At the top, they went around the galleried landing and then he stopped in front of a door, opening it and standing to one side.

"What's this?" she asked, going inside.

"It's the master bedroom." She looked slowly around the room. "What do you think?" Again the walls were white and the floor oak, there were two open doors, leading to a dressing room and bathroom, and an ornate fireplace on one wall. But what really caught Emma's eye was the window… or, to be more precise, the view from the window. She wandered over and stared out at an unbroken panorama of the Atlantic Ocean, the blues and purples of the evening sky reflected in the water.

"I think it's beautiful, Mark." She turned back and looked at him.

He came and stood in front of her. "Can you see yourself living here?" he asked, his voice little more than a whisper.

"Here?" She stared up at him.

"Yes… here." He moved closer. "I love you with every breath in my body." He closed his eyes, just for a second and when he opened them again, she saw they were glistening in the fading light. "I know I got it wrong. I know I hurt you. I hurt me too. These last few weeks without you have been the worst I've ever known, and I don't ever want to be without you again." He cupped her face in his hands. "I know you're not ready yet, and I know we've got a long way to go. But, as long as you like it, I'm gonna buy this house, because I have to be close to where you are. I've spent the last few days working things out at the office, so I can move out of the hotel and out of Boston. I'm gonna stay at the hotel in Somers Cove for now, until I can close on this place and get it ready to move into… I'm gonna have to go back to the city for work a day or so each week, so I'll be traveling around a bit, but I'm gonna make this my base from now on. I'm not asking anything of you, baby. Nothing at all. Not until you're ready. But when you are, I want you to move in here with me. Because I want you with me. Always."

Mark

"You're not serious…"

He looked down at her.

"I'm absolutely serious."

She pulled away and he felt lost without her. "We're not even back together properly yet, and you're talking about buying this place… I mean, it's gotta be worth at least five million."

He smirked. "Nearer seven."

"Seven?" She was obviously horrified. "We only broke up a few weeks ago. You came back to town just last weekend, and you're gonna spend seven million dollars on a house, just so you can live near me?"

"Yes. In the hope that one day you'll live here too. I know you wouldn't want to live too far away from where you grew up, or from your brother. You need him, and that's fine with me." He paused. "I looked at couple of other houses, but this one's got the best kitchen."

"Mark…" He heard the warning note in her voice.

"I'm in this for the long haul, Emma." He stepped nearer to her again. "I already said, I know you're not ready. I'll wait."

She looked up into his eyes. "And since when were you any good at waiting for me?"

A smile tugged at his lips, and he tried to fight it down. "It's different this time."

"Really?"

"Yes, really. If we have to start afresh, date for a while, then fine. I can do that. We don't have to sleep together. We don't even have to kiss, not if you don't want to." He put his hands on her waist and pulled her close. "Please, Emma… Please just trust me one last time. I promise you won't regret it."

She gazed into his eyes for a long moment and then, almost imperceptibly nodded her head, just once.

"I don't know why, but I can't ever resist you," she murmured and he felt his heart swell into his chest, and he hugged her to him, burying his face in her hair. Tears welled in his eyes, but he blinked them away and held on to her, until she pulled back and looked up at him again. Her cheeks were wet and he brushed away her tears with his thumbs.

"Can I take you to dinner?" he asked.

"Yes, as long as it's not to Fernando's," she replied, and he smiled.

"No, not to Fernando's. There's a nice place just a little further down the coast. I've driven past it so many times now. Let me take you there."

She nodded. "Are we dressed okay?" She was still wearing her black pants and white blouse, with a black coat, and he was in jeans, a sweater and his leather jacket.

He looked her up and down. "I don't know," he said, smiling. "I think a little jewelry might help."

She looked confused. "Then we'll have to go home again," she murmured.

"No… No we won't. I've got something that'll probably do the job." He reached into his pocket and pulled out a square box, handing it to her. "I bought you this for Christmas," he said quietly, "only Christmas never happened."

"But—But I didn't have time to get you a Christmas present before we broke up." She seemed upset.

"Hey," he said, rubbing the backs of his fingers down her cheek. "It's not a Christmas present anymore."

"Then what is it?"

He shrugged. "It's an 'I love you' present." She looked up at him. "Open it," he urged.

She lowered her gaze and opened the box, and he heard her gasp. "It's… it's beautiful, Mark," she breathed. She looked up at him again. "Why do I get the feeling this cost a lot of money."

He grinned, shaking his head. "No idea." He took the necklace from the box, unfurled it and put it over her head. Emma pulled her hair free, adjusting the necklace under the collar of her blouse, and letting it settle. It fell perfectly, just below her breasts, the stones evenly placed.

"What are these stones?" she asked, looking down at them.

"Just stones," he replied.

"Mark…" her voice held that warning tone again.

"Okay." He pointed to them in turn. "They're blue topaz, cultured pearls, and diamonds."

"Oh my God." Her voice was barely a whisper. "I can't—" she began to say.

"Do you like it?" he asked.

"I love it."

"Then you can."

Much later, after an excellent dinner, he drove them both back to her apartment and they stood outside.

"Thank you for a really lovely afternoon… and evening," Emma said.

"It's been my pleasure. It really has." He moved closer. "I'm glad you liked the house."

"Who wouldn't like it?" She hesitated for a moment. "You're really going to buy it?"

"Yes. I'll call the realtor in the morning. I'm gonna try and do a deal, of course. I know the owner's looking for a quick sale. I can do that. But I'm gonna see what I can get in return by way of a price reduction."

"And if they won't reduce the price?"

"Then I'll buy it anyway. But there's no harm in trying." He grinned. "And I'm glad you liked the necklace too." He reached out and touched one of the blue topaz stones, the one that fell just below her breasts. "It looks perfect on you."

"It's too much," she said quietly.

"It's not enough." He held her gaze for a very long moment.

"I'd better get inside," Emma said eventually. "I've got an early start."

"Yeah." He wanted to go inside with her and he felt disappointed, but hid it well. "Can… Can I kiss you?" he asked, holding his breath.

She nodded, just once and he closed the gap between them, his lips touching hers. She opened to him at the first touch of his tongue and he delved inside, tasting her again. God, she felt good… so good. He placed one hand on her waist, the other behind her head and moved her back until she was against the door, his feet either side of hers. Even through their clothes, he knew she'd be able to feel his erection, and she moaned softly into his mouth, her hands coming up to his shoulders, then behind his head and into his hair. He tilted his head to take her deeper and groaned into her as she whimpered. Eventually he slowed the kiss, nipping at her bottom lip, then reluctantly pulled back. Her eyes were sparkling and he remembered that look. He knew what it meant. She wanted him too.

"Goodnight," he whispered.

She nodded, swallowing hard. "Goodnight."

He woke early the next morning, at just before six-thirty and immediately picked up his phone, typing out a message.

— *Good morning. Hope you slept well. Thank you for last night. I'll be over later. I love you. M xxx*

He went to the bathroom and came back. Her reply was waiting for him.

— *Good morning. I slept very well. Hope you did too. I'm the one who needs to thank you. Look forward to seeing you later. E. x*

Okay, so she hadn't said 'I love you', but there was a kiss… that was something. It felt like a lot more than something and he couldn't stop smiling as he headed to the shower.

It was nearly ten-thirty by the time he walked through the door of the coffee shop. There were only two other customers there and he ignored them both. Emma was standing behind the counter and looked up as soon as he came in, a beautiful smile spreading across her face. He went straight over, leant across the counter and whispered, "It's ours."

"What is?"

"The house…"

"I think you'll find it's yours. But congratulations."

He reached over and took her hand in his. "It's ours, Emma," he said firmly. "I'm buying it for us to live in." He suddenly felt a little fearful. "I thought you were okay with giving us another chance."

"I am," she murmured. "I just need to take it slow. I've got to be able to trust you again, Mark, and you buying a house and calling it 'ours' isn't my idea of taking it slow."

"Okay." He leant back. "I get it." She breathed out and seemed to relax a little. "It's still ours though," he added and grinned at her.

She shook her head, but a smile tweaked at her lips.

"I've brought my laptop with me." He nodded down to his messenger bag that he'd put on the floor beside him. "Can I work here?" he asked, changing the subject.

"Sure." She waved an arm around the shop. "You can pretty much take your pick of the tables, the wifi is free, and I'll keep you supplied with coffee."

"With offers like that, I might never go back to my office."

Mark settled at one of the tables near the counter and started work. He'd answered most of his e-mails by lunchtime and was in the middle of a long reply to a message from Becky about the insurance claim and rebuild schedule he'd discussed with Jake earlier in the week, when the coffee shop started to get busier. He became aware of people staring at him, and a low hum of whispering, and pointed looks. It was all good natured, but felt intrusive. He wasn't used to being the center of attention like this and he felt more than a little uncomfortable.

"Come with me." Emma's voice broke into his thoughts.

He looked up. She was staring down at him.

"Where are we going?" he asked.

"Just pack up your things and come with me."

He did as she said, closing the lid of his laptop, putting it away and getting to his feet. He grabbed his jacket from the back of the chair and followed her out of the shop.

She took his hand as they walked along the sidewalk to the door of her apartment, which she opened. Then she went up the stairs ahead of him, leading him through to the familiar kitchen and putting her keys down on the countertop.

"I'll leave you with those for now," she said, "in case you need go back to the hotel, or down to the store, or something. You know where the coffee is, and how the machine works. There's fruit, chocolate, cookies… all kinds of things if you get hungry, and I'll bring you a sandwich in a little while."

He pulled her into his arms. "Thank you," he said.

"They don't mean any harm, but it was making you uncomfortable, wasn't it?"

"Yeah. I'm just not used to it. I hate it…"

"I know."

"Thanks for rescuing me."

"You're welcome." She rested her head on his chest, just for a minute. It felt good holding her there. "I'd better get back," she said, pulling away again. "It's lunchtime… I can't leave Kathryn by herself. She can't make a damn coffee."

He laughed and released her. "Okay. I'll see you later?"

"Yeah. I'll bring that sandwich up as soon as I can."

"I'll be fine."

The doorbell rang about an hour later and, breaking off from his work in the living room, Mark went downstairs, to find Emma standing there with what appeared to be a sandwich, wrapped in wax paper.

"Lunch," she announced, smiling at him, and handing over the sandwich.

"What about yours?"

"I can't stop yet. I'll take a break in another hour or so."

"I'll wait for you."

"No, you go ahead. That's still warm, and I made it specially for you."

"You did?" He smiled.

"Yeah…" She turned. "Let me know what you think," she called, and she was gone again.

He climbed the stairs, sat down at the breakfast bar and unwrapped the paper to reveal a toasted white bread sandwich, filled with what appeared to be fresh crab meat, among other things. He took a bite and decided he'd gone to heaven. It was definitely crab, but there was also tomato, and onion, and roasted pepper, and mayonnaise. And there was just a hint of lemon. He chuckled.

He went across to the living room, grabbed his phone and came back to the breakfast bar, sitting down and tapping out a message.

— *It's divine. Like you. M xxx*

He carried on eating, not expecting a reply. He knew she was busy, so he was surprised when his phone beeped after just a couple of minutes.

— *Hope you especially liked the lemon mayonnaise ;) E x*

He laughed out loud.

He worked until mid-afternoon and then went back down to the coffee shop, figuring it should be quieter now.

Sure enough, there were four customers and they didn't pay any attention when Mark opened the door. Emma looked up from the table she was clearing and he went over to her.

"You didn't come up for lunch," he said quietly.

"No. I'm sorry. I didn't have time in the end."

"You've eaten though, right?"

She nodded. "Yeah, I grabbed something earlier."

"Good." He wanted to hold her, and kiss her. But not here. "Where would you like to go for dinner?" he asked. She glanced down at her hands. "What's wrong?" Didn't she want to have dinner with him?

"Nothing. But would you mind if we didn't go out? I'm tired. I'd rather just cook something and eat upstairs."

"You'd find that more relaxing?"

She nodded. "Yes. I always find cooking relaxing. And I'm not in the mood for going out, not after what happened at lunchtime."

"We don't have to go anywhere near here," he said.

"I know, but I'd rather cook."

"Okay. As long as you're sure."

She nodded. "I'm sure. If you don't mind."

"Of course I don't mind. I love your cooking, you know that. Do you need me to go to the store and get anything?"

"Just a bottle of wine, if that's okay?"

"That's fine. Red or white?"

"White."

"No problem. And there's nothing I can do for dinner?"

She smiled at him. "No. I think you'd better leave that to me."

"That looks incredible," Mark said, watching Emma dish the food out onto the warmed plates.

"It's just onions, garlic, chicken, tomatoes, chick peas, with some herbs, stock and wine…"

"*Just*," he said.

They carried the dishes over to the table, where Emma had laid out a basket of crusty bread and Mark had opened the wine. He poured them both a glass and they took a sip before starting to eat.

"It tastes as good as it looks. And this all came out of your freezer, and the food cupboard?"

"Yes." She nodded.

"That's even more impressive." He helped himself to a slice of bread.

"I—I wanted to tell you something," she said, putting her fork down gently.

He placed the bread on the side of his plate. "What is it?"

"Between Christmas and New Year," she began, "when we weren't together, I was burying my head in work to try and keep busy, to try and stop myself from thinking about you." He reached across the table and took her hand. "There was a problem with one of the suppliers and I had to call Mrs Adams, and I asked her again about selling me the coffee shop."

"And?" Mark sat forward.

She looked up at him. "And she said yes."

He leapt off his chair, moved around the table, and pulled her to her feet and into his arms. "That's amazing news. I'm so pleased for you, Emma."

She leant back in his arms. "If I'm honest, I'm kinda scared."

"Why? This is what you wanted, isn't it?"

"Yes, and she doesn't want as much as I thought she would." They sat back down again, although he kept hold of her hand.

"Will your savings cover it?" he asked, picking up his fork with his free hand and taking a mouthful of chicken.

"No. But I won't need to borrow quite as much as I thought I would."

"Well, that's good," he said. "Why are you scared, Emma?"

"Because I don't know how to finance the upgrade, or even how much it's going to cost."

He hesitated, just for a moment. "Would you like me to take a look at the figures?" he offered.

He felt her sigh of relief. "Would you? I was hoping you'd say that." She smiled. "Last week, I was sitting here, wishing I could ask your advice. But you weren't here, and I felt like I had no-one to turn to." He heard the crack in her voice.

"Well, you do now," he said softly.

After they'd finished eating, they cleared the table, and sat on the couch.

"Can I kiss you?" he asked, turning toward her her.

"Are you going to ask me every time you want to kiss me?" she asked, a smile forming on her lips.

"Not forever, no. But for now, I think so. I think it's best." He looked at her. "So, can I?"

She leant across and put her lips against his, answering his question. He gently pushed her back into the corner of the couch, his lips crushing hers, his tongue exploring her mouth and finding hers. Her moans filled the room as he shifted position, parting her legs slightly with his own and settling between them. His hard erection pressed into her and she raised her hips to his. She wanted more. He knew she did. He pulled back and looked down at her, the sparkle in her eyes giving him more hope than he'd thought possible.

"If I'm gonna wait for you, I'd better stop this now."

She sucked in a breath and nodded her head, then sat up, straightening her clothes.

"I'm sorry," he murmured, getting to his feet.

"Don't be." She looked up at him. The sparkle was still there. "You don't have to leave though, do you?"

"Not if you don't want me to, no." She shook her head and he sat down again, leaving a small space between them.

"Can you hold me?" she asked.

He looked across at her. "Of course. Come here." She curled up beside him, resting her head on his chest and he brought his arms around her.

"I—I think I owe you an apology," she whispered, nestling further down into him.

"Why? What on earth could you possibly have to apologize to me for?"

"Because I broke my promise."

"You did?" He changed position, leaning back and raising her face to his.

She nodded. "I promised you a while back, that I'd never break up with you again. And I did. I'm sorry."

"Emma," he said gently, "I deserved everything you did. Please don't apologize for that."

"I didn't want to hurt you though."

He rubbed his thumb against her soft cheek. "I know," he said. "I didn't want to hurt you either. I was being arrogant, blind, selfish, and spectacularly dumb. Those are not a mistakes I'll be making again."

"I really hope not."

He leant down and kissed her gently, letting his lips rest against hers for a long while.

The next morning was Saturday but Mark still woke early. He didn't care. Kissing Emma last night had been magical, hearing and feeling her arousal had been incredible… and holding her had felt great. Saying goodnight and leaving her there, however, had been torture. He picked up his phone and sent a message:

— *I don't like waking up without you. M xxx*

He hoped it wasn't too much, but pressed send anyway.

Emma's reply came back immediately.

— *Neither do I. E xx*

He smiled. She'd sent two kisses. It felt like progress.

— Are you working from home this morning? M xxx
— Yes. I have to do the paperwork. E xx
— Can I come over? M xxx
— Yes. Come for breakfast, if you like. E xx
— Give me 30 minutes. I love you. M xxx
— Okay. See you then. E xx

She still wouldn't say 'I love you' to him. Or maybe she couldn't. He wasn't sure which. Either way, he still had work to do to win her round.

"Hi." She opened the door and smiled at him.

"Good morning." She looked so good. She was the only woman he knew who made jeans and a sweater look sexy. She stood to one side and let him into the apartment, then closed the door behind them.

When she turned back, he put his hands on her waist and pulled her close, kissing her… hard. He stroked a hand up her back to her neck, rubbing the skin there gently with his thumb. She stepped closer, putting her hands up under his sweater and hooking her thumbs into the waistband of his jeans. He broke the kiss eventually, leaning back just a little to look down at her.

"You didn't ask," she whispered.

"Sorry."

"It's okay. I think I prefer it this way."

He smiled. "So do I."

She climbed the stairs ahead of him and led him into the kitchen.

"Is scrambled eggs and bacon okay?" she asked. "Most of it's done already."

"It's better than okay."

She started serving up, while he sat at the breakfast bar.

"I thought I could take a look at those figures for you this morning, if you'd like me to," he said.

"Would that be alright?"

"Of course. You're probably gonna need to give me a bit more detail about your plans though, if you want me to tell you how to finance it."

Emma put the toast on the plates and added the scrambled eggs, topping them with crispy bacon.

"We'll eat this," she said, coming and sitting beside him, "and then I'll go through it all with you."

It was five o'clock before Mark had finished going through Emma's figures. She'd already gone down to the coffee shop a couple of hours before, and he joined her there, sitting at the counter.

"Can I look at the kitchens?" he asked.

"Sure."

The coffee shop was empty of customers and she took him through to the back, leaving him there with Noah, who showed him around. He seemed pleased to have someone to talk to and Mark was in there until closing time, checking over equipment and talking to Noah about Emma's ideas.

"What's the verdict?" she asked, as soon as they got upstairs again.

He sat down at the breakfast bar, while Emma stood opposite, leaning against the countertop. "Looking at how much you've got in the bank, how much you say you can afford to borrow, and how much the upgrade's going to cost, I think you're about fifteen to twenty thousand dollars shy of where you need to be."

"How much?" She was shocked.

"You want to do quite a lot of work to the front of the shop, but the kitchen's a big deal in this too, Emma. I've talked it over with Noah and, knowing what you want to offer, you're gonna need to completely overhaul it. But that's not your biggest problem."

"It isn't?" she whispered.

"No. Some of your equipment is really old. Things have changed. To get a new refrigeration unit in, you're going to need to take down the wall between the kitchen and the storage area."

She seemed to deflate and curl slightly in on herself.

"I had no idea I'd have to do that much work, or that it would cost so much." He saw a glistening in her eyes and got up, going over to her.

"Let me help you," he murmured.

She shook her head. "No. I'll just have to wait to do the upgrade."

"You don't have to wait. I'll put the money in." He took her hands in his, holding them tight. "In fact, I don't really want you to borrow from the bank. I'd like to give you all of it."

"No, Mark."

"Why not?"

"Because I don't want people to think I'm just with you for your money. And because I want to do this by myself. It's important to me. I want to make a success of this, and I want to know that *I* did it."

He pulled her into his arms. "I don't give fuck what other people think."

"Even so, Mark…"

"Emma, I know what Sarah said to you about people wanting to be with me for my money."

"How?"

"Anthony overheard her. And he told Maggie. She told me, after we broke up. I'll be honest and admit I still thought it was a misunderstanding. That was, until Sarah repeated the accusation when I confronted her about the press reports."

"She did?" Emma whispered.

"Yeah. I can't believe I didn't see all of that going on, but like I said, I was being spectacularly dumb. I told her it was bullshit. I know you're not interested in my money. I've always known that. And no-one else's opinion matters a damn, Emma."

"That's all well and good, but I still want to do this by myself."

"You would be. I'd put the money in, but that's as far as my interest would go. I don't have time to get involved… I mean, I'll advise you, if you need me to, but I really couldn't devote my time to anything major like upgrading your coffee shop. You'd be on your own, baby, and I know you can make this work." He looked into her eyes. "Of course, if you don't think you can handle it…"

"I can handle it."

"Then let me help you."

"I can't borrow the money from you. I'd hate being in debt to you like that."

"Who said anything about *borrowing* it? I'd give you the money."

Her eyes narrowed a little. "Are you offering to do this because you feel guilty about what happened with Sarah, or because you feel responsible… about the sleeping pills?" She whispered the last two words.

He stepped back, but moved his hands to her waist, keeping hold of her. "No." His voice was firm. "I'm offering to do this because I'm in love with you. I want to support you in everything you want to do. And that's all. I'd still offer you the money, even if nothing had gone on with Sarah, and even if you hadn't taken the tablets. I just wanna help you." He paused. "But if I'm being honest, yeah, I do feel guilty about what happened with my sister, *and* I feel responsible for what you tried to do to yourself…" He sighed and looked into her eyes. "I wish I could understand, Emma."

"Understand what?"

"Why you did it… why you took the tablets." She lowered her eyes. "Can you explain it to me?"

"Why?" she whispered.

He raised her face to his. "Because I need to know. Nick said I did that to you. Is that true? Was it really all my fault?" His voice cracked on the last few words.

She clasped his face in her hands. "Honestly?" she asked.

He nodded. "I have to know." He did. Even though he dreaded trying to live with himself once he knew the truth.

She took a deep breath, releasing him. "It wasn't *all* about us," she said quietly. "Not entirely… Cassie wasn't here anymore, and I missed her friendship. Jake had gone too. And Nick was focused on his work. I already felt like had no-one."

"And then I left you as well."

She nodded. "I'd been so happy with you, Mark. You'd shown me how good my life could be… and then…" She stopped talking.

"I took all that away." She didn't reply, but she didn't need to. He knew. "I'm sorry, Emma."

"I know. But I don't want you to keep saying sorry. I don't want to remember that time, or the time we've just been through. It was awful for both of us, maybe in different ways, but neither of us wanted to be apart – either time – and I really don't want to look back. I can't, Mark… I can't."

"Hey," he murmured, pulling her close again. "It's okay now. I'm here, and I'm not going anywhere."

"I just don't want our future to be tainted by the actions of our past."

"Tell me what you *do* want," he said, staring deep into her eyes.

"I want you to make it right," she whispered.

His breath caught as remembered saying something like that to her once before, the night he'd driven back from Boston with her after that shitty weekend, and they'd made love… He moved slightly closer. "What are you asking?"

"Put us back together again." Her voice broke, and now he knew exactly what she wanted.

For a second or two, the air around them stilled, crackling with unspoken emotion, then he pulled her close, their bodies fused, and he kissed her, covering her lips with his. "Where?" he murmured, panting hard.

"Here… now," she muttered back, and he felt her reaching between them and tugging on his belt.

He ripped through the buttons of her blouse, then undid her pants, pushing them down, with her panties. "Step out," he whispered into her mouth, and she did. Then, without breaking the kiss, he undid her bra and dropped it to the floor, walking her back to the wall. As she hit it, he placed one hand behind her head, the other on her breast, squeezing gently, then pinching her nipple between his thumb and forefinger. She squealed into his mouth, her tongue delving deeper.

He broke the kiss and without taking his eyes from hers, took over from her renewed ineffectual fumbling with his belt and undid it, then his jeans, pushing them down, together with his trunks, freeing his erection. He toed off his shoes, and kicked off his jeans, then yanked his sweater over his head before lifting her up. Emma stared, breathless, into his eyes, wrapping her legs around his waist as he lowered her slowly down onto his hard cock, and they both gasped at the depth of his penetration.

"Hold my shoulders, baby," he murmured, as he started to move her, lifting her and lowering her again and again.

"Oh… Oh, my God," she breathed, clasping onto him. "That's so good…"

He quickened the pace, then slowed it down again, letting her feel his length with every stroke.

"Fuck, baby, you're so wet," he whispered, nipping at her bottom lip with his teeth.

"Take me," she murmured. "Please…"

He spun her around and sat her down on the countertop, spreading her legs wide, then pounded into her, hard and deep, giving her what she wanted… what they both needed.

"More, Mark… More." Her voice hummed across his nerves.

"You're so fucking tight on my cock."

She moaned her pleasure, her cries getting louder. He pulled her forward so she was right on the edge of the surface. He couldn't get any deeper inside and he drove into her, as she gripped his shoulders, leaning forward and biting into his flesh.

He felt the ripple right in the depth of her, heard the change in her breathing. She was close… but then so was he.

"I'm… I'm gonna come…" she yelled, throwing back her head, and as she said those words, he couldn't hold back any longer and he exploded, filling her, over and over, all the longing pouring out of him, while she bucked wildly, screaming her pleasure.

"Mark…" she whimpered, calming slowly.

He leant his forehead against hers. "I know. I'm sorry. I forgot the condom again."

"That's not what I was going to say."

He leant back a little and stared into her eyes, feeling fearful. "What's wrong? Did I hurt you?"

"No. Nothing's wrong. And no, you didn't hurt me. I—I just wanted…" She breathed deeply. "I just wanted to tell you I love you. I love you so much."

He smiled. "And I love you, Emma." He kissed her, holding her tight. "Can we move this to the bedroom?" he asked.

She nodded and he lifted her into his arms, keeping them connected, his cock still hard.

"About the condom," she murmured in his ear.

He leant back and looked down at her, gazing into her eyes. "I—I'm not sure I care," he said, smiling lightly.

She shook her head. "Neither do I."

An hour or so later, she lay naked in his arms. He'd made love to her more slowly and tenderly, made her come twice more before filling her again, and now she was snuggled next to him, sleepy and satisfied.

"You're really, really bad at waiting, you know that, don't you?"

"Hey… that's not fair. You asked me this time around."

"Yeah, I guess I did."

"And besides…" He kissed her hair. "I'm addicted to you. There's no way I was gonna be able to wait long." She giggled. "We just have to accept it, baby," he continued. "We're a very physical couple."

"I don't mind that," she murmured.

"Neither do I."

"And I'll think about the money for the coffee shop," she added.

He let out a sigh. "Thank you."

"Can I make a suggestion?" Emma said over lunch the next day. It was Sunday, which meant neither of them had to work. So, they'd slept in late, waking tangled in each others arms and had made love passionately, desperately, in a wild, uncontrolled frenzy of need and lust, as though they'd just that moment realized they were really together again. Then they'd showered, washing each other intimately before making love again, under the cascading water. Mark had to smile to himself. Emma had been right; there was no way they were even remotely capable of keeping their hands off each other if they showered together.

"Of course."

"Move in here." He looked up, and found Emma staring at him. "You know it's what we both want."

"Yeah, it is."

"Then go down to the hotel after lunch, get your things, check out and come back here. You can work out of here until the house is ready."

"And then?"

She gazed into his eyes.

"And then I'll move in with you."

"You will?" She nodded and he stood, pulling her off her stool and into his arms. "I—I never thought I'd be this happy again," he whispered, kissing her. "I thought I'd blown it."

"No. I think, deep down, I knew I'd take you back, if you asked me to. I'm no good without you."

"Yeah, you are. You're an amazing person, Emma – with, or without me."

She nestled into him. "There is one thing, though Mark." Her voice was serious, with a slight warning note.

"What's that?"

"I—I think you should at least try and remember to use a condom every so often…"

He laughed. "Is there any point? I mean, isn't it a little late to be worrying about that now? We've had sex without one…" He thought for a moment. "Four times since last night."

"Well, we'll be okay this month. My period's due on Tuesday—"

"It finally arrived last month then?" he interrupted.

"Yes. The morning we broke up. I didn't get the chance to tell you when we spoke."

"I'm sorry."

"I know you are, but we shouldn't keep taking these risks."

"Why not? We both established we were okay with it when you took the test last time… in fact, we were both damn disappointed it was negative, if I remember."

"Yes, but I wasn't about to buy and refurbish a coffee shop last time."

He smiled at her. "You're gonna take the money?" he said.

She nodded. "Yes." He picked her up and twirled her around in his arms, and she squealed out her delight.

"So, you see. I can't really get pregnant, not right now."

"Why not?" He put her back down again.

She looked into his eyes. "Because it wouldn't be practical, not with all the work that needs to be done."

"Babies take nine months… you know that, don't you?"

"Of course I do."

"Which is way more time than you're gonna need to refurbish the coffee shop."

"But then how would I work… and be a mom?"

"Women do it all the time, Emma, and it's not like you'd be on your own. I'm busy, but I'd do my share… and I guess, if you wanted to be a stay at home mom, then you'd hire a manager for the coffee shop."

She studied him closely. "You've got an answer for everything, haven't you?"

He nodded. "Pretty much." He placed his hands on her cheeks. "Look, if you want to wait to have a baby, then I'm okay with that, but I really like feeling you… all of you."

"I know. I like it too. One of the things I was gonna talk to you about before we broke up was whether I should go on the pill."

"That's up to you, babe. I can't make that choice for you."

"Well, it's not something I know much about."

"Why not go and see your doctor, then? You can talk it through."

"Because the whole town would know about it."

"What? Surely, he wouldn't tell anyone."

"No, *he* wouldn't – but his receptionist would."

Mark laughed. "I'm starting to see why Jake wanted to leave this place," he said. "Okay… Come to the city with me sometime soon. We'll book you in with a doctor there instead."

"I guess I could do it while the shop's being refitted. It's a way off yet, but…" He heard what sounded like a note of uncertainty in her voice.

"What's wrong?" he asked.

"Nothing."

"You don't have to do this, if you're not sure," he said.

"It's not that. I want to at least look into it, but you hear so many negative things, like the side effects some women get."

"Well, check it out, and if it's not right for you, don't do it."

"But you've got pretty much no control, it seems. If I don't take the pill, what are we going to do? Abstain?"

He laughed. "Over my dead body."

"I'm serious, Mark."

"So am I." He moved closer and kissed her gently. "I never want you to do anything you're not completely comfortable with. If I have to, I'll try and control myself better."

"Really?" she said, smirking.

"Yes, really."

"And if that doesn't work?"

"Well, I'm in the process of buying us a house with eight bedrooms… I think we'll manage to fit a nursery in there somewhere." He smiled down at her.

She stared at him for a moment, then her lips twitched upwards and she started to giggle. "You're impossible," she said, falling into his arms.

"Yeah, I know. And yet you still love me."

"Yes, I do," she whispered. "I really do."

On Wednesday, they didn't make love when they woke up. Emma's period had started and she didn't like the idea – besides she had quite bad cramping. Mark got up and made her some herbal tea while she was in the shower, and held her while she drank it.

She said she was really comfortable lying with him, but the coffee shop beckoned and she dressed quickly, giving him a long kiss and leaving him in bed to go and open up.

Mark lay, staring at the ceiling. His day wasn't due to be that busy, but tomorrow he was going back to the city for the first time. He was going to be leaving early, probably before Emma even woke up, but it was better to do that and go straight to the office, than to leave that night and spend even more time apart. He'd be away until late Friday, so only one night, but he was dreading it. He knew Emma was too.

He sat up on the edge of the bed, and was just getting to his feet when he heard the front door crash open and a male voice shouting, "Mark? Get down here. Now!"

He was naked, but grabbed his jeans and pulled them on, running through the apartment to the top of the stairs. At the bottom, he saw Nick and Emma standing just inside the closed door. Nick was holding Emma in his arms.

"What the fuck?" he cried and ran down.

Emma turned and fell into him, and he held her while she sobbed into his bare chest.

"What's going on?" Mark looked to Nick.

"There are maybe forty reporters outside the coffee shop."

Mark felt a shiver run down his spine. "You're kidding me."

Nick shook his head. "No. I was just driving by. I saw Emma come out of the apartment and walk along the sidewalk, and they ambushed her, like a swarm of locusts. I jumped out of the car and pulled her back in here. It seemed like the best thing to do." He glanced toward the door.

Emma sniffed and pulled back from him a little. Her face was streaked with tears. "It was horrible," she muttered. "They kept shoving cameras in my face and shouting questions at me. What do they want?" she asked him.

"Me…" he murmured, then he bent and picked her up, carrying her upstairs, and through to the living room before setting her down on the couch. He looked across at Nick, who'd followed them. "Stay with her," he said firmly. "Don't leave her. Not for anything. I'll be ten minutes."

"Okay." Nick sat down at Emma's feet.

Mark went through to the bathroom, took off his jeans and showered really quickly, washing his hair and shaving. Coming back out, he dressed in casual pants and a shirt, checking in the mirror to make sure he looked presentable. He couldn't afford to give the sharks outside the door anything to work with.

He went back out into the living room and crouched down by Emma. "I'll be back in a minute," he said, holding her shaking hands in his. "Stay here with Nick. Whatever you hear downstairs, I want you to stay up here. Okay?" She looked up at him.

"What are you going to do?"

"Something I should've done a long time ago."

He looked at Nick again. "Don't leave her side," he said. "And don't let her come out there."

Nick nodded his head.

Mark got to his feet, turned and went to the stairs, walking down slowly. At the bottom, without hesitating, he opened the door and was bombarded by a rush of noise. There were shouts, questions, demands… the incessant clicking of cameras, the blinding light of flashbulbs. He stood and waited for a minute, and then held up his hand to silence them. They took a moment, but eventually, the noise died down and they stood, waiting.

"I'm only going to say this once," he said, his voice firm and abrupt. "There have been a number of inaccurate articles printed about me in recent weeks. Nothing that was said in those reports had any basis in fact. I'm not engaged to the woman in those photographs and nor is she expecting my child. I am, however, involved with someone. That someone is the lady who lives in this apartment. She's the woman I love." He took a deep breath. "As you all know, I've never spoken to the press before; I've kept my private life just that – private. The lady who lives in this apartment is entitled to her privacy too, and I'm issuing all of you with a warning now… If you come anywhere near her again, make any attempt to contact or harass her, I will sue you. Go after me, if you must, but leave her alone."

He stopped talking and, almost immediately, the clamor started up again. They wanted to know whether the lady was Emma Woods, how long they'd known each other, whether they were engaged, whether she was pregnant… the list of questions was endless. Mark held up his hand and they silenced even more quickly this time.

"I will not confirm, or deny anything relating to the lady who lives here, other than the fact that I'm in love with her, I'm in a relationship with her, and she's under my protection." He paused for a moment. "Just because I've stayed quiet in the past, please do not make the mistake of underestimating me."

He looked around at them and then stepped back inside, closing the door quietly, just as the clamor started up again. He knew his threats were hollow. Other than having a cop posted outside Emma's apartment, there was little he could realistically do to stop them. His only hope was that, with what he'd given them, plus the first 'live' images of Mark Gardner ever to be taken, they'd leave her alone for a couple of days at least… and that maybe that would give him enough time…

He took the stairs two at a time, walked quickly through the apartment and dropped to his knees beside Emma.

"I heard that," she said quietly.

"I'm sorry," he whispered, pulling her into his arms.

"Why?" she murmured into him.

"Because if I'd been less reclusive, less paranoid about my privacy, they wouldn't be so greedy for information and none of this would've happened."

She shrugged. "I understand why you were like that, especially after what they just did." She sniffled again. "I can't believe they're so horrible. But we both know they won't leave me alone."

He nodded. "I know… which means I'm not gonna leave your side."

"But you're going to the city tomorrow morning."

"Like hell I am."

"Mark, you've got a business to run."

"I don't give a fuck about my business, Emma. You're more important. I'm not leaving your side until I can deal with this."

"If it's not a dumb question," Nick put in, "how are you gonna deal with it?"

"I'm gonna close on the house I'm buying… as soon as I can. And then I'm gonna get the security system installed." He thought for a moment. "I think I can have us in there in a week… ten days at the most."

"Can I help?" Nick offered. "Being a local lawyer, rather than a big city one, I might be able to get things moving."

Mark stood, looking down at Emma's brother. "Can you hang around for a while?" Nick nodded. "Thanks," Mark said. "I need to call the realtor, and my lawyer. You might be able to help me out… Meantime, can you make some coffee?" Nick nodded and got up, heading for the kitchen.

"What about the shop?" Emma said.

He looked down at her. "You're gonna be the boss soon, baby." He smiled. "Learn to delegate. Who's on shift this morning?"

"Patsy."

"Okay, call her. Tell her what's happened and get her to open up…"

"But she can't make coffee," Emma pointed out.

"Good. Those vultures will head in there looking for gossip. It'll serve them right if they have to go thirsty."

He went to walk away, but she grabbed his hand and pulled him back.

"Can you really stay?" she asked.

"Yes. I'll do my meetings by Skype, and I'll get Becky to sit in, so she can handle things for a while, until we've moved in to the house and this circus has died down." He bent and kissed her forehead. "Don't worry. It'll be fine."

"You're sure?"

"I'm sure. I'm not leaving you here, not now." He knelt down again, leaning into her, "I told you I'd keep you safe, and I'm going to. No-one's ever gonna hurt you, Emma." He kissed away the tear on her cheek. "You're mine," he whispered.

She nodded, and murmured back, "All yours."

Epilogue

Mid-February

Emma

It actually took until the end of January for Mark to close on the house and get it ready for them to move into, but in all that time, he didn't once leave Emma's side. He went everywhere with her, sitting with her while she worked in the coffee shop, going to the store… even to the post office. The press continued to hound them, and she was scared. She was really scared. She'd got a taste of living in the public eye and she didn't like it one bit.

They moved into the house on the last day of January. In the end, there had been little Nick could do to move things along further and Mark's Boston lawyers had taken care of everything. The most time-consuming aspect was the state-of-the-art security system Mark had installed, which included a high fence that bordered the property, and a huge gate that kept out all unwanted visitors, both of which were monitored by CCTV cameras. Still, Emma didn't mind the delay because, for the first time in weeks, she felt safe. She especially felt safe waking up in Mark's arms every morning and looking out onto the ocean. That was something she'd really gotten used to over the last two weeks.

Today being Sunday, neither of them were working and Nick had come round for brunch. They'd talked about Emma's purchase of the coffee shop, which was due to go through in the next few weeks. Nick had been handling the legal side of things for Emma and had made sure everything had gone smoothly. As they ate and talked, Emma was finding it hard not to smile, even though she thought Mark and Nick might wonder at her inane cheerfulness. Her life seemed so damn perfect now, she didn't honestly believe things could get any better.

It wasn't until the end of the conversation that Mark really got involved, and that had nothing to do with the coffee shop. He took a long sip of coffee and looked across the kitchen table at Nick.

"Do you handle much commercial law?" he asked.

Nick looked surprised. The question was a little random. "As a company, no. It's not really Tom's field of expertise. If we get asked to, then I handle it. Why?"

Mark hesitated a moment. "Because I've been thinking about putting some work your way," he said at last.

Nick seemed even more taken aback. "If you don't mind me asking… why? I'm sure you can afford to pay Boston rates, and besides, you'll probably find far better qualified lawyers there than here."

Mark smiled. "You're right, I can afford their rates. I have a lawyer already in Boston. He's worked for the company for years… as to him being better qualified, well, that's not always what it's about. With a lot of those guys, it's just about getting the business done. They don't really care about the people." He paused. "But I've noticed the way you've dealt with Mrs Adams over the coffee shop… I mean, you obviously had Emma's best interests at heart, but it seemed to me, you never forgot Mrs Adams was selling up the business she'd had for over thirty years. You showed great tact in dealing with her… I like that. And I'd like to see more of it."

Nick blushed, which wasn't something Emma had seen very often. It made her smile.

"I'm not suggesting I'd give you all our work," Mark continued, "but I'd like you to think about handling our takeovers. They sometimes need a gentler touch."

Nick was staring at Mark, but eventually managed to speak. "I don't mean to sound ungrateful," he said, "but I'd have to discuss it with Tom."

"Okay," Mark replied, nodding.

"It's just, it wouldn't feel right, taking on a major new client without talking to him about it first."

"I understand," Mark said. "Discuss it with him. I'll happily come and meet with him, if you think it's necessary."

Nick nodded. "I'll let you know."

Emma glanced across at Mark, wondering if he really needed to place his work with Nick, or whether this was an olive branch to her brother. She looked into his eyes and knew straight away the offer was genuine. Mark didn't need to make gestures.

They were standing on the driveway beside Mark's car, waving goodbye to Nick when Mark's phone rang. Nick's truck had just disappeared around the corner as Mark pulled his phone from his pocket and checked the screen.

"It's Becky," he said to Emma. "I'd better take it. I'll go indoors… it's too windy out here."

"I'm gonna go and look at the ocean," Emma told him as he wandered toward the house.

"Don't get cold," he called after her, putting the phone to his ear.

She wandered around the side of the house and down the lawn to the edge of the garden, which overlooked the ocean. Mark was right, it was freezing out here, but she didn't care. She had a couple of layers on, and a thick scarf that she'd grabbed before coming out to see Nick off… Besides, she loved the garden, and the view.

She smiled to herself again and stared up at the sky. She'd really never felt this happy. Not even when she'd been with Mark before. Then, she'd always felt as though there was something that could threaten them… but now, she knew how much she meant to him. She knew he'd move heaven and earth to keep her safe and make her happy. And she was happy, because she had Mark, she had his love, and she had a secret. It was a secret no-one knew… not even Nick. She hadn't told anyone yet, because she'd only found out for sure herself that morning.

She was planning a special meal for that night, and she was going to tell Mark then. She turned for a moment and looked back at the house. She saw him standing at the living room window, the one that opened up onto the deck, watching over her protectively, and she waved. He waved back and blew her a kiss; she blew one back. She was so glad he was being as protective as he was, because she was going to need him more than ever now.

She looked down at herself and placed her hand on her flat stomach… and she smiled.

Mark

"I know we didn't plan it this way, but I need you up here," Mark said.

"I thought you were going to handle it…" He could hear the reticence in Becky's voice.

"I was, but you know you're so much better at dealing with personnel than I am." The new hotel – the one Jake had been working on since last summer – was due to open at the beginning of March, and Mark had decided he wanted to have Becky there to help settle the new staff in, deal with any initial problems, and generally make sure things ran smoothly for the first week or so. "Is it a problem?" he asked.

"No. I've just always tried to avoid going up there, that's all." He thought about it and realized she was right. She'd never once visited the site.

"Why?" he asked.

There was a long silence, then she said, "I used to know someone from near there… from a town called Somers Cove."

"Oh my God, not you too. That's where Emma's from."

"I didn't know that." She sounded shocked.

"Yeah. She's lived there all her life."

Becky didn't say anything.

"Look, if it's really a problem," he said, trying to sound soothing.

"No. This is part of my job. It's fine. Besides, it's not like I'll be going to the town itself. The hotel's twenty miles away, and I haven't seen this guy since I was at college." She paused. "I don't even know for sure he went back there when he graduated. He could be anywhere."

"Exactly. So, you'll come?" he asked.

"Of course. I'll clear my diary and come up there."

"Thanks, Becky."

"How's the house?" she asked.

"The house is amazing."

"And Emma?" He heard the smile in her voice.

"She's better than amazing." He was watching her out the living room window, and she really was amazing. She was wrapped up in a thick jumper and woolen scarf, over the tightest jeans he'd ever seen and her hair was blowing wildly in the wind. She looked so damn sexy...

"I'm really happy for you, Mark." Becky's voice cut through his thoughts, but he realized her tone was sad.

"Is everything okay?" he asked.

"Yes. Everything's fine." She sounded too bright now, and he knew she was lying, but he couldn't push her. She'd tell him when she wanted to. "I'll speak to you tomorrow."

"Sure." He wanted to say more. He wanted to offer to help her with her husband again, being as he was fairly sure the asshole was the cause of her problems... but he didn't want to interfere.

They ended the call and he stood, staring down at Emma. God, she made him so damn happy. Living here with her was perfect and she was so good for him. He recalled his conversation with Maggie from that morning. Emma had persuaded him, over the course of the previous few days, that he should go and visit Sarah. He'd said he'd go, if Emma came with him, but she said no, his first visit should be by himself, and maybe should be somewhere neutral. Emma could stay with Maggie, while Mark took Sarah out. Mark had discussed this with Maggie and she'd agreed. She thought Emma's plan was a good one. Sarah was a lot better, but she was missing Mark and Maggie thought a visit might help her. She needed to know he still loved her, even if he was struggling to forgive her. She suggested that Mark should go visit, take Sarah for a coffee, just for an hour and see what happened.

That plan suited Mark really well, because he wanted to take Emma to the city anyway. Now they had the house, he felt safer leaving her alone for the odd night, and he'd been traveling into Boston every so often for work, but he hated staying at any of the hotels… and all the while he was staying in hotels, Emma refused to come with him, knowing he'd taken other women to his hotels in the past. So, he'd found a small apartment. It was nothing grand, just a small two bedroom place, near Jake's old apartment in the Back Bay area. He'd been to see it the last time he was there, and now he wanted Emma's approval. He'd worked out, they could go next Saturday, after she'd closed the shop, stay at one of his hotels outside the city – one where he'd never taken anybody before – and then he'd drive them into the city on Sunday morning. He'd take Sarah out for an hour, while Emma stayed with Maggie, and then he'd go back for Emma, and they could go to see the apartment. He felt it was important for them to have a base in Boston too; somewhere he could call home when he wasn't with Emma, but also somewhere they could stay together when they were both in the city. Emma wanted him to go there to try and rebuild his relationship with Sarah, and he couldn't do that without her by his side.

He put his phone into his back pocket and then tapped his front one gently, feeling for the small ring box inside. He'd picked up the engagement ring two days before and planned to propose to her tonight. He knew they'd only been back together for just over a month, but he didn't care about that. It wasn't about time, it was about love. He loved her completely; she loved him and he wanted her in his life forever.

He gazed down the garden, just as she turned and spotted him. She waved and he waved back, blowing her a kiss. She returned it and he smiled. She looked out over the ocean again and he saw her rest her hand on her stomach, looking down at herself… and in that moment the realization hit him. *Could she be…?* He thought for a moment. It was possible. It was, if anything, more possible than the last time. Despite his promises to try and show more self control, he'd forgotten the condom on more than one occasion in the heat of the moment, most notably on the night they'd moved into the house, which was around three weeks ago now… His cock stiffened as he remembered taking her on the stairs, giggling and so excited, they hadn't been able to wait; then again in the shower, real hard, breathless and heady, and filled with longing; then a third time in bed, much slower, their eyes and bodies locked. On none of those occasions had the thought of a condom even crossed his mind… not until the following morning, when Emma had reminded him. She hadn't seemed too unhappy about it though, and he'd made love to her again – also without a condom – telling her that there seemed little point in worrying, considering what had gone on the night before. So, thinking about it, yeah… it was *really* possible. And it made sense of that morning's events too. It had struck him as odd that Emma had taken a little longer than usual in the bathroom. Maybe she'd been taking the test… And then, when she'd come back to bed, she'd asked him to make love to her, and he had, taking her real slow and gentle. She'd insisted he didn't need a condom, and when she'd come, she'd cried his name with such love in her voice and tears in her eyes, it had taken his breath away, and she'd clung onto him so tight, much tighter than she usually did…

He opened the door, stepping outside and walking down the garden, unable to wipe the smile from his face. To hell with waiting until tonight. He wanted to propose before she could tell him her news. He wanted to give her the reassurance that he was entirely hers, that he would always be there for her, and that nothing could divide them… ever again.

The End

Keep reading for an excerpt from Suzie Peters' forthcoming book
Rebels and Rules
Part Three in the Wishes and Chances Series.

Available to purchase from June 1st 2018

Rebels and Rules

Wishes and Chances Series: Book Three

by

Suzie Peters

Chapter One

Nine Years Earlier

Becky

"I suppose you ought to get dressed," Nick said. She heard the reluctance in his voice. It mirrored her own, but it gave her a warm glow to know that he wanted her to stay naked and curled up in his arms just as much as she did.

"Do I have to?" She looked up at him. God, he was gorgeous, even with his clothes on. He was wearing jeans, a white shirt, and a pale gray waistcoat. This was what he wore all the time – it was like Nick's trademark, as was his dark disheveled hair, which he wore at collar length.

"We're already late," he murmured, leaning down and kissing her. She felt his stubble brush against her skin and shivered at the contact. "I told Eliot we'd be there." She sighed and went to move away from him, but he pulled her back. "Doesn't mean I wanna go," he said, smiling, and she just had to smile back.

He'd arrived about thirty minutes beforehand, just as Becky had stepped out of the shower and wrapped herself in a bathrobe. Kelly, whose flat she shared, had opened the door to him, only wearing a towel herself, which she'd wrapped around and tied just above her ample breasts. She was gushing and simpering to the point where it was embarrassing and, to escape her, Becky had suggested that Nick join her in her bedroom. He'd agreed, removing the robe almost as soon as they'd closed the door, and they'd been lying on her bed ever since. She'd suggested that he could get undressed too, and he'd told her, in between kisses, that he wanted to, but if he did they'd never get to Eliot's party. As far as Becky was concerned, that would have been absolutely fine. She didn't want to go anyway. And not just because she wanted to be in bed with Nick. Kelly was going too, and Becky knew she'd be wearing something revealing and sexy; something bound to grab Nick's attention, which made her feel even more insecure than usual, especially as she also knew Nick had asked Kelly out before her – he'd been honest enough to tell her that.

"Hey…" He waved his hand in front of her face. "You're daydreaming."

"Hmm." She nestled into him again, not wanting to tell him about her jealous fears.

"C'mon," he said. "Time to get up."

She pulled away from him unwillingly and shifted to the edge of the bed, clambering off and walking round to the dresser, where she stood with her back to Nick, combing out her long, straight, dark hair. Then she opened the top drawer and grabbed a pair of white lace panties, bending over and pulling them on. She heard the soft groan from behind her and turned to face him. He was watching her intently, his steel gray eyes on fire.

"Keep doing that, and we won't be going anywhere," he murmured, his voice deep and sexy.

She smirked, then turned and bent over again, this time to pick up her shoes from the floor. She didn't need them yet, but wanted to tempt him all the same.

"Jeez, Bex," he said and she heard him move, then felt him come up behind her, his body pressed against hers, his arousal obvious through his jeans. She dropped her shoes, stood upright and leant back into him, his hands coming around her, cupping her breasts. "What are you trying to do to me?" he asked.

"I'm not trying to do anything," she whispered.

"You're a tease," he murmured into her hair, before planting gentle kisses on her shoulder and moving up to her neck.

"No, I'm not. I deliver on my promises, Nick."

"Yeah… don't I know it." She felt his right hand move down, across her flat stomach and inside her panties, his fingers finding her sensitized clitoris. He rubbed gently and she rocked her head back against his shoulder, sucking in a deep breath. "You're really wet," he whispered into her ear.

"Because I want you." She ground her hips back into him, feeling him hard against her.

He groaned again, more loudly. "I want you too."

He increased the pressure on her clitoris, moving his fingers faster and harder over her swollen nub.

"I—I'm gonna come," she stuttered.

"Not yet, you're not." He pulled his hand away and spun her in his arms so she was facing him, panting hard.

"Nick…" she breathed.

"I want you like this all night," he murmured, his eyes dark with desire. "And later, I'm gonna take you back to my place and make you come so fucking hard."

"Oh God… yes." She felt her legs giving way and he held her up.

He waited until her breathing had calmed a little. "You okay?" he asked.

"Apart from feeling frustrated, yes," she said, looking up at him.

"I can handle frustrated," he replied, grinning at her.

"We're going back to your place after the party?" she said, her brain finally unscrambling a little.

"Yeah. Didn't I tell you?"

"No." She leant back in his arms. "No. You didn't."

"Ah, well… Tony's already gone home for the summer. He left this afternoon. So we've got the place to ourselves for once." Nick shared a flat with another law student, Tony, who didn't like him having women to stay over. Nick thought it was a little weird, but it was Tony's place and he respected the guy's rules, so they hadn't yet spent a whole night together, being as Becky didn't like the idea of Nick sleeping at her place either, not with the too tempting Kelly in the very next room.

"We do?"

"Yeah. I guess you could pack an overnight bag…" He left the sentence hanging, and looked down at her, expectantly.

"My dad's coming to pick me up tomorrow morning, to take me home, but…"

"But?" he queried.

"But I can stay at your place tonight, if you want me to?"

"Oh, I want you to." He leant down and kissed her, his tongue finding hers and letting her feel his need.

"I guess I'd better pack then," she said, when he finally broke the kiss.

"And maybe get dressed too?" he suggested. "You can't go to the party like that."

"Do we have to go to the party at all?" she asked, picking at one of the buttons on his shirt. "Can't we just go straight to your place?"

He chuckled. "We'll just go for an hour or so, then we'll make our excuses and leave."

"Okay," she said reluctantly. She knew that if Nick had promised Eliot he'd be there, he wouldn't let him down. She put her arms around his neck and leant into him. "I can't wait to sleep with you," she whispered.

He pulled her close, crushing her against him. "We won't be sleeping, baby," he said softly. "This is gonna be our first night together, and our last for a while too. I've got no intention of letting you sleep at all."

Becky didn't get around to packing. They spent the next ten minutes kissing, before she finally got dressed. They agreed they'd come back to her apartment and she'd pick up her things then – they had to drive past her place to get back to Nick's anyway. It wouldn't be a problem.

Nick held her hand as they went out into the living room, where Kelly was waiting for them. Becky sucked in a breath and knew that her mouth had dropped open. What on earth was Kelly wearing? Whatever it was, it left nothing – absolutely nothing – to the imagination. There was a trend on the catwalks for sheer fabrics, and Kelly had gone to town with it, whilst evidently deciding to abandon underwear at the same time. Her dress was cream in color, with a silver embroidered pattern, which strategically covered her nipples, but left the outline of her breasts showing. Becky allowed her eyes to drop, and let out a gasp. It was so obvious Kelly wasn't wearing any panties, even though the embroidery just about hid the essential area, but as she turned to pick up her purse, her ass was completely visible.

"Jesus," Nick muttered under his breath, but Becky wasn't sure if that meant he liked what he saw, or not, and she didn't want to look at him, fearful of what she might see in his eyes. All of a sudden her red sundress, that Nick had told her looked sexy a few minutes earlier, seemed wholly inadequate.

"Do you like it?" Kelly asked. "It cost a fortune." Becky wasn't in the least surprised. The Youngs – Kelly's family – had money, lots of it, and affording the dress would have been no problem for her. Whether her parents would have approved of her wearing it without anything underneath was another matter, but they were back home in Fall River, where the two girls had grown up. Although they hadn't technically grown up 'together', because Becky's parents weren't from exactly the same part of town, when they'd arrived at Boston University and discovered they were both from the same place, it had made sense for them to room together… Well, it had felt like it at the time. Becky had started to regret that decision almost as soon as it was made; like the first night, when Kelly had come home the worse for alcohol, with an athletic-looking guy, who she'd dragged into her bedroom, and entertained loudly until the early hours of the morning.

Luckily, both she and Nick were both saved from having to make up an answer by the ringing of the doorbell.

"That'll be Tyler," Kelly said, moving to answer it.

"What's he doing here?" Nick whispered to Becky.

"He's taking Kelly to the party," she replied.

"Really?" Becky glanced up at Nick's face. He was clearly surprised. "I didn't know he was interested in her."

Becky wondered if Nick was envious of Tyler, but didn't get the opportunity to dwell, before the man himself entered the room. He was the antithesis of Nick; blond, tidy, perfectly groomed in smart pants and a button-down shirt. He seemed to be the light to Nick's dark. But she preferred Nick's dark.

"Good evening," he said, formally, looking Becky up and down. "You look lovely."

"Thank you," she muttered, feeling embarrassed.

"Shall we go?" Nick suggested.

"We could all go together, couldn't we?" Kelly suggested.

"No." Nick and Tyler spoke at the same time.

"It's not practical," Tyler continued.

"No, it isn't," Nick confirmed, giving Becky's hand a squeeze. Then he gave her a tug and they headed for the door, followed by Tyler and Kelly.

As they began their drive to Eliot's house, Becky looked over at Nick, wondering what he was thinking, whether his mind was full of images of Kelly and her obvious attributes, and whether her own were now diminishing in his eyes.

She blinked back her tears and looked out the window.

It was exactly a week since Nick had taken her virginity, but she'd already lost count of the number of times he'd made love to her… and it was always glorious. He always seemed to know exactly what she wanted, and he delivered – every time. She smiled, just for a moment, before recalling yet again how Nick had wanted to go out with Kelly for months and months before he'd given up on her and asked Becky on a date instead… just five weeks ago. And in that one spectacular evening, had put an end to her years of pining for him.

Nick had filled her head, her heart – her life, really – since she'd first seen him three years ago, at the beginning of their Freshman year. Now, as their third year was drawing to a close, he was finally hers… well, she hoped he was. He was certainly dating her, taking her to the movies, for walks, and out to romantic dinners. He kissed her – a lot. She liked his kisses; they were warm, passionate, exciting. He held her in his arms all the time, and she really enjoyed the feeling of his strong muscles binding them together. A couple of weeks ago, he'd used his tongue, and his fingers to bring her to orgasm and, for the first time in

350

her life, she'd experienced the other-worldly joy of letting herself go completely; letting the man she loved take her to that place beyond pleasure. And as of last Friday night, he'd become her lover. He'd called himself that, smiling down at her as he'd entered her for the first time, so tenderly. He hadn't said 'I love you', so she didn't really know how he felt about her, but then she hadn't said those magical words to him either; even though she knew he was everything to her... and more.

She brought her hand up to her neck, fingering the silver locket Nick had bought her last Friday – a really sweet gesture for their one month anniversary. He'd given her that just before taking her to bed...

"What the hell is Kelly playing at?" Anne-Marie murmured in Becky's ear.

Becky shrugged. She couldn't reply. She couldn't talk, because she knew if she did, she'd cry.

She was confused, hurt, embarrassed... and deeply humiliated.

When they'd arrived, nearly an hour ago, Nick had told her he'd go and get them some drinks, leaving her standing near the living room window, while he'd headed into the kitchen. But he'd only gotten halfway across the room when he'd been accosted by Kelly, who'd managed to keep his attention ever since. Becky had stood there watching them, and on three separate occasions – just three – he'd looked over at her and either winked or smiled, but he'd made no attempt to get away from Kelly... none whatsoever.

"Are you okay?" Anne-Marie asked.

Becky nodded.

"Can I get you a drink, or anything?"

"No, thanks," Becky managed to say, although she knew her voice wasn't normal. Anne-Marie drifted away into the crowd and Becky looked over to where Nick and Kelly were talking. Why was he doing this? He'd implied that he couldn't wait to take her home to his bed, that he wanted to make love to her – all night. When they'd pulled up outside Eliot's house, he'd leant over and kissed her, and told her they'd spend some of the night, in between making love, talking about how they could try and get together over the summer break. She knew already that he was planning on working at his dad's boat yard and she had a job lined up at a hotel in Fall River, but he'd said nothing was insurmountable… not if they wanted to be together. So, what had changed?

"You don't look very happy." The voice was too close and she flipped her head around, to be faced by Tyler. She stepped back instinctively, although the window was right behind her, leaving her nowhere to go.

"I'm fine," she murmured.

"You don't look fine." He moved closer still. He smelt of strong liquor and an aftershave she didn't like. It was sweet, cloying. "You look very uncomfortable."

Maybe because you're in my space, she thought, but she didn't say anything. She was far too polite.

"They get on real well, don't they?" She looked up at Tyler, his blue eyes gazing down at her, and he nodded toward Nick and Kelly, still deep in conversation on the other side of the room. "You should see them in class," he added. "They're inseparable."

Becky felt her heart lurch in her chest. She had no idea what Nick got up to during his classes. He, Tyler, and Kelly were all at the Law School, while she was studying Hospitality Administration.

"To be honest, I don't know why I bothered inviting Kelly tonight," Tyler continued. "It's so obvious she's only really interested in Nick." He looked at Becky. "And he's always had a soft spot for her, hasn't he?" He hesitated for a moment. "I mean… I know he's seeing you, but that's just a casual thing, right?"

Becky wanted to scream at him that it was anything but casual… it was *everything*. Well, it was to her, anyway.

"I'm sure Nick would have asked Kelly out again, if she hadn't been seeing Dale…" Tyler's voice droned on in her ear.

Dale and Kelly had shared precisely two dates – and Kelly's bed – over the weekend that she and Nick had got together. Becky couldn't really see how that would have stopped Nick from trying again with Kelly, if he'd really wanted to. He'd only have needed to wait a day or so…

"And he never stops talking about her," Tyler continued, leaning back on the wall beside her and folding his arms.

They stood in silence for a moment and Becky watched Nick and Kelly. They talked animatedly; he waved his hands around, and listened attentively, like he was interested in what she had to say. She moved closer to him and said something that made him laugh, throwing his head back a little. Had this been what he'd wanted all along? Had the rest of it – the dates, the walks, the dinners, the words, the necklace, taking her virginity – had it all just been a series of lies… lies he'd told her to get closer to Kelly?

She sucked in a breath and tried to stop the tears from falling, just as Nick glanced over, then turned back to Kelly again, before the two of them headed across the room straight toward her and Tyler, who pushed himself off the wall as they approached.

Becky stared down at the floor, unable to make eye contact with anyone.

"Hey," Nick said as he came to stand in front of her.

She didn't reply.

"I'm sorry," he said eventually, "I never got you that drink, did I?" She looked up now. He was smiling down at her. "I'll go and get you one."

She wanted to tell him not to bother. She wanted to tell him to take her home, but he'd already turned and was walking away.

"Nick!" Kelly called after him. "Hold on. I'll come with you."

He slowed and let Kelly catch up with him, and Becky gazed after them as they left the room. Just as they turned to disappear into the kitchen, she noticed Kelly lean up and plant a kiss on Nick's cheek. She heard herself gasp and bit back the tears.

"Oh, Becky," Tyler said, moving closer again. "Don't let it get to you. Some guys just can't help themselves."

She turned to him and noticed the concerned look on his face, his eyes piercing hers.

"Dance with me," he said, nodding to the other end of the room, where the furniture had been moved to one side and a few couples were moving vaguely in time to the music. "It'll take your mind off things."

Becky hesitated for a moment, then realized that, whatever she'd thought she had with Nick, she'd clearly been wrong. It might have been love for her, but it was obviously just a game to him; he wasn't serious about her at all… and now that Kelly was interested in him, Becky knew she didn't stand a chance. Kelly was the one he'd always wanted, and she was making herself more than available. Hell, she was positively trumpeting her availability.

"Okay," she said to Tyler and offered him her hand.

He smiled down at her and led her through the crowd of drinking, laughing, talking people. Then, as if on cue, the music changed and a track started playing that was much slower. Becky thought she recognized it. She thought it was by The Fray… maybe? She wasn't sure, and at that moment, she really didn't care.

"Just forget about him, he's not worth it," Tyler whispered, pulling her into his arms. She let him, going limp, like a rag doll. Someone turned up the music, and she felt it wash over her, just as Tyler placed his mouth next to her ear and echoed the lyrics now filling the room, murmuring, "I'll look after you," as she started to sob into his chest.

Nick

He laughed at Kelly's observation of the way the class had handled the juvenile delinquency seminars they'd been attending for the last few weeks of the semester. Nick had to agree with her that some of their classmates had been fairly juvenile and delinquent themselves. He glanced over at Becky again. Tyler was standing beside her, although she was staring at the floor now, rather than looking at the weasel. Thank God. 'Weasel' was a good description of Tyler. He had a kind of pointy face and beady eyes. Well, Nick thought he did, anyway. He also took way too much interest in Becky, or at least he had done for the last few weeks, ever since Nick had been seeing her. What the hell he was doing here with Kelly was a mystery to Nick, not that he seemed to be paying much attention to his date. He seemed far more keen on talking to Becky…

"We'd better be getting back to our dates, don't you think?" he said to Kelly.

"Oh… I guess." She sounded disappointed. "Thanks for helping me out, Nick. I knew you'd know the answers."

"It's no problem." He turned to walk away, but she pulled him back again.

"You're sure you didn't mind helping me?" She looked up at him through her thick eyelashes.

"No, Kelly. It's fine." She was pushing her breasts forward, her hard nipples poking into the sheer fabric of her dress and Nick was finding it hard to know where to look. He thought her dress was cheap… although he knew it was probably anything but, knowing Kelly and her ability to spend money. He wondered how she could show herself off like this, and marveled at how he'd ever been interested in her. Well, he guessed that was obvious really. She was flaunting the reasons for everyone to see. And, for Nick, that was the biggest turn off of all.

He glanced back at Becky again, wishing Tyler would just leave her alone.

"Come on," he urged Kelly and this time, she let him lead her over to where Becky and Tyler were standing by the window.

"Hey," he said, standing in front of his girl. She looked beautiful, but kind of doubtful, and he wanted more than anything to take her away from this place, back to his apartment and to his bed, to spend the night with her for the first time ever, and maybe – just maybe – tell her how he felt about her.

She wasn't responding, but maybe she was a little mad with him. He'd promised her a drink, probably about an hour ago? And he had let Kelly kind of monopolize him.

"I'm sorry," he said, "I never got you that drink, did I?" Now she looked up at him and he thought he saw something in her eyes. He wasn't sure what it was… Hurt? Uncertainty? Either way, he didn't like it. He smiled down at her. "I'll go and get you one." Then he could come back, they'd find a quiet spot and talk, and then he'd get her away from here.

He turned and had just moved away when he heard his name being called. It was Kelly – again.

For Christ's sake. "Hold on…" she yelled. "I'll come with you."

Really? Couldn't she just give him a moment's peace?

He slowed his pace just slightly and let her catch up as they headed toward the kitchen, and then, just as they turned the corner to exit the room, she leant up and kissed him on the cheek.

He stopped. "What the hell did you do that for?" He glared down at her.

"Because I wanted to," she purred.

"Well don't." He didn't dare look back into the living room, but he hoped they'd gone far enough into the kitchen that Becky wouldn't have seen that little display.

"Oh, come on, Nick…" Kelly simpered.

"Leave it, Kelly." He moved away from her, and went through the kitchen, down the short corridor, to the bathroom beyond, which was – fortunately – vacant. He locked the door behind him and sat down on the closed toilet seat, leaning forward and putting his head in his hands.

What had he ever seen in Kelly? He was willing to admit he'd been interested in her for… well, years. They'd met in their first class together in that first week, and he'd been utterly smitten – as had every other guy in their class – by her long blonde hair, pale green eyes, and pouty lips, and her hour-glass figure didn't hurt either. He'd followed her around like a lapdog for a few months, and then he'd seen some guy leaving her apartment block – enjoying a passionate farewell kiss on the doorstep – early one morning, while he was out for a run. It was then that Nick had realized she was maybe a little faster and looser than the girls he was used to, back home in Somers Cove.

Still, the attraction hadn't waned, although he'd stopped following her so much… well, there were only so many times he wanted to watch her with other guys. And Nick wasn't idle, or lonely. He'd taken the chance to sleep around a little himself. He'd even admitted to himself that he was doing it in the hope Kelly would be jealous. She hadn't been, of course – she hadn't even noticed – but he'd had some fun, so what did it matter?

And then, one evening just before last Christmas, he'd finally had the opportunity to ask her on a date. He'd been quite cool about it, despite his nerves, and she'd looked him up and down, as though appraising him before giving him her decision, and then she'd laughed, real loud, and told him that she wouldn't be seen dead with a guy who dressed like him, who didn't even know how to comb his own hair… and she'd flounced off.

He sat back and stared at the ceiling, shaking his head. Considering her reaction, he might be inclined to wonder why she was behaving the way she was tonight – except he'd already worked that out. He knew exactly what Kelly was doing and it made him dislike her even more. She hadn't been interested in him when he was single, but now he was dating Becky – her friend – he'd suddenly become a whole lot more tempting. *What a bitch…*

He let out a long breath and tried to calm down. He thought about Becky and smiled. She looked real sexy tonight in that red sun dress… much more so than Kelly in her see-through effort. Becky exuded sensuality and an innocent charm that had him hooked from the first time she'd served him in the coffee shop, where she worked on Tuesday and Friday afternoons, and all day on Saturdays. Of course, he hadn't known she was Kelly's friend at the time… After her rejection, he'd kept himself to himself for a couple of months. Then, as winter was just starting to fade, he'd discovered the coffee shop and started using it as a quiet place to study. He liked it there, it reminded him of the coffee shop back home, where his sister Emma had a part-time job. He missed Emma – a lot. And one Friday, when he had the place pretty much to himself, Becky had come over to clear his table and see if he wanted anything else. Her voice was all shy and tentative, and he'd looked up into those golden brown eyes and, when she'd smiled down at him, he'd just fallen for her. It was that easy. All thoughts of Kelly, and every other girl he'd ever known simply evaporated.

He'd waited a couple of weeks, spending as much time there as possible, and discovering that while her name tag said 'Rebecca', everyone called her Becky, and that she was studying Hospitality Administration in a completely different part of the campus, which was why he'd never met her before, and then one Friday evening, five weeks ago, he'd plucked up the courage and nervously asked her to the movies. She'd smiled, that slow, beautiful smile of hers and said yes, and he thought he'd died and gone to heaven. Finding out that she shared an apartment with Kelly was tricky, but there wasn't anything he could do about it.

Becky seemed shy and self-conscious and, after they'd been seeing each other for a couple of weeks, she finally told him that she'd liked him for a long time. He'd wondered how she'd even known he existed, and she'd explained that she'd seen him around, looking at Kelly, watching her. He'd felt embarrassed then, and had clarified that Kelly meant nothing to him – not now. He explained his dumb infatuation and she'd seemed to understand. He'd been tempted that night to tell Becky how he really felt about her – that he was in love with her – but he'd wondered if that might seem a little crass in the circumstances. Instead, he'd kissed her tenderly, and held her in his arms… and things had become quite heated. In between breathless moans and sighs, she'd made it clear she wanted more, so he'd given her what she needed, bringing her to orgasm, firstly with his fingers, and then his tongue. He'd asked for nothing in return, making that whole evening about her… And just watching her come apart had given him more satisfaction than any sexual experience of his life.

He shifted on the seat. Just thinking about that night made him hard.

A smile settled on his lips as he recalled the nights that had followed… her orgasms – and there were a lot of them – and his. Her innocence was beguiling, but she'd learned fast, and the end results had been spectacular.

And then, a week ago, he'd happened to be passing the antique jewelry store between his apartment and one of his lecture halls, and he'd seen the necklace in the window. It was perfect; a silver chain, with a heart shaped locket, featuring a geometric pattern. It was an art-deco piece and it was beautiful, like Becky. He'd bought it there and then. He hadn't put anything in it; he'd left that for her to do, and after he'd given it to her that evening, he'd taken her to bed and they'd made love for the first time… and it was her *very* first time. Even as he was taking her virginity, he knew the memory of that night would stay with him forever.

As she'd lain in his arms afterwards, all satisfied and sleepy, he'd reached a decision… Becky may not have been the first woman he'd ever made love to, but she was going to be the last. That was one of the ways he knew he was in love with her. He'd always taken his chances when they presented themselves, and he'd never really waited for any woman. He'd slept with quite a few different girls over the years, while he decided what to do about Kelly – because, as much as he'd thought he wanted Kelly, he wasn't willing to sit around and wait for her to be available – but with Becky, it was different. He knew that, from then on, he'd be faithful to her. There would be no-one else for him, ever again.

"Hey… can you hurry up in there?" The male voice from the other side of the door woke him from his daydream.

"Sorry," he called and got to his feet.

He opened the door and passed through, letting a tall, skinny-looking guy go in after him.

Nick made his way back to the kitchen. He hoped by now that Kelly would have given up waiting for him, but he was out of luck. When he went back in, she was standing by the door and her eyes lit up like a firework display when she saw him. He grabbed a couple of sodas from the countertop and made his way over, hoping to bypass her.

"Nick," she said softly. "What's wrong?"

"Nothing. I'm just neglecting Becky. I should get back to her."

"Why?" Kelly asked. That was a dumb question if ever he'd heard one.

"Because she's my girlfriend?" He said it like a question, to try and show her how dense she was being.

She laughed, but not in the vicious way she'd done when she'd turned him down. This was more of a tinkling giggle, with a softer tone. "Oh dear," she said mildly. "You don't get it at all, do you?"

"Get what?" he asked, trying to duck past her again.

"College isn't the place to do serious relationships, Nick."

It obviously wasn't for Kelly, and he knew a lot of other people who slept around. Hell, he'd done that himself for the last couple of years, but he and Becky were different.

She moved a little closer. "Why don't you come upstairs with me?" she whispered, taking the sodas from him and putting them down on the countertop beside her. "I'll show you a much better time than Becky ever could."

"Kelly, I'm not interested—"

"How do you know?" she interrupted. "Look, it doesn't have to be upstairs. We can go out to your truck, or even back to your place, if you want. I don't mind where we go…" She moved right next to him, her body touching his. He could feel her breasts against him, and he tensed. She wasn't turning him on – not in the least – but he knew he had to be real careful about what he did next. He couldn't afford for her to misunderstand or misinterpret his actions. "I guarantee you won't be disappointed," she murmured softly, running her hand down his chest.

He took a step back. "No, Kelly. I've told you, I'm not interested. I'm with Becky, and you're with Tyler."

Now she did laugh… loudly. "I'm not with Tyler," she said, "not in the way you think. And if you honestly believe you're with Becky, you're a lot more naive than you look."

He felt his skin crawl. "What do you mean?" he replied.

"I mean," she said slowly, moving closer again, "that Becky gets it, even if you don't. Do you honestly think she's sitting around the apartment when she's not with you?" She looked up at him, but her face had become a blur as his blood pumped loudly through his ears, disorienting him. "She's playing the field, just like everyone else, Nick. You need to wake up."

He was frozen to the spot, unable to believe the words spewing from her mouth.

"Come with me," she said, taking his hand, "I'll prove it to you."

Nick let her lead him back into the living room, and stood with her to one side of the door. Becky and Tyler weren't by the window anymore and he scanned the room, looking for them. It didn't take long to find them, and when he did, he felt his blood turn to ice, watching as his life disintegrated in front of him.

At the other end of the room, a space had been cleared, and a few couples were dancing to a piece of music he didn't recognize. It was a slow number, and Tyler was holding Becky close in his arms, swaying her gently from side to side, his hands resting just above her backside. Her head was lying on his chest. They were lost in the music, and the moment, it seemed.

"See?" Kelly whispered in his ear. "She's not the person you thought she was, is she?"

Nick shook his head slowly, unable to take his eyes from the woman he loved, even though she was in the arms of another man.

The track ended and he watched as Tyler leant back a little. Even from this distance, he could see him looking down into Becky's eyes. She had her back to Nick, so he had no idea what she was doing, but he knew the expression that would be written on her face. He'd seen it for himself often enough in the last five weeks.

Then Tyler placed a finger under her chin, raising her face a little, and he leant down and kissed her, his mouth on hers. It was then that Nick felt the pain. It started in his chest, cutting him in two, cleaving its way through his body and wrenching his very soul apart.

How could she? How could his Becky do this?

Except she wasn't *his* Becky, was she? That much was obvious.

"I'm sorry," Kelly said and he dragged his eyes away from the car crash in front of him and looked down at her. "I wish you hadn't had to see that." He studied her face for a moment. Her eyes were twinkling and she wore the pout so well…

"Come here," he said, and took her hand, just as the music started up again. He pulled her onto the dance floor and held her body close to his, feeling her breasts crushed against his chest. Over her shoulder, he watched as Tyler pulled back from the kiss, keeping a firm hold on Becky and moving her in time to the music again, a soft satisfied smile on his face. Tyler started to turn them, and Nick knew that in just a few seconds, Becky would be facing him. He'd have to see that same contented expression on her face too, and he couldn't bear it.

"Hey," Kelly said, leaning back a little in his arms. "Remember me?"

He looked down at her. "Yeah… I do."

Without thinking, he leant down and captured her lips. They were warm and soft. He felt her tongue enter his mouth, delving for his. He responded, a little half-heartedly, letting his tongue caress hers, as her hands moved down between them. *No way!* He wasn't in the mood for that, certainly not with Kelly. He grabbed her hands and, holding them in his, kept the kiss going a little longer…

… to be continued

Printed in Great Britain
by Amazon